WARLORDS
ASCENDING

BOOK 2 OF WARLORDS
AN ADVENT MAGE NOVEL

HONOR RACONTEUR

 RACONTEUR HOUSE

Published by Raconteur House
Murfreesboro, TN

WARLORDS ASCENDING
Book Two of Warlords
An Advent Mage Novel #8

A Raconteur House book/ published by arrangement with the author

PRINTING HISTORY
Raconteur House mass-market edition/ June 2018

www.raconteurhouse.com

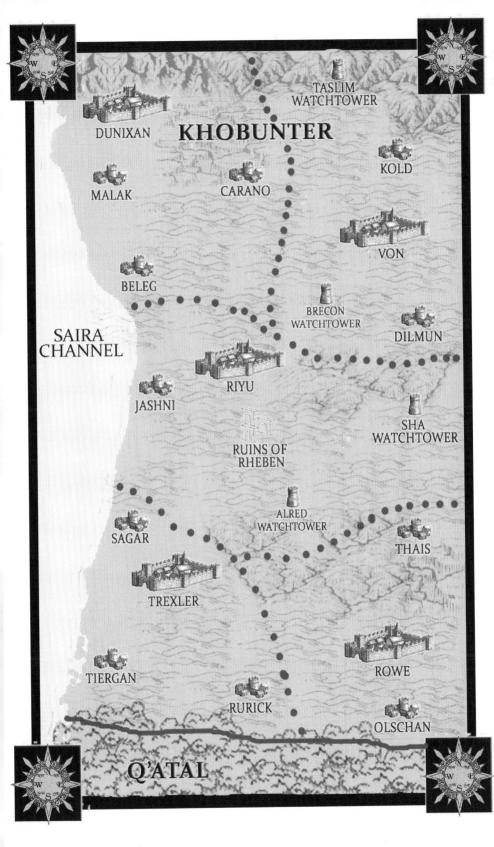

Other books by Honor Raconteur
Published by Raconteur House

THE ADVENT MAGE CYCLE

Book One: Jaunten
Book Two: Magus
Book Three: Advent
Book Four: Balancer

ADVENT MAGE NOVELS
Advent Mage Compendium
The Dragon's Mage
The Lost Mage

Warlords Rising
Warlords Ascending
Warlords Reigning

THE ARTIFACTOR SERIES

The Child Prince
The Dreamer's Curse
The Scofflaw Magician
The Canard Case

DEEPWOODS SAGA

Deepwoods
Blackstone
Fallen Ward

Origins

FAMILIAR AND THE MAGE

The Human Familiar
The Void Mage
Remnants*

GÆLDERCRÆFT FORCES

Call to Quarters

KINGMAKERS

Arrows of Change
Arrows of Promise
Arrows of Revolution

KINGSLAYER

Kingslayer
Sovran at War

SINGLE TITLES

Special Forces 01

The Midnight Quest

*upcoming

People assumed that because Shad was a soldier, he knew how to follow orders. And naturally, because of his reputation as a Super Soldier, he must excel at them. Right?

Aletha nearly laughed up a lung every time she heard that.

Shad never appreciated his wife more than at this moment as he snuck out of Strae Academy in the wee hours of the morning. As a soldier herself, she understood orders. She also understood when to ignore those orders. Garth had told Shad to stay put, but Shad's heart and instincts couldn't abide the thought. His little girl was in the middle of a desert land known for violence and a carelessness with life that made his blood run cold. He absolutely could not leave her there. Hundred dragons or no hundred dragons, he needed to make sure she was alright.

So he left. Was tricking a student into thinking he was on a secret mission a nice thing to do? Likely not. Shad ruthlessly did it anyway, letting the young Elemental Mage build him a skinny bridge for him to run across. He hopped off that, waved a cheerful goodbye to her, and hoped that Garth wouldn't tear a strip off her hide when he put all the pieces together.

A few hundred steps down the road, something moved on his back. Shad came up short, startled at first, then resigned as the obvious hit him. Sliding a strap off his shoulder, he slung the pack around and opened it to find a very smug, white cat curled up in the top. "Now when did you get in there?"

Tail licked a paw and groomed his right ear, not deigning to reply.

"I suppose it was silly of me to think that I could go to Becca without you tailing me." He thought about dissuading the cat, as there would be no supply of anti-aging potions where they were going, but Tail knew this. Knew it and chose to go anyway. Well, a short time away from the potions wouldn't kill him. Shaking his head at himself, Shad offered a hand, which the Jaunten cat took, using it to climb up comfortably on Shad's shoulder. "Alright, Tail, let's go find our girl."

The cat gave a purr of agreement, the sound vibrating through Shad's skin.

Boat to shore, then he bought a horse, heading straight into Ascalon. He needed preparations and a dragoo, and the only person who could help him was Xiaolang.

For two days, Shad had rehearsed what to say to his friend and former captain, the argument that would make Xiaolang help him instead of tie him up and ship him back to Garth.

To his complete lack of surprise, Xiaolang met him at the gates of the city, sitting astride a dragoo with an air of extreme patience. Knowing very well that Xiaolang, as an empath, could read him like an open book, Shad met him with a reckless grin and casual salute. "Hail, friend!"

"Hail, you idiot," Xiaolang responded dryly, blue eyes twinkling. "You got here in good time. I actually didn't expect you for another two hours or so."

"Ah, well, you know. Traveling light is always faster."

"That it is." Acting as if they had all the time in the world, Xiaolang leaned forward on the pommel of his saddle. "How fares your beautiful wife?"

"Six months along and thriving. I'm assured that the baby is fine too, and believe me, we have very anxious Life Mages gathering around her like a herd of mother cats. If the baby so much as twitches, she gets examined." Shad personally laid odds on Aletha's temper snapping at some point and her sending everyone rolling in the near future. His wife did not handle being coddled well. "And how is your brood doing?"

"Also thriving. A little too well, actually, I feel like I'm constantly chasing someone before they can get into trouble." Xiaolang lifted a single brow. "Speaking of…."

Shad upped his grin a notch. "I know I'm in trouble with Garth, don't worry. In her defense, Parmalysian had no idea what I was doing when she helped me over."

"Oh, Garth knew you'd snookered her into it, he didn't blame her." The way Xiaolang said this promised that allll of the blame would rest solely on Shad's shoulders. "I only have one question for you. Do you plan to haul the Problem Children back?"

Shad squared his shoulders and let his grin drop. With only a little reluctance, he answered, "No."

Xiaolang searched his face for a moment, and probably on some level, Shad's emotions as well. Then he nodded and swung out of the saddle, drawing the reins over the dragoo's head and extending them to Shad. "This is Gen. His saddlebags are stocked with a week's worth of food and water. Tent and two spare outfits are packed on top. Map and reports of everything I know, which includes the intelligence reports of this morning, are in the top right bag."

Wait. What? "Xiaolang. You're just handing me supplies?"

The Ascalonian Captain gave him an enigmatic smile that Shad had come to know and dread. "You need to go. None of us can stop those three, we don't have a leg to stand on considering what we were doing at their ages, and I frankly agree with them. Someone had to step in and fix the mess that is Khobunter. As long as you don't intend to bring them back, why should I stop you?"

Neither of them said the obvious, that Shad was the only one that could go and help. Garth and Xiaolang both, with their positions in their respective countries, couldn't go into Khobunter without implicating their rulers. Shad was one of the few with the right expertise and political neutrality to head into a foreign war. Relieved that he didn't have to argue the point, Shad swung off his own horse and exchanged reins. "Hug Asla and the kids for me."

"I will," Xiaolang promised. "Shad, one thing."

Pausing with a foot in the stirrup, he looked at his friend. "What?"

"Well, two things, actually. There's something that has… changed." From the way that Xiaolang struggled to form the words, he himself didn't clearly understand what it was. "I caught this flash when talking with Garth. All I got was the sense that Becca's future has changed."

The words swirled in Shad's head and then stilled, forming a picture. A picture he might not like. "You're saying what, exactly? That by going into Khobunter, the path she was supposed to walk has altered?"

"Yes, I think that's precisely it." Xiaolang gave him a shrug, a helpless motion. "I might be wrong, but that's what I saw."

"Great Guardians, but I'm not sure I wanted to know that. Alright, what's the second thing?"

"Ascalon is becoming…anxious." The way Xiaolang said this made it sound like the biggest understatement of the century. "They're not sure what to make of three teenage mages that are conquering a country with brute force. Osmar and Warwick are just as concerned. It would behoove those three to reach out, send a message to the respective leaders that states their intentions. Maybe do a few peace talks."

Shad rubbed his head and gave a grunt. "Diplomacy. Not a bad thing. I'll let Nolan handle that, he's the best trained for it. Anything else?"

Shaking his head, Xiaolang denied, "That's it, for now. When you do find them, send me word so I know where to send updated reports to. I think those three will gladly accept your help, but remember, you're not dealing with your little sister and two rambunctious teenage boys anymore. You're facing two warlords and a prince who have fought very hard to achieve that position."

Shad let himself slump against the dragoo's side for a moment, eyes closed, just breathing in the scent of leather and warm, reptilian skin. "Where are they now?"

"Alred Watchtower, according to our last report."

"It takes, what, a week of riding to get up there?"

"More or less," Xiaolang confirmed. "You might make it before they move on."

Letting out a sigh, Shad forced himself upright again and swung smoothly into the saddle. "Maybe by the time I get up there, the idea will settle in my head a little."

Xiaolang's expression was sympathetic and not unamused. "Good luck?"

Grunting, Shad gave him a salute. "I'm going to need it."

The Gardener extended a hand, beckoning them to her.

Nervous and shaking, Becca, Trev'nor, and Nolan obeyed that silent summons and walked forward. For all of their sakes, she hoped they would be told they could stay in Khobunter.

If not, she might be the first person in history to ever argue with a Gardener.

The Gardener smiled at Dunixan and made a staying motion with one hand. He blinked, startled, and pointed a finger at his chest. "Me?"

She smiled, inclined her head, then turned and walked toward the mages.

Becca watched this interaction with a speeding heartbeat. The Gardener intended to talk to him next? Just who was this man?!

The Gardener motioned for both boys to kneel down, which they promptly did, although they looked close to fainting any second. Becca remembered, belatedly, that this was actually the first time they'd seen a Gardener in person. Hearing stories about it did not have the same impact as a living, breathing version right in front of your eyes.

She took their hands, one in each of hers, and stared at them steadily. Becca waited, not very patiently, at their sides.

When two full minutes elapsed, she prompted, "What is she saying?"

"This is our task," Trev'nor managed, voice strained. "Khobunter is our task."

Becca felt like the ground tilted under her. "Whaaaa?"

"The reason why we had to be awakened early as mages, why we needed to be friends, all of it was preparation for coming in and changing Khobunter," Nolan clarified, still steadily staring back at the Gardener. "Nothing less than rock-solid friendship would carry us through this."

The Gardener reached up and patted them both on their heads, exactly like a doting grandmother would do, which set the boys to blushing. Becca didn't need a translation on this one as it was obvious they had been praised for their actions so far.

Letting go, the Gardener released them and turned to Becca, holding out a hand.

Slowly, Becca sank down to one knee and accepted that hand, feeling unbelievably nervous about what would be said next. She knew, after all, that when a Gardener spoke to you, your life would be turned topsy-turvy afterwards.

"Riicbeccan," she greeted, voice cool and calm like a mountain spring. "Our Balancer. You have worked very hard the past few years and overcome much. We are proud of you."

Becca felt her eyes fill up with tears. To be told this by the beings that took care of this world meant more than she could ever express.

"When we awakened you as a mage, we wished for you to change the deserts back into what they were meant to be. We thought you would do so from Strae, as you have little need to travel. We did not expect you to take on the responsibility of this land, as your friends have done, but we are exceedingly glad that you have. The road ahead of you will be hard and dangerous but your life will become all the richer for traveling it. Do you wish for this place to become your home?"

"I do," she responded shakily. "Can I stay here?"

"It was not our original intention, but you have earned the right to say where you plant your heart. If you wish this land to be yours, then we will make the changes necessary for it to be so."

What she had just been told was huge. Becca struggled to both breathe and think, as doing both while under a Gardener's influence was something of a struggle. "Once I change the deserts back, will my task be over?"

"No. What you have been given to do will take your lifetime. You are our Balancer until you are put in your grave. Likewise, your children and grandchildren will take up this role. A garden cannot be ignored for any length of time before reverting."

Of course, if you stopped watering a plant, it would whither. Consistent watering would be necessary to keep a land healthy and green. This made perfect sense to her. "I understand."

"Yes, I feel that you do. You are not alone here. We have awakened others to help in this. You have met some of them."

Really?! Who?!

"We have others who are coming even now to help you. Do not lose heart, or courage. Keep walking on your path." With her free hand, she patted both of theirs before releasing her and walking away.

Becca sat there, heart trying to thump its way out of her chest, watching as the Gardener calmly walked straight to Dunixan and motioned him to get down. His guards did not like the proximity of this strange creature near their warlord—in fact one of them had a weapon out and at the ready. Dunixan had to wave them back, gesturing for them to stand down, before they attacked.

The warlord knew very, very little about Gardeners, but even he seemed to feel the raw power of the being in front of him. Or at least her authority. He knelt, somewhat hesitantly, then started when she took up his hand. Becca was a little far away to see every nuance of his expression but watching his mouth drop open gave her a perverse satisfaction. Wasn't so unflappable now, was he?

"A Gardener is talking to a warlord," Trev'nor stated, having regained some of his balance and voice. "What's wrong with this picture?"

"The only reason a Gardener talks to anyone is to give them a task or to help verify that they're *on* task." Nolan pointed at him, finger shaking a little. "That man has to be trustworthy. She wouldn't be talking to him otherwise."

"I guess that answers his question of an alliance." Trev'nor let his head fall back, breathing deeply before asking, "Becca? What did she say?"

"She said that I wasn't supposed to be in Khobunter." Seeing their looks of alarm, she hastily added, "That's not a bad thing. She said it wasn't in their expectations, but they were proud of me coming here and taking on the responsibility of fixing the country. So she said that if I wanted to stay here, I could, and they'd make the necessary adjustments."

"What adjustments?" Nolan asked, still a little alarmed.

"I should have asked that," Becca groaned, belatedly realizing her mistake. "I got the impression that I wasn't supposed to leave Strae, as it wasn't necessary for me to travel and do my work. So me living here has a ripple effect? Somehow?"

Nolan scrubbed his hands over his face several times. "I have the feeling we're going to be analyzing this conversation for the next few months. At least. She say anything else?"

"That there were people awakened to do this task too, and that we've already met some of them." Who, she would dearly love to know, although she had a few suspicions.

"Who?"

"She didn't tell me. She did say others were coming even now to help us. So more help on the way, yay?"

Trev'nor grumbled under his breath, "Garth is right. Talking to a Gardener leaves you mostly frustrated and second-guessing everything."

Becca was more interested to hear everything the boys had learned. "Was that all she said to you? That Khobunter was your task?"

"No, she also assured us that she had told Garth we were doing our task and he wasn't to interrupt us."

Now that must have been quite the conversation. Becca was extremely sorry to have missed it.

While they talked, Danyal sprinted out of the city, several other soldiers with him. He almost stumbled when he caught sight of the Gardener, studying her in bewilderment. "What…is that?"

"A Gardener," Nolan answered, regaining his feet and pulling Danyal in to explain everything in a rapid undertone. Becca kept one eye on that conversation, and the rest of her attention on the warlord. Dunixan became increasingly quiet, if more rattled. The Gardener finally let go of him, turned to give the mages a little wave, and then disappeared into thin air.

"That poor man." Becca actually felt a twinge of sympathy for him. Here he was, having no real knowledge of magic at all, and suddenly a Gardener was in his head with little preparation. "Let's go unscramble him. He's surely overwhelmed by now."

"If we can," Trev'nor agreed, pushing up to his feet. "I'm still feeling scrambled. Garth told us the stories, but he didn't explain how intense of an experience that is."

"I'm not sure if that's something that can be explained." Nolan offered Becca a hand up, which she gratefully took, as her knees were prone to wobble a little. "He might need to lie down and just absorb for a little while."

Guardians, but Becca loved that idea. "Why don't I create some shade clouds and we all lay down until this settles in our minds?"

"Do it," the boys commanded in unison.

Simin the First Guard did not like having a strange creature near her warlord, nor did she like the effect said Gardener had after it left. She kept shifting on her feet, hand on the hilt of her sword, as if itching for a target. The other guards copied her, facing outwards in a rough circle, now on the lookout for any other strange creatures that might pop by. Becca sidled in a little closer to her to speak even as she formed clouds above her head. "First Guard Simin, do not be alarmed. I can assure you no harm has been done to Warlord Dunixan."

Simin's dark eyes narrowed, anxiety rising off the woman's muscled shoulders like steam. "He is not a magician, like you. He cannot protect himself from such a being."

"Gardeners will never attack or harm a person," Becca soothed, briefly glancing up at the sky to make sure that she had the clouds she wanted. Hmm, not quite. She tweaked a little more to get the cumulus clouds she needed. "And they speak to more than just magicians. My own brother got orders from a Gardener on how to rescue me as a child and he's not a magician, but a soldier."

Eyebrows rising, Simin took this information in for a moment. "And he had no ill effects?"

"None whatsoever." Becca realized belatedly that Danyal had closed in behind her, standing in her shadow, and Dunixan had gotten out of his dizzy spell at some point and listened in on this conversation with sharp attention. Turning a warm smile on the man, she said in some sympathy, "It's just overwhelming as a Gardener speaks directly to your mind and emotions with images and feelings. Takes a bit to unscramble it all. Do you mind my asking what the Gardener said to you?"

Dunixan grabbed hold of the stone bench behind him and pulled his body back onto it, sitting like a fragile man of advanced years. "She said quite a bit to me. She first explained exactly who all of you are. I understood and yet didn't. What, exactly, is a Balancer? I received the impression that this is a very important role, one that changes the world itself, and very few are called to be one."

The boys flopped onto the opposite bench, Danyal choosing to stand just behind them, intently listening to this conversation. Nolan answered the question, although he kept rubbing at his temples while doing so. "A Balancer is a person specifically called to a task that will help restore the balance of the world. For instance, our mentor Rhebengarthen was tasked with restoring magic to Chahir, which he did. It took him several years of work to do so and he is no longer called to be a Balancer. Becca is a Balancer," he waved to her with a few fingers, smiling at the double take of his listeners as they turned to stare at her with wide eyes, "and will be for the rest of her life. Her duty is to turn the world back into the green paradise it is meant to be. Khobunter is specifically one of the areas assigned to her."

Dunixan chewed on this, staring at her with wide eyes,

before blurting, "They'll call a teenager to this position?!"

Finding this funny, Becca laughed. "I was actually called to be a Balancer at eight."

Everyone but the boys choked, making her laugh harder.

"Not everyone that a Gardener speaks with is a Balancer, you understand," Trev'nor tacked on. "Sometimes they just need you to do something specific, and that's it. They'll actually call you Balancer if you are one."

Dunixan released a pent up breath. "I am relieved to hear this."

"What else did she say?" Becca encouraged, taking a seat next to Nolan now that her clouds were done.

Dunixan looked desperately in need of a stiff drink. "She wanted me to understand that all of my experience, all of my knowledge, was to prepare me to meet you. To work with you. I am to be your ally."

A thrill went through Becca. Yes! Finally, finally, an ally they could truly trust, that had the resources and knowledge they needed. She glanced at Danyal, checking his response to this, and he looked equal parts bemused and relieved. So, even he knew this to be a good man? He would have said something by this point otherwise.

"The last thing she said was that there were others prepared, like I was, and we were to welcome them. That she was proud of me." Here Dunixan paused, mouth working, as if searching for the words. He put a hand to his heart, tapping it lightly. "That touched me deeply. I felt as if I was speaking to a grandmother who knew me."

"That's not a bad analogy," Trev'nor agreed, tone soft. "Gardeners are rather like mentors to us, as they watch over and help us in our lives as much as they can. Sometimes, though, they leave things up to us. Now, I'm sure you're wondering what she said to us?"

Dunixan nodded fervently. "Can I ask?"

"Of course," Nolan assured him, then launched into the short version of their story, catching the man up to speed.

Becca let this pass through one ear and out the other, instead watching the other men in the group. They moved and stood like soldiers, neither of them anxious to join in on the conversation, instead watching and listening with true intent. Second and Third Guards, perhaps? Becca had to give Dunixan this: the man had moxie for traveling through enemy territory with just five people.

Her attention returned to Nolan as he said her name.

"—and Becca isn't actually supposed to be up here, not originally. But because she took the duty on, they're changing things so she can stay in Khobunter."

For some reason this impressed Dunixan, and he gave her a look of profound respect. "You negotiated with them?"

Shaking her head, Becca corrected, "I didn't need to. They saw my determination here, how I felt about this place, and let me have the option. Gardeners never force anything. They suggest, maneuver, influence, but never force."

Dunixan didn't know what to make of this answer. He kept giving aborted shakes of his head. "Why would you choose this?"

"She's crazy," Trev'nor explained seriously.

Becca reached around Nolan and slugged him in the arm. Danyal, behind her, snickered.

"Ow, Bec!" Trev'nor complained, rubbing at his abused skin with a wounded pout.

Dunixan's eyebrows rose in sharp amusement as he took in the exchange. "You are engaged, then?"

Trev'nor and Becca exchanged a weary look. "You want to straighten him out, or shall I?" Trev'nor asked with a sigh.

"Treat us like siblings," Becca requested of the warlord.

"We were raised that way."

"Ah, I see." Dunixan, unlike others who had said the same thing, appeared to truly understand this. "Well, Warlord Riicbeccaan, Warlord Rhebentrev'noren, Prince Vonnolanen, I would like to negotiate a formal alliance. Are you willing?"

"I think we are. I vote we introduce you to the dragons first, so no one gets accidentally eaten," Trev'nor opined. "Then, let's move this conversation inside the city. We have a lot to discuss."

Alred still felt very unsettled. The citizens cautiously came out of their houses, reluctant to do so, but aware they couldn't hide forever. Trev'nor saw more than a few of them speaking with the soldiers, relieved and half-disbelieving expressions on their faces when they realized who had conquered the watchtower. Part of Trev'nor wanted to go to some of these people, speak to them personally, but that would have to wait. He needed to have a good conversation with Dunixan first.

He cast a quick glance over his shoulder at the man following them. Strange character, this one. Dunixan seemed some sort of strange cross between fighter and businessman. He looked and moved like a soldier but his eyes evaluated them in a way that suggested deals and profits. It was an interesting juxtaposition to be sure. The easy way he used the correct terms when addressing them, the knowledge he had of magic, all spoke volumes as well. This was an educated man and no one's fool. Trev'nor just wasn't sure if he could be blunt with the man or if he preferred political roundabout.

Hopefully blunt. Trev'nor had no tongue suitable for political backtalk.

They reached the building Becca had claimed as an

impromptu office, nothing more than the commander's office with a few more chairs thrown inside. Chaos reigned inside, stacks of reports on the floor and nearly toppling over, the desk shoved under the window, maps dominating the walls. It smelled like man sweat and dust, not a pleasant combination, and someone had opened the window to help combat it. Becca did not sit at the desk, but instead chose a chair. Trev'nor didn't blame her. He didn't think evil was catching, but he didn't care to test that theory by sitting in that chair. He chose somewhere else as well, as did Nolan after a moment of hesitation. Danyal refused to sit at all, putting his shoulders to the wall right next to the door and firmly planting his feet in a parade rest.

Dunixan caught this evasion as he stared at the chair in question for a moment before pointing to it and asking, "Something wrong with this one?"

"Previous commander's chair," Nolan explained succinctly, tone clipped.

"Ah." Wisely, the warlord shoved it out of the way, grabbing a folding chair and sitting in it instead. "As I stated earlier, I wish to offer an alliance. I believe we're all amiable to this, especially after our special visitor, but I need to know exactly what you require of me. I need you to understand as well that I will retain my position as Warlord of Dunixan."

With everyone settled, Becca seemed to take in a breath before speaking, words chosen carefully. "Warlord Dunixan. I, for one, don't see the need to take you out of power. There are certain things that we need you to do, and if you can agree to them, then certainly I won't fight you. Trev, do you agree?"

"I certainly do." Trev'nor had to phrase this right, to make sure he wasn't misunderstood. His Kobuntish had grown by leaps and bounds, but nowhere near fluency, and that left lots of room for misunderstandings. They were managing well so far, but they might have to call for Amir at some point. "First question, do you have any slaves?"

"Not magical slaves," Dunixan responded promptly. "I have taken some hundred or so due to conflicts with Riyu and Von, but they are all former soldiers. Is this an issue?"

"We want slavery outlawed completely in Khobunter. You can take people prisoner, certainly, but you cannot enslave them." Becca cocked her head, offering, "We can find a way to send them home, either for ransom or bargaining power, or offer them another life. I've found so far that if you treat a released slave decently, they'll bend over backwards to be good citizens."

"Is that what you've done so far? You told me all of the magicians were sent to an academy, but I noticed that absolutely no slaves were in Trexler. I thought it strange."

"We've released every slave we've come across," Nolan answered simply. "Will you agree to this condition, Dunixan?"

"I will. I've never had the taste for it, anyway, and my economy is not built upon slave labor. It is no great loss. I take it that you want to make this illegal because of the magicians?"

"You are correct." Trev'nor let out a small breath, relieved this first point had been taken so well. "Your attitude is very refreshing. Can I ask why you don't have magical slaves?"

"When I visited Bromany, I saw magicians living like every other citizen. I saw what it did to the economy, the culture, to have magic free instead of chained. It made a deep impression on me and, after that point, magical slaves were no longer bought or sold in Dunixan territory. It's made me somewhat unpopular with my neighbors, but I couldn't bring myself to do it."

The Gardeners sure knew how to pick them.

Danyal stirred and for the first time spoke. "Warlord Dunixan, can I interpret your words to mean that you will not treat any magician as a tool? That you will always treat them as free citizens in Khobunter?"

"You may, Commander."

Satisfied, Danyal went back to holding the wall up.

Trev'nor cast him a glance, making sure he didn't have anything else to add, before continuing, "Second thing we must agree on: You must change your laws to agree with the ones we've put into place."

Dunixan's eyes narrowed. "I cannot agree to that unless I know what your laws are."

"You're familiar with the ancient laws of Khobunter, the ones your founding warlords created?" Nolan asked, waiting only for a nod before continuing. "Good, that makes this easier. We've basically adopted those laws with a few tweaks. Mostly dealing with slavery and updating the laws dealing with economy. We found them to be good laws, fair ones. We didn't need to adapt them much."

"If memory serves, Amir dropped off our paperwork here already…" Becca trailed off as she went to the desk, rifling through several boxes before going, "Aha! Here, this is the short version of the laws. Read through this."

Dunixan took the pages she handed him and read with considerable speed, eyes panning the page back and forth. He stopped mid-way through the second page and glanced up at them. "You have eliminated the laws about taxes. Why?"

"We don't actually agree with the tax system in Khobunter," Becca explained, perhaps a trace apologetically. "It seems to be counterproductive. Most of them are far too high and drain the economy to the point of poverty levels. I want to redo those laws, but we haven't had the time to come up with a thorough enough system to replace them; hence we left it blank for now."

Dunixan's expression cleared slightly, although a faint frown lingered around his mouth. "I understand your concerns, but that needs to be addressed."

"I'm perfectly willing to do so," Becca assured him. "We have basic taxes in place now as a place holder of sorts. Once the economy recovers enough to support true taxes, we'll sit down and revisit it."

He gave a noncommittal hum and continued to read. When he reached the last page, he settled them in his lap, thinking hard before his head came back up. "I do not find anything to object to except the taxation laws. And those, I think, we can come to an agreement on. Very well, I accept the second condition. Do you have any others?"

"Only one, and I think you've already done that," Trev'nor responded. For his first negotiation, things were going swimmingly. He might as well enjoy it while it lasted, as he doubted the second would go as well. "You have to recognize us as warlords in our own right and accept us as rulers."

Dunixan's eyes crinkled up in the corners, a faint laugh coming from him. "Yes, Warlord Trev'nor, that I can agree with. I now understand what you need from me. Can I list my needs, now?"

"Please do," Nolan encouraged.

"I need your acknowledgement of my power and position as Warlord of Dunixan, as discussed. Any issue with that?" Pleased with their shakes of the head, he continued, "I saw the gardens, irrigation systems, and water reservoirs that you put in Trexler. I want the same done to Dunixan, throughout my territory."

"Done," Trev'nor agreed instantly. "I don't know when we'll be able to, but I think we can work up a timeline and tackle it in stages."

"Agreed." Dunixan looked very pleased by this. "I agree to supply military support to you during this war if you agree to supply military support to me whenever I need it."

Becca nodded firmly. "Agreed. Not that we'd ever ignore it if you were attacked, you understand. If any part of Khobunter is invaded, we're going to respond."

"I don't actually expect anything else, but it needed to be said," Dunixan acknowledged. Setting the papers aside, he loosely clasped his hands together. "My final point is that when we have Khobunter settled under your rule, I want magicians stationed in Dunixan. I want the same environment and perks that I saw in Bromany, and that requires magical power."

Trev'nor thought that was obvious, but perhaps in Khobunter, it wasn't. He looked to his co-ruler, and Nolan, and saw no objections. "I think that's common sense, Dunixan, but we agree. You'll have magicians in Dunixan. Anything else?"

"No." For the first time, the man relaxed enough to actually smile at them. "We'll need to write something official up, but you have my verbal agreement of an alliance."

"Excellent." Becca clapped her hands together, beaming at him. "I'm so glad. One thing, though. You've said that you have experience with magicians. That you visited Bromany and saw for yourself what a country is like when they accept their magicians. If you're wondering what our end game is, then you can use Bromany as your example."

Dunixan went taut in his chair, attention riveted to her. "Just like it?"

"Well, no," Trev'nor felt he had to step in and correct this a little. "We don't mind the Khobuntian culture. Some of the rules and customs here are quite lovely. We like this people as a whole. It's your rulers and current laws that are the problem. So we're keeping true Khobuntian culture, what it was in the beginning before slavery and greed messed you up."

"Right, right," Becca agreed, nodding along. "But we make it more. Greener, lusher, more inviting to people. We give it the land necessary to support cities and dragons. We make the laws more humane, like the rest of the world's, so people can actually thrive here."

Dunixan swallowed hard and he ducked his head, coughing into a hand, clearing his throat. "Forgive me. I'm quite overcome."

In that moment, Trev'nor saw the man beneath the title and his heart felt touched in turn. So this was the man the Gardeners had prepared to help them? A man who loved his country but wanted more for it—who felt emotional at the idea of what it could become. In such a small room, it was no challenge to reach out and lay a hand on the man's shoulder, and he grasped that warm, hard bulk of muscle like a comrade in arms would.

"Dunixan." Trev'nor waited for those dark eyes to meet his and grinned the most outrageous grin he could manage. "You have no idea. You only saw Bromany. You didn't see Coven Ordan, right?"

As if he sensed something wonderful would come next, Dunixan slowly shook his head, lips parted in anticipation. "No. Coven Ordan is the home of the Bromany magicians, is it not?"

"That's precisely what it is. And it's a very amazing place." Not that Trev'nor had seen it with his own eyes, but he'd had plenty of descriptions of it. "When we're done with this country, there will be water fountains, living memory stones, floating cities, irrigation canals, lush gardens the likes of which Khobunter has never seen. *That* is what we want to build in this country. You'll help us."

Dunixan seemed to realize this wasn't a request, and he didn't hesitate to agree. "I will. My grandfather was the first to visit Bromany. He came home determined that his province, at least, would become like that country. He did his best, as did my father, but the pressure of two warring provinces as neighbors prevented them from doing what they truly wanted. I've been just as hedged in. I want what you describe. I want what I've seen with my own eyes, both in Bromany and what you've managed here in such a short time. I am your ally in this, Magus."

"Good. I want you to be my ally, Dunixan, but I also want you to be our friend." He looked to Becca for support on this.

She beamed at both of them. "Yes, Dunixan, please be our friend. Friends are so much better than mere allies. They look for ways to help each other. And they're more honest with each other, too. We need honesty and true communication if we're to accomplish everything we've set out to do."

"I must agree." Something in Dunixan's posture, a rigidity, eased. "I prefer to be your friends, certainly."

"Good, that's settled." Nolan clapped his hands together, grinning from ear to ear. "Now. A few things we need to discuss. My friend, would you like to have a few dragons claim your territory as their new home?"

Dunixan blinked. Then blinked again before blurting, "Can I?"

"Certainly!" Nolan assured him brightly. "You know, the reason why so many of them volunteered to come with us is because they ran out of room in the home nesting grounds. They don't have the space or resources to support the next generation. Because you're bordering the sea, they'll have plenty to eat and good space to start a nest in. They've already been badgering me to request this of you. How about six mated pairs to start off with?"

The warlord looked a little overwhelmed by this offer, his mouth opening and closing several times before he got a grip on himself. "I'll happily accept them. They will help me protect the province?"

"Let me explain." Nolan leaned a little forward in his seat, as casual and at home as if he were back in Strae. "When a dragon claims a territory, absolutely nothing dangerous is allowed anywhere near it. They will squash it flat or burn it to cinders before it can even get a toe over the border. So if you offer them a home, sincerely, and they claim it? No army in the world will get over your borders, not without a serious fight."

Dunixan exchanged a look with Simin, the First Guard looking as overwhelmed by this offer as Dunixan likely felt, although the warlord had better control over his facial features. Simin looked happy but also dubious, as if wondering what the catch would be.

"No catch," Nolan assured them, smile crooked. "Just let them fish in the sea and give them a good territory to build a nest in. Something tall, like a mountain, will do fine. Explain the rules to them, introduce them to the people, and they'll be the best guard dogs you've ever seen."

"Be a friend to them, in other words." Dunixan's eyes became shrewd. "Be a friend to them and they'll be a friend in return?"

"Kindness and friendships always opens doors," Trev'nor stated simply, repeating the Tonkowacon wisdom, the words falling from his lips almost in a cadence.

"That it does." Satisfied, Dunixan nodded sharply. "Introduce them to me later, these dragons. I want to meet them. We'll discuss what areas work best for them and make a plan."

"I'll be pleased to." Satisfied, Nolan leaned back.

Trev'nor hated to bring it up, but someone had to. "Good things aside, we need to talk about what happens next. I really, really do not want a repeat of this place."

"What happened?" Dunixan took in their expressions and guessed grimly, "Riyu pulled his usual trick of lining the walls with hostages?"

"Got it in one," Becca answered sourly. "I hate that man."

"Trust me, my friend, no one likes him. And he's the main reason I haven't been able to let down my guard this past decade. I agree it's a dirty tactic, but there's no real way around it. You'll have to press forward," Dunixan counseled, although his tone was gentle and sad.

Becca shook her head grimly, mouth pursed, hands clenched together so tightly the knuckles shone white. "We're mages. We've been trained by the best. We'll think of a way around this. Right now, I want to figure out what our next step should be."

"I think we should hit Riyu dead on," Trev'nor opined. When he got three looks of disbelief, he hastened to defend himself, "Otherwise, we repeat the hostage situation with both Sha Watchtower and Jashni. Do you want to do that? I sure don't."

Nolan rubbed his chin, staring off into space. "You think that if we take Riyu on we can order the other two cities to stand down?"

"It has a good chance of succeeding," Dunixan conceded, although the frown on his face suggested doubt. "I'm just not sure how we'll get into Riyu. I know you have dragons and magic, but that place is heavily fortified. Riyu keeps the very best magicians to protect himself. The city won't be easy to conquer, not like the rest of his territory."

"I actually have another, more immediate concern," Becca admitted. "Rheben."

Trev'nor looked to her askance as he didn't see what she meant by that. "Rheben? You mean the ruins?"

"Yes, them."

"Not following, Bec," Nolan admitted, brows twisted up in a quizzical expression. "The ruins have been there for centuries. I don't see how leaving them alone for another few months is going to hurt anything."

Becca didn't like this response and glared at Nolan. "Someone failed to instill in you the proper amount of paranoia. Can you think like a bad man for a sec? Three mages appear out of nowhere, conquer a place, disappear for a week, appear again, and then start taking Khobunter by brute force. One of them is named with the same surname as the site of some famous ruins. A paranoid man would link the two."

"Actually, even one that isn't paranoid would wonder if there's a connection," Dunixan offered. "I wondered about it myself when I received the initial reports."

Trev'nor realized what they were driving at and groaned, rubbing his fingertips against gritty feeling eyes. "You think they'll try to invade the ruins? Possibly for information?"

"Or just destroy them outright. They don't know what connection you and the ruins have, but they likely don't want to find out, either. Just destroy it, check a possible problem off the list." Becca caught her bottom lip between her teeth for a moment, worrying at it. "I have to say, I don't like this idea. But it occurred to me earlier, and if I can think of it, you know someone else can too."

"There's a lot of information there that we didn't get to properly study," Nolan agreed uneasily, shifting in his chair. "We barely skimmed the surface. And there's still a great deal of infrastructure that I think is still usable, with some patching. I know it might not be immediately serviceable, but Trev, don't you think you want to restore that city to its glory days at some point?"

Raising both hands in surrender, Trev'nor said, "Alright, alright, you make a good argument. So, Bec, what do you want to do? Go there now, put up a barrier around it?"

"I think we need two more days here to start a garden, get these people sorted, but yes. That's exactly what I want to do. While we're traveling up, we can strategize, think of which target we want to go for next." She looked at Dunixan hopefully. "I don't know how long we can keep you?"

"At least another two weeks," he assured her. "I didn't plan to catch up with you this quickly so I built in some extra time. Especially if I can ride a dragon home?"

"Trust me, not an issue," Nolan assured him, eyes crinkled up in laughter.

"Then I can stay for a good while longer." Dunixan grinned back, as delighted as a child with the promise of a new toy.

Trev'nor fully understood the delight of having dragons at hand and didn't judge the man for it. Especially since he still got that heady rush whenever he got near his own dragon. "Look, I know we just started this meeting and all, but I'm starving. Let's break for an early lunch, then maybe we can continue talking while working outside. If you're set on staying here only for a few days, Becca, that doesn't give us much time to work."

"True," she agreed, going back to worrying her lip. "I

can't explain it, just an uneasy feeling we need to protect the ruins sooner rather than later."

Her instincts might or might not have been peppered with paranoia, but Trev'nor wasn't in the mood to question her about it. Not in Riyu's territory especially. "Ain't arguing. Let's go." Heaving himself up to his feet, Trev'nor felt a decade older. But then, nothing about entering Khobunter had been easy. He felt exhausted to his bones some days. At least today he felt lighter. Having a Gardener come in and tell him he was in the right place, doing the right thing, helped ease the burden significantly.

Not that he wouldn't be up half the night wondering about the *rest* of what she said.

Shaking the thought off for now, he left the office and then maneuvered so that he could walk next to Dunixan. "While we're outside working, stand next to me. I want to talk about the changes you need in your own land."

Dunixan's head snapped around, eyes widening. "You'll do my province next?"

"At least get started, sure. If we condition the soil right, and get some rain in, it'll be far easier for Nolan to plant later. Raw power can only overcome so much." Seeing the open joy on that face, he couldn't help but chuckle. "I told you. It's better if you're friends with us."

"I have the feeling, Rhebentrev'noren, that you'll be an amazing friend." Looking about them, Dunixan added quietly, "I realize that this battle was rough on you, and I can see that you're not really ready to welcome anyone in just yet, but I'm glad that I came when I did."

"So am I." Trev'nor meant every word of it. "Trust me, so am I."

As usual with their plans, their thought to stay in Alred for two days didn't last more than a few hours. Becca really should stop being optimistic about how much time it would take to settle a place they had just conquered. It never went as well as she hoped.

In the end, they sent some of the dragons ahead to the ruins to guard the place while they took a solid week to build up the defenses in Alred, reorganize the government, and plant a rather extensive garden. The people still flinched when anyone spoke to them, but at least they began to tentatively voice an opinion after five days of being charmed into talking.

The former slaves lingered as well, just a little while, burying and mourning their dead. It tore Trev'nor to pieces every time he saw someone at a grave. Becca sympathized whole-heartedly, but she couldn't afford for her co-ruler to become an emotional wreck every day either. She quickly found him things to do away from the graveyard and kept him busy on the other end of the city.

They had the rest of the day before leaving for Rheben. She planned to use that time to get a good storm coming this direction. Partially to top off the water reservoirs here but also to water Nolan's garden. If she let it die due to lack of rain, he'd murder her in the dead of night.

Sitting on the edge of the watchtower, she aimed her eyes directly west, focusing on the storm coming in off the sea. She'd been patiently nurturing it for a few days now, and by the time it arrived, it should be the perfect gentle, steady rain that Trev'nor and Nolan needed.

"Becca."

Without turning her head, she responded, "What is it, Cat?"

"Dunixan asks where you are."

Craning her head about, she looked up, but could only see the underside of Cat's jaw from this angle. The dragon loved it when her partner came up to sit on the watchtower, as it gave Cat the perfect excuse to lounge on the top of it and sunbathe. "Tell him he can come up."

"Will." The dragon let out a low crooning noise, like a cross between a purr and a vibration, mixed with a few high pitch notes.

Figuring that she must be passing the message along via dragon, Becca went back to staring at the sky and her gathering clouds.

An indeterminate time later (Becca never kept good track of time when she worked), she heard footsteps coming up the stairs. Knowing who it must be, she hailed him without looking, "Sorry to make you climb all the way up here. I can't move just yet; I'm babying a storm system."

"Your dragon explained," Dunixan assured her, coming to crouch at her side. "Can I speak with you while you work?"

"Sure. Right now I'm just riding herd on it to make sure it doesn't get sidetracked by a random air current." She patted the rough stone on her right, inviting him to take a seat.

Dunixan promptly sat, at ease despite the fact that a simple railing separated him from a thirty foot drop. So, not afraid of heights, apparently. Good. Otherwise that flight home would induce heart failure.

Continuing, she explained, "Someone up here keeps messing with my air currents, which in turn takes off with my storms, and it's severely aggravating. It's half the reason why I came up here in the first place, to figure out who's the culprit and to stop them."

"I see. It can't be another Weather Mage, correct?"

"Correct. Probably an Air Mage, I can't think of anyone else who has the magical ability to do this. And he's up north, somewhere, that much I know. We'll find him eventually." Becca smacked a fist into her palm, smile feral. "And then I'll have a little chat with him."

"I feel sorry for him when you do." Dunixan grinned at her.

Shrugging, she let that pass and asked, "What did you need to talk to me about?"

"There are a few things I want to clarify." Dunixan wrapped his arms comfortably around the banister as he spoke, the pose oddly childlike. "I know we've touched on this before, but…you're not expecting help from home?"

"No one really can," Becca confirmed with a sad smile. "Most of our mentors and teachers hold political positions in Chahir and Hain. They literally can't move without implicating their countries. The one person that might be able to help is my older brother, but his wife is six months pregnant, and I can't force that decision on him. Besides, there's a good chance he'd try to drag me home."

"Ah. I did wonder about that." Dunixan studied her from the corners of his eyes. "You are from a long line of mages?"

"No. My brother is my adopted brother. He's a soldier." Becca could have left it there, but this was a good chance to give her friend and ally more background. Information on their history had more or less come along in context, but not all of it, and he needed to know who they were to understand why they reacted the way they did. "You heard about how a Gardener came to me when I was eight, and Shad took me out of southern Chahir to Strae at that point. Nolan didn't elaborate much more than that."

"Correct."

After so many years, she could say this now with only a pang, and not an urge to cry. "My birth family abandoned me at the first signs of magic ability."

Dunixan hissed in a sharp, shocked breath, hand rising to grip at his neck in an instinctive move. Of course, to him, the idea was unfathomable. The one iron clad rule in Khobunter that everyone stuck to was that you didn't abandon family. No matter what they did. To this culture, the idea of her being thrown away was unfathomable.

Giving him a sad smile, she kept going: "It's still a death sentence to have magic in certain provinces in Chahir, although King Vonlorisen decreed otherwise. I was cast out of the family, given enough provisions to give me a head start, and my mother told me to run for northern Chahir. As if an eight-year-old had any real prayer of making that kind of journey. The Star Order Priests, of course, could detect me and hunt me down. Shad was ordered by a Gardener to come get me, to guard me. He and his wife, Aletha, somehow managed to find me before the priests could and rescued me. It was his choice to adopt me as a little sister and I have to say, the world has never seen a better big brother than him. I feel blessed by that. But Dunixan? If you wonder why I am so adamant about protecting magicians, and restructuring this country, it's because I know *exactly* how these people feel. I have run for my life. I have been hunted down like a rabid dog. I've known betrayal and heartbreak and ground-shaking fear. I refuse to let it continue."

Becca forced herself to stop and breathe, as just saying the words brought back dark memories. Breath shuddering in her lungs, she looked to the sky, unable to meet Dunixan's eyes for a long moment. When he didn't say anything, she dared a glance.

Dunixan watched her face, his own expression one of infinite dismay. When he finally did speak, his voice was low and laced with a rough catch. "Magicians in other countries always seemed to live a charmed life to me. I never once considered that they might experience such terrible beginnings. Was Trev'nor like this, too?"

"Trev'nor and Nolan experienced something similar. Not as bad as mine, fortunately. Their powers both awakened when they were five. It was still very illegal then to have magical ability. Vonlorisen hadn't changed the laws yet. Nolan was smuggled out of the palace in the dead of night by our mentor, Garth, and a team of mercenaries from Ascalon. Trev'nor was actually picked up by a Tonkowacon tribe when he was two, and he lived with them until his magic ability awakened. Then the shaman of the tribe ran across Garth and made a request of him. Garth took him back and found Jaunten foster parents to raise him."

"So you've all lost your homes because of your magic." Dunixan shook his head, mostly in disbelief, and he stared blindly out over the horizon. "Unbelievable."

"Has your conception of the world just been turned on its head?" Becca asked, not unkindly.

"I rather feel like it has." He considered this, silently, before asking abruptly, "If you know what this is like, why do you keep sending the magicians away as soon as you rescue them?"

"Not much other choice," Becca admitted. "Although

it kills us to do it. Their magical power has to have either a limiter on it or the magician has to be able to control it. Otherwise you get some rather spectacular magical accidents. You're not following this, are you?"

Dunixan shook his head helplessly. "Why would magic be out of control?"

"Magic follows intents. And it doesn't have to be true intent, it can be the most random thought that crosses your mind. Say, for instance, that you looked about this tower and you wondered what it would look like if the bricks were pink. If you were a magician, one without any control of your magic, it might latch on to that and turn the walls pink." Chuckling at his expression, she assured him, "I'm not exaggerating. I actually saw that happen once in school. One of my classmates, who's a witch, turned our room pink in the middle of the night. Her dreams were rather interesting, shall we say. Our professor got a good laugh out of it before she changed them back. See, magic likes to be used. It will use any excuse to be used. So until these magicians are trained, we can't trust them to run around unsupervised."

"And you can't just take along untrained magicians into one battle after the next, especially since most of them are children or old people," Dunixan completed with new understanding, although he looked a trifle vexed by this. "I understand the problem, but we need to find a long-term solution to keep magicians in this country."

"I completely agree. Strae Academy is being overrun with our rescued people. We don't dare send them to Hain, we'll never get them back. Chahir's second magical academy is still in the process of being built and can't possibly accept students at this point." She spread her hands into a helpless shrug. "We can only send so many people there before they literally can't take another person."

Dunixan rested his chin on top of the balcony railing, brows furrowed as he thought.

Becca let him think as she checked in on her storm system. Lovely, it had gotten side tracked by a northeastern air current while she was distracted. With a mental crook of the finger, she yanked it back in the right direction and ordered that naughty air current to go away. There, better.

"Why not ask Coven Ordan for help?" Dunixan turned his head again to face her. "I'm sure we can afford to hire at least a few instructors."

"Give them a temporary building, throw together a makeshift academy, then build something more proper in one of our already conquered cities? That's what you're thinking? Honestly, I'm not sure if they would come. Don't get me wrong, Coven Ordan loves to send out people this direction as they're highly invested in the future of magic on this continent. I've had the thought before of reaching out to them for help, but there's two issues with that. One, I don't know if they would come. The code of ethics for magicians is that we will not abuse our powers. Conquering Khobunter is…"

"Possibly walking a razor thin wire?" Dunixan offered, mouth thinning. "You really think so?"

"We've done it for very good reasons and with completely pure intentions. Well, mostly pure, as I have an unholy desire to squash the evil men in this country. Murderous intent isn't pure, really. But it's definitely treading a line that most magic councils will not agree with. I'm not sure if they would be willing to help us considering that. The second problem is I honestly have no idea how to reach them," she admitted frankly. "I've never had to speak with them before. Trev and Nolan have no idea either. We'd have to physically send one of us over there and we've all been so crazy busy trying to stay alive that we didn't feel comfortable sending anyone away for long."

"Then we might need to stop, take a defensive stance, and take the time to send one of you." Dunixan's head kept waggling back and forth as he mentally fought through issues. "Although I'm honestly not sure when. How many more students can we send to Strae before they refuse anymore?"

"We're probably at that limit already. Although they'll have to take this next lot, small as it is. We don't have any other place to put them."

Dunixan growled out a half-hearted curse. "I had a feeling you'd say that. We need more help, Warlord."

Beaming at him mock-cheerfully, she clapped her hands and exclaimed, "That's why we were so happy when we got you."

"That, and it meant one less province to conquer."

"And that," she agreed promptly, still with that falsely bright smile.

Snorting, he let that one go. "So our next goal is to find a way to train magicians in this country."

Becca nodded in vigorous agreement. "We're going to be in a world of trouble otherwise."

They left the next morning after breakfast. Trev'nor wanted to leave at the crack of dawn, of course, but his wishes could not be met when moving a whole army. It did not escape Becca's notice that Dunixan simply stood by and watched as she got the army formed up and ready to move out. Seeing her military leadership skills in action? In his shoes, she'd certainly have done the same.

Nolan and Trev'nor put a ward around the town as she formed everyone up. It set the inhabitants of Alred quivering and shaking again, but Becca had already explained about it three times and didn't have the patience to soothe frayed nerves again. They'd get used to it.

She did steal a few peeks upwards as they formed the ward, noting how it came together, frowning a little at the speed of it. Normally, a ward made by two mages went up a little faster than this. Then again, Trev'nor likely felt more than bagged out this morning. He'd gone and dropped off their rescued magicians yesterday, which meant he'd gotten back late last night. If he'd had more than five hours of sleep, Becca would be surprised.

It took twice as long as it should have, but that meant the barrier went up nearly at the same time she had everyone ready to go. Trev'nor came around to her side, looking over everyone and giving a grunt.

"Do I take that to mean, 'Good job, Bec, let's move out'?" she teased him.

"When we get there, I'm finding a nice, shady spot and taking a nap," he informed her, stifling a yawn.

"That's fine. I can manage the rest." Turning, she gave Danyal a nod, as he was the one with the lungpower.

"ASSUME SEATED POSITIONS!" Danyal bellowed.

With them settled on the earthen magic carpet, Becca grasped Cat's saddle pommel and swung herself up and aboard. Danyal surprised her by readily swinging up behind, strapping himself in. Normally she had to order the man up. What had brought this on?

Deciding to question it in the air, she didn't say a word, just gave the boys and Dunixan a casual salute. "We'll scout ahead."

"Go," Nolan encouraged, already heading for Llona.

Cat very nicely went out a distance before launching herself up, avoiding sending the mere humans scattering from her backdraft. Becca waited until the dragon had good speed going and fell into a natural, easy going glide before risking a half-shouted conversation with the man behind her. "It's unusual for you to come up with me."

"I wanted to speak to you about Dunixan."

Ah. This now made more sense. "You wonder why we trust him so easily?"

"Yes."

Danyal had missed the first part of the Gardener's visit. Becca had tried to explain, but apparently her explanation had left holes. "The Gardeners are the most pure race ever created, Danyal. They are incorruptible. Their only focus, at all times, is to keep the balance of this world. That means keeping it as the garden it is meant to be. It means riding herd and protecting the people that will help maintain that balance. If a Gardener has prepared Dunixan to help us, he is vital to our mission and completely trustworthy."

The silence behind her rang loud enough to be a shout. She let him stew in it, coming to his own conclusions and asking his own questions.

"As you say," he finally responded.

Becca's ears quirked at this. 'As you say' was one of Danyal's catch phrases. It didn't mean he agreed with you, he was just willing to drop the argument and let time prove who was right. She could live with that.

"I heard that you are currently the only Weather Mage?"

That question came out of the blue. Becca had to switch mental tracks before responding. She half-turned, an uncomfortable position, just to steal a glance at the man's face. He looked remarkably stony, his expression revealing nothing of his true thoughts. "That's correct. It's part of the reason why the Gardeners called a Guardian for me."

"I also heard that mages are all required to marry?"

Becca wondered just where he'd hear all of this from. Nolan, likely, as he was very free with all information regarding magicians. "Well, yes. No other option," she agreed equably. This command didn't bother Becca much as she wanted a husband and family.

"You will consider Dunixan?"

Becca choked on air, and she heard Cat laughing in her dragonish way. "What is it with this culture?! You people are constantly suggesting prospective marriage partners to me!"

"You won't consider him for marriage, then?"

Why did the man sound relieved? Becca stole another glance at him, truly wondering what was going through his mind. He had lost half of his reserve, now looking as hopeful as a puppy with a bone in view. "No, likely not. He seems a fine man, but he's not my type."

Danyal didn't seem inclined to argue this point, just nodded amiably. "It will be difficult to decide on a bride price for you. We must consider this now, have it settled, as you'll soon have suitors coming for you."

So many parts of that statement disturbed her that Becca dearly wished she had a headache potion on hand. Sometimes being a mage instead of a witch aggravated her sorely. "Danyal. I realize in this culture that you still have bride prices, and dowries, but I really hope to discontinue that practice. It drives people into poverty. It's not a good financial practice. Think about it. How many men do you know, good men that would be good husbands and fathers, who aren't married because they literally can't afford it?"

The wind picked up a little as Cat flapped, gaining more speed before coasting again. The dragon, Becca felt sure, listened intently in on this conversation. And likely reported every word to Nolan, just for the boys' amusement. Dragons were sneaky that way.

When the air steadied around them again, enabling them to speak without shouting, Danyal ventured cautiously, "All dowries?"

"All," Becca stated firmly. "In fact, I'll set the example. There will be no bride price or dowry with me."

"This is not something done in Chahir?"

"Not among magicians, certainly. I think the aristocracy still does it to some degree but it's a tradition that's losing steam."

"I see."

He didn't, clearly, but when Becca stole a glance, he seemed happy about this declaration. As he should, since it would mean his own chances of getting married just improved drastically. As Becca understood it, the man actually had debts to pay off because he'd been on short pay for so long he could barely afford to eat.

Feeling as if she should say something else, she tacked on, "I'll only marry for love, Danyal. Not for any other reason. Duty might demand it of me, in many senses, but I look at it this way. I've been handed a very difficult road to walk, one overrun with obstacles and heartache. I think that I am due some personal happiness, don't you?"

He grasped her arm in a gentle squeeze, voice rich and warm. "I certainly do, my Raya. I most certainly do."

They made good time to the Ruins of Rheben. Trev'nor brought them in just after lunch. He still found the method of creating a moving earth platform for people to sit on cumbersome and slow, at best, but half the army still had a fear of being underground and couldn't tolerate it at all. Even above the ground, he was supposed to hold to a certain speed, nothing faster than a trotting horse. Supposedly. (He might have moved a little faster than he told people he would.) His whole plan that morning involved taking a nap as soon as they arrived, but once the ruins came in sight, he experienced a surge of energy. Something about this place always teased at his curiosity.

He stopped just in front of the southern wall, or what remained of it. Before they moved on, he really wanted to fix as much of that wall as possible. Maybe scout around and fix a few buildings, too. Over the last few weeks, they'd spoken several times about needing a magical academy of their own, of not sending all of their rescued magicians on to Strae. Trev'nor didn't have any idea where they would find instructors, but he knew this much: He wanted to build the academy here, in the ruins. It seemed only appropriate to do so, in this place where magic had been introduced to Khobunter.

So maybe while they were here, he could find a good building for it, get the structure sound and ready.

Only when the ground came to a dead stop did people cautiously get off. From the air, Cat swooped in, landing gently. Trev'nor could hear Commander Danyal bellowing out orders, for people to set a perimeter line, for others to start scouting the area, for yet others to find good buildings to set up camp in. Trev'nor automatically assigned himself to the camp group, as they'd definitely need his help.

As he got up, he noticed that something during the trip up here had changed. Danyal always possessed this expression of adoration on his face whenever he looked at Becca. Usually covered by a mask of professionalism, granted, but even a blind man could tell the man had a crush on her. But something had changed, and now that expression shone more open, a little more noticeable. Trev'nor bumped Nolan's shoulder and jerked his chin to indicate the two as Danyal helped Becca down from the dragon.

"I see it," Nolan said softly, eyes narrowed in a speculative manner. "She's said or done something to give him hope. I wonder if she sees it?"

"Shad shut every boy down that tried to approach her. I'm not sure if she's got a lot of experience with men." Trev'nor would bet she had none, in fact. "Maybe one of us should cue her up?"

Nolan took a half step in, making this conversation even more private. "You think we should?"

The way he asked this concerned Trev'nor. Lowering his head a smidge, he asked in a near whisper, "You don't think Danyal's a good catch?"

"He's got a good decade on her, at least, in age."

Well, true. Not that it bothered Trev'nor any. The Tonkowacon didn't care about age differences and that attitude had stuck with him. "Yup. And?"

Nolan gave him an odd look. "Not an issue with you, apparently. You think Danyal's a good match for her?"

"I think he fills the shoes that Becca's prospective husband needs to. He's a good soldier, he's savvy enough to protect her, and he's smart enough to know when to back away."

Nolan snorted, putting a fist in front of his mouth to mask a smile. "True, it takes a certain amount of survival instincts to live with her."

While he wanted to talk a little more about this, Trev'nor saw several soldiers peeking hopefully in his direction, which meant they needed help with something. Recognizing that duty called, he shrugged. "More on this later. You handle dragons, I'll handle camp."

"Done." Nolan turned and sauntered off, calling out in Dragonese as he went.

Belatedly, Trev'nor called to his friend's back: "Warn them about the fuzzies!"

Nolan swore, then shouted back, "I'll take care of it!"

Trev'nor rolled up his sleeves and went to work himself, pointing out the safer structures to use for camp, repairing areas that proved dangerous, fixing a few of the roads so equipment could easily be brought in. Rheben had been built with space in mind, the roads wide enough for three carts abreast, the arches over the roads tall enough that a dragon could saunter underneath with no trouble. The long ago Earth and Elemental Mages who had constructed the place had not cut corners, as the main structures still held up very well. Most of the damage came from the broken irrigation systems, sun rot, and wind.

The earth and stone in the city leapt to obey his command, making it easy to restore the section near the gate into a more habitable place. As he worked, he explained to the soldiers nearby what they were seeing—how the aqueducts worked, how the city's supports had been built, how that narrow bed over there was actually a dry fountain, and so on. The soldiers peppered him with questions, curious about the use of magic in crafting the structures.

Perhaps Ehsan or Azin heard him. Perhaps one of them spoke to the other about it. All Trev'nor knew was that he came out of a building, looking for the next thing to fix, and found that all of the water fountains in this part of the city suddenly worked. On every corner, water came tumbling out of the interior fountains, tracing down the sandstone walls. Pure and clear, it streamed along the narrow routes, sprouting up sometimes in a courtyard fountain, or flowing gently down stony walls into dry garden beds. The smell of the air changed, turning from dusty to slightly moist, the sound of moving water echoing like music through the deserted structures. It brought more life to the city and Trev'nor beamed to see it.

Catching Ehsan's eye as the man jogged by, he cupped a hand around his mouth and shouted, "Good work!"

Ehsan flashed him a smile in return, proud and smug, then waved and disappeared around a corner. Clearly the man was on a mission to get more of the fountains going. The more water sources, the better, so Trev'nor left him to it.

He went for the building next door, as frankly the thing looked like a strong gust of wind could blow it over, and started on the first story. It had two levels to it, maybe they could put people to sleep upstairs?

From behind, someone sprinted in and skidded to a stop. "Trev'nor!"

Turning, he found Dunixan wide eyed and a little breathless behind him, half-stooped as he fought to regain his breath. This alarmed Trev'nor and he stopped working on the wall mid-way, ready to leap into a different action. "What's wrong?"

"There's water in this place?!" Dunixan blurted out, eyes wide as saucers.

Trev'nor scratched at the back of his head, not sure why the man was so surprised. "Well, sure. Why do you think our ancestors chose to build here in the first place? We're sitting on a huge underwater lake."

"Khobunter is nothing but desert, water is hoarded more preciously than gold, and you didn't think it was important to mention that the ruins you want to rebuild is sitting *on a natural source of water*?!"

Well, alright, put like THAT... "Dunixan, you have to understand, water is the least of my worries. I can have water at my fingertips at any time because of Becca and Ehsan."

Dunixan spluttered some more, incoherent and incredulous.

Trev'nor had a flash of clarity, a perfect moment where he suddenly saw Khobunter the way that Dunixan must see it. A savage place with no water, limited vegetation, harsh conditions and even harsher enemies constantly pressing from all sides. Nothing about this country could be taken for granted, not even a basic necessity like water. It occurred to him that perhaps he should tell his new friend and ally what the Gardener had said to him. "Dunixan. Do you know why Nolan and I were called here?"

Rehinging his jaw, Dunixan managed hoarsely, "You said it was because Khobunter was your task. Reclaiming it was your task."

Shaking his head, Trev'nor corrected, "Reclaiming it is only half our task. The number one main reason why an Earth Mage and Life Mage were called to this was because between the two of us, we carry a garden. We literally are gardeners, in a sense. I can take any soil and remake it into something rich and fertile. Nolan can create seeds and plants out of thin air and willpower. Granted, having Ehsan and Becca along makes watering a lot easier, but even without them, we would have managed."

Dunixan lost his incredulity, but now he studied Trev'nor the way a business man would at a negotiation table—intensely, his weight balanced on his toes. "You said before that this place will be a garden before you're done with it. You meant that literally? The whole country?"

"Might take me a few decades, but trust me, we'll get it done." Grinning a little cockily, he added, "So you see, we look at Khobunter and see totally different things. You see a harsh land that will kill you in an instant. I look at a space ready for a garden. And this place," he flung out his arms to indicate the entirety of the ruins, "will be the crown jewel."

Dunixan's mouth twisted in a sad, bitter way. "It must be nice to have that kind of power."

"Trust me, it has its pros and cons. I try to live in the pro moments and ignore the cons as much as possible."

"Ah. Yes, I'd nearly forgotten." Dunixan shook his head, his bitterness disappearing.

What, now? Trev'nor's head cocked a little as his response had been beyond cryptic. What did Dunixan mean by that?

Before he could ask, Dunixan pressed, "Then is this where you will set your capital city?"

"If I have my choice, yes. I think it's the best option, as it's more or less central to the whole country. I hope to put a magical academy here someday as well." Trev'nor went back to working on the wall, as they steadily lost daylight and he wanted people to have a good roof over their heads when the cold night air arrived.

"I think it will be a good place, for political reasons. If you chose any other city to claim, it would influence people to think that you prefer that territory over another's."

Trev'nor winced. "I hadn't thought of that. Ooh, that would have been bad. I'll have to convince Becca it needs to be here, then."

"I don't think it will take much convincing."

He didn't either. Becca normally had good sense about this sort of thing. It's what reassured Trev'nor about having her as a co-ruler. "Dunixan, are you free?"

"Well, yes. Is there something you want me to do?"

"If you're willing." Trev'nor could think of three things off the top of his head, but settled on the easiest first. "It's about time for our weekly check-in with Trexler. Becca, Nolan, and I normally contact them via dragon and get a status report, issue any rulings that need to be done, and whatnot. I don't think Nolan or I have the time today, we need to get this place situated before we run out of daylight. Can you sit in with Becca?"

"I certainly can. Do you know where she is?"

"No, but any of the dragons will be able to tell you."

"I'll assist her," Dunixan promised before turning to leave.

Calling after him, Trev'nor requested, "If you see Azin, snag her! I need her help!"

"Understood!"

Well, that had been an interesting conversation. Just when Trev'nor thought they'd given the man all the basic information he needed, Dunixan surprised him like now, incredulous that they could just make water appear in deserted ruins. How much did Trev'nor take for granted that was a matter of survival for these people?

And did he really want to know the answer to that?

Shaking his head at himself, he went back to work.

Trev'nor absolutely refused to let them put a ward up until he had most of the outer walls rebuilt. The wards would have to be redone anyway after the wall was repaired, why waste the magic? Just wait until the repairs were done and do it right the first time. It took two days with him and Azin working nonstop to finish the wall. Then Nolan refused to let them put up the barrier until they could get the outer gardens started. Becca thought they were both being a little silly, starting gardens now. Granted, Nolan was planting trees and little else, and the water system now worked perfectly so it should be fine for a little while. But it meant that someone would need to come back here on a semi-regular basis to check up on things.

Something about this smacked of maneuvering and Becca had a suspicion what the boys were up to. They wanted to get the city up to a certain level of repair and then try to talk her into making it the capital. After living with them for nearly a decade, she knew how they thought. But they weren't as clever as they believed they were and she'd already made the decision that the Ruins of Rheben should be their capital.

Although they'd have to change the name, of course.

She stood on the newly repaired western wall, calling in a storm to help top off the water reservoirs, and watched with amusement as Trev'nor and Azin repaired the gate nearby.

Danyal came up the stairs at a smart clip and saluted her, which she returned, before reporting, "Everything is secure. We've found the fuzzies in the grain bins again, however. Raja Nolan assures us he'll have a firm talk with them."

"It's good those things are cute as they're certainly a lot of trouble." Eyeing her commander sideways, she asked suspiciously, "How many of the men are asking permission to take one along when we leave?"

"A lot," Danyal admitted, mouth twitching in an aborted laugh.

"For Guardian's sake." Becca rolled her eyes and wondered sometimes if she was actually leading an army. "They can't safely take them from here, the fuzzies aren't able to survive in open desert. But you can tell them that after the fighting is over, they're welcome to come back and take one home with them."

"That will make them happy, my Warlord. I will tell them."

Cat lifted off from the ground outside, stretching her bulk up so that she caught the edge of the wall and heaved herself on top, head coming around to Becca's level. "Brother-soldier coming."

"Brother-soldier coming?" Becca repeated with considerable confusion. Was she supposed to know who the dragon meant by that? "Can I get a name?"

"Soldier at southern gate," Cat continued her report, lifting her head a little to peer toward the direction of the southern edge of camp. "Says brother of Becca."

It hit her like a bolt out of the blue who it must be. She had a moment of pure elation, with concern and determination nipping at its heels. Grabbing her dragon's harness, she swung herself nimbly on board, startling Danyal, who scrambled to leap after her. "Cat, take me there. Tell Nolan and Trev'nor that Shad is here."

Cat gave her a nod even as she spread her wings, readying for takeoff.

"Shad?" Danyal repeated in confusion. "You mean your

brother? But how by the gods did he even track you down here? He's three countries away!"

"*Was* three countries away, and you have to understand something, Danyal. Riicshaden is *the* soldier. He is the finest soldier that Chahir ever produced, preserved by the Guardians and Gardeners themselves in order to protect this generation of magicians." Twisting in her saddle, she pinned Danyal with a look, although it proved to be unnecessary. Danyal's eyes were wide enough to pop out of his face. "Do not underestimate this man. He went into the heart of dangerous territory, with only one soldier and a cat for backup, and managed to retrieve me safely. Coming after us here? Is a cakewalk to him."

She had no time for anything more. Cat back flapped a little as they landed just outside the edge of camp. Becca turned her head, spied Shad, and her heart let out a clutch of relief. Her eyes burned, the emotion hit her so strongly, and she had to take a moment to collect herself. As anxious as she might be about his reaction to all of this, a part of her would always feel better seeing her brother. Nothing in this world could defeat Shad. The idea of it was unfathomable to her.

He looked well, if a little sunburned, standing beside a dragoo she'd never seen before. Several other men and women stood behind him, clearly Chahiran themselves as they all sported fair hair and sunburns. Something about them looked a little strange, as if they had magic themselves, but it was muted in an undefinable way. Becca shook the puzzle off as something to dig into a little later.

Shad's head tipped back as he discussed something with the dragon on gate duty, but at their entrance, he turned and spied her. A bright smile lit his face and he ran to her without any hesitation.

Becca dropped from the saddle and straight into his outstretched arms, embracing him fiercely. He smelled like earth and sunshine. She closed her eyes, and for a moment, just a desperately needed moment, indulged in the feeling of being perfectly safe. They lingered there, her toes not even touching the ground. Neither spoke. Words, at this moment, weren't needed.

"SHAD!" two male voices exclaimed in delight.

The moment broken, Shad slowly lowered her and half-turned, an arm outstretched to Trev'nor and Nolan as they raced to them. "Ah, there's my other problem children."

Laughing, the boys fell into his arms as well, forming a group hug.

"How in the world did you find us?" Trev'nor demanded, an unrelenting grin on his face. "Although of course you did."

"It was easy." Shad looked at him with considerable asperity. "You leave quite the trail behind you, young warlord. I just followed the path of green."

Trev'nor's face formed a perfect 'oops, right' expression. Giddy with happiness, Becca threw her head back and laughed. "He's got you there, Trev. With all of the terraforming we've been doing, of course it would be easy to figure out which direction we've been going."

"This last stretch proved to be a bit of a challenge, as you hadn't done any conquering or planting yet," Shad added with a knowing glint in his eye, "but I did train you three after all. I knew what your strategic choice would be."

Becca drew a little out of the hug and belatedly realized a white cat sat on the back of the dragoo. "Tail!"

With a litheness that belied his age, her Jaunten familiar hopped to the ground and lifted his front paws up. She picked him up instantly, cuddling him in close. "Ahh, I missed you. How did you convince Shad to bring you along?"

The cat regarded her with an expression that stated, Please, as if I had to do such a *mundane thing*.

"You stowed away, didn't you." Becca chuckled, rubbing her cheek along the cat's. Moments like these made her wish she could purr. "You clever, clever rascal."

"It always amazes me she can understand every facial twitch of his," Shad observed to no one in particular.

Feeling like they were being rude, Becca drew back, still cuddling Tail with one hand, and gestured for Danyal and Cat to come in closer. "Shad, this is my dragon, Cat."

Cat leaned down to touch her nose to his hand. Shad, being an old hand with dragons, didn't hesitate to reach up. "A pleasure, pretty lady."

Rubbing slightly against his palm, Cat purred at him. "Nice brother."

"Glad you think so."

Reaching out, she caught Danyal's arm and pulled him gently forward. "This is my right hand, Commander Rahim Danyal. Danyal, my brother and Guardian, Riicshaden."

The two men clasped hands strongly, but warily, neither quite sure where they stood with the other. She'd been so happy to see Shad, her emotions blinded her to the fact that none of the soldiers watching looked all that welcoming. Tension rose off of Danyal in visible waves, curtailing her elation. Becca saw the situation but didn't know how to soothe out that eddy of tension.

"Riicshaden," Danyal greeted before slowly letting go.

"Commander," Shad returned, eyes roving over the man in a blatant study.

"Before we enter the city, I must ask you a question," Danyal informed him. "Do you intend to bring these three home again?"

Shad produced an enigmatic smile on his face that would

rival Xiaolang. "I do not."

Becca didn't expect him to say that. Her jaw dropped a little. Trev'nor outright spluttered while Nolan went statue still, blue eyes sharp and fierce as they watched Shad.

The enigmatic smile grew a notch wider as Shad stated, "If I had said yes, you wouldn't have let me in the city, would you?"

"I would not," Danyal agreed steadily, not at all fazed. "We need them. Desperately. We will not allow them to be taken away from us."

"Well, it's not a fight we'll need to get into, thankfully. Actually, I'm here to bring help." Turning, Shad indicated to the group standing nearby. "Come on, everyone, come a little closer. These are your new bosses. Bec, Trev, Nolan, the Gardeners sent this group up to help you."

Nolan came forward, offering a hand. "Vonnolanen. A pleasure to exchange names."

A woman, tough and thin with spiky blonde hair around a heart shaped face stepped forward to grip his hand. "Magus. I am Carjettaan, a Legend."

Becca's attention abruptly sharpened. Yes! That explained why her magic looked muted and strange. She wasn't a proper magician at all, just someone with magical talent in a focused area.

Nolan's lips parted in an expression of true delight. "Carjettaan, I am very, very pleased to meet you. I can't tell you how desperately we need someone with your abilities. Are all of your companions Legends?"

"No, Magus," one of them corrected. He came around to stand at Carjettaan's side, so that they could get a better view of him. He was a middle-aged man with a bit of a belly, a pleasantly husky, deep voice, and a kind smile. "Some of us are specially trained gardeners."

"Specially trained," Trev'nor said slowly, green eyes going wide. "As in specially trained by the Gardeners?"

"Precisely," he confirmed, pleased.

It hit Becca who these people must be, and she instinctively recoiled two steps, hugging Tail tightly to her. Shad moved with her, putting a hand at the small of her back, halting her retreat. He leaned in to whisper in her ear, "I know, kid, I know, but don't balk. I've met and worked with reformed Star Order Priests before. Trust me, when a Gardener reforms someone, they're completely reformed."

Becca understood that, intellectually. But the memory of being hunted by the Order still lingered in the back of her mind like a ghost. She could not just accept these people so cavalierly.

The two boys clearly didn't have the same issue as they went about introductions, shook hands, exchanged smiles, all around pleased at having expert help come in. Becca let Trev'nor handle this, as it would take a while before she could interact with them. She tried to keep her face neutral, to not give her emotions away, but she was aware of both Cat and Danyal watching her like hawks. They knew something was up.

A dragon beat overhead, then another, and people shifted to allow the two newcomers room. Shad looked around and let out a low whistle as his eyes went upwards. "That is quite possibly the largest dragon I've ever seen. An elder?"

"Yes," Garth answered, lowering his head to a more comfortable conversational level. "I am Garth."

Shad blinked, eyes widening, then he grinned in an unholy manner that spoke of mischief. "You don't say."

"I know, I know," Trev'nor came to stand at Garth's side, reaching up to scratch a sensitive spot behind the right ear. "I find it funny as well. Don't you dare spoil it, Shad, we want to introduce these two ourselves."

Shad cackled. "It will be priceless. Make sure I'm there, I don't want to miss the show."

"Promise," Trev'nor assured him. "Garth, this is Becca's brother, Shad."

"Ah, Teacher-Shad," Garth answered with a pleased purr-rumble.

"That's me," Shad agreed.

Nolan retreated to his dragon's side to make the introductions. "This is Llona, my dragon."

Llona stretched forth her nose past Garth's bulk to touch Shad. "Riicshaden, pleasure."

Touching her nose with his open palm, Shad greeted her warmly. "Pleasure, Llona. You pronounce n's very well."

Llona purred and bumped her head against his hand, tail thumping gently in pleasure.

"Why don't we take a moment, relocate to a nice, shady spot, and we can talk properly?" Trev'nor invited.

"You went through all that trouble to come to this city," Shad drawled. "Be a shame not to use it."

Becca turned to the soldier standing on duty, a face she thankfully knew, and asked, "Sergeant Mose, can you see that his dragoo is taken care of? Bring his belongings into my tent. Everyone else can settle in whatever buildings or tents we can make available."

Sergeant Mose snapped out a salute. "Of course, my Warlord."

"Everyone, go with Sergeant Mose for now," Trev'nor instructed. "Once we get a good game plan of what to do, we'll come and talk to you, divvy out assignments. If you need anything, ask Mose, he'll arrange it for you."

Returning Mose's salute, she gestured for the men to follow her, which they amiably did. Half of her attention was on Shad as she walked along the reconstructed part of the city and to the building designated as their command building. He didn't intend to bring them back? Becca would never, in a million years, have predicted that. It boggled her mind. Was he the only one with this opinion or did the others feel the same way?

Word of Shad's coming leaped ahead of them so by the time they reached the building, someone had thoughtfully put in a tray of fruits and two jugs of water. Becca passed out cups of water to everyone before taking a seat herself. With this many people inside, they didn't have quite enough chairs to go about, so Trev'nor borrowed a little dirt from outside and crafted a chair for himself.

Relieved to be in the cooler interior, Becca placed the cool cup against her face for a moment, waiting for the lingering heat to leave her skin. Ah, better. "Shad, we're very, very happy to see you."

"Feeling's mutual." He grinned at them. "Alright, I know the gist from Garth, but tell me the full story."

The three mages exchanged looks of surprise. Trev'nor asked hesitantly, "Didn't you read the letter?"

Blankly, Shad repeated, "What letter?"

Becca let out a groan, frustrated and resigned in equal measure. "Why are men such terrible communicators? We sent a letter along with all of your new students that told everything that's happened."

"Must have slipped Garth's mind," Shad defended mildly. "Five hundred plus students in one go will do that to a man. So tell me the story. What sent you up here in the first place?"

Resigned, Becca started them off. "It was my fault, actually…"

They took turns, as none of them could tell the full story alone. Sometimes one of them would choke, either from grief or rage, and another would pick up the thread and continue to weave the tale. Shad had to stand several times, pacing back and forth, so shocked and dismayed he didn't know how to respond.

When they reached present day, ready to conquer the next city, they abruptly stopped and dead silence reigned for almost a minute. Shad may have said he had no intention of bringing them home before this story was laid out, but surely he had second thoughts about it now. Likely third and fourth thoughts as well.

Not being one to stay still under any strong emotion, Shad leapt up again, grabbed Becca by the shoulders and started shaking her back and forth. "I'm so proud of you."

"Really?" Becca's head kept bobbing back and forth, but she still managed to talk. "'Cause you look mad."

"I'm madly proud of you." He gave up the shaking—finally—and hugged her tight enough to restrict breathing. "Mostly because you got this wonderful fight going and didn't think to invite me. Shame on you, little sister."

Grinning, she hugged him back. "My bad. I'll invite you to the next war I start."

"You better." Finally easing up a little, he half-turned to face everyone else. "I'm sure you're wondering what everyone else's take is on this."

"We're desperately curious," Nolan admitted with a half-wince on his face and a slight hunch to his shoulders. "Do I dare ask how my family is reacting?"

"It's mixed," Shad admitted easily. "Your grandfather is pleased and tearing his hair out in intervals. Your father is secretly pleased and outwardly worried. Or so I understand. They're not going to send an army after you, and you're not going to be disinherited, so don't worry much on that front."

Nolan heaved out a breath of relief.

"Do send a letter home soon informing them of your plans, though," Shad tacked on. "Because I'm not sure how much patience they have left."

"I will," Nolan promised faithfully.

To Trev'nor, Shad continued, "Your family is relieved to know that you're safe and anxious for you at the same time. A letter home to them wouldn't be amiss."

"I've already started it," Trev'nor assured him with a wry smile. "I'm not sure how to get it delivered is all."

"We'll figure it out." Shad seemed to draw in a breath before he focused on Becca, still in his arms. "Aletha has a message for you: Little sister, you're nuts. We love you, but you're nuts. If you have to do this, know that we have your back anyway."

The way he delivered those words, Becca could hear Aletha's voice in her head. She felt tears burn her eyes and had to blink them back. "I know that. You always have my back."

Shad gave an exaggerated look around, as if referring to the situation and country as a whole. "I actually blame her for this. She was the one that kept telling you that you could do anything you wanted to. There's limits to that, kiddo, you know?"

She grinned up at him, full of snark and ginger. "I know no such thing."

"Apparently." Shad wrinkled his nose at her, making her giggle. "Crazy woman. I knew you'd grow up to be a crazy woman. Ah well, that's how life goes, I suppose."

Trev'nor raised a finger in the air, drawing attention to himself. "Do we dare ask how Garth and Chatta are taking this? Xiaolang? King Guin?"

"Garth says we have no room to throw stones, we were also getting into trouble as teenagers." Shad paused so they could laugh, which they did, in agreement and delight. "I know, I didn't expect him to say that either. Xiaolang was of the same opinion, funnily enough, although I think he's relieved too. With you two in charge of Khobunter, Ascalon's job just became easier. Defending borders is no fun. King Guin is anxious to see you succeed, I think, although officially he has no stance as of yet."

Nolan nodded, not surprised. "I expected him to wait before taking a stance on this. The Trasdee Evondit Orra?"

"I didn't ask." Shad's expression became sharp, blue eyes glittering in icy disdain. "As I frankly don't care what they want."

"Neither do we," Trev'nor stated flatly. "We just want to know if we have to fight them on this matter as well."

"Garth, I believe, is already maneuvering around them. He's done so quite handily by borrowing help from Coven Ordan to deal with the influx of students."

Becca felt more than a little relieved to hear this. Of course Garth would handle the magic council. He was an old hand at doing so. With this information, she dared to ask the one question still left unasked. "How long do we get to keep you?"

"Until you have the country under control." Shad turned somber, shifting so that he faced her head on. "Becca, I know the Gardeners told you that they would make it so that you could stay in this country. But they haven't released me from being your Guardian. Not yet, anyway. I feel that I should stay and help you, until you're in a more stable situation. I know that you have lots of help around you, quite capable help, but—"

She put fingers to his mouth, stopping him. "Shad, we always want you with us. You have no idea how many times we lamented that you weren't here with us. I have very good men under my command, yes, and the dragons are life-savers. I'd be lost without all of them. I still want you with me."

"*Can* you stay?" Nolan asked, more practically. "Aletha and the baby—"

Shad intoned with a droll roll, "I am under my wife's orders to not leave until it's safe to do so. She informed me that if I returned even a minute sooner, our first child would be our last because she would have me by the balls."

Danyal, who up until that point just quietly watched, choked.

Trev'nor nearly fell out of his chair laughing. "She would, too! Danyal, if we ever get the chance to introduce you to Aletha, you'll be in for an experience. She's a former Ascalonian soldier, now one of the weapons professors at the magical academy we were all trained at. Nothing fazes that woman."

For a moment, Danyal considered him, then his eyes moved on to Becca, studying her. "This woman, she helped to raise you?"

"That's right," Becca confirmed.

Danyal gave a sage nod. "All is now explained."

Trev'nor and Nolan nodded along with him, grinning. "Isn't it?" Nolan agreed. "Well, Shad, welcome! You bring us a lot of good news, not to mention good help, and we needed it."

"I expect so. I got a good look on the way in." Shad jerked a thumb to indicate the northern territory. "That does not look easy. One question, though, as I'm sure Garth would have wanted me to ask: How many more students do you anticipate you'll send home?"

"We honestly have no way of knowing," Nolan answered helplessly, spreading his hands in an open shrug. "We find anywhere between fifty to four hundred magical slaves in any city. It's impossible to predict."

"You realize Strae is not able to accept all of those students?"

Becca groaned, rubbing at her temples. "We know. We just don't know what else to do. We don't have the teachers or resources to teach them here. Believe me, we'd love to, as we don't have good odds of getting most of those magicians back."

Shad gave them a look that only a mentor could, one that screamed patience at his students' obtuseness. "May I suggest, oh formidable warlords, that you take a page out of Garth's book and ask Coven Ordan for help?"

"I've considered it, but—"

"You think they will?" Trev'nor voiced the doubt they all harbored. "I mean, it's one thing to help Garth when he's calling. But Shad, we're breaking some serious rules, here. Mages are not supposed to be involved in politics, and they're certainly not supposed to go around conquering countries."

"Gardeners gave you permission, you're fine," Shad dismissed easily. "You're thinking too deeply about all of this. Remember, Coven Ordan's populace is also descendants of the refugees from the Magic War. They're highly invested in Chahir's magicians, people that you are even now trying to rescue. You think they won't help?"

Until he said it that way, Becca hadn't considered it from that angle. But he was exactly right, Coven Ordan would likely be willing to help here, rescuing these lost descendants. "You really think so?"

"Remember, when they first reached out to Garth, they were doing so while stamping all over Vonlorisen's toes," Shad reminded them. "Chahir absolutely did not want magic anywhere near them. They barely tolerated it in Hain.

Coven Ordan has their priorities right. They don't care about politics. They care about people. Trust me, they'll help."

Said like that, it seemed obvious. Becca let out a breath she didn't realize she was holding. "You're right. Guardians, you're right. We've been overthinking this. Alright, someone needs to go and ask Coven Ordan officially for help. Who goes?"

Trev'nor and Nolan exchanged looks before shrugging and looking back at her. "You go," they said in unison.

Pointing a finger toward her nose, Becca exclaimed, "Me? Why me?"

"I need to finish the walls around Rheben and get the ground ready for Nolan to plant in," Trev'nor responded mock-patiently. "Nolan needs to be here for planting. Ehsan can find us water enough to get things going. The only one expendable, at least for a few days, is you."

Becca considered this for a moment. "Really? You think you can spare me for several days? 'Cause I have to tell you, I'll be gone at least seven days, I would think."

Nolan folded down fingers as he counted the days. "Two days, maybe two and a half to fly there. Talk to people, charm them into sending help. Then two and a half days back. Yes, I think seven days at minimum. Bec, we got a lot of work here to do. We have to make this place defendable, we need to assign the gardeners and Legends that were sent to us, and probably get a building ready for our new magic academy. Trust me, we won't even miss you before you're back again."

All of that was likely true. "Alright, if you're sure?"

"Sure," Trev'nor assured her. "And you need to leave soon. After we conquer Riyu, we're going to be in a quagmire all over again, overrun with students and no teachers. The sooner you can get help coming, the better."

Also very true. "Well, that's fine, I can leave in the

morning. But you realize that I have to take Shad with me."

That set the boys to squawking. Becca regarded them with exasperation, setting both hands on her hips. "Think, you idiots. I've never been to Coven Ordan. Neither have the dragons. Someone who knows the way has to go with me."

"That'd be me," Shad agreed cheerfully. "You'll be fine, boys, I'll be back before the fighting starts. I can poke holes in your tactics then."

"Oh joy," Nolan deadpanned. "Fine, go with her. Just Shad?"

"No," Becca corrected instantly. "Tail and Danyal go with me too."

Tail sniffed in disdain, conveying that of course he was going with her. Danyal twitched in surprise, jaw dropping a moment before he recovered himself and went professional once again. "Raya, why me?"

Turning to him, Becca regarded the man that was her cornerstone in this strange land. Her smile became bittersweet as she went to him, taking up a hand and giving it a squeeze. "Because I want you to see it. Danyal, we keep describing to you how this land will look when we're done with it. How it will be lush, and green, and full of magic. How beautiful it will be. But I also realize that it will take decades to bring it to that point. I want you to see what a land that's been taken care of looks like. What Khobunter will look like when we're done with it."

Danyal's dark eyes searched hers uncertainly. "You think I do not believe you, my Raya?"

"I know you do. But I want you to see it, regardless. The memory of that place will help you." Releasing his hand, she gave him a wink and canted her head to look over her shoulder. "Well, brother mine, you tired of traveling yet?"

"Never." Spreading both of his hands out, Shad gave her an elaborate bow. "Warlord, I am at your disposal."

Flying to Bromany via dragonback presented its challenges. Mostly for the human passengers. The dragons, suitably fueled up and rested, could fly straight for three days without any issue. Crossing the channel into Bromany presented no real difficulty and they were excited about visiting another country.

The humans, on the other hand, were aware that bathroom breaks would be very difficult under the circumstances. They chose to eat and drink very sparingly during those three days, which made the trip unpleasant in several ways.

As soon as land came within sight, one of the smaller no-named islands off Bromany's coast, Becca ordered the dragons to land. They did so with alacrity, which she appreciated, as she wanted *off*. Becca clambered down, wincing at her screaming bladder, and hobbled over to the nearest big bush she could find. She could hear the two men also finding privacy.

When she walked out again, Becca wanted nothing more than a bath, clean clothes, and a decent meal. It reminded her strongly of when she'd escaped the slave chains, although her reasons for being in this state were radically different. She came and touched Cat's side, drawing the dragon's attention to her. "Let's camp here for the day. I know we have daylight left, but you're tired, I can't face anymore flying, and I want a proper meal."

Cat turned her head to look at her companion, Dawn Rising, a golden dragon that had kindly offered to take Shad over. Dawn Rising dipped her head in agreement and stated in very careful Solish, "We hunt."

"Please do," Becca encouraged. "We'll be fine here for now. Just leave the saddles. Here, let me unstrap both of you."

Shad came out while she worked on Cat's buckles and unstrapped Dawn Rising. Both dragons shook themselves, eerily like wet dogs, then dove directly into the sea, sending waves out in every direction.

After three days of nonstop flight, they likely had gotten very hot. The cool water would be welcome right about now. Becca watched the dragons splashing about for a moment, smiling, but her protesting stomach didn't let her linger on that for long.

Turning to her brother, she asked, "Food or bath first?"

"How about we get food started, and we can take turns bathing while it cooks?" he riposted practically. "I request a rain shower."

"Done," she agreed easily.

Danyal approached at a steady lope, slowing as he joined them. "A rain shower?"

"I can create a single rainstorm and fixate it in place," Becca explained. She'd seen what Khobuntian bathing practices were like. The idea of filling an entire tub with water, or showering, was anathema to them. They didn't have enough water for that kind of luxury. A washcloth and a basin sufficed for them. "You're in for a treat, Danyal. Showers are blissful."

"Especially when we're this ripe," Shad agreed, then

clapped his hands together and rubbed the palms briskly together. "Right. I brought a cast iron oven. Baked fish and vegetables, anyone?"

Becca had seen Shad teach a survival class on more than one occasion, which included cooking, so she knew exactly which recipe he referred too. "Ooooh, I haven't had that in the longest time. But you really want to take the time to fish?"

"Don't need to." Turning toward the dragons, he called out, "Ready!"

As if on cue, Dawn Rising turned and flung a fish at his head that looked as big as a man's torso. Shad caught it full body, hanging onto the slippery, wriggling mass of it with considerable difficulty. Beaming, he told his dragon fisherwoman, "You're a goddess!"

Dawn Rising chortled in delight, then went back to diving in the sea for her own lunch.

Of course he'd charmed the dragon into fishing for him. Likely on the trip here they had been trading fish stories. Rolling her eyes, Becca let this pass. "You clean, then. Danyal, if you'll help him get a fire going? I'll hunt down a good spot for the shower and get it started."

"Leave us a rain cloud here?" Danyal requested, pointing to a spot nearby. "We need fresh water to cook with."

"Certainly." She concentrated for a moment and formed a small raincloud, something that would release as much water as a kitchen sink back home. Satisfied, she anchored it in place. "There?"

"Perfect, my Raya, thank you."

Looking around for Tail, she almost asked if the cat intended to follow along, then realized her familiar sat at Shad's feet, eyes riveted to the fish in the man's hands. Never mind, that was a stupid question. If there was fish to be had,

Tail would not leave until he got at least a bite of it. Shaking her head, she went into the tree line, looking for a shady spot that would offer privacy but enough of a clearing to shower in.

Uninhabited islands like this had no trace of mankind. Which meant the vegetation grew wildly, often mixed up with its neighbor, growing in and around each other. Trees soared overhead, bushes grew large enough to be small trees themselves, and Becca couldn't go two feet without tripping over a vine. She finally stopped ten feet in, convinced that if she went any deeper, she'd never find her way out again. Instead, she went sideways, trying to keep the men within earshot, as she didn't want to get too far from camp. They had to find the shower themselves, after all.

At first, she paid scant attention to their conversation until Shad said her name. Then she paused, head swiveling that direction. What was that?

"—Becca seems to be universally adored among your soldiers. I grant you, she's a cute kid, but it seems to go deeper than that. I'm a little surprised. Khobuntian culture isn't one to encourage women in their military. Isn't having a female warlord strange to you?"

"A little, at first," Danyal admitted. Clinking sounds accompanied the words as he unpacked the cooking gear. "But our Raya is a good leader. She cares for her people. She uses tactics that safeguard us instead of using us like cannon fodder. For that alone, we would swear fealty to her. But she does more than that. She strives to make our lives better. We've never before seen a leader like her, or Warlord Trev'nor, or Raja Nolan."

"Which is why you said that if I came to take them back, you wouldn't let me into the city." Shad sounded unusually serious for once, nothing of his usual joviality in his tone.

"Yes."

"Commander, no offense, but it's a really sad state of affairs when three teenagers do a better job at ruling than your regular warlords."

"I know it, Riicshaden. But those three teenagers have moved heaven and earth for us. Their methods are sometimes rough, and I do not always understand why they do what they do, but they work very hard to give Khobunter a future. Their intentions are good ones. I will support them because of that. We all will."

"Gardeners," Shad said in a gusty sigh. "They sure know how to pick them."

"I'm sorry?"

"Becca mentioned to me that the Gardeners have prepared certain people to help reform Khobunter. I'll bet you my left eye you're one of 'em."

She nearly stopped breathing. Becca didn't know whether she was happy, confused, or what, but part of her felt stunned at just the possibility. Danyal was?!

"Me?!" the commander spluttered. She heard a muffled *thunk*, as if he had just dropped something heavy onto the sand in his surprise.

"Think man, think. What those three needed more than anything was a capable commander they could trust. They wouldn't have gotten past that first major city without one. And there you were, in the perfect place, in the perfect time, being exactly what they needed. You think all of that was coincidence?"

Becca didn't think it was. Not put like that. Perhaps even Danyal saw the other man's point, as he gave no rebuttal.

"But I've never seen a Gardener," he finally protested, weakly.

"Don't need to in order to be one of their tools. I never

saw one either, not when I first got stuck in a crystal. I didn't see one at all until they gave me directions on where Becca was. But I was prepared for her, to guard her, centuries ahead of time. You see?"

"I think I do," Danyal agreed slowly. "But there's no way to verify if I am one."

"Not unless a Gardener chooses to put us out of our misery, pop in, and verify all of this. I have to tell you, odds are slim on that. They're rascals that way. They love to leave us guessing. I think it's cheap entertainment for them."

Becca was actually sure of that. Otherwise why be so cryptic?

Shaking her head, she went back on task. Create a shower, take said shower, then gorge herself on fish and baked vegetables. She could wonder about this conversation and all of its implications later.

It took extreme willpower on her part to get on Cat's back again the next morning. Becca was very glad she would be spending three or so days in Coven Ordan as it would take those days to recover enough to be willing to climb on dragon's back for the return trip. Unless she could charm a Water Mage into taking them back.

That would be lovely. She should totally do that.

Shad, of course, had told her the stories of how Coven Ordan looked, as if it were a floating island surrounded by mountains. Seeing the thing with her own eyes was a different experience altogether. It frankly took her breath away. The island shone in the morning sun like an untarnished jewel, magical enough to belong to a myth instead of reality. As they came in closer, she started to notice the finer details.

The city was a hodge-podge of different architectures, with every possible roof line. So much magic permeated the structure of it that the air shimmered around the island.

Danyal breathed out a blessing as he took in the sight of it, his arms tightening instinctively around her waist. "That is Coven Ordan?"

"You understand now why I wanted you to see it!" She had to half-yell this as Cat started her descent, but she caught the look of childlike wonder on his face, and in that moment, three days on a dragon's back became totally worth it.

An alarm went up as they approached the city. Becca would have been surprised if it hadn't. They were coming without any warning, after all. Cat and Dawn Rising landed just outside the main gates, although there was precious little space to do that in, and they jostled each other slightly in the process.

Shad hopped lightly to the ground and called out, "Riicshaden to speak with Raile Blackover!"

"And that," Becca said to Danyal frankly, "is why I wanted Shad to come with us. He not only knew where to go, but he knows who to talk to."

The message got passed along, but the guard at the gate kept up a staying hand, indicating they couldn't go in yet. He looked like a wizard to Becca, a young one, likely near her age. He took in the dragons with a dropped jaw, eyes roving over their forms and back again.

Danyal, of course, asked the practical question. "How is the city floating?"

"An insane amount of magic."

He accepted this with a nod, not expecting a different answer. "If they do not have dragons, how do these people come and go from the city? I see no bridges."

Becca carefully removed goggles and riding helmet,

knowing that she likely had weird patterns in her hair because of it, but grateful it kept hair out of her mouth during the flight. She fluffed it out a little, trying to be more presentable. "They create a bridge whenever they want to leave, I guess?"

"There's actually a bridge here," Shad corrected. He rocked back and forth on his heels, totally at ease while waiting to be let in. "It's just heavily glamoured so we can't see it."

Oh. Well that did make more sense, actually.

Danyal angled his body around so he could see more clearly through the open gate. For several minutes he studied everything he could see, lips parted, eyes as big as saucers. Becca looked at the city as well, impressed with what she saw. She knew that some elements of Strae had been copied from Coven Ordan. The glamour of the sea parting around the island, for instance. But seeing it like this now, she realized that Garth's whole inspiration for the academy came from this place.

"This is a city of wonders," Danyal finally stated, voice husky and a little subdued. "Raya, this is what you want to build? This is your vision for Khobunter?"

"Yes," she confirmed simply. "You see it, now?"

"I do," he answered, eyes bright. The next time he spoke, it was with unshakeable resolve. "I do. I will help you."

Becca linked her arm in with his for a moment, beaming up at him. "I know you will. Take notes. I love some of these designs, so I'm stealing them."

A rasping voice chuckled off to the side. "I take that as a compliment, young Magess. Shad, you rascal, don't you age?"

"Right back at you, old man," Shad shot back with a wide grin, his hand outstretched. "How are you, Raile?"

"Ancient," the wizard responded, grasping the offered hand, the other firmly planted on a cane.

So this was Raile Blackover, unofficial mayor of Coven Ordan? He did look like he had one foot in the grave and another on a banana peel. Becca had been told that Raile was actually a little younger than Shad, being a child when the Magic War had started two hundred years before. He must be consuming anti-aging potions daily to be still alive now. His skin looked like aged parchment, hair white and nearly nonexistent, but those eyes were sharp as they looked over these uninvited guests. "Shad, don't tell me this young woman is our Weather Mage?"

"She is. Raile Blackover, this is Riicbeccaan, and Commander Rahim Danyal."

Raile likely didn't miss the uniform, but he greeted them both cordially. "Welcome to Coven Ordan, Magess, Commander."

"Thank you, sir." Becca took in a breath. She'd spent nearly four days thinking of how to phrase things and she prayed she had it right. "Sir, first I apologize for dropping in unannounced like this. I had no way of contacting you beforehand. I've come here in an official capacity to ask for your help."

"In what capacity are you speaking?" Raile asked, eyes penetrating, both hands braced on his cane. "Not as a Weather Mage."

"No. I'm asking as Warlord of Trexler." Everyone within earshot sucked in a shocked breath. Even Raile did a double take. She kept her game face on through sheer effort. "Sir. I realize I've likely broken about a dozen rules, but you need to hear me out. We had very good reason for turning Khobunter on its head and conquering it."

"I certainly hope, for your sake, that you did," he agreed

neutrally, his head canting a little to the side, as if he could divine every thought in her head if he wished to. "But let's sit and talk this over first. My knees can't handle standing for long periods of time and I have a feeling that you're about to deliver a whopper of a story."

Not for the first time, Becca heartily wished she had been able to bring Nolan in with her. He was the one trained in diplomacy, after all. But she also had to learn how to do this eventually, and now would be a better chance than most, as she had Shad with her to help guide the direction of this conversation.

Raile didn't take them far, just to a modest house tucked along the outer wall with a pretty garden lining the front and a very Chahiran pitch to the roof. Obviously his house, as he pushed the door open with complete confidence, leading them inside to a dimmer interior that smelled strongly of books. He brought them into a sitting room, small and quaint, filled in every nook and corner with knick-knacks and stacks of books. He gestured for them to sit, which they all did.

"Don't worry about your dragons, they'll be seen to."

"I have no doubt they'll be pampered and petted within an inch of their life," Shad agreed, quite comfortable in this space as he took a chair. "Coven Ordan hasn't seen dragons ever."

Chuckling in a raspy way, Raile agreed, "Too true. Now, Warlord, do tell me what drove you to the edge. By any chance, is it connected to all of these untrained magicians popping up out of nowhere?"

Puzzled by this, she looked to Shad. "You and Garth didn't tell him?"

"No," Raile grumbled petulantly, glaring at Shad. "They wouldn't utter a peep, no matter how I threatened them."

"This is her story to tell," Shad defended himself mildly.

They hadn't told him what was going on and Garth still got Raile to send help over? Becca would have paid dearly to be a fly on the wall for *that* conversation. Pity she'd missed it.

Before they'd left, Shad had advised her that in order to gain this man's attention, she had to start from the very beginning. Becca knew precisely what that meant. "Wizard Blackover, when the magicians were forced out of Chahir two hundred years ago, some of them went to the Isle of Strae. Some of them came to Bromany. But some of them went east and were never heard from again. I know where that third group went."

Raile slowly leaned forward, every line in his body screaming tension. "How do you know this?"

"Because they left a memory stone. They went to Khobunter and founded a city. Rheben." She held her breath and waited for his reaction.

"Rheben," he breathed, exultant with the discovery. "Rheben. It still stands?"

"The ruins of it remain, yes. Trev'nor and a few others are rebuilding some of it now." They were getting sidetracked. Becca almost wished they could just talk about ruins, as what she had to tell him next made a clump rise in her throat. "Sir, there's a reason why only ruins remain. Some hundred years ago—I'm sorry, we don't know the precise day at this time— Rheben was attacked by an army. All of the inhabitants were carried off and made into slaves."

Raile lifted his cane and slammed the butt of it into the

floor with both hands, his face turning red with apoplectic fury. "WHAT?!"

"Their descendants are still enslaved today throughout Khobunter," she continued, trying to keep her voice level, trying to keep from seeing with her mind's eye all of those people kept in slavers' trains.

Danyal reached over and grasped her hand, squeezing it hard.

She cast him a grateful glance and took in a breath, regaining her composure.

"They're still slaves." Raile repeated this as if it didn't make any sense, as if she had just told him something preposterous. "They're all still slaves?"

"Except for the ones we freed. The ones we sent to Strae."

"*That's* where they're coming from?" Raile shot Shad a hard look. "Is this why you and Garth wouldn't give me a proper explanation?"

"I told you, we wanted one of the three to explain it to you. They've earned that right," Shad responded with no trace of apology in his tone.

Not wanting an argument to break out over this point, Becca pressed forward. "Sir, it's not limited to the magicians in that country. We discovered this ourselves because they caught us just as we crossed into Khobunter and put us in slave chains."

If Raile was angry before, he crossed the line into furious at these words. "You're telling me that they'll enslave any magician they can get their hands on?"

"Yes, sir."

The ancient wizard stared at her, torn between raging and crying. She could well understand why, as she battled between those two emotions on a regular basis. Abruptly he turned to Danyal, sitting at her side. "What is your stake in this? You're a soldier of Khobunter."

Danyal winced at these words, recognizing them as a semi-accusation. "With respect, Elder, our rulers are monsters to their slaves but they're not much better with the other citizens. We do not wish for them to have power over us. Warlord Becca, Warlord Trev'nor and Raja Nolan are good leaders. They want to turn our country into a garden, a free place. I support them in this."

"Khobunter's original laws have been warped, overwritten, or twisted by the warlords over time," Becca explained quietly. She dearly wished that Nolan had come to do this instead. She had a bad feeling all she had done was make Raile mad, and mad people were never inclined to be helpful. "These are good people, sir. I know this. They helped us once we freed them. They don't like their current governments any more than we do. They don't know what to do with magicians, there's some very deep cultural prejudice there, but they're willing to change. They're willing to give those magicians a chance. Some of them even hired a few wizards and were delighted about it. I've got two provinces under control at this moment, two cities in Riyu, and half a country still harboring magical slaves. We find anywhere between fifty to four hundred with every city we conquer. You want to know why I'm here, telling you all of this? I need your help."

"We need your help," Danyal surprised everyone by saying next. His voice was passionate, raw emotion pouring off of him in waves. "Elder, I did not understand until the moment I saw your city what has happened to my country. Greed has robbed us of magic. We've lost hope, water, freedom, and any chance of the fantastical happening in our lives because we lost magic. Our warlords, they fight to give this back to us. Help them."

Raile lowered his eyes and stared at the floor for a long moment. The silence felt claustrophobic, the tension thick enough to slice and serve on bread. Becca barely dared to breathe.

When he finally lifted his head again, the anger had simmered to a cold burn, his jaw tight enough to break. "Warlord. You're aware that every magical council in the world will pitch a fit if I aid you in this."

"Yes, sir."

"You're aware of this and you came to me anyway."

"Yes, sir." Becca shrugged, not knowing what else to say. "Shad told me once that Coven Ordan has its priorities straight. You put people over politics."

Raile gave Shad quite the look for that. Shad beamed back at him, completely unrepentant. "Be that as it may," Raile said pointedly before facing her again, "you still must understand that I will face serious repercussions if I openly help you."

Becca's ears perked at the word 'openly.' That sounded like room for negotiation to her. "Yes, sir, I do understand that as well. However, I think there are still other options."

Shad cleared his throat and murmured to her, "Aren't you forgetting to tell him something?"

Something she'd forgotten? Oh, duh. Mentally kicking herself, Becca hastily set about rectifying her idiocy. "Wizard Blackover, there is something I didn't tell you. We had a Gardener visit the three of us about two weeks ago. She told us that Khobunter was our task."

If she'd surprised Raile before, it reached another level now, as his eyes nearly popped out of his head and he had to scramble to get his jaw back into socket so he could actually speak. Voice wobbling, he squeaked out, "Khobunter. Is your task."

"Mine, Trev, and Nolan's," she clarified. "The Gardener did tell us they had prepared several people to help us with the task. I believe Commander Danyal is one of them. And they just dropped off a load of reformed Star Order Priests recently as well, which is all very helpful, but it doesn't give us the experts we need to help with our magicians."

Shad had that enigmatic smile on his face, the one that said he knew a secret that not everyone was privy to. Sitting back, he crossed one leg over another. "Bec, something you might not know about our esteemed wizard, here. He himself is a Balancer."

Becca nearly fell out of her chair. "He is?!"

"He is?" Danyal breathed in amazement, eyes darting between wizard and mage. "I thought Balancers were extremely rare."

"They are," Shad assured him. "I think there's only about four in existence. You know all four, by the way, you lucky dog. Raile's task is to restore the lost bloodlines of Chahir, which includes training them. Garth shared that responsibility at one point, but half the reason why Raile is still alive is because the task isn't done yet."

Raile looked at Shad steadily, a look which Shad returned, his expression one of challenge. The words weren't spoken, but they hovered visibly in the air: Well, Balancer, what are you going to do?

"The councils," Raile announced firmly, "can go hang. Alright, Warlord, what do you need?"

"I need a magical academy," Becca answered bluntly. Some part of her screamed in excitement and it was all she could not to launch herself at the old man and squeeze the stuffing out of him. "I need it built in Khobunter and I need it operational yesterday."

"You'll have it," he promised her. "My word as a

Blackover."

At that, she couldn't contain herself any longer and she did go straight to him, throwing both arms around his neck and hugging him hard. He smelled like peppermint and potions, a heady combination. "Thank you so much," she whispered against his hair.

Chuckling, Raile reached up and patted her back. "I've never been hugged during negotiations before. I like it. They should always end like this."

"You're only saying that because a cute girl is hugging you," Shad drawled.

"Yes, and your point is?"

"Just saying."

Stepping back, Becca beamed at him. "Seriously, thank you. We didn't know what to do, and we can't afford to lose any magicians."

"We'll help you. They are as much our responsibility as yours," Raile responded, already levering himself up to his feet.

Becca gave him a hand, gently pulling him up, then lingered there as she seriously didn't understand how he managed to stay upright. He felt like stringy muscle and bone to her.

"Young man," Raile addressed Danyal forthrightly, "I want a detailed account from you about your culture. You'll be in charge of preparing everyone that I send to Khobunter, so they don't make any cultural gaffs."

Danyal's hand went up in a habitual salute, then realized he couldn't salute and settled for a sharp bow instead. "I will be honored to help, Elder."

Belatedly, Becca realized that bringing Danyal along was a stroke of genius on her part. Even she didn't understand Khobunter's culture all that well, despite being there for months and directly changing several customs. Danyal would be far better at preparing their teachers than she would be. "Danyal, please don't worry about keeping track of me while we're here. Help them in whatever way you can. Getting the teachers properly prepared is the priority."

"Of course, my Warlord."

"Good. Wizard Blackover, I should tell you that before we left, Trev'nor had found a building he said would make a good magical academy. Actually, we believe that's what it was before the city was destroyed. He and another Elemental Mage are doing their best to get it structurally sound but it will take more than their magical talent to get that building operational again. Also, the city is basically deserted. I can post several men there to help guard the place, and four dragons have already claimed it as territory, so it should be safe enough, but there's not going to be much in the way of supplies or equipment. Everything that you possibly need either needs to be sent along or be bought before entering Khobunter."

"Don't worry, young Magess." Raile patted her hand reassuringly. "This isn't the first time that I've established an academy. I do hope it will be the last, however."

The way he said this suggested…no, surely not.

"Wait, Raile." Shad pointed an illustrative finger over his shoulder toward the east. "You're not suggesting that you, yourself, are going to go?"

The expression on Raile's face depicted the epitome of forced patience. "Of course I am."

Actually, there was no 'of course' about it in Becca's mind. She was thrilled to hear it, though. She couldn't help but bounce a little on her toes. "Sir, truly?"

"I could leave the other academy to Garth, as training up the rising generation was his task as well, but this one I think should be mine." Nodding decisively, pleased with his own decision, Raile headed for the door. "I'll need a few hundred anti-aging potions and a little help from a Life Mage for this one, I think, but I don't dare send any of the younger ones off without my help. It's a harsh environment they're going into and none of them have the faintest clue on how to set up an academy."

All true, all of which explained why Becca was ecstatic that Raile was coming. "Sir, may I suggest bringing along at least one historian as well? We barely tapped into the memory stone and there's a lot of records and such that we haven't dared to touch."

"Oh, trust me, child, we'll be sending along a whole passel of historians. In fact, they'll kidnap your dragon and race off without you once they hear this news."

Somehow she didn't doubt that. Well, the kidnapping of the dragon wouldn't happen, but she could see the rest of it.

Raile paused just outside the doorway and regarded her, eyes squinting a bit against the sunlight. "How long can you stay before you must return?"

"Three days, sir." Becca half-winced saying this as she knew that three days would not be sufficient time to prepare these people. "And we'll only be in the Ruins for about two days before we have to leave for the next city."

"There's a certain momentum to war," Shad agreed behind her. "If you don't keep it, it gets harder. And if they don't strike Riyu first, he'll come for them, and we want to avoid that at all costs."

"I understand," Raile assured them. "Then we'd best pack quickly."

At no point had Becca suggested that he actually be ready to come with her on the return trip home. She figured she'd leave them instructions on how to get there, maybe Dawn

Rising, and they'd wing it as best they could. "You really think you can pack everything you'll need, draft everyone, and prepare them enough to leave for Khobunter in just three days?"

"Only if we stop lolly-gagging about and talking it into the ground."

Snapping her mouth shut, Becca promptly skipped off the front step. She could take a hint. "Let's go, then."

Trev'nor stared at the building, sucking down water as if it were air, and tried to feel some sense of accomplishment. Standing eight stories tall, with arched risers leading to both east and west wings, his hopefully-an-academy dominated the space like some majestic castle. It had quite possibly the most unique and awe-inspiring architecture he'd ever seen. Part of him had been *oohing* and *ahhing* the entire time he worked to restore it, amazed at the architectural detail in everything from the patterns in the sandstone to the trim along the ceiling.

And while he'd been building and restoring for nearly eight days straight, it was hard to feel like he'd gotten anything done when he looked around the city and realized he'd barely made a dent.

Dropping down next to him on the bench, Azin let out a groan, rubbing both calves with her hands. "Main structural beams are all restored."

"Bless you," he praised in heartfelt tones. With the beams being metal, it fell just outside of his comfort zone, and while Trev'nor could work with metal, it felt like slogging uphill in mud while doing it. It was so much better to have an Elemental Mage do the work instead. "It wouldn't be such a massive project if this place wasn't so, well…"

"Massive?" she finished. Taking out her own canteen, she turned it nearly upside down, gulping water.

"Yes, that. I'm glad it is, mind, because that means they'll be able to handle all of the students they're about to get. But it sure is hard on the ones restoring it." Trev'nor would bet the place could give Strae a run for its money when it came to size. And Strae was one of the largest magical academies in the world.

"Are we done?" Azin asked uncertainly. "With this building, I mean."

"Actually, I think we've done all that we can." Trev'nor sat on the bench he'd fixed yesterday, staring out over a desolate courtyard that had once sported quite the garden. There was still so much to do, windows to replace, floors to install, kitchens and bathrooms to repair, but his magic wasn't suited to do any of it, not really. "We're going to have to rely on whatever help Becca brings in with her to finish up. As soon as she's back, we have to figure out how to deal with Riyu and move. We can't afford to sit much longer."

From behind, he heard a pebble skitter and footsteps before a familiar voice announced, "Just heard from Dawn Rising and they'll be back in a few hours, actually."

Trev'nor twisted, craning around to see Nolan. "A few hours? Really?"

"Yup. I didn't get all the details, as Dawn Rising didn't know everyone's names, but she informed me that 'lots of people' are coming and they're coming in three groups."

Excited by this news, he straightened from his slouch, gesturing for Nolan to come around so he didn't have to stare at him at that awkward angle. "Three groups? She's bringing that much help?"

"The girl's persuasive. It's one of the reasons why I wanted her to go." Nolan rubbed his hands together, excited. "Can you help me clear and prepare some of the land over here? I want to get a garden started for them before they arrive."

That was an excellent idea and Trev'nor really should have thought of it before. After all, the academy would have to be totally self-sufficient until they could get this city properly restored again. "Sure. Where do you want it?"

"Most of the vegetables and fruits that I want to plant actually like shade or semi-shade, so maybe over here, near the porticos?"

Trev'nor could actually work that magic while staying seated, so he did, as he had no more energy at the moment. He'd been on his feet for days and needed a break, especially if Becca was coming back so soon. No doubt he'd be press-ganged into helping people unload things when they arrived.

While he worked, Nolan turned to Azin and said kindly, "Azin, I want you to understand that when these people arrive, you're welcome to stay here and start studying. You don't have to keep fighting with us."

Wait, what? Trev'nor stared bug-eyed at Nolan, not quite believing what he had just heard. Since when had Nolan come to that decision?

Azin looked between the two of them uncertainly, worrying at her bottom lip for a moment before asking tentatively, "Do you not want me to go?"

"You are a tremendous help when you fight," Trev'nor told her firmly, not wanting her to think she was unwelcome. "Of course we want you with us."

"But we also recognize that you've got limited training and you might have some questions to ask another Elemental Mage," Nolan tacked on.

Trev'nor felt the urge to kick his friend. "I think what Nolan is trying to say is that if you want to take a break from fighting, and get a good grip on your magic, you're welcome to stay."

Her expression cleared a little although her frown remained. "I would like to think on that."

"Do, just be quick to make a decision." Trev'nor shot Nolan an exasperated look.

His friend mouthed, 'What?' with an innocent shrug of the shoulders.

Like he didn't know that he'd just thrown Trev'nor for a loop, telling one of their strongest fighters she could sit the rest of the war out. He'd get Nolan for this later.

They worked steadily, the three of them, Ehsan pitching in when they needed water. It still looked like a young garden, more sprouts and saplings than anything, but Nolan assured him it would be fully mature in three days and ready to harvest. Trev'nor kept one eye on the sky, marking the time, and his excitement grew as the sun set. Three different groups? Who had chosen to come help? How had Becca persuaded them? Did they think to bring everything they would need with them?

He actually sensed them before he saw them, as someone working earth magic approached at wicked speed. "Someone's using the Earth Path," he blurted out, head snapping to face west.

"They're here?" Nolan called back to him, voice rising in excitement.

"Just about. Let's meet them at the gate." Trev'nor lifted his head and called, "Garth, can I get a quick ride?"

"Always, fledgling." The massive elder dragon unfurled from the building he'd been sunning himself on and stretched out, grasping all three of them to hold tight to his chest before lifting off in a half-glide, half leap toward the western gates. Trev'nor appreciated the hold, as he felt much more secure squashed against warm scales than he would just dangling from a dragon's claws.

In minutes Garth deposited them on top of the wall, and they scurried down the stairs, wanting to be on the ground when their new teachers arrived. Trev'nor noticed that Azin kept tugging at her clothes, messing with her hair, and reached out to still her hands. "You're fine, you're fine. These people appreciate hard work and they know we've been building a city."

"I look so dirty," she complained to him, tugging at her hands. "And these are people of legend."

"No, they're just people, living in a legendary place," Nolan corrected with a gentle smile. "There's a difference. Speak of the devil, here they are."

The earth sloughed in every direction as their guests came out of the ground, leaving the Earth Path. Trev'nor's eyes roamed over the group and his pulse quickened in an exultant rush. There must have been at least fifty people in the group, with crates and bags and more equipment than he could catalogue in a quick once-over. So they *had* come prepared, then. So many people, and this was only the first wave?

His eyes caught sight of a familiar blonde in the front and he let out a whoop before racing forward. "Sallah!"

Sallah flung out both arms wide and caught him in a hard embrace, nearly lifting him off the ground, despite the fact she was a good half-head shorter. "There's one of my favorite people. What were you thinking, Trev, stirring up trouble without inviting me?"

Hugging one of his favorite cousins tight, he rocked them both back and forth. "I never in a million years should have doubted you'd come, but somehow I did. What about the kids?"

"Bah, they're practically grown, they're fine." Standing

back, she held him at arm's length, eyes tight with worry even as she tried to smile. "Your magic is far too low, cousin."

"I know, trust me, I know. I was trying to get as much ready for you as I could before you arrived." He patted her arm reassuringly and then looked around at everyone. He saw more than one face filled with disbelief, as if they hadn't been able to believe it all until they saw the city with their own eyes. Putting on his official face, Trev'nor called out, "Welcome to Rheben! Thank you so, so much for coming. I'm Rhebentrev'noren, Warlord of Trexler. As you can see, the city is still very much in disrepair, so watch your step. I've fixed a certain section of it, so that's structurally sound, and you can rest easy there. If you have questions or concerns, you can ask any of the dragons and they'll either help you or be happy to pass the message along to someone who can."

"We are pleased to hear that, Warlord," a creaking, somewhat familiar voice responded.

Trev'nor went completely still, doubting his ears and memory. No, surely not. Surely Becca hadn't managed to convince *him* to come too.

People parted, giving the man room, and Raile Blackover appeared. He looked a little healthier than he normally did, not relying so heavily on his cane, better color in his skin and his stoop was now nearly gone. Trev'nor imagined quite a bit of magic went into restoring the man to such good health. As if in a daze, he went forward, extending a hand. "Sir. You've come to help us?"

"I wouldn't dream of sitting this one out, Trev'nor." Raile clasped hands with him, the grip strong and reassuring. "And before you ask, the magic councils can go hang, as far as I'm concerned. The work here is too important and I believe that when a Gardener says you're on task, you don't argue the point."

He seriously wanted to hug the old man. "Couldn't agree more, sir. Come, meet one of our rescued magicians." Turning, he caught Azin's elbow and pulled her forward. She looked beyond nervous and stumbled a little, eyes wide in her face. "This is Azin, an Elemental Mage. Azin, this is Raile Blackover, a wizard from Coven Ordan."

Raile grasped her hand and smiled at her gently. "A pleasure, Magess."

"Oh, oh, no sir, I'm not a mage," she denied hastily. "Not yet. I haven't been trained, just know a few tricks."

"Trust me, child, you're either a mage, or you're not. There's no middle ground on that." Releasing her hand, he gave her a wink before greeting, "Vonnolanen, you're looking rather more tan than I last saw you."

"This climate will do that to you, sir." Nolan clasped hands with him, beaming. "But come inside, all of you, we've set some buildings aside for your use. I'll introduce you to the dragons as we go."

Trev'nor let Nolan briefly play tour guide as people carried things into the city. He sought out Becca, found her, and gave her the hardest hug he'd ever done in his life. "I love you, you're amazing, how did you convince RAILE BLACKOVER of all people to come?"

Laughing, she hugged him back. "It's quite the story. I'll tell you later, when we have Nolan. Well, Trev, how do you think I handled my first diplomatic mission?"

"You are amazing. This is so much more than I anticipated." Stepping back, he beamed at her. "Seriously, though, did they bring everything they needed to?"

"Sallah said if they did forget something, they were all magicians, they'd make it themselves. She was quite firm on that point." Becca shrugged, grinning, stating silently it wasn't her problem.

Ehsan darted through the gate, eyes wide, panting a bit for breath which suggested he'd sprinted here. "Trev'nor, is—she is. Becca, you got them? Those are the teachers from Coven Ordan?"

"That's them. Well, some of them, others are still en route." Becca went and caught his arm, drawing him back into the city. "Come with me. Come meet our new dean. He's amazing, the oldest man living."

Trev'nor watched her go, still dazed and reeling a little. She'd done it. He'd only given it 50-50 odds for her to succeed, and even then he imagined only a handful would be willing to brazen this dangerous land. Instead she'd brought enough staff to actually run a huge academy. "Shad. How did she do it?"

"Hugs," his mentor intoned drolly. "Hugs will change the world."

Knowing that tone, Trev'nor rolled his eyes. "No, seriously."

"I am serious," Shad rebuked with mock hurt. "Why does no one believe me when I'm being serious?"

Danyal cleared his throat, eyes sparkling with muted laughter. "Warlord, in fact Riicshaden is not pulling your leg. Hugs were involved. But in truth, Raya Becca simply laid out the facts. Wizard Blackover was so outraged he immediately agreed to help. I myself am impressed with how quickly he pulled teachers and supplies together, but all are eager to help, and none of them are inclined to leave anytime soon."

Hearing this, Trev'nor really wanted the full account. He told himself firmly to be patient. "Good. I can't wait to get the story later. Come inside, let's get people sorted. Danyal, if you can help me figure out who to permanently post here? I'd like to start introducing people so everyone knows each other."

"Certainly, Warlord, I would be pleased to."

Falling into step with the men, Trev'nor encouraged him with a smile of anticipation, "And tell me, what did you think of Coven Ordan?"

"It is a wonderful place, one beyond my dreams," Danyal responded promptly, lighting up like a child. "In fact, Raja, do you think you can create a floating island here?"

Trev'nor had only contemplated the idea a few hundred times, growing up. "You know, Danyal, I've thought about this before. I certainly want to try. Where do you think we should put it, though?"

"I've considered the matter on the way over here, and in fact I do have a few ideas."

They bantered the idea back and forth as they walked into the city, Shad inserting absurd suggestions as they walked, prompting all three to laugh. Trev'nor's face ached under all of the smiles and laughter, something that hadn't happened in a long time, and he realized what this buoyant feeling currently occupying his chest was: hope. He hadn't felt it in so long that he'd nearly forgotten the emotion altogether.

But with the arrival of Coven Ordan's teachers, that's what came with them. Hope. Trev'nor felt like they'd finally crossed a cleft point, that rehabilitating this country really was possible after all.

Well. Maybe they weren't as crazy as he thought.

Trev'nor had assumed that once people arrived, he would have to ride herd on them, at least to a certain extent. Perhaps the mentality came from being in charge of people here. The Khobuntians he had conquered were so unaccustomed to having the freedom to think for themselves that they had to be led in almost everything.

Coven Ordan's magicians didn't have that problem.

He went to the building site the next morning, fully expecting a lot of questions, only to find that people were well underway and not one of them did more than smile and wave before getting back to work. Stunned, he watched them competently put the academy back to rights, only conferring with each other on what should be done next.

Raile came up to him, smiling in greeting. "Good morning, Trev'nor."

"Good morning, sir." Trev'nor bounced a little on his toes, grinning from ear to ear, unwilling to contain his general happiness. "I love people with initiative. I thought I would need to come out here and tell people what to work on."

"No need. That's what I'm here for."

"True, I'd forgotten. Or maybe I'm just in the habit now of people constantly plaguing me for orders." This lack of demand felt quite refreshing. More seriously, he asked, "Is there anything you need?"

"Information, young man, information. Your co-ruler gave me general parameters to work off of, but I feel the need for particulars. Here, let's sit in the shade while I ask questions."

Trev'nor still felt the effects of having worked for nearly two weeks straight without a break, so sitting and chatting sounded heavenly to him. He promptly sat on the nearest shady bench, one leg tucked under another, angled so he could comfortably face the wizard. Raile sat a little more heavily, also angled.

"Ah, there. I'm feeling better than I have in years, but even Life Mages can only do so much."

That brought up a point that had bothered Trev'nor for years. "Sir, if you don't mind a personal question? I always wondered how you're still alive. My understanding is that there's limits to anti-aging potions and Nolan told me once he couldn't fathom how you made it past a hundred and fifty."

"He's correct to question it." Lowering his tone, Raile admitted, "The Gardeners step in and help from time to time. That's how we all knew I wasn't done yet, that there was still the last of the Chahiran bloodlines out there to discover. I never knew where, even though I searched for them."

"So you were surprised to hear they were in Khobunter, but not really."

"Surprised they were in the one place I never thought magic would thrive. Angry with myself for being so prejudiced that I didn't properly consider it. Ah well, I suppose that's why you and Nolan and Becca were called to this task."

Trev'nor shrugged, unable to disagree. "What questions

do you have for me, sir?"

"Becca mentioned to me that you only have half of Khobunter under control. Which half?"

Gesturing to the ground, Trev'nor borrowed a little dirt and made a map of Khobunter. "These three provinces: Trexler, Dunixan and half of Riyu. We're dead-set to conquer the rest of Riyu before the month is out. Dunixan, by the way, is an ally of ours. He was educated differently than the other warlords. In fact, he actually visited Bromany as a child."

Raile's eyebrows, what was left of them, rose sharply. "Did he, now."

"He's far more comfortable with magic than anyone else in this country. He actually approached us, wanting an alliance, and sir, I know for a fact that he is one of the people the Gardeners prepared to help us. In fact, I witnessed a Gardener speaking directly to him."

The ancient wizard let out a low whistle. "Rare, that. So this man can be trusted."

"Yes. He's one of the few that refused to participate in the slave trade, so there are no magicians in his territory." Trev'nor had a notion that was the real question.

"That's part of what I wanted to know," Raile stated with a nod. "But you still have half of Riyu, Von, and Rowe. That's quite possibly a very large student body for us."

"Yes, sir." Trev'nor cleared his throat and dared to ask the question that no one else was sure whether they should ask. "Do you want us to go and fetch the students from Strae and bring them here?"

"I think we'd better, don't you?" Raile responded dryly. "I understand that quite a few families have been separated. It will be better for their sake, and Garth's sanity, if we bring them back."

Trev'nor put a hand to his chest, letting out a relieved

breath. "I thought so as well, I just didn't want to hit you with a huge amount of students right off the cuff like this. You don't even have the academy finished yet, after all."

Raile flicked a hand, both accepting and dismissing this. "We'll take another three days to properly set up, then I'll send Sallah down to collect everyone. They'll all be relieved to hear it. Nolan tells me that his dragon is the record keeper?"

"Yes, sir. She'll be happy to recite the names, if you want to take note here."

"I'd prefer that. It will help us sort everyone but also it will tell us who might still be out there, who to expect." Raile looked off, toward the building, but his expression suggested his eyes saw much farther north. "This troubles me, young Warlord, more than you can know. My heart aches for my students, even though I haven't met them yet. My heart aches at the knowledge that you were in chains yourself. I feel that I have failed whole generations just because I didn't ask enough questions."

"Is that why you were so quick to come when Becca called?" Trev'nor asked quietly.

"Part of it. Guilt is a powerful motivator." With a sad smile, he patted Trev'nor's knee with a gnarled hand. "I am so sorry."

"Sir, you have nothing to apologize to me for. I admit it wasn't pleasant, but the men that chained me paid for it." Trev'nor's lips pulled back into a grim baring of teeth. "Trust me, I got my revenge. And I think, odd as this might sound, that my experience in those chains was necessary. It gave me true understanding of what these people were living through. It connected me to them in a way I can't explain. Without that, I would never have become as devoted to them as I am, and I would never have considered staying and taking this country on as my own."

Raile considered him with eyes that masked his true thoughts. "You think so?"

"The Gardeners do everything for a reason. They waited until we had conquered two provinces before showing up and telling us that Khobunter was what they'd prepared us for. You think that was coincidence?"

Snorting, Raile shook his head. "No. No, I do not. Point taken, young man. Well, I might be late to this particular party, but we are here now. Do not worry about your magicians. I will take care of it."

"I have no doubt of that, sir." Trev'nor in fact felt downright relieved that Raile took the responsibility on. Partially because he knew the old man could handle it all but also partially because if any of the magical councils came knocking at his door and issued demands, Raile knew exactly how to handle them. "Before we go, is there anything else I can do for you?"

"You go get me the rest of my students," Raile ordered, jabbing a finger at Trev'nor's chest, although a smile tilted the corners of his mouth up. "That's the only thing you can do for me."

Cockily, Trev'nor grinned at him, giving him a half-bow. "That I can do."

By the time Trev'nor made it back to the unofficial office, he found not only his two friends, but Shad, Dunixan, Simin, and Danyal all clustered around the map of the country. They all stood, as there was no way to cram that many chairs in this small of a room, and Nolan had to stand sideways to give him room to enter. He knew a war council when he saw one and chose not to ask stupid questions. "Just spoke with Raile. He said that he'll go and fetch the students from Strae in about three days, after they have the academy here more or less ready."

Everyone let out a relieved breath, for different reasons. Becca tilted her torso forward, leaning enough that she could look past Shad and Nolan to see him. "Is there anything he needs?"

"More students. We've been ordered to collect them," Trev'nor deadpanned.

Snorting, she gave him an analyst's salute. "That we can do. Well, let me catch you up. So far, we've argued and made no decision."

Shad chuckled, head rolling around on his shoulders, relieving the strain. "That about sums it up. I understand that taking Alred Watchtower was gruesome because of Riyu's tactics. You don't want a repeat."

Just those words made a wave of bile rise in Trev'nor's throat. He choked it down to manage a single, clipped, "Yes."

His mentor caught the reaction, eyes sharp, but thankfully asked no further questions. "Right, well, I have a few ideas of how to avoid a repeat but we definitely have to be sneakier, and I think we'll have to use a Legend."

And that would be the first point of contention, right there. Becca still didn't trust the reformed Star Order Priests. Nolan had been in danger, but never hunted by them—unlike Becca, he hadn't faced that danger personally. Garth had rescued him before it could come to that point. Trev'nor didn't understand her bone deep fear of them, but he respected it enough to not patronize her about it.

"I'm sorry, can someone explain exactly what a Legend is?" Dunixan requested with a slightly raised hand. "I've never heard of this."

"Legends have one of the most unique talents of all the magic users," Becca sought to explain, scratching at her cheek thoughtfully with a finger. "They can sense everything around them—and I do mean everything. People, buildings, rivers, mountains, everything down to a single pebble. They are like a living, breathing map legend."

"Hence the term," Dunixan responded in enlightenment. "I see. That talent will be extraordinarily helpful to us in the future. No wonder everyone's excited. And we have two of them?"

"We do. The problem is we can't keep many of the people the Gardeners gave us," Nolan chimed in. "I know we left detailed instructions behind on how to care for the gardens, but…"

"These people are entirely too stingy with water and the plants are likely wilting or dead by now." Trev'nor rubbed at his forehead, feeling a headache brewing already. "I've had the same fear. So, what, we keep a single Legend and send everyone else out?"

"No, we keep two Legends, one for me and one for you," Dunixan corrected. "You've got two Legends here and I want one."

"That's fair," Becca said neutrally.

It relieved Trev'nor that she was at least willing to use the additional manpower even if she didn't like having them. Then again, needs must. "So what are we arguing about?"

"Who to hit first. Riyu or Jashni." Shad smiled genially at the table in general, an expression that every student of his knew well. It meant that someone had overlooked the obvious and Shad merely waited for the right time to point it out.

Nolan blew out a gusty breath, shoulders slumping for a moment. "Alright, Shad, what did we miss?"

With that devil-may-care grin he was famous for, Shad stabbed both locations on the map with two different fingers. "Hit both."

His mouth opened instinctively to object, then Trev'nor's mind stopped him, hearkening back to those numerous lessons with Shad. Trev'nor might not be inherently sneaky, not like his teachers, but they'd drummed certain lessons into his head the hard way. He saw it the moment that Nolan and Becca did, as all three said in unison, "A diversion."

Dunixan looked between the three of them, head cocked a little in question. "A diversion. Which city is the diversion?"

"Jashni," they all answered in unison once more, then looked at each other and grinned in amusement.

Shad raised a hand to knuckle an imaginary tear from the corner of his eye. "My darlings, all grown up and going to war. Oww, Bec, that's my rib. I'm quite attached to it."

With the ease of a sibling, she ignored this protest. "Let me see if I can spell out what Shad is thinking. We send in a Legend, Trev'nor, and Dunixan's army to Jashni. Dunixan makes a ruckus outside the city, acting as if he's intent on conquering the place, drawing Riyu's attention—and hopefully most of his troops. While they're doing that, the Legend helps Trev'nor pinpoint the slaves' exact locations, and he just pops them out via Earth Path."

"I think I should go with them, Bec," Nolan disagreed. "I can go in cat form and scout out the situation ahead of time, help get everyone out of chains and ready to retrieve. I can also intervene if it looks like they're going to bring more slaves out as hostages."

His childhood friend inclined her head, agreeing. "If you want. While everyone's doing that, we'll march to Riyu and leave the army just out of sight. Shad and I will sneak into Riyu and capture the warlord. With him out of commission, the city will be in complete confusion. Then we call in our army, conquer it, no problem."

"From your lips to the Guardians' ears," Trev'nor prayed. "So far, none of our battle plans have really survived intact on the first try. We always have to adapt on the fly."

"Battle plans never survive first contact, it's a golden rule," Shad informed him. "But this, I think, will work. Jashni and Riyu are close enough that mirror communication should work, correct?"

"They should," Trev'nor allowed, thinking hard. "I bet we can charm Raile into making us a few before we leave."

"Let's do that. The timing on this has to be precise, kiddos. Very precise. If we linger too long around Jashni, we make it obvious that we're not really intent on getting into that city. But if we don't give them enough time, we don't draw Riyu's troops out. It's imperative that we get at least half of Riyu's standing army out of the city, otherwise our own troops don't stand much of a chance. They outnumber us significantly. Dragons can only make up so much fighting force."

Trev'nor agreed, and it was that timing that worried him. Would they be able to pull this off? If they didn't, they risked getting their own men needlessly killed and possibly losing a lot of innocent hostages in the process.

He saw from the corner of his eye that Simin ducked in low to speak to Dunixan quietly, but paid it no attention until Dunixan cleared his throat. "Raya Becca, if it's all the same to you, Simin wants to go in with you. She's been in Riyu's castle once before, as an ambassador for me, and is semi-familiar with the layout."

"It's been some years," Simin admitted frankly, "but I believe I remember most of the main routes, at least."

"Please come with us," Becca invited, expression

calculating. "Your familiarity with the place will be very helpful."

Trev'nor really, really wanted one of the Legends to go with Becca. He knew she would need that help. Just as he knew she wouldn't be able to accept having someone like that in her scouting party. He caught Nolan's eye, saw from his friend's expression that he thought the same thing, but Nolan gave him a minute shake of the head. Best to let it lie. She had Simin with her, hopefully that would be enough.

Shaking his head, he moved on. "When are we doing this?"

"We need to move sooner rather than later," Becca opined, frowning down at the map and tracing routes with her fingertip. "I say we nail down the timing on this today, organize troops tomorrow and get people in position, then start marching the day after."

"If you want me to organize my own troops and march on Jashni in time to meet you there, I'll need to leave tomorrow, and you'll need to give me a head start," Dunixan disagreed. "It will take me a solid week of travel to get home, after all, and I've already stayed longer than the two weeks I'd planned."

"No, it'll take about two hours," Becca disagreed while smiling pointedly at Trev'nor.

"Trev'nor Travel Service, coming up," he drawled. "Dunixan, I'll take you up. In fact, I'll take all of our gardening experts to their new homes as well. Nolan, you better tell me who needs to go where."

"I'll give you the list later," Nolan promised. "But I think Dunixan should go up via dragon. It'll be just as fast and he has dragons to settle in before he leaves home with an army."

Good point. Trev'nor had almost forgotten about the dragons.

Dunixan inclined his head in agreement. "Let's do that, then."

"Shad," Nolan inquired, "how much time do you think we should feasibly give Riyu to send troops out?"

"Depends on how war ready they are. They've got semaphores to pass messages with, right? That shortens the amount of time he needs to get a message from Jashni, so there's that, too."

"I believe I can answer some of that," Dunixan volunteered. "But before we talk about the timing, I think we have skipped over a rather major concern. Why do all of you assume that he will not utilize the slave magicians in Riyu?"

Trev'nor shared a confused look with his friends before responding slowly, tone lilting up in question, "Because he didn't do that before? He used them as hostages. That's why we're focused on rescuing them first."

"Indeed," Dunixan responded patiently, eyebrow arching ever so slightly in challenge, "he used them as hostages. And Alred Watchtower still fell. You think he'll repeat the use of a tactic that failed?"

"The man makes an excellent point," Shad acknowledged. "Alright, Dunixan, you know the ruthless snake better than we do. If hostages don't work, what will he try next?"

"He'll try using them." Dunixan didn't look at all happy with his own words; his mouth twisted as he spoke them, but there was no doubt in his voice. "Riyu hates magicians, thinks of them as nothing more than cattle, but the man is good at using the tools available to him. Not always in the way you'd predict, but he's not the type to ignore a weapon in his arsenal. I swear upon my name and the sand under our feet, he'll use the magicians in the next battle as a fighting force."

Becca groaned, slumping to rest her head in both hands. "Dunixan, I really want you to be wrong about that. As much as I hate them being used as hostages, I like them in the cages, they're easier to rescue that way. If they're actually on the battlefield, that means fighting around them somehow."

"Do I sound thrilled at the possibility? Still, it's very likely he'll do this. He unfortunately has a precedent to follow, as Von always uses their magicians as soldiers."

That was the first Trev'nor heard of it. "Do they really?"

"Yes, it's why Riyu has never won a battle against them," Dunixan explained. "And why the man actively buys up magicians as much as he can before Von can get his hands on them. Trust me, as distasteful as he finds the idea, he knows that this will work. Von has shown him it will."

And this was why the Gardeners had sent them Dunixan. Trev'nor would not have anticipated this new tactic otherwise. "Then we better train our own mages on how to deal with magical attacks. If that's the case, though, then we need to divide our labor up a little. Someone needs to go with Dunixan to protect his army from magical attacks, and someone needs to go with Commander Danyal."

"I vote Azin with Dunixan, Ehsan with Danyal," Nolan stated, rubbing at his chin thoughtfully while he stared at the map. "Ehsan will need water to work with, which Becca can supply. Azin doesn't need any support from us, so she'll be ideal to send with Dunixan."

Made sense to him. Trev'nor glanced at Becca, got a nod of agreement, and shrugged. "We'll do that, then. Bec, you want to teach them shielding?"

"Sure, I'll do that after the meeting."

A thought hit Trev'nor and he leaned into Nolan's side to ask, "Did Azin actually say that she'll keeping fighting with us, then?"

"She did, told me so earlier."

Thank all Guardians for that. "Alright, if that's settled? Dunixan, let's go back to the question of timing and semaphores. The land between Jashni and Riyu, what's it like? I assume that if they're using semaphores, it's mostly flat?"

"Almost completely so," Dunixan replied, gesturing to the map and tracing a line with his finger between the two cities. "From here to here is a large highway and there's very little variation to the landscape. Barely anything more than a few dips in the land."

"How quickly can they get messages back and forth, and how fast do you think they can deploy?"

As Dunixan replied, Trev'nor borrowed stone from the walls, widening the area somewhat and created little stools for people to sit on. After all, they were going to be here a while.

Becca clapped her hands together, looking at her two students and feeling a little inadequate to the task. A mage's shields all worked the same in theory, but every one's magic manifested it in a slightly different way. Finding that was not always easy. Becca dearly wished she could ask one of the Coven Ordan mages to teach this instead, and she still might do that, but they had only just arrived and were in a frenzy to get things settled and the academy up and running. Becca felt she should at least attempt the lesson first before calling in help.

"Right. You're probably wondering what I'm teaching you now and why we're so far away from the city. I'm trying to avoid property damage. Not that what I'm about to teach you is dangerous, but the application of it is." And that had only confused them further. Right. "Have either of you seen us use our mage shields?"

Ehsan thought for a moment before snapping his fingers. "Those glowing domes of power you sometimes have around you?"

"Yup, them," Becca confirmed. She frankly couldn't remember when and where they'd used those, as none of them had really needed anything but weapons shields since arrival, and even that rarely. Wait, she had used a magic shield once, hadn't she? Anyway, apparently someone had, and that made this a little easier. "Dunixan has a terrible theory that Riyu will use magicians actively in the next battle instead of just as hostages. Unfortunately, I think he's right. I want to teach you mage shields not only for your own protection but to protect our troops as much as possible. Now, first thing you must know—the shields will do nothing to you as it's your own magic, but it will hurt anyone else that comes into direct contact with it."

Their shy Elemental Mage didn't like the sound of that. Anxiously, she queried, "Hurt them? How badly?"

"Mostly it throws them back a few feet and knocks them unconscious," Becca explained, trying to alieve her worries while still relaying the danger. "It's a strong shock to the system. It'll take a certain set of conditions to permanently damage someone, like them standing in water when they touch the shield, or if they hit another weapon when they're thrown back, something like that. What you have to understand is that there are two types of mage's shields. There's a shield against weapons, and another against magic. You're not going to be able to use both of them at once."

Ehsan lifted his hand a little, signaling a question. "Why can't you use both at once?"

"Magically speaking, you can, that's not an issue. It's a mindset problem more than anything." Becca didn't recall if she had ever asked that question. Although she instinctively knew the reason, it was hard to put the answer into words. "Think of it this way. When you're using your magic, do you try to do something with your right hand and something totally different with your left?"

"Use water in two different ways at once?" Ehsan's eyes crossed and he shook his head. "Hard to imagine I can pull that off. It takes a lot of concentration just to do one task."

"And that's the problem," Becca acknowledged. "It takes practice to be able to do it. You can, mind you, every magician can. But you have to be perfectly comfortable with both shields individually before you can progress to the point that you can carry both at once."

"Sounds challenging," Azin responded dryly. "So, one at a time. Do they have to be in dome shape?"

"You can shape them however you need to," Becca assured her. "We use the dome because it's one of the stronger shapes, just by its nature, and it's the most effective in protecting a small area. Like one person. We'll start with the dome, but I'll need you to learn how to do walls at the very least so you can protect a wide area. Magic shield first."

Using the same words that Garth had, so many years ago, she walked them through the basics of shielding. The first few tries staggered and failed, as they normally did, then Azin caught the trick of it and hers held steady. Ehsan struggled a little more with the concept until he too caught the idea of it.

Becca found their barriers an interesting manifestation. Most mage shields glowed the same color as their magic, especially the weapons shield, and these two weren't exactly an exception to that. But mixed in with Azin's grey and Ehsan's blue were flecks of highly polished spots, scattered throughout the shield like fine glitter. It took her a while to understand what she saw.

Sand.

How integrated was this desert life into their psyche that even in their barriers, the sand was part of it? Shaking the thought off, she asked them both, "Do you feel like you have a good hold on it?"

Ehsan stared at his shield before nodding slowly. "I think so, yeah."

"Azin?"

The Elemental Mage didn't look as confident but answered, "Mostly?"

"Alright." Without any warning, Becca shot a small bolt of energy straight at Ehsan. It bounced off the barrier, of course, but the surprise of it made him yelp and jump back, losing the barrier in the process. Her second bolt hit him square in the chest, making him leap again and rub at his abused skin.

Glaring at her, he grumbled, "Alright, so I didn't."

"No, you did," Becca disagreed, trying not to laugh and somewhat failing at it. "My first bolt bounced right off. But you lost it after that point when your concentration broke. No matter how surprised you are, no matter what happens, you have to keep that shield up. Lives other than yours depend on it."

With a final pat at his chest, Ehsan resumed his spot and erected the barrier. Ready, he gave her a go-ahead jerk of the chin.

Becca hit him again, and it still startled him a little, as impacts against a barrier felt jarring to the one holding it. He held it through three bolts before it faltered. A fine sweat developed on his forehead, not unexpectedly in this afternoon heat, but Becca thought it more because of the concentration he put into this.

"Rest a minute," she advised. "Alright, Azin. Ready?"

Azin did not look at all ready but responded firmly, "Hit me."

Knowing what Becca would do, Azin lasted twice before the shield faltered, then yelped and danced around when the bolt hit her arm. To Becca's eyes, it looked like that third bolt barely slid in, the shield still having some strength to it.

Panting, Azin asked her, "Are you sure we can learn this

fast enough for the battle?"

"We have a few days before everything can be in place," Becca reminded her. "And the first day is always the hardest, for some reason. After the first day, you sleep on it, and it's much easier the second day. I think your subconscious mind has to get used to it. We'll go a few more rounds before we'll stop for the day, get dinner and all of that."

Ehsan braced himself in a fighter's stance, lifting the shield up again, and this time it looked far more opaque. Determination written all of his expression, he demanded, "Again."

Now that looked like a proper magic barrier. Grinning, Becca obligingly hit him again. One, two, three, four bolts and still it stood. Curious to see just how strong it was, she gathered a larger strike and hit him with a quarter of her normal strength. It held, only just, then splintered.

Spluttering, Ehsan demanded, "Are you trying to kill me?!"

"The barrier held," Becca pointed out sweetly. "I believe in you."

"Don't believe!"

A crunch of boot on sand mixed in with a low chuckle heralded Shad's approach. "Bec, be nice to the kids."

"That's rich, coming from you," she retorted, turning just enough to watch him. "You beat up on kids regularly."

"Training requires speed, not my fault they don't always dodge well," he responded airily.

"Uh-huh." Becca, being one of his students, knew very well that he never fought full force against them. Still, she'd come away from a few training sessions with some pretty spectacular bruises. Shad might know how to pull a punch but he didn't know how to go easy on someone in training. "So what are you here for? To watch the show?"

"Nope, thought I'd help. You've been doing magic barriers for nearly two hours. About time you switch it up, you think?"

Actually it probably was. "Azin, Ehsan, you ready to switch? Alright, then, same concept only we do a variation for physical attacks."

Shad patiently stood by while they learned the concept, and tried it, and tried it again when it protected more against magic than weapons. It always took a moment to switch mental tracks when first learning the barriers. Becca knew from the look of the shields when they finally had the right one up.

"Ah, there we go." Shad clapped, beaming at both of them. "Now I can see it."

"Only magicians can see the magical barriers," Becca explained, mentally kicking herself for not mentioning this before. "But everyone can see the weapons shield. It's one of the advantages, makes people stop and question before they do a full-bore attack."

Azin thought that through before asking, "So does that mean we'll need to be extra careful with magical shielding so no one accidentally runs into it?"

"That's precisely what it means. Alright, everyone ready to be tested? Good." Pointing a warning finger at her brother, Becca cautioned, "No more than quarter speed. Go easy."

"Becca," Ehsan said in exasperation, "you just shot a lightning bolt at me!"

"He's more dangerous than lightning, trust me," Becca answered, not at all kidding.

Shad grinned at her. "Aw, you say the sweetest things."

Taking four prudent steps back, Becca mouthed to the other two, 'Be ready to duck.'

Nervous now, they went into guard stances beneath

their glowing shields. Shad pulled sword and long dagger from his waist, gave them a twirl, then charged. Well, sort of charged, he knew better than to go full force against the barriers. It was more a scare tactic than anything, as he never once made contact with the actual barrier.

There was something inherently unnerving about a soldier charging you with weapons in hand. Even with these two, who had seen battlefields, they'd never been directly in the line of fire before. Instinctively, they flinched away, and that cost them their concentration. The barriers faltered, and they ended up with blades against their necks.

Azin stared up at Shad, wide eyed and panting, holding perfectly still. "You are *terrifying*. That's a quarter speed?!"

"Maybe a smidge faster," Shad acknowledged, grinning at her. "Granted, not many people are as fast as I am."

"Thank all guardians, saints, and pink elephants," Becca mumbled under her breath. From her peripheral vision, she saw Trev'nor standing at the gate and waving at her. "Looks like I'm being summoned. Shad, I expect my students back in one piece."

"I got them," he assured her, waving her off.

Knowing very well that by the time Shad finished with them, they wouldn't flinch from a charging dragon, Becca left the two with him. They might blame her for it later, but they'd also survive the upcoming battles, and that's what was important. Becca walked to Trev'nor's side, drinking steadily from her canteen as she moved. She really needed to get another storm heading this direction, this heat was unbearable. Didn't Khobunter know what Fall was?

"Bec," Trev'nor greeted, his hand shielding his eyes so he could stare at the training session. "How are they doing?"

She flattened herself to the wall, taking advantage of the meager shade offered there. "They have the basics down pat.

It's just a matter of practice now. I figure we should both take a run at them every day until we leave."

"It's a good idea. I'll take them in the morning." Lowering his hand, he turned to her. "Listen, I've been thinking about who to leave here in Rheben as security. How do you feel about leaving Captain Hadi's squad?"

"I think that's a great idea." In fact, Becca hadn't thought about who to leave just yet, but Hadi definitely made the top of the list. "He's comfortable with the magicians, most of our rescued people will recognize him as a good guy, and he certainly knows how to protect a city."

"Man's got at least a decade of experience," Trev'nor confirmed. "I think he's one of the best fits for the position. If you'll assign him here?"

Becca shook her head. "How about you ask him, and if he agrees, I'll assign him. I don't want to leave someone here that's unwilling. They won't do as good of a job."

"Ah. Point. Alright, I'll ask. Also, I'm not sure if anyone told you, but while you were gone both Azin and Ehsan were claimed by dragons."

Having gone through the experience herself, Becca knew very well that was exactly how it worked, and not the other way around. "Excellent, I hoped that would happen. Who claimed who?"

"Orion for Azin, Ginger for Ehsan."

"Now that's an interesting combination." If Becca had thought to play matchmaker with dragons and other people, those would not have been the ones she'd put together.

Trev'nor's rueful look illustrated his own thoughts on the matter. "Isn't it, though? Who'd have thought that our shy Azin would partner with what is quite possibly the burliest bad-boy of a dragon in the entire clan?"

"Or that Ehsan would attract Ginger, who can be a

sweetheart, but has the shortest temper known to man. How many things has she set fire to, again?"

"All the things," Trev'nor answered dryly. "All. I'm actually grateful for that pairing, at least that way our Water Mage will be on hand to put out whatever she's set on fire."

"Amen." Becca considered the matter and couldn't help but wonder, "Is that why Azin chose to keep fighting? Because of her dragon?"

"I think it might have played into the decision, yeah. But Azin's got family that's still missing. I don't think she wants to stop until she'd found them."

Becca had known that, actually. Azin remained very private with her own affairs but she did share some things. "I don't blame her."

"Neither do I, I'd choose to do the same." Gesturing to the trio still training out in the desert sand, he asked softly, "Do you think they'll be ready?"

"I think they'd better be ready, especially if Dunixan is right about Riyu's possible tactics, and I'm pretty sure he's right." Becca's internal eye turned toward the memory of Alred and for just a moment, despite the extreme heat, her blood ran cold. "Danyal once said that when fighting with Riyu, even if you win the battle, you still lose. For once, I'd like to turn the tables on that man so that he's the only one that loses."

Trev'nor put an arm around her shoulders and gave her a comforting hug. "From your lips to the Guardians' ears."

They stood in silence for a while before Trev'nor broke it, his voice low and subdued. "Are you absolutely sure you won't take a Legend with you? Dunixan said he was half-kidding, he feels like you need the Legend more than he does."

Becca couldn't make herself look him in the eyes and she

shook her head firmly. "I can't. I'm sorry, I just can't."

"These aren't the same people that chased you as a child," Trev'nor argued, trying to get her to see reason. "They're not even Star Order Priests anymore. Their magic isn't even the same."

"I can't ignore what they were," she snapped back. "I know they're not the same now, that the Gardeners would never have given them to us if they weren't trustworthy, but I only know that in my head! I can't accept it emotionally."

"Becca—" he started in a near growl of frustration.

"I can't trust either of them, and I don't want them at my back when I go into enemy territory."

Trev'nor paced three feet away, struggling with his own fears and frustration with her, then walked back, growing more resigned with each step. "I can't convince you, can I?"

"Give me time," Becca requested softly, staring out over the desert. "When I get to know them better, maybe I'll be able to look at them and see something other than a former enemy."

He clearly wanted to argue that the one thing they didn't have was time, but he bit back the words, standing with her in an uneasy silence instead. Finally, he capitulated, "I don't like it, but alright. You sure you'll be fine without one, though?"

"I think we'll be alright with Simin leading us."

He let out a soft breath, almost a sigh of resignation, but didn't push the matter any further. She knew that she'd disappointed him with that answer but the idea of taking someone into enemy territory that she couldn't trust made her stomach revolt. No. Just…no.

They'd be fine.

They really had to get more magicians trained up and some designated mirrors in place for these long-distance communications between their cities. Doing all of it through the dragons was as tedious as plucking all the hairs off a meuritta. Nolan didn't find it so, but Nolan could communicate directly with the dragons. Trev'nor and Becca were the ones who wanted to pull their hair out. The delay in communicating back and forth with Nolan acting as their medium could be anywhere between fifteen seconds to fifteen minutes, depending on the length of the message.

Today's session they spoke with Sagar, and while it appeared they had nothing serious to report, they did have a few issues to clear up. Trev'nor waited patiently for the messages, trying not to yawn or think too much about food. This late in the evening, he could either go for food or sleep, depending.

Something loud happened outside, multiple voices rising in either anger or fear, and Trev'nor shot up to his feet automatically. He couldn't hear it clearly through the office walls, but he could certainly tell something bad had gone down.

"That does not sound good," Becca observed in worry, also rising, going to stick her head out of the doorway. With the door open, the voices grew sharper and more distinct, the language in the rough Khobuntish slang the soldiers favored. "Cat, what's going on?"

"Bad fight," Cat mourned, sounding more sorrowful than anything. "Soldiers and magicians fight."

Swearing, Trev'nor glanced at Nolan, who instantly gestured for them to go ahead. Trusting him to take care of Sagar's minor issues, Trev'nor immediately left the office, right on Becca's heels. The shouting lowered to an unhappy murmur, which conversely worried him even more. What had happened to stop them?

They barely got down the street when Danyal appeared, running for them, although he skidded to a halt at their approach. "Raya, Raja, we've had an incident."

"Incident is not a word I like, Danyal," Becca growled, her agitation clear in the sharp tones in her voice. "It usually means trouble I won't approve of. What happened?"

Wincing, Danyal tried to keep a stoic face on. "Some of the men were being a little too rough on our magicians. The magicians tried to appease them at first, then one of them argued back, and it became physical. Garth fortunately stopped it before things could escalate."

Trev'nor saw red. The Alred magicians were still with them, as they hadn't the time to take them to Q'atal just now, and so they'd carted them along up to Rheben. Of everyone they'd rescued, he felt more than a little partial to this group, as he'd shed blood saving them and still felt guilty down to his core for not being able to save all of them. To think that some of his own men were tormenting them even further....

Magic sparked around Becca in a visible flash of light before she clamped down on her temper. "Lead me there."

Distinctly uneasy, Danyal obediently turned and moved off at a quick walk, fast enough that Trev'nor nearly had to jog to keep up with the man. They left the main street and went into the kitchen area, three buildings that surrounded a fountain courtyard. Everyone had voted to keep it for a mess hall, as it was one of the most structurally sound areas in the city and by far the prettiest. It didn't look at all tranquil and inviting now, not with multiple soldiers standing uneasily in groups and the magicians huddled in the far corner.

Without thinking, Trev'nor immediately went to them, stroking Garth's neck as he walked past in greeting. The dragon turned his head slightly to watch his rider but said nothing. Trev'nor focused on one of the women, a witch he knew by name, and used the gentlest tone he could muster. "Halia, what happened? Who's hurt?"

"The soldiers wouldn't eat with us," she responded, edging out of her protective clutch around her daughter, her hand reaching out for his sleeve but not quite touching. Her dark eyes darted nervously over to the side, teeth catching her bottom lip and worrying at it. "They said we didn't have the right to eat first. We argued, of course, that wasn't what you told us. Then they punched Sameel, and my daughter screamed for the dragons, and Garth came instantly to stop it all. Trev'nor, we can eat with the soldiers, can't we?"

"You can," he assured her firmly, catching that uncertain hand and squeezing her fingers reassuringly. "You were right to argue with them and they were very, very wrong to even try and stop you. Sameel, are you alright? Where are you hurt?"

Sameel had twenty years on him at least, but still ducked his head deferentially, the area around his right eye already bruising into a molten pattern of different colors. "I'm alright, Raja, I've had worse."

"I will fix this," Trev'nor swore to them. "Go ahead and eat, no one will stop you."

When they nodded, still a little hesitant and uncertain, Trev'nor felt like killing something. He turned and stomped toward the group of soldiers who were on their knees, clearly the guilty party, before he started glaring at the wrong people. He could feel his magic writhing under his skin, reacting to his emotions, and had to physically fight to get it back under control. It had been a while since he'd felt this kind of rage.

Becca stood in front of the five kneeling soldiers, arms crossed over her chest, feet shoulder length apart, glaring down at them as if they were insects she'd just peeled off the bottom of her shoe. "Did I hear that right? You told our magicians that they didn't have the *right* to eat first? Or eat with you?"

All of the men looked uneasily at the dirt, refusing to answer her.

"ANSWER ME!" she thundered, her voice ringing off the walls.

Everyone watching jumped, and not just because she yelled. Visible sparks and waves of golden magic swirled around Becca, a magical manifestation of her temper on the rise.

"My Warlord." Danyal walked right into that whirl of magic, braving what no sane man would, and put his hand on her shoulder. "Calm yourself, please. Angry people do not make wise decisions."

Some part of Trev'nor witnessed this and had to hand it to the man. Danyal certainly knew no fear. But the rest of him agreed one hundred percent with his co-ruler and felt like bashing a few things.

Becca took in a deep breath and let it shakily out again, her magic calming, although it lay over her form like a glowing halo. And not in a good way. "I am well aware that not all of you share our agenda. That some of you joined with our army because it was the best option available to you, in order to maintain your freedom. I don't ask that you understand what we're doing, but I do demand that you respect it. People are not cattle, they are not worms for you to squash under your feet, and you do not get to put yourself above former slaves just because they once wore chains. *I,"* she pounded a fist to her chest, voice rising in crescendo, *"wore those same chains."*

"We both did," Trev'nor informed the quaking shoulders coldly. "And we won't forgive this kind of attitude. I, personally, will not forgive anyone that hurts these people. I fought to free them and have the scar to prove it. You dare trample on what I fought to protect?"

Danyal, either fool hardy or brave, cleared his throat and offered, "I believe that they didn't think that far, Warlord. I believe it was habit more than anything. I make no excuse for them, but please calm yourself as well. I don't wish the earth under our feet to suddenly upheave."

Only then did he realize that his magic, too, had gone a little out of control. It swirled around him, ready and eager to destroy something, just waiting to be released. Taking in a deep breath, Trev'nor sought to calm himself and found it far harder than it should have been. He hadn't been this angry since Rurick.

"Danyal." Becca didn't take her eyes off the men, voice flat. "I believe that military law states that anyone who disobeys a direct order is to be fined for a minor offense or incarcerated for a major one. I believe under the definition, this falls under the 'minor' category, am I right?"

Whirling on her, Trev'nor slashed a hand through the air. "No. I will not have this settle on a fine."

"Trev, I can't justify incarcerating the men," Becca argued, looking distinctly unhappy with her own words.

"The wording of the regulations is fairly clear on this."

Stepping in closer to her, he switched to Chahirese, leaving everyone else out of this conversation. "I do not want our soldiers to think that this is something they can get by with. You really think that a simple fine will correct this behavior?"

"I don't, but I can't incarcerate them for this, Trev'nor. If we don't uphold the laws that we ourselves made, then that makes us as bad as the rulers we replaced," she argued back, voice low and heated. "We can't change the rules just because we're angry."

"Then maybe the rule needs to be changed. I don't agree with a fine."

"I can't change the regulations on the spot, either," she retorted, temper flaring again. "Think, you idiot. Doing that doesn't make it any better."

Throwing a finger toward the watching magicians, he hissed, "I will not have them abused by our own soldiers. I won't tolerate this, Becca."

"You think I like it?" she hissed back, like a coiled snake ready to strike.

"Stop, stop." Shad appeared between them, waving a hand down in a chopping motion. "Time out. Becca, I agree that a fine is not enough, there was physical damage done to one of them. You and Danyal put your heads together and get creative. Trev'nor, come with me."

Trev'nor snapped around, a retort ready to fly. He absolutely refused to move until he had this settled the way he wanted.

Grabbing him by the arm, Shad ordered with a smile that was all teeth: "Now, Warlord."

He knew that tone. Ten years of being Shad's student, of obeying the man unquestioningly, kicked in like a habit or an instinct. He followed without arguing, still steaming mad and wanting to do damage.

Shad led them far away from the kitchen area, down a road he hadn't repaired yet on the opposite side of the gate, well away from the area they'd made camp in. Only when they were far enough away to be out of earshot did he stop and turn again. Sympathy reflected in his eyes. "Trev. I know you're angry. I have a feeling I know why, as well."

"Because those five did something inexcusable," Trev'nor snarled, slamming a fist against the outer wall and leaving a crater behind. Shrieking hinges, he'd have to repair that later.

"That, I agree on. I don't think anyone would disagree. But your anger, and Becca's, is a little too extreme for the situation. I know Alred Watchtower was bad, young'in. I can see it in the way you flinch, the sad way Becca looks at the city. How bad was it?"

None of them had been able to bring themselves to talk about it. Even now, Trev'nor didn't, but the rational part of his mind realized he had to. Shad wouldn't know what Riyu was really capable of if they didn't tell him. Woodenly, he rattled out the explanation without taking a single breath. "Riyu left standing orders that if we approached, they were to use the slaves as hostages. He had them in cages all around the top of the watchtower and along the top of the gates. If we still attacked, they were to kill the rest of the slaves still in the pens, then kill any non-essential civilians left in the city."

Shad's head fell back and his eyes closed, sickened and resigned all at once. "No wonder everyone hates that man. What did you do?"

"We attacked. Garth dropped me onto the roof of the watchtower as a night drop. I went through the ceiling—" Trev'nor choked on the rest of the words, unable to force them past a constricted throat. Even now, he still relieved that moment in his dreams and every morning he woke up with tears smeared all over his face.

"Trev'nor." Shad wrapped him up in a hug, his embrace tight, murmuring words of comfort against his ear. "I know you did all you could, saved as many as you could."

"We shouldn't have done it," Trev'nor choked. "If I'd known you were coming, we would have waited. You're so much faster than I am, they all would be alive if you were the one to go in—"

Pulling back, Shad gave him an odd look. "Wait, now, hold on. I know I'm faster than you are, but Trev, I can't move inhumanely fast. And it sounds like that's what it would have taken. How many levels did you have to go through, how many soldiers did you have to face?"

"Three levels, about twenty soldiers, but—"

"Whoa, whoa, three levels? You fought through three levels? Twenty soldiers, by yourself?"

"Well, no, Garth helped. He came in from the outside."

"You seriously think that I could have done better in that scenario?" Shad demanded incredulously. "Kid, you were in a kill box! A really tall kill box, I grant you, but that's worse than a fatal funnel, you know? In fact, I think a watchtower is more a combination of a kill box on top of a fatal funnel, which is the worst combination in history. Even if I had been with you, we still would have had to clear each level one at a time. You couldn't have dropped me through on my own, I'm not an Earth Mage, you'd have to go with me through each roof."

Trev'nor's mouth opened to protest, then he stopped and really thought about. The angles, the logistics, the timing it would take to bring a passenger along in that scenario.

"You just realized I'm right, didn't you? Now, I grant you, we might have been able to save more if I'd been with you.

The two of us together, we would have been able to clear each level faster. But Trev, you didn't know I was coming. You can only make the best decision on the information you have at the time, you can't predict the future. No one's blaming you for doing the best you can, right?"

"I blame me," Trev'nor whispered.

"Why are you blaming yourself for what evil men did?" Shad rebuffed him gently. "Did you take a sword to those people? Did you kill them? No, right? The only thing you're guilty of, Rhebentrev'noren, is saving people."

Trev'nor turned away, scrubbing his face with his hands, eyes still hot with unshed tears. It all made sense, what Shad said. His heart just couldn't accept it.

"Trev, the hardest person to be angry with is yourself, and I think that's the problem here. You and Becca are still very angry about Alred, feeling like you didn't make the best decision, that you could have done something differently. I think you made the best decision you could at the time. Did you know about that standing order before you breached the city?"

"No," Trev'nor admitted hesitantly. "No, we only knew about the hostages."

"So you personally went to safeguard the ones you knew needed your protection. Nothing wrong with that. Let's lay the appropriate blame at the right door, shall we?" Shad grabbed his shoulder and shook him gently. "And let's not put our guilt on other people."

Blowing out a breath, Trev'nor looked up at the sky blindly for a long time, feeling his anger cool as he did so. As much as he wanted to argue with Shad, his mentor made entirely too much sense, and he found he couldn't even scrape up a word in contradiction. "Since when were you wise, Shad?"

"Hey, I have my moments. Don't you roll your eyes at me, I'm your illustrious mentor, remember?"

"Right. Illustrious," Trev'nor agreed deadpan, taking in a fortifying breath. "Come on, illustrious mentor, let's go see what my co-ruler has decided to do."

Shad fell into step with him, studying him from the corner of his eyes. "You're going to let her decide?"

"Yup. For two reasons: One, she's calmer than I am at the moment, so her judgement's going to be fairer. Two, the army is kind of Becca's domain. I've learned not to mess with it, she demands more respect from the soldiers than I do."

"Hmmm," Shad hummed thoughtfully. "I wonder why?"

"She was the first to salute them back, the first to put on a uniform. I think that's why." Trev'nor kind of regretted not doing either, now. He'd had to earn their respect the hard way and he wasn't convinced he had it yet.

They returned to the courtyard and found that the watching crowd had more or less dispersed. The magicians sat gathered around two different tables, eating slowly, and the rest of the soldiers carefully gave them space. Becca stood near the courtyard gate, talking quietly with Danyal, but at his approach she stopped and watched him warily.

Opening his arms to her, he silently invited her in for a hug, sighing in relief when she instantly went to him, hugging him without hesitation. Folding her in, he whispered against the top of her head, "Sorry."

"I know, I know. You don't need to say anything else."

"Whatever you decide to do in punishment, I'm alright with it. I trust your judgement."

Still wary, she stepped back and informed him slowly, "I fined them three months of pay and put them on latrine duty for a month."

"Alright," he agreed. Privately, he felt like that wasn't

quite enough, but he didn't fully trust himself right at that moment.

"That's it? No argument?"

Shaking his head, he assured her, "No argument. I apparently have too much anger and guilt left over from Alred. I just want to kill anything that hurts them."

"I know, and it's worse coming from our own side, but Trev—I promise you, this won't happen again. The way we reacted sent a message loud and clear to our soldiers. They treat the magicians with respect, or they incur both our wraths."

"They won't dare to repeat this behavior again," Danyal assured them both. "Thank you, Raja, for keeping your temper."

"Fortunately Shad talked sense into me," Trev'nor replied with a crooked smile. "Becca, I think I need to eat dinner with everyone here. Can you handle the rest of the meeting with Nolan?"

"I will, don't worry about it. You're right, they need some moral support right now." She gave him another quick hug, then snagged Danyal and retreated back to the office with him.

Trev'nor didn't actually feel up to sitting down to dinner and acting like things were normal. He really wanted to curl up somewhere and just sleep this off. Shad perhaps sensed this, as he put a supportive arm around his shoulders as he lead the way into the courtyard. "I'll eat with you."

Casting him a thankful look, Trev'nor murmured, "I'm so glad you came up."

"Me too, kid. Me too."

"Carjettaan, how are you with enclosed spaces?"

The Legend gave him a blatantly amused look, both eyebrows arching. "You're asking this now? While we're sitting under Jashni?"

Trev'nor could admit his timing might be a bit off. "We were rushed this morning, I didn't think to ask."

"I'm fine with it. In fact," she turned about in a slow circle, looking all around her, "it's quite fascinating. When you said you'd take us down into the earth, I envisioned a tomb or just a box of stone, something along those lines. But this is more like a cocoon. A cocoon of magic and earth. I feel like I'm in a cave with glowing walls more than anything. The Gardeners told us that Earth Mages understand the earth very well, and that it will conform to their will, but I didn't fully understand that until you took us down here."

Between rushing about getting their new gardeners in place, sending Dunixan home via dragon back, making sure the academy was up to spec, and transporting part of their army to a waiting spot near Riyu, Trev'nor hadn't possessed much free time. Certainly not enough to question his new… helpers? Retainers? What was he supposed to call them, anyway? And lurking underneath a city he was about to infiltrate might not be a good moment to ask any questions, but they were sitting there waiting on Nolan to give them the signal, so at the same time, Trev'nor didn't see the harm. "What was it like? Living with the Gardeners."

"Incredible, in many senses of the word. Also very confusing and overwhelming. They just don't think the way that we do. I came to understand that they speak to us like we would a young child. Our understanding is very limited compared to theirs."

Trev'nor had precisely one encounter with a Gardener, but he understood immediately what she meant. "Did you see them day to day?"

"No, that was too much for us. They would come for about an hour at a time, speak with us, do alterations as necessary, then give us a task to complete before the end of the day. The area we were in…" she paused, mouth searching for words, but coming up empty. Frowning, she started again. "I don't know where we were. Somewhere on the planet, certainly, but I can't tell you specifically what country. It was the most amazing garden I've ever seen. They sometimes would take us out of the garden, let us see the damage done by careless people, and those of us talented enough would help fix it. Not everyone was happy being there, though. There are still some up there grumbling."

"I don't doubt that." Trev'nor's attention caught something in particular that begged to be clarified. "Alterations?"

The older woman gave him a sad smile. "Our magic became incredibly warped by being in the Star Order. It took them years, almost a decade in my case, to undo the damage. Originally, my magic was never suited to be a witch, but was always meant to be a Legend. I was so glad the day it finally settled back into my body correctly. Most of my life, I felt very out of tune with my own skin. Having my magic flowing again was amazing. Like I could finally breathe."

Everything she said fascinated him and just brought up other questions. Trev'nor began to regret the timing of this conversation. "I want to talk to you about this more later, when we actually have the time. And please, please write down everything you can remember. We have such limited documentation on the Gardeners. Everything you can tell us will help the rising generation."

She gave him a slight bow. "I will do so, Warlord."

For some reason, having this woman who was at least twenty years older than him bow and call him warlord disturbed Trev'nor. Should he correct it? But technically, she was right to address him so.

"If I may, one question?" Carjettaan waited for his nod of encouragement before asking, "Your co-ruler, Becca, is not comfortable with us. Have we done something to offend her?"

Trev'nor winced. He really, really didn't want to answer that question but at the same time she needed to know. "It's not you, any of you, personally. It's just that the Star Order hunted her when she was eight years old. Shad had to swoop in and rescue her."

The former Star Order Priestess winced. "I was afraid it was something like that. I understand her dislike, then."

"I'm sure she'll adapt and realize you're not the same but it's going to take time." At least, Trev'nor hoped that this would be smoothed out in time. It'd better; he didn't know what else to do otherwise.

From the mirror broach pinned to his collar came the tinny sound of Nolan's voice: "*Trev.*"

Heaving a silent breath of relief, Trev'nor blessed his friend's timing. "Here."

"*Dunixan's army is now in sight. I just saw a soldier racing up to the semaphore tower, so looks like they're sending off a message pretty quickly."*

So they bought the ruse so far. Well, the semi-ruse, as Jashni would still be conquered either way. "Got it. Did you tell Becca?"

"She hasn't checked in yet and I don't dare contact her first. If I give their location away, Shad will never let me live it down."

"Wait, then." Trev'nor eyed the ceiling. "And tell us when to move. We're right below one of the holding cells."

"The one near the northern gate," Carjettaan tacked on helpfully.

"Don't move quite yet. Also, we're going to be in for a whale of a fight out here."

Trev'nor didn't like the sound of that at all. "Why?"

"You know how Dunixan thought Riyu would use the slaves to fight? Turns out he was right. The stronger of the magicians are already lined up on the walls. As soon as Dunixan is in range, they're going to start hurling spells."

What spells, that was the question, as none of them had formal training. What attack spells had been orally passed down? "Did you tell Azin?"

"I did, and she's already got a shield up. Bless Becca for teaching her so well, I can tell from here that shield is incredibly strong. I think our soldiers will be alright as long as she holds it."

The words went unsaid: How long could she? Azin, as a mage, possessed an insane amount of power at her fingertips, but at the same time she was new to shields. Trev'nor knew exactly how much concentration they took until the bearer got used to carrying them. With multiple attackers flinging spells at her, how long could she hold that barrier?

Not wanting to plant that doubt in anyone's head, Trev'nor asked a different question instead. "Did you call

Ehsan and warn him? If they're doing it in Jashni, you know they'll do it in Riyu."

"I'm calling him next. Stand by."

The broach went still and quiet once more. Trev'nor reached out with his senses, but of course he could only feel earth and the weightier feel of the buildings sitting on it. His magic wasn't as suited to this as the Legend standing at his side. "How many groups are you detecting, again?"

"Six, with multiple magicians strung out along the walls. The group above us is the largest."

Six. Trev'nor's cheeks puffed up as he blew out a steady stream of air. This was going to get tricky.

Becca had never tried sneaking before, not seriously when lives were on the line, and she found it far more nerve-wracking than she expected. Watching her brother move steadily ahead of her, slipping past sentries around the base of Riyu's fortress, one would think they were on some kind of grand quest. He grinned from ear to ear, excited, nearly glowing with happiness.

In contrast, Simin moved as silently as a shadow, grim faced and with a hand clenched permanently on her short sword.

Part of Becca's mind irreverently wondered if Danyal and Cat still pouted. When they had split ways this morning, her commander had not worn a happy expression and her dragon openly huffed and puffed, making her displeasure clear to all. But they couldn't risk either of them being within sight of Riyu's walls. Becca left firm orders for them to march for the city slowly and to halt if things went wrong. She didn't want them parked outside of Riyu's gates if this plan didn't work.

Getting into the city had not been at all challenging, as Trev'nor had dropped them off inside of it and near the fortress before speeding off to Jashni. They'd had no other viable way to get in that wouldn't take several hours, and if they had an Earth Mage that could circumvent the walls, they might as well use him.

But that only carried them so far. Now they were near the fortress, and that was a different kettle of fish altogether.

The city of Riyu was one of the oldest cities in Khobunter, and the state of the buildings reflected that. It was made of the same sandstone, mortar, and bricks that most cities used, but the age of it shown in the wear and tear along the seams. Years of wind and sun had worn this place down so that it looked half-decayed in areas, like the buildings were infected with leprosy. People had crammed buildings in together, so that barely a foot could pass between the buildings, and clothes lines strung out over the tops of the streets. It brought some color to this brown-on-tan colored city but even that ended once they came close enough to the fortress. The street wrapping around the base of the eight story building had nothing crowded near it, and no one dared to hang laundry to it, either. It made the road almost seem wide in comparison to the others, but that wasn't actually the case, it just didn't have the same amount of clutter.

By wits and will, Simin led them along to an inner gate, one used mostly by the servants, then past it altogether. "Water route," she whispered back, eyes intent on the very narrow way ahead of them. Between the fortress wall and this back alley, Becca barely had the room to pass through without her shoulders touching both walls. Had the designers planned it to be this narrow on purpose or did it just sort of end up this way when the city started encroaching? At least it didn't smell like a sewer, even though it rather looked like one.

"Not following you," Shad admitted, still happy at the idea that trouble might leap out at any point. "I see no water."

"About every five years, they get major storms that blow through and drench everything for three weeks," Becca explained quietly, following right at Simin's heels. "They have reservoirs and water canals for those seasons that lie dry the rest of the time. I learned about it the first city we took. I assume Simin wants to use some of these to wriggle through the walls?"

"We can breach the outer wall that way, at least," Simin confirmed.

"Simin~" Shad sing-songed mischievously. "How do you know exactly where this is, hmmm?"

"You really think I was here for peace talks, all those years ago?" Simin snipped back, casting them both a quick wink.

"Not for a moment," Shad admitted, chuckling.

Exasperated that her brother would *chuckle* while trying to sneak into a heavily fortified building, Becca poked him in the ribs. "Why do you find danger so funny?"

"I find absolutely nothing funny about fatal funnels, which we're in," he assured her, so deadpan that she knew he was laughing internally.

"You are so totally laughing on some level right now. Aletha was crazy for marrying you."

"Let me tell you something, little sister. Aletha is actually crazier than I am, she's just better at hiding it."

"Tell me something I don't know." Snorting, she realized she was bantering while on a stealth mission and felt slightly appalled at herself. Maybe Shad's crazy was contagious.

Slinking a little lower to the ground, Simin motioned for

them to stop and slid one eyeball around the corner of the fortress's outer wall. She stayed that way for a few moments before she gestured them onward with a flick of the hand. "Clear for now. The narrow opening with the blue door. Go."

Praying this all worked out according to plan—Becca really didn't want to set fire to the whole city while fighting their way out of here—she scurried for the door in question.

Trev'nor looked at the ten soldiers clustered around him. Becca had suggested he take soldiers along, to help deal with the rescued slaves, as they had no way of knowing if anyone would panic. Also, after Trev'nor brought everyone out, he needed to park them a safe distance away and the soldiers would help manage them all until he could return and fetch them back again. These ten were handpicked by Danyal himself, good men that had grown very accustomed to magic, but even they cast leery glances toward the faintly glowing earthen walls.

Thinking it best to remind them of the plan, to take their mind off being a hundred feet underground, Trev'nor cleared his throat. "Gentlemen. I realize you know the plan, but let's review it. I will literally drop people in here all at once. Nolan will warn them ahead of time, but they'll likely panic. All of you speak better Khobuntish than I do, so I'm trusting you to reassure them. As soon as I have them all, we'll zip to the next location, grab more people. I need you to pull every person off to the right side as soon as you can, give me room to bring more people in."

"Your right, sir?"

That was an excellent question and one Trev'nor should have considered before. "Yes, my right. Do you all remember what to tell them?"

One lieutenant in the front dutifully recited, "We're soldiers of the new warlords and we're freeing all of the magicians. We'll bring them safely into the Ruins of Rheben, where they can be reunited with friends and family. It'll be safe there, they won't be slaves any longer."

"Excellent." Trev'nor could only think of one more thing to add. "Make sure no one touches the walls. It'll shock them rather badly. If anyone starts panicking, knock them out without hurting them if you can. Sit on them if you have to. We absolutely cannot afford panic down here."

"Yes, sir!" the men barked in unison.

"Good, thank you." Trev'nor eyed the ceiling again, anxious and trying not to show it. How much time had passed down here, anyway?

Silence descended once more, thick and heavy. It grew uncomfortably warm as well, between his magic and being enclosed in a space with no air currents. Trev'nor's magic made the air breathable, but that didn't automatically make it comfortable, and he really wanted to open up and give them some air. Unfortunately he didn't dare, not until it became absolutely necessary. A stray thought passed through his mind, a remembrance of a time Garth had been in a similar situation. Had he the same thoughts, the same wish for fresh air? For all that his mentor freely shared experiences with them, Trev'nor just now realized that he'd been stingy with the details.

Of course, thinking about one Garth made him think of his dragon doppelganger. Garth had been seriously unhappy with this plan, as he couldn't reach Trev'nor if something went wrong. Any assurances that he'd be fine, that being under the earth was the safest place for him, were soundly ignored. Trev'nor had a feeling he'd be soothing a dragon's ire later for this plan, despite it not being his idea.

Sergeant Mose cleared his throat and sidled in a little closer. "Raja?"

"Yes?" Trev'nor, thankful for the interruption of that silence, gave him a quick smile.

"Commander Danyal said earlier that Raya Becca wants to dissolve the tradition of bride prices. Will that happen or…?" the man trailed off invitingly.

Trev'nor stared at him, nonplussed, as this was the first he'd heard of it. Then again, the idea of bride prices made no financial sense whatsoever and Trev'nor was not personally in favor of the tradition. He knew for a fact it had kept at least three of these men from marrying, as they couldn't afford it, and he didn't like the idea of anything interfering with a man's happiness. Certainly not his soldiers, whose lives were hard enough already. "Raya Becca and I are in agreement that it should be dissolved." There, that sounded official.

The soldiers looked around at each other, smiling, looking happier than they ever had. Trev'nor took in the reactions and made a mental note to himself to talk this over with Becca. Soon. Practically, he added, "I haven't had a chance to plan anything official with her about this, but know that we feel like it's preventing good people from marrying, which we're not in favor of. It'll be one of the things in this culture we'll change once we get everything else settled down."

This didn't daunt them at all, in fact they seemed to hear "it will be changed" and nothing else. Ah well, if Danyal reported that Becca said this, then she certainly had. Danyal didn't know how to exaggerate. And Trev'nor thought it was a great idea.

The mirror broach lit up and Becca's voice came through clearly, if softly: "*Trev, Nol, the order just went out. Troops are assembling right outside of the gate. I think in another hour or so, you need to move. How are things there?"*

"*Dunixan's army is putting up a really good distraction. He's assembling catapults here, like he's going to siege the place or die trying,*" Nolan reported. Very smugly, he continued, "*They're buying it hook, line and sinker. But the city commander has also deployed magicians along the walls, so I think we're running out of time here. I'll have to quietly subdue people when I can, buy us some time. Trev?*"

"I'm waiting on you to tell me when I can move." And Trev'nor's nerves hoped that would be soon, as he couldn't do this waiting thing much longer. He preferred action and dealing with bad consequences to sitting around biting at his nails.

"*They're assembling quickly over here. I think they've drilled for just this event as no one's needing much direction.*" Becca paused, seconds ticking by. "*Almost completely assembled and curse that goat of a whoreson, he's got magicians lined up with the soldiers. Dunixan was unfortunately right. We're in position to go down and find Riyu himself but I'm not moving until the army is at least out of sight.*"

More time passed. Trev'nor didn't want to chat incessantly as that might give Becca's position away, so he kept his mouth shut even though he really wanted to ask her just how far she'd gotten into the fortress. She had two sneaks with her, so he had to assume she'd made good headway.

"*Army has left Riyu. They're double-timing it toward Jashni. Nolan?*"

"*Commander's lost his nerve, he's ordered magicians to start firing. It's a rather interesting mix of spells, not all of them lethal. Azin's holding for now but I'm not sure how long she can last—it's quite the barrage. I'll have to react in a few minutes. Is the army far enough out yet?*"

"*No. We need a little more distance. They can still easily retreat at the moment."*

Nolan swore, soft and vehement, the hissing of a cat's growl in his tone which told Trev'nor that his friend hadn't changed out of cat form yet. *"Tail reports that they're not heading toward the big holding pen near you, Trev. They've got another group stashed along the eastern wall."*

Blessing Tail for helping with the spying, Trev'nor demanded, "Is he sure?"

"He's sure. I don't know why, though."

"Not as strong of a magic source over there," Carjettaan reported, troubled. "I think they're mostly the useless slaves, the ones without any magical talent."

The expendable ones, in other words. Trev'nor made a snap decision. "Becca, I have to move. Nolan, I'm grabbing what's above my head first. You subdue those soldiers if you can. If not, we'll just have to deal with the fallout."

"No other choice," Nolan agreed, breathing a little harder, as if he were already sprinting. *"Bec?"*

"We absolutely can't afford for those soldiers to return to the city. Nolan, can you communicate with the dragons long-distance?"

"I can, and I think I know what you're going to ask."

"Whatever you two are planning, do it, we don't have time." Looking around him, Trev'nor trusted his friends to do their jobs and ordered the soldiers: "Get ready. We're about to have company."

Becca had done some rather surreal things in her life, but straddling a dry water canal, on top of an enemy fortress, calling down an air strike, had to make the top of the list. She felt like every cell in her body sat on a trip wire, ready to spring into action at the slightest indication her small group had been discovered. Shad, lounging just below her at the T of the canal, seemed perfectly at ease. He actually had his legs swinging back and forth as he stared down. Simin, at least, seemed aware that even though they were technically out of sight of the guards patrolling the battlements below them, someone looking up at the right moment and from the right angle would be able to spot the intruders.

Riyu Fortress certainly commanded quite the view. Most of the fortress edges didn't have a square shape—instead each tower was a large circle, with the base being half again as wide as the very top level. It dominated the city, giving a bird's eye view of the streets below. The architect had taken advantage of the height, and along the top of each level, the wall was not made of thick stone, but instead a water canal to help capture any falling rain. Four water reservoirs sat on the very top of the fortress, canals running down from each to connect with each other, leading to larger reservoirs at the base of the fortress. They were nothing more than wide squares of cement and stone, hot under the blazing suns and not a trace of moisture to be found in this season. Becca knew from the feel of her nose and cheekbones she was burning. Nolan would have to heal her tonight because she didn't dare call in shade clouds.

Trying to ignore all of the discomfort, she kept the mirror broach up at her mouth and her eyes trained on the troop movements outside of the city. "Nolan, the semaphores."

"Dragons are on their way. They're actually happy they can destroy something. I think they were getting bored just flying around up there."

Of course they were. "Remind them we need to destroy just ONE semaphore, alright? We'd like to be able to use those ourselves later."

"I'll try but I don't think that's going to sink in very well. Not with the mood they're in."

Becca prayed this worked. Rule number two—or was it three?—of combat was disrupt enemy communications as much as possible. If your enemy couldn't coordinate an attack or talk to each other, it made your job much easier. If Jashni couldn't relay they were under attack via magical means, that they had lost their hold on the defenses, then Riyu wouldn't realize what was really going on. Or at least, that was the hope. Becca had Dunixan's troops attack Jashni for a reason—she wanted them to believe this was the same ole' same ole', just another border conflict with Dunixan.

Not a new conflict with the magical warlords.

From this distance, the troops couldn't really be seen. Just the trail of dust behind them as they marched steadily westward. Becca certainly couldn't see any hint of the dragons swooping in and targeting the semaphores. She sat there for another moment, indecisive, then glanced down at her brother.

Sensing her gaze, he craned his neck around to return the look. "No sense sitting here, kiddo. They either make it or they don't. Let's find a warlord."

Huffing out a breath, she nodded agreement, then carefully half-climbed, half-skidded her way back down. They'd climbed up to this height just for the vantage point to confirm troop movements, but this wasn't where they needed to be. Simin claimed the war room was on the third level of the fortress. They had five levels to scale back down, and then the lovely task of finding a way actually inside.

"Shad." Becca frowned down the side of the building, and all of the guards making regular patrols, and honestly had no idea how to get past all of them. "How do we get inside the building, anyway?"

"Doors," he explained, expression mock somber and earnest.

Rolling her eyes, Becca willed herself to have patience. There was simply no helping Shad in these moods, he was as bad as a child in a candy store. "No, seriously, how do we get past all of the guards and inside?"

"Watch and learn, kiddo." With a wink, he slid his way down to the next level.

Trusting that he knew what to do, she gamely followed.

"I now seriously regret only bringing eleven people with me," Trev'nor complained under his breath.

"Did you say something?" Carjettaan asked, breathless from all her yelling to be heard over the many, many cries of their rescued slaves.

Trev'nor waved her off, indicating it hadn't been anything important. He knew, intellectually, that rescuing everyone at once wouldn't be easy, but 'not easy' was the understatement of the century. People were panicked, even with the warning they got from Nolan, and not handling being underground well at all. They tried to climb the walls, and the soldiers couldn't always stop them in time, which led to hurt people. Hurt people do not make wise decisions. They screamed, cried, tried to climb over each other, frantically looking for an exit.

He dearly wished he could give them one, but Trev'nor didn't have the time to zip out to some desert location, dump people temporarily off, then come racing back to the city for the next load. He was barely able to keep ahead of the Jashni soldiers as it was, following Carjettaan's instructions on where to go next.

Eleven soldiers did their level best to contain the situation, loudly explaining the situation over and over. Some people calmed, some were too hurt and scared to listen, and more than a few had to be physically stopped before doing something stupid. It was nothing more than a din of noise and chaos and Trev'nor had to ignore all of it or risk sending them into a ley line.

Trusting his people to do their jobs, he grimly continued on, hitting five locations as quickly as possible. A few times they accidentally dropped a Jashni soldier in with the slaves, which made things more than a little exciting.

Sweating profusely, dying for a drink, Trev'nor focused on his Legend for the last time. "Where next?"

"Straight north," she directed, then did the count down. "Five, four, three, two, one…a little more. Stop. Directly overhead. I count thirty-three."

Following her instructions to the letter, Trev'nor carefully dropped the last group inside of this already crazy bedlam. Good, now that he had everyone, he could move them out of the city altogether, to some safer place where they could wait the battle out. He didn't have time to take them all the way to Rheben, unfortunately, but perhaps to the back of Dunixan's army would wor—

A scream of warning, nearly lost in among the other screams, was his only hint before searing pain hit him in the back. White hot, it robbed him of all breath for a moment, but it didn't stop his training from kicking in. Trev'nor had an elbow up as he spun around, another arm up to block the next attack. He saw his attacker in a split second, a young soldier that looked too white around the eyes, frantic and literally fighting everything within reach of him. Multiple people dodged, frantic to get out of his way, most of them quick enough to avoid serious injury.

The soldier dodged the elbow Trev'nor threw his direction, but he couldn't dodge two very upset enemy soldiers, and he went down in seconds, dead before he hit the ground. Trev'nor couldn't pay much attention to him, as abruptly he went sideways, the searing pain demanding more and more of his attention.

"Raja." Sergeant Mose dropped to his knees, already stripping off his pack, reaching for something. "Raja, stay with me. You, Legend, take hold of him and don't jostle that knife."

"Shouldn't we pull it out?"

"No, not until Raja Nolan says we can. I saw a man walk around for thirty minutes with a knife in his gut, hurting but alive, and when they removed it he was dead in minutes. Better to leave it. Raja?"

Trev'nor forced himself to focus. "Guardians, getting stabbed hurts. Don't worry, Mose, I'm still aware." Not for much longer, though. He could feel the blood leaving him too quickly, soaking the back of his shirt and pants, and that was not good. That was in fact very, very bad. If he lost consciousness down here, he would bleed to death before Nolan could get to him, and if he died, everyone else down here died with him.

Some part of his mind realized that he couldn't afford to pass out, but darkness and the idea of sleeping was tempting. So tempting. He shook his head, fighting to stay awake. "Carjettaan. Dunixan's army. Find me his army."

Strain laced her voice, but her hands on his side stayed steady as she directed, "Go left a little, good, straight twenty. Almost there. Three, two, one, go up."

Trev'nor brought them carefully to the surface, gasping now in pain, silently crying from it. He really, really hated being stabbed. The earth melted away, revealing the blazing suns and a slight breeze that momentarily felt good enough to override the pain. He reveled in that one moment, fingers fumbling for the mirror broach and missing it.

Mose grabbed it and held it up for him. Trev'nor fuzzily decided to promote the man, he was doing excellently in a crisis. It took more focus than he really had, but he activated the mirror and called into it hoarsely, "Nolan."

"*Trev? Did you get everyone out?*"

"Nolan," he repeated, knowing he should ask for help, but the words escaped him. He couldn't bring them together long enough to force them out of his mouth. "Dunixan. Hurt."

"*Wait, what? I didn't catch that.*"

Mose leaned over, putting their heads on the same level. "Raja Nolan, Raja Trev'nor has been stabbed. We're at—"

Trev'nor didn't hear anything after that.

Becca now appreciated just how much Shad had NOT taught her the past nine years. He made sneaking into the building look easy, nothing more than a lark, using techniques she had never seen before. Her brother and Guardian really had had no intention while raising her to let her out of Strae, had he? He'd taught her self-defense and strategy because to him not knowing that was suicidal, but he'd not carried it farther than that. Part of her felt miffed at this, that he didn't think she'd go out and face the world, but Becca grudgingly admitted she couldn't blame him. Even she had thought she'd stay in Strae or at least Chahir for the rest of her life. Khobunter had changed her mind on that.

Shaking the thought off, she focused on the here and now. They were inside on the third level of the building, Simin leading, Shad rear guard, with Becca in the middle. She had magic ready and waiting on her fingertips but prayed she didn't have to use it. It would be a dead giveaway to their position and she couldn't really afford that just yet.

The halls thrummed with noise, almost a visible echo as people rushed back and forth, calling out information and orders to each other. The interior seemed more opulent than some of the fortresses she had been in—and that said something. Trexler's office had been a gilded nightmare but the interior of the Riyu Fortress gave even it a run for its money. This hallway alone had enough gilded edging along the trim work, rare rugs, and priceless statues to run a country for a month.

And as soon as she had control of this place, that's exactly what she would do with it. Displays of wealth like this were wasteful and insane.

Simin stopped at the end of the hallway, where another bisected it, and lifted a closed fist. Recognizing the universal signal to stop, Becca instantly did, nearly holding her breath.

The retainer's head swiveled back and forth as she checked both ways, then she ducked back in a little further so no one could easily see her from the other hallway. Keeping her voice low, she explained, "Riyu's war room is three doors down from here on the right side. I think the time for stealth is over."

"Gotta agree," Shad responded, hand reaching for the sword hilt at his side. "Simin, how many do you think are in that room?"

"You'll have a full council in there at least, with a few runners and officers."

"So, at least twenty people," Becca translated this with ease. "Shad, want to breach?"

"Yes." He flashed her a quick smile, already moving. "Simin, secure the doors once we're through."

"Understood."

The voices coming out of the war room were loud enough to hear clearly in the hallway. People argued at the top of their lungs, trying to out-shout each other. Most of the shouting seemed to be done by Riyu, as she heard pleas addressed to him several times to calm down.

After so many battles and horrendous ordeals she'd survived, Becca was past being scared, but her pulse still quickened as adrenaline shot through her system. She'd already been on edge but now it kicked up to another level, heartbeat loud enough to be a war drum in her ears. That war drum went into a triple beat when Shad strode through the open doors.

For a moment, no one seemed to realize they were there. Men of various ages and dress, some in uniforms, some not, ranged around the large square table in the center of the room, sometimes pounding on it to emphasize some point. Runners scurried between the desks lining the walls and the main table, passing along messages, usually ignored in favor of the generals yelling at each other. It in no way resembled her own war councils, where people rationally spoke to each other, communicated ideas, and didn't try to push their own agendas. How had Riyu managed to keep his territory intact with these idiots as his advisors?

One of the officers noticed first, taking them in and swearing even as he pulled a sword free of its sheath. "INTRUDERS!"

That shouted word made adrenaline spike then sing through her nerves. The time of stealth was over. The men nearest the door rushed for her, swords leaving their sheathes in a ring of metal on metal, war cries bursting free from their mouths. Baring her teeth, she raised both hands, shooting out precise lightning strikes and hitting men dead in the chest. They flew backwards, impacting the table and sending papers flying. Shad was a whirlwind, taking down opponents quicker than she did. Becca hadn't seen him in action like this in years, but age had obviously not slowed him down.

In close quarter battle situations like these, it was very easy to lose situational awareness, to focus only on the enemy in front of her. Becca blinked, forced herself out of that narrow field of view, and actively kept track of both Simin and Shad as they moved. She could hear a few people fighting Simin behind her, trying to break for the door, but no one managed it. Simin had not acquired her position as First Guard because of her diplomacy skills, after all. Becca spared her a glance, just to make sure the woman wasn't overwhelmed, but Simin had it well under control. She'd even managed to close the doors and lock them so help couldn't come in from the outside.

After that glance, she focused on the men still charging

her, some of them leaping over each other, eager to take the attackers down. Magic whirling around her like a miniature storm, she shot bolt after bolt, hitting them in the chest, forcing them back. She moved steadily forward, not allowing them to maneuver her into a corner.

She didn't want everyone in this room dead. She needed Riyu alive, if possible, and everyone was clear on what the man looked like. Late fifties, black hair touched with grey at the temples, usually in uniform with decorations all over the left breast pocket. A few men semi-fit that description so she incapacitated them, using just enough power in her lightning to stun them or render them unconscious. Simin would be the one to confirm his identity.

In minutes the room fell still, men either dead or lying comatose on the floor. Shad wasn't even breathing hard or sweating. He turned, gave both women a once over with his eyes, then beamed. "That went swimmingly."

Taking a moment to draw in two large lungful's, Becca got her breathing back under control enough to respond, "It did. Simin, I knocked out a few men. Tell me who Riyu is."

Simin straightened her uniform jacket with a jerk as she moved forward, sometimes using a boot to flip men over on their backs so she could see their faces. She moved steadily, a frown deepening with every person she overturned. She stopped at the last body at the far end of the room, turning to face them. "He's not here."

Groaning, Becca slammed a fist against the table. "I heard people address him, I thought for sure he was in here. My mistake, we didn't double check first before attacking."

"No, I did," Simin disagreed, her eyes scanning the room. "As soon as Riicshaden came in, I verified Riyu was here. He was sitting in the chair at the head of the table."

"What is this, a locked room mystery?" Shad asked

rhetorically. His expression warred between being disturbed and intrigued. "He was here, now he's not. The windows are too narrow for a man to get through, the doors are locked, there's no other points of access in this room. So where did he go?"

Simin opened her mouth, paused, then went to tap thoughtfully at the paneling on the nearest wall. "Many warlords have escape holes built into their fortresses."

Through new eyes, Becca saw the way the room was built. The bottom half of the walls had decorative wood paneling on it shaped in large squares. She hadn't thought anything of it, being more focused on the people than the decorations, but now that Simin had brought it to her attention, she found it very suspicious indeed. Wood was ridiculously precious in Khobunter and people didn't use it for pure decorative purposes, no matter how wealthy they were. Wood was used for furniture, sometimes for structure, but never anything else. "One of these panels opens to an escape route."

"I'm afraid so." Simin ducked into a bow, tense and contrite. "Apologies, Warlord, I did not consider this."

Becca shook her head. "Damage done now. Let's focus on where he would go. We have to catch up and capture him or it leaves me with the fallback plan of taking the city by brute force. I don't like that option, it's a terrible one, so let's avoid it if we can."

"If his fortress has been compromised, wouldn't he head for the military headquarters next, take up a defensive stance there?" Shad asked Simin, twirling his sword idly in his hand.

"That would be the logical choice, yes. I can't think of another place for him to go."

Becca had to admit that in his shoes, that would be where she'd retreat to. In order to take back the fortress and deal with the enemy, he'd need access to his army after all. "Where is that?"

"Fortunately, not far." Simin strode for the doors, for the first time her expression giving away her own trepidation at the situation. "You realize the alarm is sounded now. We'll be fighting our way out of here."

"It's alright, Simin," Becca assured her, believing every word she spoke even if she didn't know how they'd manage it. "We'll make it."

As a child of the Tonkowacon, Trev'nor had woken up in various circumstances, some of them downright strange, but this was definitely a new one. Incredible heat from two different sources, one of which rumbled under the force of angry growls, like an earthquake throwing a tantrum. Pain radiated from his back like a live entity, robbing him of breath, and rendering the idea of moving absolutely impossible. Just breathing hurt. It took him a fuzzy moment to get both eyes open, a harder task than usual, but when he managed it, he rather wished he could just go back to sleep. Sleep was easier.

Garth wrapped around him like an overprotective mother hen times ten, snarling at anyone and everyone except Nolan. His best friend knelt at his side, tears streaming down dirty cheeks, both hands firmly on his skin and pouring Life Mage magic into him like a living pulse. Well that explained why Trev'nor felt like he had two sources of heat burning against him.

He tried to figure out where he was, but couldn't see much around green scales and a gigantic wing stretched overhead. Sounds nearby of shouted orders, the uneasy murmurs of voices overlapping, and the very familiar noises of battle clued in him. Back lines of an army. Either Dunixan or his own, but he had a vague memory of heading toward Dunixan. Or thinking he should. Had he made it?

Neither of them seemed to realize he was awake, so he tried to speak, only to realize his mouth felt like a sand monster had crawled inside and died, very messily. Swallowing did not improve the situation and all he could manage was a croak.

Nolan's eyes snapped up to his. "Trev. You awake?"

Giving up on the whole speaking thing, Trev'nor nodded.

His dragon, at least, seemed to sense the problem as Garth bellowed out, "Bring water!"

Someone hastily obeyed that command, hesitating only to make sure that Garth wasn't going to snap him in half for daring to approach, then knelt at Trev'nor's other side. Mose. Of course it was Sergeant Mose. Trev'nor was definitely promoting the man after this.

Greedily, he latched onto the water canteen pressed to his mouth and sucked it down dry. It felt a little awkward, not to mention painful, to do so while entertaining a hole in his kidney. But Nolan patched him up beautifully so that the pain faded to a mutter in the background.

Releasing the canteen, Trev managed a smile for the very worried trio hovering at his side, not to mention everyone else gathered around and watching. "Thanks. That's much better."

"Trev, we talked about this," Nolan joked, although his tone and expression strained under the jocularity. "No dying. Becca will make me raise you from the dead just to kill you again if you make her rule Khobunter by herself."

"Is it my fault I was stabbed from behind?"

"Yes, yes it was. You are one of the Super Soldier's students, you're supposed to dodge everything." Nolan's façade broke, revealing the terror and desperation underneath. A new spate of tears threatened to spill over and he ruthlessly wiped them with the edges of his sleeves before he reached forward to grab Trev'nor in a fierce hug. "Seriously, don't scare me like that."

"Fledgling no go without me," Garth informed him firmly.

Trev'nor returned his friend's hug, but eyed his dragon. That did not look like an expression he could argue against. Garth hated being underground for long lengths of time, but Trev'nor had to use the Earth Path sometimes, it was their fastest option. He wasn't sure who was going to win this argument, but he imagined that one of them wasn't going to be happy with the compromise.

"We'll figure out a way," he promised. "Nol. Did I get everyone out?"

Releasing him, Nolan sank back onto his heels, although he went no further. "You did. By some miracle, you did. Llona sent a message back to Rheben about where we are. Hopefully Sallah can come fetch everyone soon."

That would certainly make Trev'nor's life easier. He tried to sit up, only to have shooting pain stab through his side. Hissing, he froze, breathing through it.

"Don't move just yet," Nolan cautioned him, easing him back against Garth's side. "My magic is still working."

"Nol, warn me ahead of time, will you? Your early warning system needs work." Trev'nor breathed a few more times, pain fading, and indeed he could feel his friend's magic still knitting the skin back together. He sometimes forgot that even life magic wasn't instantaneous.

From the other side of Garth, he could hear someone jog closer. "Nolan, is he up?"

Dunixan. So he had made it. He turned his head, looking for his ally, and called out, "I'm up. Sort of."

With a weather eye on a still grumpy Garth—who let out some alarming steam at regular intervals—Dunixan approached, coming in to kneel at Trev'nor's feet. With Garth's wing stretched out overhead, everyone had shade over them, but Dunixan wore the signs of being out in the desert heat for the past several days. Even for his toughened skin, the suns had been too much, and he sported quite the burn across his nose.

The other warlord took him in with worried eyes. "You were bleeding very badly. Can you stand yet?"

"Not yet," Nolan cautioned, putting a staying hand on Trev'nor's chest. "It wasn't just the wound I had to close, I had to worry about replacing all of the blood he lost as well. Trev, I know you want to get back in the swing of things, but you really should stay put the rest of the day. You lost so much blood I almost wasn't able to revive you."

And that would explain why Trev'nor still felt lightheaded. "Can we afford for me to stay down?"

"The only major job we needed you to do, you've done," Dunixan assured him, worry still clouding his expression. "I think we can manage the rest. Please don't push yourself, if you go down again, we're all going to end up as dragon snacks. Garth was not pleased with us."

Garth let out a snort hot enough to scorch everyone nearby. Seriously, that steam had more than a little fire to it. Trev'nor put a hand on his dragon's hide, soothing. "I promise to move only if things get desperate."

Appeased, all three males relaxed.

"I'm glad you're being sensible." Dunixan paused before adding, "I hope you don't mind, but I borrowed Carjettaan. We needed a Legend to help track the approaching troops from Riyu."

"That's fine," Trev'nor assured him.

Nolan's head turned, his eyes going a little dragon shaped, a clear sign that his usual control was in tatters at the moment. He only did partial transformations like these when his emotions ran too high to keep his magic in check or when his magic ran a little too low. Trev'nor bet at this moment it was a little of both. His head cocked, neck turned to an odd angle, then he straightened out again before announcing, "Llona reports that Sallah is on her way to collect the new students. Trev, maybe you should go back to Rheben with them?"

And thereby be safely out of danger of rejoining the battle? Trev'nor shook his head firmly. "I'll stay on the sidelines, but I'll go crazy if I don't know what's going on. I'll coordinate between you and Becca."

Reluctant, Nolan finally nodded acceptance. "Alright. Garth, I'm trusting you to keep him down until he's fully healed."

Garth gave a grunt and settled in even more firmly around Trev'nor. The young Earth Mage glanced up at his dragon, and that stubborn gleam in those golden eyes, and had the feeling he was absolutely never going to live this down.

"Warlord!" Carjettaan came speeding up, skittering to a stop, a wild look in her eyes. "We have a problem."

Trev'nor glumly looked at that expression and just knew that he was going to hate what came out of her mouth next. "What's gone wrong this time?"

"The army out of Riyu is retreating back to the city." Agitated, she shifted from foot to foot, her head turning eastward, still tracking their movements even now. "They suddenly reversed directions about a minute ago."

Letting out a curse, Dunixan shared a speaking look with the two of them. "Did Raya Becca somehow fail? Or did they figure out we're a ruse?"

Snatching up the mirror broach, Nolan demanded, "Becca. Becca, answer me."

It took an agonizingly long moment before any sort of response came through, and when it did, Becca's words came out in pants. "*Nolan, we have a problem. Riyu escaped.*"

This day just got better and better. Trev'nor resisted the urge to bang his head against a hard surface. He'd already suffered enough trauma today.

"Escaped how far?" Nolan asked, jaw clenched. The skin around his eyes and temples went scaly, as if he were ready to fly off and pound the man into the sand.

"*We're not sure. Out of the fortress, I think, but I have no way to confirm it. We had to fight our way to the top and I'm waiting on Cat right now. Nolan, I'm hard pressed on all sides here. A little reinforcement wouldn't hurt.*"

"Becca, it's worse than you think. The army that left Riyu has turned around and is heading back toward the city. You need to get out of there."

Dead silence.

Trev'nor stared at the mirror, quiet but still active, and felt like his heart had relocated to his throat. Had she been attacked, was that why she wasn't trying to respond? Was she just thinking? He had no idea what the situation over there was. He couldn't imagine that anyone could get through Shad, but they were in an enemy city with no backup. Sheer numbers could overwhelm even him. Had not Rheben fallen because of that very tactic?

"*Nolan. Is Trev'nor nearby?*"

He let out a breath at her voice. So, thinking, then.

"Yes, but he's been badly hurt." Nolan glanced his direction as he answered, jaw rhythmically clenching. "I healed him, but you can't ask him to fight today. Perhaps not even tomorrow. He lost a lot of blood, Becca."

"*Can he hear me?*"

"I can hear you," Trev'nor answered, pitching his voice a little to carry.

"*You are hereby banned from getting injured for the rest of this war, do you understand me? I know men like to show off battle scars, but this is getting ridiculous.*"

Even though she couldn't see it, Trev'nor grinned. "Yes, dear."

"*Eww. Seriously, you just gave me goosebumps. Alright, so you're out of commission for the moment. There's only one way to deal with this since that's the case. Nolan, send word to Danyal to attack Riyu.*"

While she was right, Trev'nor instinctively protested: "But our army doesn't stand a chance! If they arrive too quickly, they'll be between Riyu's defenses and the army coming in from behind. They'll be squashed like a grape in a wine press. They can't take the city fast enough to prevent that from happening!"

"*They don't need to worry about that army. I'll handle it.*"

She couldn't possibly mean...

"Uh, Bec?" Nolan stared at the mirror in growing alarm. "You mean just little ole' you is going to fight? You sure?"

"*I can finally use tornadoes.*"

"She sounds entirely too pleased about that," Dunixan noted. Even though he sounded calm, he looked distinctly unnerved. "Can she really defeat an army by herself?"

"No, even she'll get overwhelmed." Trev'nor thought that was the case, anyway. Becca was so untested when it came to true combat, where she didn't have to hold back for fear of hitting an ally, that they didn't know what her true potential was. He did know, though, that she would likely run out of magical energy before she ran out of enemies. "Bec, we're sending Ehsan to help you."

"Sure, I'll take the help. Nolan, you and Tail stay with Dunixan and help him. Just get our army moving. I have to stop Riyu's advance before they get any closer to the city, so have Ehsan meet me there. Go." The connection abruptly died.

Nolan shifted into dragon before the last syllable faded from the air, his head lifting up as he let out a long, sonorous note.

Having never seen this transformation, Dunixan stared wide eyed at Nolan's dragon form for the longest moment before he shook his head, snapping himself out of it. Only then did he focus on Trev'nor. "Trev'nor, I have to ask. Can we still win this?"

Unsure, Trev'nor gave him the best answer he could. "We're in the middle of the river, Dunixan. It's too late to turn back now. We either sink or swim."

Understanding, if unhappy with the answer, Dunixan gave a slow nod. "You're correct. If I were alone in this, I think I would have drawn back by now."

"And that would have been the wise decision to make. But we have another army and honestly, five mages are basically an army themselves. We need to press forward. The next time we try this will be that much harder, the odds even more stacked against us." Trev'nor looked up, his head tilting to the side to see beyond Garth's wing. "I thought I heard storm clouds. Becca's already gearing up for the fight."

"You really think just the two of them can manage?"

"Well, Dunixan, would you want to fight around tornadoes and lightning?" Trev'nor responded dryly.

Grimacing, the warlord shook his head. "But you sent another mage to help her."

That statement sounded more like a question. Trev'nor

sat up a little more, carefully, as it felt beyond awkward to have this very serious conversation while lying on his side. "I'm afraid she'll magically exhaust herself before she runs out of enemies. But I also hope that with Ehsan there, we won't have as many casualties. Surely not every man fighting in Riyu's army is a bad one. Like the other provinces we've taken, good are often mixed in with the bad. Ehsan will help contain them until we can send in reinforcements."

"I see." Dunixan sat back on his heels for a moment, thinking hard, then twisted about to stare at Jashni's walls. "If Riyu is being attacked, and Raya Becca is dealing with the army, then I think it's time we took this battle seriously as well."

"I think you're right," Trev'nor agreed. "And the faster you can do it, the better. Garth, can you help in this battle?"

The dragon's eyes narrowed to mere slits of gold, steam rising off of him in visible waves. "Will."

Belatedly, Trev'nor realized this might have been a bad thing to ask. Garth was so mad he would likely flatten the city. "Try to remember that what you break, I have to fix."

Garth carefully maneuvered into an upright position, readying himself to launch into the battle. Only when he was free of Trev'nor's weight did he eye Jashni, tail lashing like an angry cat. "Bad city," he finally pronounced.

Uh-oh. "Wait, Garth—" Trev'nor frantically called, but it was too late, Garth had already bounded out of reach and launched himself into the sky. Leaning against Mose's supportive hand, he growled in resignation, "Shrieking hinges."

Dunixan watched the dragon go, mouth turned upwards in what might have been a smile. "Can I translate that as, 'It's a bad city anyway, no loss if I flatten it?'"

"That's exactly what he meant." Trev'nor honestly didn't

know if this day could get any worse. Then he watched Llona and Orion, the other two dragons with them, leap right after Garth. Clearly, things could get worse. Groaning, he buried his head in his hand and advised, "Dunixan, you better pull your men back."

"Before they go squish? Good idea."

Becca was not happy. Mostly with herself.

They had no prayer of tracking Riyu. The bottom levels of the fortress sounded an alarm, the building thundering as people rushed back and forth, shouting orders to each other. She had no way of knowing where that secret passage of Riyu's had led, if he was simply a level below her, or if he had abandoned the fortress altogether. If she had just taken a Legend along with her, as Trev'nor urged for her to do, they would have been able to track Riyu. Even if they'd lost him in this maze of a city, she would have known before Nolan contacted her that Riyu's army was doubling back. Her prejudice had kept her from trusting a Legend enough to bring one along, and now she was paying for that mistake dearly.

With Shad and Simin's skills, they got free and managed to get back to the top of the fortress. At this stage, trying to go down and fight their way back out of the city would be tantamount to suicide. Becca didn't even try. Ignoring Shad's grumbling about it being a hard core rule to never go up, she led them to the top, calling for Cat as she went. Her dragon swooped in, Dawn Rising coming as well, both of them catching onto the top of the fortress and clinging there like giant lizards on a sunny rock. Becca wasted no time in climbing into the saddle, Shad throwing himself on behind her, and they barely got one strap on before Cat took to the air again. Simin followed suit on Dawn Rising, both dragons flying hard and fast away from the fortress before someone could scramble archers and fire at them.

As they flew over the city, Becca stared hard at the walls, absently buckling herself in, hands moving automatically. While she was in the fortress, Danyal had arrived, but just barely. She could see him on the horizon, not close enough to attack, and he hadn't even formed ranks yet.

Someone called for the slave magicians to be used in defense of the walls. They scattered over the top of it like worker ants, throwing whatever attacks they knew how to do. Becca had hoped they wouldn't think to do that, but of course they did. It was probably standard protocol.

Signaling them to land, Cat led them out some distance, well out of range of fire, and landed heavily, wings still spread as if she knew very well they'd have to take off again in a minute. Becca waited until Dawn Rising landed nearby and called to Simin, "I need to go! The army isn't going to Jashni, they're coming back to Riyu. I have to head that off! Can you go to Danyal, update him on what happened?"

"I can, yes!" Simin responded, sounding worried. "What about the magicians on the wall?"

They'd assigned Ehsan to the army to deal with such a contingency, but now she was pulling him away to help her, which left their own army defenseless to magical attacks. Becca muttered curses under her breath.

"He'll need to fire at the city long-range for as long as possible, keep them occupied until we can get a mage to him that can counteract the attack."

Simin put a fist to her heart in salute. "Yes, Warlord."

"Thank you." She took two minutes to double check her

straps, making a few adjustments. "Shad, are you perfectly settled? Good, let's go. We have an army to defeat."

"Excellent." Shad bounced a little in the saddle, as happy as a puppy with a new mud puddle. In fact, if he'd possessed a tail, it would be wagging furiously. "I've never faced an army with just three people before. This will be *funnn.*"

He looked so delighted, that even though Becca felt the strain of the situation, even though it threatened to crush her, she still had to smile. "You crazy man."

Shaking a finger at her, Shad gave her a mock pout. "Don't think you're forgiven for not inviting me before. Just this won't make up for it."

What in the wide green world would she do without Shad? Smile stretched from ear to ear, she reached over and gave him a quick, one-armed hug. "You're the best brother ever, Riicshaden."

He hugged her right back. "You know it."

That she did. Reaching forward, she stroked Cat's neck. "Thanks for coming. Let's go west, toward the army, alright?"

Cat lashed her tail, crouching low in the front, grumpy and not even trying to hide it. "No tornadoes," she informed Becca with a growl.

It had briefly escaped her mind that with her dragon along, Becca would once again have to keep track of air currents. In a near whine, she protested, "But it'll be hard to fight with just lightning!"

"No," Cat maintained firmly.

The sacrifices she had to make, seriously. "Fine, no tornadoes." Now grouchy herself, Becca signaled for them to go. Seriously, this battle couldn't be going worse if she tried. First she lost the warlord, then she had to escape from the city, and she didn't want to even think about what Danyal would do against the magical attacks, and now she had to keep one of her tactics holstered because Cat wanted to be with her. "Tell me Ehsan is coming."

"Coming," Cat assured her as she started flapping, gaining elevation. "Soon."

He had been with Danyal and the rest of the army, so it would take him a little longer to reach her, but not by more than a few minutes. Or so Becca hoped. This was going to be difficult otherwise.

Shad settled in behind her, hands at her waist, and leaned in enough to say next to her ear, "All joking aside, you sure you can defeat an army of that size?"

She had to save her response as Cat launched into the air, as the flapping and wind noise would have drowned out her words. Once they were airborne, however, she shouted back to him, "I'm not trying to! Just going to hold them off!"

He tapped her arm in acknowledgement, but didn't try to speak.

Becca didn't know if she had the kind of magical stamina to defeat an army, but she didn't intend to answer that question today. If her experience in Khobunter had taught her anything, it was that good men were forced to work for evil ones, and she couldn't assume that everyone in Riyu's army deserved death. If she'd had that opinion, she would have lost the good soldiers she had in her command now. So whatever anyone else thought, Becca flew westward with only one goal in mind: stop their advance.

One of two scenarios could happen. She could halt them long enough for both Jashni and Riyu to be taken by her own people, cutting off all lines of retreat, and force Warlord Riyu to surrender. Or he could refuse to surrender and she would have to use force to subdue them. Becca really, really hoped for the first scenario but was glumly aware that a man of Riyu's reputation wasn't about to surrender easily.

Coming in from the air gave her a distinct advantage, but also a disadvantage. She could see exactly from here the entirety of the army, stretched out along the highway in marching file, four abreast. She couldn't count them fast enough while Cat flew overhead, but she didn't need to. Experience had taught her how to eye an enemy's ranks and get an estimate of the number. If there were less than fifteen thousand troops down there, she'd eat her boots.

Becca looked the situation over and re-evaluated how important her dragon's happiness was. This definitely looked like a situation that called for tornadoes. What had Riyu done, grabbed part of the city's guards on his way out? Was he part rabbit or just all coward?

With her palm, she smoothed a line down Cat's neck, signaling for her to slow down and hover as much as possible. Without the wind rushing in her ears, she was able to turn and speak to Shad, if a little louder than usual. "Keep an eye on their movements for me! If you see signs of magic, tap Cat on both flanks, she'll duck and roll!"

Nodding understanding, he loosened his hands from around her waist, prepared to move if necessary.

With will and magic, Becca formed clouds over their heads, drawing on the storms she'd prepared beforehand, bringing them in closer to her. The air grew humid and heavy, the sky a rolling pitch of darkness and thunder. No one in Riyu had seen a storm like this, they'd never been in the right conditions for it, and the soldiers underneath clearly felt unnerved as they kept breaking formation, their attention on the sky over their heads.

The very first thing that Becca had to do was scatter the ranks. She had to break the idea of moving forward, get them scrambling for cover, not that there was much to offer in this flat desert landscape. Right before she released it, the men reformed into square formations, then the magicians moved up from the back of the ranks and formed a second row around them.

Becca realized in horror what Riyu had just ordered. The slaves were both a living barrier to his soldiers and the first line of offensive tactics. Even as she paused, lightning charged and ready to be thrown, the first wave of magical attacks from the ground seared through the air.

As Shad gave the signal, Cat ducked and rolled, barely missing some of the attacks, the heat of the magic so close that it felt like it singed the side of her legs. Sensing Becca's turmoil, Cat flapped hard three times, gaining altitude and buying her another second to think.

"That's dirty," Shad yelled, sounding half-cross and half-admiring. "Ethics aside, it's a good tactic, keeps us from blasting him willy-nilly."

Becca couldn't help but agree even as she cursed Riyu and the dogs that bred him. Out in the open like this, she should have full advantage, but with the magicians directly in the line of fire, she didn't dare just throw lightning around.

"What are you going to do?" Shad yelled to be heard over the wind.

"Scare them, try to scatter the ranks!" Becca yelled back, thinking hard. She'd have to be pinpoint precise every time or risk doing serious damage to the very people she was trying to rescue. Never before had her control been challenged like this. Taking a deep breath for courage, she guided Cat back around and asked her to dive.

The wind rushed past her face, tearing at her clothes and making them flap hard against her skin. She ignored the sensations and focused like she had never done before. With precise strikes, she called lightning down from the sky and hit just to either side of the highway.

If she put holes in the highway itself, Trev'nor would skin her.

The front ranks broke for cover, diving for any rocky crag or heap of rocks they could find, no matter how small that might be. She was too far up to hear any screaming, but she imagined there were more than a few cries of alarm. Still, not everyone was faint enough at heart to break, and they grabbed the slaves that tried to run, hauling them back into formation.

Someone down there had the guts to aim at Cat with a crossbow, not that it came anywhere near the mark. The dragon lazily dodged it with a quick barrel roll and then spat out a fireball, scorching the highway. It was hot enough to leave a smoking crater in the center of the stonework.

Aw, busted buckets. Becca eyed the crater glumly. Maybe Sallah would fix it for her?

Another wave of magical attacks flew at them, forcing them to duck and evade once again, throwing Becca's aim off. She had to wait until Cat turned back around to try again, this time hitting a little closer. People screamed and ducked again, but others kept their feet, sending fire spells and arrows their direction. One enterprising group in the back ranks stopped marching long enough to crank a ballista up and fired that, forcing Cat to duck sharply down or get skewered.

It brought them dangerously low, right above the army's head, and anyone with the brains to do so took full advantage, attacking while they could. Cat gave a grunt of pain as something hit, then spat out another fireball over their heads, forcing the rest of them to duck.

"Cat, you alright?!" Becca demanded in alarm.

"Scratch," the dragon assured her dismissively, more annoyed than anything.

Shad called from behind, "They're loading another ballista! Duck, Kitty-cat!"

Flapping hard, Cat went sideways, slicing neatly through the air. Becca craned her head around, trying to target an area with lightning, but at this angle and speed, it was hard for her to focus well enough to do a precise pin-point strike. She threw some lightning in that general direction, not close enough to harm anyone, just to buy her another second to think.

Horns sounded, calling people back into rank, and her heart sank a little as she realized they weren't buying the lightning strikes. Riyu wasn't going to be put off with her one-manned attacks. He was still advancing toward the city.

Making a snap decision, she yelled, "Sorry, Cat!"

The dragon turned her head just enough to eye her rider suspiciously. "Why sorry?"

In answer, Becca called upon the wind, twisting and twirling it, mixing hot air with cold to create several dervishes on the ground. This, finally, broke up the ranks and people dove for cover, or ran for it. Becca sighed in relief. Alright, dervishes worked and didn't upset Cat's flying too much. Maybe this would work? She created three more as her earlier versions took off into the desert.

Whatever people still standing on the road really ran then, scrambling in all directions, ignoring the orders of their superiors. Several horns went off, calling repeatedly for soldiers to reform the ranks, but it only met with partial success.

Becca knew that her time was limited with this tactic of firing at the enemy but not actually doing damage. They'd catch on sooner or later that she didn't actually intend to harm anyone and get bolder in trying to attack her as a result. She wanted the casualty count to be as low as she could make it, so it would behoove her to have a few 'close calls' to draw out the game for as long as possible.

She threw some more lightning out there, making it seem as if she aimed for pockets of men. Some she scorched a little, as she saw several drop and roll, putting the fire out on their uniforms before hastily scrambling away. It drove fear into them, that she only targeted the groups. They split up even further, moving away from each other, not wanting anyone near them. Becca tried to herd the magicians together, pull them away from the rest of the soldiers, and it worked to a limited degree. They no longer hovered quite so strongly around the soldiers, at least, and most ran for any cover they could find in this flat stretch of land.

The officers went mad, blaring the horns constantly, sometimes getting off their dragoos and physically hauling men up, forcing them into line. Becca would wait until they got about twenty together and then would aim a lightning strike at them, scattering them all over again. It became mental warfare more than anything, a tactic that Shad and Aletha had taught her well, a skill that Khobunter had honed to a fine edge.

"Warlord's figured the game out!" Shad called to her. "I don't think you'll get by with this for much longer!"

"I know!" she called back, anxiously eyeing the horizon. Her efforts to divide the magicians from the soldiers failed as they were yanked back into formation. Where was Ehsan? If he didn't get here soon, she's really have to fight and that wasn't the plan.

Cat let out a pleased purring rumble, a sound more felt than heard, vibrating through Becca's legs. She turned to look, and it took a moment to spot them, dark grey against a dark sky, but finally she did.

Ehsan had arrived via dragon back, Ginger already

spitting fireballs.

She raised the mirror broach and shouted into it: "EHSAN!"

Faintly, almost too faint to be heard, Ehsan responded. "*I hear you!*"

Over enunciating every word, she yelled as loudly as she could: "THEY'RE USING MAGICIANS TO RING THE SQUAD FORMATIONS! BE CAREFUL!"

"*I will!*" he promised strongly.

Praying he'd understood her, as the wind and the storm made it difficult, Becca unleased the heavens and gave him more than enough water to work with. It drenched everyone, including her, within minutes and reduced visibility down to ten feet. Despite the desert heat, the rain cooled her considerably and she shivered a little. If not for Shad's heat at her back and Cat's from under her legs, this weather would be perfectly miserable. Grimly, she let it linger for a few more minutes, as she honestly didn't know how much water Ehsan needed to pull this off, then she lowered the intensity of the storm to a light drizzle.

There, now she could see what she was doing.

Unfortunately, as soon as the magicians below had visibility again, they started firing every spell they knew upwards, forcing both dragons to dodge. Becca swore all over again as she was forced to roll, or evade, time and again. She literally could not get a target lock on anything down there. The ballistas kept firing as well, now targeting Ginger as well as Cat.

At this rate, Becca and Ehsan would lose.

Becca could feel Cat tiring under her, not used to doing all of these acrobatics in the air for long periods of time. One slip on her dragon's part, she'd take a hit full force. Becca absolutely did not want to risk that, but she didn't know what else to do. She couldn't erect a magical barrier around her dragon, it was too odd of a shape and wouldn't protect her from the ballistas. If she tried to do something for a weapons shield, it wouldn't protect from the magical attacks. And she couldn't afford to use both shields, her magical core was draining rapidly, she didn't have the strength to keep both of them up for long.

Tapping her shoulder, Shad yelled into her ear, "CALL AZIN!"

True, one more mage might make all the difference, especially Azin. She could unarm everyone safely and within minutes, leaving only the magicians left as combatants. Did Becca dare? "BUT WHAT ABOUT JASHNI?"

"THEY'LL MANAGE! YOU TWO CAN'T DO THIS ALONE!"

Not knowing what else to do, Becca trusted his advice and lifted the mirror broach once more. "AZIN!"

It was faint, hard to hear, as Azin wasn't loud at the best of times. "*—here!*"

"I NEED YOU!" Becca yelled, over enunciating each word.

"*—ming! Do...hear...I'm com—*"

I'm coming. Is that what she'd said? Becca prayed that was what she heard and tapped Cat, asking her to rise and give them the safety that the wind and clouds could offer. She turned the storm back up to full volume, unleashing a torrential rain that would buy them a little more time as well.

Circling about, Ginger came to fly at their side as they did large, lazy circles around the army on the ground. No one moved down there except reforming their formations, from the look of it. Becca found this odd. Were they so blinded by the rain that Riyu couldn't advance? Or were they still trying to form up? She was only catching snatches of movement on the ground.

The mirror broach emanated a faint light and sound and she held it up again to her ear. "SAY AGAIN?"

"*WHAT ARE YOU DOING?!*"

Ah. "WAITING ON AZIN!"

The mirror went still again. Becca put it back up before she could accidentally drop it, then prayed fervently Azin would get here before the army could get back underway.

Perhaps no one listened in the heavens, as barely any time passed before Riyu started marching for the city once more. Becca turned Cat around, slowing the rain enough that she could see, and set off several small dervishes again. This time, she didn't try to avoid direct contact, but let people be picked up and flung about. It wouldn't seriously injure anyone, and right now minor injuries were acceptable if it meant halting that advance.

With the rain slowed, magicians turned to fire off spells, forcing Cat to evade again.

They repeated this cycle several times, Becca feeling the drain of her magic as she kept a raging storm going overhead while throwing out multiple attacks of her own. She didn't know how much longer she could keep this up.

Like a streaking shadow, Orion arrived with Azin, bellowing loud enough to make the thunder overhead seem muted. He unleashed a torrential stream of fire right alongside the highway, forcing people to evade or get scorched. It was so hot the stone itself steamed and glowed for a moment before the rain cooled it. As he moved, so did Azin, her power in full swing, everything metal from helmets to shields to spears yanked from the soldiers, going flying off onto the desert floor. She couldn't disarm them all in one sweep, but she certainly got a huge chunk of the army disarmed, and had already turned, ready to make another pass.

Becca seriously wanted to hug both of them for getting here so quickly. Orion must have set a new speed record. She so owed him a cow for this.

Relieved, she let the storm overhead recede a bit, nothing more than dark clouds pitching and rolling overhead, giving her two friends the visibility they needed.

Now unarmed, the soldiers turned to the magicians, trying to huddle behind them. Becca sent out several dervishes, forcing them apart, breaking their concentration as they did with her earlier. The ballistas no longer had any ammunition to fire, thanks to Azin, and with that threat gone, she could put a flat magical shield under Cat's belly that would protect her from the brunt of the attacks. "Cat, you're safe, go!"

The dragon might not understand what her mage fully meant by that, but she took Becca at her word and dove for the ground.

Ehsan wasted no time getting to work. Water rose in streams under his command, shooting forward and forcing people to duck or get knocked sharply off their feet. He scattered them like petals in the wind.

Orion swooped around, Azin making another pass, and whatever weapons she missed the first time, she claimed the second go round. Men cried out, desperately clutching at their swords at least, but the weapons were wrenched away without any trouble.

Between Ehsan's attacks and Becca's dervishes, the army's formation thoroughly broke, leaving people on the ground or madly running for the city. Ehsan switched from attacking to whirling water at high speeds, starting out in wide circles and tightening slowly, drawing men together and keeping them hostage. Anyone that tried to breach the water barrier was thrown back for their trouble. Becca had experienced such harsh water only once and it had skinned her elbow and nearly broken an arm, that's how hard it had been. She knew that it would keep the men in line, once they realized the force of it.

No one in this desert had ever seen water like this, certainly not used like this, and it confused them so much that at first they didn't know how to respond to it. Ehsan used that moment of confusion to full advantage, bringing several groups together. By then, the secret was out, as the others learned from observing what it would do if that band of water started up around them. They tried to leap over it or roll underneath it to escape.

Becca went to work when they did, using lightning and strong winds to herd them back together. It was not unlike herding cats, especially since she actively tried to keep the officers away from the foot soldiers. A little hard to determine insignia from this distance, so she likely missed quite a few, but the ones that had kept a banner carrier and trumpeter near them were clearly officers. Those she could maneuver away.

The magicians, they were the hardest to deal with, as some of them could use magic that would repel the water.

Orion, to her complete surprise, landed in front of the largest group of magicians and spat a fireball at them, sending the puddles of water on the ground steaming. The magicians, not used to fighting a dragon, frantically either ran for it or tried to stand their ground, unleashing a flurry of attacks at him. Azin hadn't let him land without a shield in place, however, a flat plane right in front of him that sent every magical attack bouncing back at their users.

Rearing up a little, Orion bellowed a war cry, scaring everyone half to death, including Becca. He could make the heavens shake with a voice like that!

It broke whatever nerve the magicians had left, and several of them huddled right there on the spot like a frightened child. Azin gathered the shields and weapons she'd thrown aside earlier and used them to form a wall around the magicians, caging them in. Trusting that those two had the magicians in hand, at least, Becca's attention turned to the rest of the army.

Cat kept doing slow passes, nothing more than one large circle after another as they used magic to contain the army. Grimly, she kept working, throwing one lightning bolt after another, forcing them to fall prey to Ehsan and Azin. Becca could feel her magic grow low, dangerously so, and she knew that she'd have to stop soon or become useless altogether. With a pat on Cat's back, she urged the dragon to go up a little, well out of range of any stray fire.

Shad leaned in, putting his mouth near her ear. "You're getting low on magic, aren't you, kiddo?"

She nodded. Of course he would be able to tell. Shad had lived and worked with magicians for decades, he could recognize the signs well enough, especially with her. "How many left, do you think?"

"You've got maybe five hundred still loose. Ehsan and Azin can finish up. Cat, pass along that message, will you?"

Taking the canteen from the saddle pouch, Becca drained it halfway and felt better for it. Something about magical drain always dehydrated a person severely. It felt ridiculously similar to blood loss, or so she'd been told. Becca had never been hurt enough to experience it, so she'd have to take Garth's word on that. It would be even better if she could eat something, but there was nothing on hand, so she'd have to just deal for now.

Ehsan either realized she was low on magic or was

determined to deal with the army to the bitter end, as he didn't hesitate to entrap the rest of them. Azin started in on the other side, also caging people in with the metal she had on hand. Becca lost count of how many groups they did, but she was satisfied to see that neither of them put more than two hundred men in the same group.

Letting out a high whistle, Shad commented, "Your friend Ehsan is nothing to shake a stick at. That's some skill, right there, being able to hold that much water in formation."

"I know. He's extremely formidable. It makes me very glad he's on our side." And this was him half-trained. Becca couldn't wait to see what he was like after he'd gone through Raile's academy. "I think they got all of them. You see anyone else?"

"Nope. They've done good. Now comes the hard part," Shad added more somberly. "What are you going to do if you can't convince Riyu to surrender?"

Becca bared her teeth in an ugly smile. "Oh, I'm really hoping he doesn't."

Trev'nor tried to look on the bright side. At least Garth had only smashed half the city. That was something, right?

The citizens of Jashni had only gotten one bellowed warning from the enraged dragon before Garth sent a tail through the outer wall. People had been running in every possible direction since. Even Dunixan's men had retreated from the city, not daring to get in the dragon's way for fear of friendly fire.

Of course Garth alone couldn't destroy half a city in a few hours. Llona and Orion had cheerfully joined in, just as mad in their own way that a friend had been hurt, and took great delight in lighting anything with a government banner on fire. If not for the storm Becca had called in, the entire city would have gone up in flames already.

Dunixan came to sit next to Trev'nor on the folding cot Sergeant Mose had set up for him. They hadn't bothered with a tent, just a hastily erected lean-to over him so that he wouldn't be battered by the elements while he recuperated. Trev'nor might very well be the only person dry in this entire region.

"Well," his new ally stated, staring at the city, mouth kicked up in what might have been a smile. "I see the age old adage is true. Never upset a dragon."

"They're not supposed to be used in combat," Trev'nor mourned, staring at the city glumly. It was going to take him three solid weeks to fix all of that, he just knew it.

Snorting, Dunixan put elbows to knees and leaned forward, letting that one pass without comment. "Carjettaan informs me that most of the citizens who fled went toward the coast. Sensible of them, it's the only source for water and food nearby. I'm not quite sure what to do about them."

"Let them be for now. They'll find their own way back, or go to you. They don't have many options and I've learned to not force people. If they come in on their own terms, it's easier on us." Trev'nor turned his head, regarding the very small area that held their prisoners. Maybe two hundred altogether, all under guard. That couldn't possibly be the entirety of Jashni's soldiers. "Where's the rest of the enemy troops?"

"Most fled with the civilians. Some are holding out in a defensive position inside the city." Lowering his voice a notch, Dunixan leaned in a little to confide, "I honestly think that if you give them good terms for surrender, they'd give up without a fight. They're between a rock and a hard place right now. Riyu won't forgive them for the loss of this city."

Somehow that didn't surprise Trev'nor. Bad rulers were quick to assign blame. "Let's do that." Blinking, he peered up at the sky as the rain slowed from a torrent to a drizzle. "That's the third time she's done that."

"You mean the heavy rain?" Dunixan peered up at the sky as well, holding out a hand to catch some of the rain drops.

"She does this when working with Ehsan," Trev'nor explained, still peering thoughtfully upwards. What did this on-again, off-again storm pattern mean? Azin had left earlier to help, so Trev'nor assumed they'd more or less be able to handle things on their end, as he hadn't heard another peep from Becca calling for help after that. He dearly wanted to ask but was afraid of calling at the wrong moment. A moment of inattention at the wrong time in battle could get you killed. "She'll unleash a torrent of rain at first, give him plenty to work with, then slow it down to a drizzle when she feels he has enough. It gives them better visibility but still a steady source of water, so Ehsan doesn't feel as if he has to ration what she's given him to work with."

Dunixan withdrew his hand, regarding the sky thoughtfully. "I see. This is a normal pattern, then?"

"Not quite. She normally only has a heavy rain in the beginning of the battle, nothing more than a drizzle after that. I think it means she was having trouble."

"She did call for Magess Azin," Dunixan observed, a little troubled. "Should we help her?"

"I'm not sure if she needs it. And Nolan might be the only person who can go." There was one person, at least, that he could talk to. Picking up the mirror, he said clearly, "Nolan."

"*Here. Trev, I think I should head to Riyu. You basically have the situation in hand here, right?*"

"I do, and I was about to suggest the same thing. Check in with Bec on the way, see if she needs help first. I'm more worried about that situation than the other."

"*Alright. I'll take Tail with me and Llona.*"

"Go." Trev'nor huffed out a not so secret breath of relief. He did not want to deal with that furball if Tail was separated from Becca much longer. The cat could and would make their lives distinctly unpleasant. Dropping the mirror, he tapped his fingers against his leg, thinking hard. "Dunixan, let's come up with some reasonable terms for surrender and see if we can't wrap this up."

"Of course."

Becca knew only from Simin's description what Riyu looked like, but the warlord proved to be very conspicuous. He had banners with him, a full dress uniform on, and he was the only person that didn't carry a weapon on him. Granted, Azin had disarmed everyone earlier, but he should still have a belt and sheathe on him somewhere. And yet he didn't. That alone screamed arrogance as in this harsh land, everyone went around armed in some fashion, even the warlords. Did he really think his guards could handle everything that attacked him?

"Cat," she called to her dragon, leaning a little forward, "I think we should land. See that man with all of the shiny, sparkly things on his chest? Take me to him."

"Will," the dragon said hesitantly, adding in a questioning tone, "Nolan coming?"

Becca blinked, looking toward the horizon. "He is? How fast?"

"Fast."

So in other words, fast enough that it would behoove Becca to wait for a few minutes for him to arrive. True, she likely should, as it would be better to have one more of them on hand for this. "Then land a little nearby, we'll wait for him to come."

Obligingly, Cat swooped down in lazy circles, landing gently several paces away with a slight thud. Shad was out of the buckles in a thrice, hopping lightly to the ground in a guard stance that didn't even pretend to be casual. It took Becca a little longer to get the wet leather straps undone, then she too hopped down, wringing her hair out over one shoulder as they waited. She needed to invest in a rain poncho or something similar for these situations. Being stuck in soaking wet clothes was no fun at all, even if she did dry quickly.

Nolan swooped in, air nearly vacuuming in his wake, then did a backwards flip as he came in for a landing. He changed shape as he approached so that by the time his feet touched the ground, he was nearly human. It was always a little awe-inspiring, watching this transformation, but it also made Becca's joints hurt in a sympathetic ache. Tail leaped lightly from his hands and wasted no time in coming to stand at her feet.

Taking in the situation with a pan of the head, Nolan gave them both a thumb's up. "Good work."

"Why thank you, Raja," Becca intoned, giving him a curtsey. She dropped a hand to give Tail a quick rub behind the ears as she asked, "Jashni?"

Snorting a laugh, he assured her, "Under control. They're doing mop-up right now." His eyes turned to Riyu and his expression became hard and unreadable. "So that's Riyu."

"Sure is." Straightening, she took a breath and summoned some energy into her flagging body. What she wouldn't give for a nap about now. Shaking the thought off, Becca marched forward, everyone moving with her. Ehsan dropped the water barrier around Riyu and the few officers standing with him, making it easier for everyone to talk to each other. Five paces away, she took the man in from head to toe. He looked like a drowned rat, like they all did, black hair plastered to his skull, uniform sticking to him, but what caught her attention were his eyes. He blazed with fury, glaring at her as if he wanted to slice her open from stem to stern. That expression made him look like the monster Becca knew him to be. It felt distinctly unnerving, facing that, and she had to take a deep breath for courage before she felt she could speak in a firm tone. "Warlord Riyu. I am Riicbeccaan, Weather Mage and Warlord. You will surrender to me or be executed."

Spinning, Riyu grabbed the nearest weapon to him, the flagpole in his guard's hands, then charged at her like an enraged bull, screaming inarticulately as he came. The attack came so suddenly Becca flinched from it instinctively. Was he mad?!

In a blur of motion, Shad sped past her, sword already out in his hand. He met Riyu head on in a clash of metal on wood, then spun like a dancer, sword flashing up and around, cutting a neat slice across Riyu's neck.

Riyu dropped dead, pole spinning free of his lax hand.

Everyone froze, stunned at the speed and ferocity of the attack. Becca had fully intended to execute Riyu, as she didn't imagine the man would willingly surrender, but she'd also intended to do a trial of some sort first.

"Oops," Shad finally stated, looking down at the corpse. He did not sound apologetic.

Nolan let his head fall back, staring up at the heavens in a clear bid for patience before saying, "Shad. We meant to hold a trial first."

"Reflex," Shad responded with a splay of the hand, manner suggesting: 'killing bad guys is a habit, what can I say?'

Not knowing whether to laugh or groan, Becca stared at the corpse, but really the damage was done now. And she couldn't chide Shad. He'd only been protecting her after all. Tail actually gave a pleased purr at the outcome, which spoke volumes. "Haul him up. We might as well put him to use."

Nolan cottoned on to her plan almost instantly and nodded approval. "Good idea. Now." Turning to the rest of the soldiers, most of them staring in horror at their fallen leader, he announced loudly, "Jashni has fallen! Our army is attacking Riyu as we speak! Surrender now, and those that are willing to accept our rule will be allowed to live as full citizens. Refuse, and we will turn you loose in the desert."

These men understood better than she did what a death sentence that meant. Without the proper supplies— sometimes even with the proper supplies—a man could not survive in this place for more than a few days. If the lack of water didn't kill you, something else would. Bandits, poisonous reptiles, starvation, almost anything.

Without any instructions, the men dropped to their knees, putting folded hands on top of their heads, signaling their surrender. Satisfied, she stepped in closer to Nolan and conferred with him in a low voice, "I think I'd better head to Riyu with the dead warlord. Maybe I can get them to surrender too."

"It's certainly worth a try," Nolan agreed readily, although he frowned at the other soldiers. "I'll stay here and help Ehsan and Azin bring this lot in. Your magic is too low to be doing any more fighting today anyway."

That obvious, huh? "I'll leave this to you three, then. Jashni is really taken, though? Trev'nor's alright?"

"Trev'nor's fine," Nolan assured her. He had a strange expression on his face, as if he were trying not to laugh and wince at the same time. "Jashni isn't. Garth, ah, got a little mad that Trev was stabbed. Llona wasn't much better. Orion kinda just took advantage and joined in."

Closing her eyes in a fatalistic gesture, Becca didn't even feel the need to ask. "They destroyed Jashni. Didn't they."

"Half the city's still standing?" Nolan offered.

"In the name of all of the gods, saints, angels and pink elephants, why did you let them loose on the city?!" she hissed at him.

"You think I can stop a dragon with a mad on?" Nolan asked, shaking his head in amusement. "You overrate my persuasive powers."

She hadn't had a headache before, but it arrived with blinding speed. Rubbing at her temples, she thought about it, but really there was only one conclusion to be reached. "It's Trev'nor's dragon. He can clean up the mess."

"You know, that's exactly what I said."

Seriously, as soon as her back was turned…shrugging this off, she turned away. "I'm leaving this to you, then. Cat, pick up the body. Let's go to Riyu."

Carrying a dead body in order to threaten a city had to be one of the most macabre things that Becca had ever done and she hoped to high heaven she wouldn't need to do it again. It squicked her out so badly that constant shivers raced across her skin and she couldn't even glance toward Cat's claws without feeling nauseous. The only thing that kept her on this plan was the sure knowledge she would save a lot of lives by using this scare tactic.

And that was well worth the price.

They barely got any air under Cat's wings before Riyu City came into view, that's how close the battle had been. Becca couldn't see the finer details from this height and she didn't dare just swoop in willy-nilly. Riyu's gates were not open and her own forces were battling it out with the city's defenses with ferocity. The magical attacks weren't as fierce as what she had battled, which indicated that Riyu had taken the best magical fighters with him. But they were certainly creative, she gave them that. Her own forces waited several lengths away from the gates, just far enough away to be out of an archer's range, backed up behind overlapping shields and some hastily constructed trenches that looked to have been dug out by dragon's claws. This reeked of a stalemate to her. Appearances could be deceiving, however, and she needed to speak with Danyal before doing anything theatrical.

Either Becca had become entirely too predictable, or Cat read minds. Either way, the dragon bypassed the city's battlements and headed straight for the commander. She landed in the back lines, tossing the body distastefully a little distance away, then settled on her belly so people could climb off.

Tail leapt lightly from her hands and to the ground, preening an ear as soon as he settled on the sandy soil. Becca had to struggle again with the damp leather straps, then followed, blissfully thankful she wouldn't have to ride any farther today. Or at least she hoped not. It felt very good to have solid earth under her boots.

"Warlord Becca!"

Turning, she found Sergeant Amir hailing her, relief visibly on his face. He slid a little to a stop on the sand, offering a sharp salute, which Becca immediately returned. "My Warlord. Commander Danyal urgently requests your attention."

"Lead me to him." She had her own orders to issue and moved with as much alacrity as her cramping thighs would allow.

Tail and Shad followed without a word as they weaved through the back lines. Becca saw a few wounded already being taken care of, several dragons on the ground, although the way steam came out of their nostrils, they were itching to fight. Then they entered the fighting ranks, with catapults in use, and flaming arrows being regularly released. The snap and twang of firing sang like a badly tuned instrument in the air.

Their banner stood proudly in the wind, although a little limply thanks to the recent rainstorm, and marked Danyal's location. Amir headed straight for it, announcing in a loud and sharp voice once he was close enough to be heard, "Our Warlord Becca has arrived!"

Every soldier in hearing distance turned and snapped a salute, which she immediately returned, although her eyes focused on Danyal. The man looked as professional as always but there were lines of worry around his eyes and mouth she didn't like, and he gave off the vibe of being a hair away from exploding with stress, which she really didn't like. He turned sharply to her, one hand reaching out that didn't quite touch her. Eyes giving her a quick, if penetrating scan, he demanded, "Raya. You are well?"

Despite the fact she'd had little choice in the matter, Becca instantly regretted leaving Danyal alone with the army. Clearly she'd worried him sick by taking off as she'd done. "I'm well, don't worry."

He didn't look at all convinced and Becca had the strangest impression that if they weren't in the middle of a battle, he would have bundled her up in something dry and forced her to sit next to him for a spell. Or maybe that was her wishful thinking.

Shaking the thought off, she assured him more strongly, "I'm fine, just a little magically depleted at the moment. Give me an update on the situation here."

Danyal had to visibly swallow what he wanted to say before he could answer her. "We're having trouble getting through their defenses, but we've at least held the city so they can't send out more reinforcements to Jashni. Streaming Clouds informs me that Jashni was taken."

Never before had Becca blessed the dragons' ability to exchange information with each other over long distances. It had been vital during this battle. "Yes. They've gotten the city to surrender. Danyal, Warlord Riyu is dead."

That got everyone's attention. People froze and stared

at her as if she'd announced the world had just ended. Shrugging, she added with a jerk of the thumb, "Shad did it."

Not at all bothered by this semi-accusation, Shad intoned grandly, "I find death has greatly improved his disposition."

Snorting, Becca had to duck her head to hide a maniacal chortle as she really, really couldn't disagree.

Danyal gaped, floundered, and finally managed to get his jaw back into the socket long enough to croak, "You just killed him?"

"In all fairness, he'd grabbed a banner pole and charged me," Becca explained with a soothing hand on Danyal's arm. "I think Shad killed him out of reflex more than anything. Guardians' reflexes are no joke. Now, that said, no one else really knows this yet and I think we can play it to our advantage."

The commander looked more than a little disturbed by this news, but happy as well, a mood shared by all. Riyu had been one of those people that if on fire, people would throw kindling on, so no one lamented his premature death.

Trying not to grin openly, and failing badly, Danyal asked her, "Does Magus Ehsan have the other troops well contained?"

"It's actually Azin, Nolan, and Ehsan over there. And yes, for the time being, but that's a serious strain on them. We need to send him help. Nolan contacted Dunixan, and he's sending troops, but they will take a while to arrive. Whatever soldiers we can afford to send via dragon back to Ehsan should go as soon as possible," she directed firmly.

"Consider it done," Danyal assured her before giving Amir a go-ahead nod.

The sergeant saluted and left again at a dead run.

Stepping in a little closer to her, Danyal ducked his head slightly and said for her ears alone, "You want to use Riyu's corpse as a scare tactic."

How had the man learned to read her so well in such a short amount of time? "Yes. Do you think it will work?"

"I do." Danyal hesitated before looking toward the city walls. "You shouldn't go by dragon. They've been firing ballistas at them. We've already had one hurt, although thankfully it was a torn wing and not anything truly serious."

That would explain the steaming dragons sitting around. Becca couldn't quite suppress a wince. Garth and Nolan were going to have to handle them later, when they all caught back up with each other. "So, what, just waltz up to the city gates?"

"I'm not sure we can," Danyal cautioned. He encouraged her to turn, following his pointing finger, leaning in a little next to her side. "Come, see that line of buildings against the base of the wall?"

"Yes, I do," she acknowledged slowly, shielding her eyes with a hand in a vain effort to block out the suns' glare and get a better look. "What are those?"

"Shanty lean-tos, for the most part." Danyal eyed her sideways, a little cautious, as if he knew she wouldn't respond well to what he said next. "Raya, the very poorest can't afford to live inside Riyu itself, so they stick as close to the city as they can. I believe procedure normally dictates that the inhabitants of this section be allowed inside during siege."

"Danyal, I have this bad feeling you're going to say 'but they didn't.'"

He nodded unhappily. "They didn't. I have a terrible feeling why. You see those cauldrons that line the top of the wall? I will bet you my eye teeth they contain oil."

For the second time today, Becca's blood ran cold then boiling hot as his meaning registered. "You don't mean to tell me that they're going to set fire to all of those people's homes if we approach too closely?!"

"I'm afraid that's the standing order, yes. And it makes sense, strategically. If their defenses on top of the wall have failed to halt our advance, the only thing left to try is to ring the city with fire, physically stop us from advancing. Unfortunately, those shanty homes are made of fragile and very flammable material. It's the perfect kindling."

Becca grasped her hair with both hands and let out a muted scream of raw rage. Riyu's standing order was to burn his own people alive?!

Stepping forward, Shad took a better look himself. "It's evil, but it would work. At least short term, and short term might be all you need for reinforcements to arrive. Danyal, how sure are we that there're still people in those houses?"

"Unfortunately, we're certain. We saw movement in there upon first arrival. In fact, I was worried that there were soldiers hiding in there at first, trying to spring some sort of ambush on us. It's become clear after the past few hours that instead, it's very poor and terrified civilians." Danyal rubbed at both eyes with the pads of his fingers, tired and very unhappy.

Becca was past 'unhappy' and heading for livid. "Shad."

"Yes, dearest sister?"

"Good job killing Riyu."

Grinning at her, he patted her on the back, comforting more than anything. "I knew you'd see the light. Alright, Danyal, I take it that the reason you're so far back is because you don't want to test that standing order?"

"I didn't dare, not without having either Magus Ehsan or the Raya on hand," Danyal confessed. "We have no way of putting those fires out."

Smart of him. Becca blessed the man silently for being both observant and smart. "Alright, in your expert opinion, can I approach with a small party without setting them off?"

Danyal spread his hands in a helpless shrug. "My Raya, if I knew their exact orders, I could answer that question. Right now I only have an educated guess. I wouldn't think that your approach would set them off, but I can't be sure."

Right. Becca stared at the city, weighing options, their pros and cons, not sure what was the best option.

Some kind of exchange happened between the men, as Shad murmured in a soft voice, "She's very low on magical power right now. I don't think it's wise to push it."

"Is that why she's hesitating?" Danyal whispered back.

"That's why," she confirmed for them, equally soft. "If I approach, and they set those fires, I'm not confident I have enough in me to call up another storm to put it out."

"Call Ehsan first," Shad suggested. "Send the troops over to deal with our prisoners, bring Ehsan over here, and between the two of you surely you can handle it."

That sounded like the most feasible option. Becca went with it. "Danyal, scramble the dragons and a platoon to send that direction."

Snapping out a salute, he immediately turned, calling out orders.

Becca dug out the mirror and lifted to her mouth. "Ehsan."

"Here. How are things over there?"

"Tricky." Becca explained the situation as succinctly as possible before requesting, "I need you back here, just in case this goes pear shaped. As soon as the platoon gets there, come back this direction. You're close, so it won't take long."

"*Understood, I'll do that. You'll wait until I've arrived?*"

"I will. Oh, and stay in the air, out of range if you can. You'll need full visibility of the city if this goes wrong."

"*Alright.*"

The mirror went dark again and Becca put it away. Hopefully this was the right decision.

Danyal turned back to her, once again standing very closely to her side. "Ehsan is coming? Good. You have a shield to protect against magic?" Knowing she did, he didn't wait for anything more than a nod. "Then take me and Riicshaden, and we'll carry the body forward to them. Let them see it, make your demands, and walk away. Perhaps we can negate their standing orders if they see their Warlord has fallen."

It sounded so simple the way he stated it, so obvious, that Becca's mind threw out several objections. Wouldn't someone else try to step in and fill the void, try to claim the position of warlord, wouldn't the people still object to being conquered, and so forth. But there was a good possibility that none of that would happen. Dunixan had briefed them before about Riyu's political state. The man had been so greedy, so paranoid, that he gave the minimum amount of power to his people and delegated as little as possible. No one was a named successor. Certainly someone would want to be in his position but they wouldn't get enough support to instantly defend the city from the enemy at the gate. Riyu's very tactics to keep his people in line could very well lead to the city's downfall.

While she agreed, she chose to change just one thing. "We'll ask one more person to join us, to carry Riyu's body. I want both you and Shad's hands free while we approach."

Hessen, one of the burlier soldiers, stepped forward, giving a salute. Becca hadn't interacted with him much, but he'd quickly become one of Danyal's favorites, as the man wasn't the type to shirk the dirty work. "My Warlord. Request permission to carry that thrice-cursed son of a goat."

Grinning at him, she saluted him sharply. "Only because

you called him a son of a goat. You'll find him next to Cat. Oh, and Lieutenant?"

"Yes, my Warlord?"

"Don't touch my shield once I've erected it," Becca warned seriously. "It will hurt you badly. I'll give us plenty of room on all sides, but make sure to keep up with us and don't extend your arms out to touch the sides."

Hessen gave her a sharp nod. "Yes, my Warlord. I'll be back in a moment."

She watched him jog away before her eye was distracted by several dragons taking off, soldiers either in saddles or clutched in their claws. Good, Ehsan would soon be on his way here. Bending, she scooped up Tail, requesting of her familiar, "Stay on my shoulder, will you? I need an extra set of eyes."

Tail rubbed against the top of her head, agreeing, then settled snuggly on her shoulder. He'd occupied that seat often over the years and they both knew how to balance his weight.

Becca had enough magical energy to hold a shield for a while. It thankfully didn't require much to maintain, otherwise she might not have been able to pull it off at this point. She tried not to let her exhaustion show but she had a feeling that neither Danyal nor Shad was fooled. Shad already knew, of course, and Danyal pressed a canteen into her hands with a firm look that meant 'shut up and drink it.'

Despite being soaked earlier, she felt perfectly parched, and drained half of it in one pull before handing it back. There, that was a little better.

Hessen returned after several minutes, again at a jog but this time with the body slung over his shoulders in a fireman's carry. He didn't look at all winded or strained by the burden despite the fact that Riyu could hardly be described as a small man. Then again, Hessen looked like he could wrestle even a dragon to the ground, so one person's weight shouldn't pose much of a challenge.

The mirror went live in her pocket and she pulled it out. "Becca here."

"*Becca, I've got the city in view,*" Ehsan reported.

Close enough. "Thanks, be on standby. We're going to try approaching."

Replacing the mirror, Becca motioned for them to follow her, erecting a magical shield above their heads as they moved, although she kept it flat and well away from everyone. Danyal bellowed the order as they moved: "CEASE FIRE! CEASE FIRE AND MAINTAIN POSITION!"

As the order carried through the ranks, people put weapons down, retreating behind shields, watching avidly as their commanders moved past them. Becca could hear a wave of words follow in their wake as people spotted the dead warlord. Before they could reach the city, Becca bet herself that the whole army would know what they were doing.

Only when they went past the front lines did she extend the shield all the way around them in a dome that grazed the ground. Enemy fire continued to rain down on them, and especially at her shield, but it all just bounced off with sparks. It unnerved Hessen and Danyal badly, who had no real experience being under the shield, so she sought to reassure them, "It's fine. Nothing can penetrate this shield. Not even dragon's fire."

"And believe me, we tested it," Shad inserted jovially. "Multiple times. That was a very fun experiment."

"You mean the experiment where you lost both eyebrows? That one?" Becca grinned at his wounded expression.

Mock-pouting at her, Shad whined, "You're not supposed

to tell all my secrets."

"Shad, you were playing fire dodgeball with a *Fire Mage and a dragon*. That's far too good of a story to not tell."

"Perhaps later," Danyal requested in exasperation, "while we're not walking through a battlefield?"

He did rather have a point. Becca lost all common sense when around her brother. He was a corruptive influence that way.

Becca gauged the distance. She didn't want to get too close to the gates, not with the danger of setting some protocol in motion. Was this close enough they could hear her?

The thought barely formed in her mind when Shad swore and pulled her back, his arm a band around her chest. "Too close, too close!"

She saw what he meant in the next moment as several of the pots of oil tipped, splashing out over the roofs of the shanty houses. This close, she could see how it was mostly made of fabric, little else, and terror seized her. Even wet, with the oil, the fabric would catch fire instantly and offer no protection to anyone inside.

Frantically, she snatched out the mirror even as she turned, running back for the front lines. "Ehsan! Ehsan, they're pouring out the oil!"

"*I can't see any—*" He broke off with a vicious curse in Khobuntish slang. "*Multiple fires are breaking out. I'm suppressing them as fast as I can.*"

Becca stopped running and spun sharply, forcing everyone to stop with her or plow into her shield. Fires blazed along the pitched tents and lean-to roofs, mostly eating at the oil, but it dried out the fabric enough that the flames started to carry across. "No, no, no, no, no! Ehsan! Front gates, there're fires at the front gates!"

"There are fires at every gate. I think someone panicked. Becca, I don't have enough water!"

For the first time in her life, Becca didn't feel up to calling a storm. Just holding the shield took concentration. But she couldn't ignore these innocent people huddling in the only homes they had, nor could she ignore the desperate plea in Ehsan's voice. "Gentlemen, I'm dropping the barrier."

"Got it," Danyal and Shad said in unison, moving to standing as a living shield in front of her. Seeing that, the soldiers still on the wall lost no time in firing their direction. Shad moved like a whirlwind, intercepting every arrow, knocking them aside, the shafts cleanly cut in two. Danyal moved with his round shield in front of him, blocking whatever might get through Shad's defense from hitting her.

Praying she had the strength for this, she called on the storm already formed overhead, saturating the clouds, forcing it to rain just one more time. What strength she had sapped from her bones as all of her energy flew straight into the heavens. Even then, she didn't have the reach or stamina to pour rain over the whole city. It hit the front gates, right in front of her, and didn't spread any further than that.

Ginger swooped about, Ehsan drawing on the rain straight from the clouds, wielding it with the finest control she'd ever seen a Water Mage perform. He moved the water in a spray, dousing the fires as Ginger took him on a tight circle around the city's walls.

Her knees started to shake, breathing labored in her lungs, and Becca gave it two minutes before she was so tapped out that she'd collapse right here. "Ehsan. Is that enough?"

"Not quite. Almost."

She wanted to chide him for not using the water puddled on the ground, but actually she saw him doing exactly that.

This area was so dry it had soaked up most of the rain, which would come in handy later, but she cursed it now. It left very little for him to work with from the previous storm.

Proving to have the worst timing in the history of timing, her air-tampering magician chose that moment to throw the air currents into a spin, yanking on her storm and pulling it off-course. Becca swore viciously, every cell in her body protesting as she demanded more magical power, jerking the storm back on course. When she got her hands on that starveling, eel-skinned, whoreson fool, she'd gut him for this.

Hessen dropped the body with a thud and moved to support her, his chest to her back. "Pardon, my Warlord."

"Bless you, Lieutenant," she panted, not sure she could keep upright anymore without his help. It might be a breach of etiquette for him to touch her, but she wasn't about to call the man out for it. "Ehsan, I'm done, I can't keep it going anymore."

"I think I can manage this last part. Let go."

Thankfully, she did so, black spots swimming in front of her eyes. As soon as she stopped, the rain dissipated like fine mist, the clouds above breaking up a little to let streams of light through. The storm spun out of control, moving on as the air currents from the north pushed it off. Danyal spun, dropping the shield and catching her up in his arms. "Hessen, the body. Riicshaden, guard our retreat."

"On it," Shad assured him calmly, not even out of breath.

Becca hadn't been picked up like this since she was a child, and found it a slightly strange experience to be hauled back like so much luggage. At least Danyal hadn't thrown her over his shoulder in caveman fashion, though. Tail snuggled against her stomach, not willing to run back with them. Becca felt like she shouldn't be showing any signs of weakness, not in front of an enemy or her own troops, but didn't have the energy to argue.

They hit the front lines at a fast jog, her own troops automatically opening up to let them through, then closing the shields fast and tight to guard their rear. Becca let her head rest against Danyal's shoulder for a moment, tired and frustrated.

As soon as they got close enough to the center, Cat muscled her way through and nuzzled her. "Hungry?"

Of course, to a dragon, hunger was the only reason for acting like a wilting damsel in distress. "Starving, Cat."

"Fix it," Cat promised. Turning, she bellowed out for a plate of food and water. With that kind of no-nonsense tone, a dozen cooks were likely to respond.

Danyal cautiously set her down, easing her to the folding command chair like she might break. Gently squeezing his shoulder, she assured him, "Magical depletion is nothing serious, just taxing on the body. As long as I rest and eat something, I'll be fine. But it does mean that we can't carelessly approach again today. I have no magic to call on a storm right now."

"We'll find another way," Danyal promised, worry still reflected in his eyes. "Rest, my Raya."

Trev'nor arrived at Riyu's gates two hours before sunset, cradled against Garth's chest in one giant paw. He would have chanced the saddle, but honestly he became lightheaded when in the air. The swoops up and down made his eyes spin in his head. Nolan said the blood loss would set him back two days and Trev'nor believed him. Still, he felt able to walk around and at least direct matters, which meant he really should help Becca. Riyu was the last problem they had left to solve to win this battle.

As he passed over the highway, he saw Azin hard at work erecting temporary barriers off to the side to hold the soldiers. The structures looked like prison walls with no roofs, metal constructs at least ten feet high. Dragons and their soldiers oversaw this endeavor and Ehsan stood nearby, at the ready. He spotted Trev'nor overhead and gave a wave but didn't signal for help, which meant they had it all well in hand.

If they were building a temporary holding cell out here, then Becca hadn't taken Riyu yet and wasn't sure if she would be able to get them to surrender tonight. Frowning at this, Trev'nor started praying he was wrong and his co-ruler just didn't want to introduce an army back into the city so soon after a surrender. Just in case someone got ideas.

The city and waiting army came slowly into view, nothing more than moving dots that gradually grew into human beings. Garth slowed to start his descent, warm evening air swirling about them and tugging at the loose strands around Trev'nor's face. Somewhere in the insanity, he'd put his helmet in a special place, and the goggles had not been sufficient to keep his hair back. He was going to have to find a moment to re-braid his hair. It was past the point of aggravation.

From the smell of it, the back lines were busy cooking dinner for everyone. So Becca didn't think they'd enter the city tonight? Or she was feeding everyone while they were just sitting around with their faces on, either one. Trev'nor really, really hoped it was the latter.

With a soft thump, Garth settled them toward the very back, avoiding knocking anyone over. He released Trev'nor slowly, keeping a paw at his back until Trev'nor felt steady on his own feet. Good thing, too, as it took a minute for his head to stop swirling.

"Trev."

Trev'nor's head came up and around until he spotted Shad jogging toward him. "Hey. How goes it?"

Lifting a hand, Shad see-sawed it back and forth. "Not sure yet. How're you doing?"

"Mostly recovered," Trev'nor assured him, even though he desperately wanted to sit down and wait for this lightheadedness to pass. "Where's Becca?"

"Straight ahead, stuffing her face." Shad slid in next to him, putting a supportive arm around his back, avoiding the wound at the waist so neatly a person would think he could see through clothes.

Grateful for the support, Trev'nor leaned against him, putting a hand on his shoulder. "It's very convenient that you're a little shorter than me."

Shad shot him a dirty look. "See if I do *you* favors anymore."

Chuckling, Trev'nor let his mentor guide him, addressing Garth as he went, "Find some food and water, will you? You've been fighting all day."

The dragon gave a snort, expression saying he didn't need some fledgling to give him orders. Trev'nor rolled his eyes and let that one pass. Garth was in a mood right now, it was impossible to reason with him.

Shad took him a short distance, toward the 'eating grounds.' Trev'nor didn't know what else to term it, as no one had erected tents or tried to find boulders to sit on. They just spread out uniform jackets and sat cross-legged, balancing plates on their knees. It was like a picnic without the fancy baskets. Becca sat right in amongst the men, exchanging smiles and words, which pleased everyone around her. She'd gotten better at the language over the past several months and only occasionally did Danyal, seated right next to her, have to supply a word or phrase she needed.

Trev'nor gave her a once-over as he approached, mentally wincing at her state. That had to be the lowest reservoir of magical power that he'd ever seen. That battle had sapped her pretty badly, it seemed. She was apparently recovering, as the food and rest helped her regain some strength, enough at least that she could move about normally. Trev'nor wrote off all possibility of her doing magic before tomorrow afternoon, though.

Trev'nor nearly missed it, but the reactions of the men around them clued him in that something obvious was going on. Then he realized that Becca and Danyal shared the same jacket, likely Danyal's jacket, as the man was in shirt sleeves and Becca in full uniform. Of course the jacket wasn't all that big, so the two of them had to sit with legs overlapping to fit on it. It looked immediately couplish to Trev'nor's eyes, and that was from a Chahiran perspective. Khobunter was even more uptight about this sort of thing.

"I know," Shad said from the corner of his mouth in a low tone. "Pretend you don't see it. Danyal hasn't actually made a move yet and Becca's still a little oblivious. Give 'em time."

So Shad was aware of this and not saying anything? Well now.

Courting even under the best of circumstances could go easily awry. Danyal had the odds stacked against him, trying to do it under these harsh conditions with his boss. Trev'nor wished the man luck and decided to cut him some slack, deliberately turning a blind eye to his friend being cozy on a battlefield. "Bec."

She stopped mid-sentence, head coming sharply around. "Trev! Why aren't you in Jashni?"

"Dunixan and Nolan have that well in hand," he assured her, coming to stand nearby in one of the only clear spots left. He eyed it sideways, trying to estimate if it offered enough space for him to sit. Maybe? "I stayed long enough to hand over all of our rescued magicians to Sallah and Raile. Llona straightened out people on who was where, so a lot of who we rescued knew they'd be reuniting with friends and family soon, which put fears to ease. They were a lot happier going on the Earth Path the second time. Sallah stayed long enough to put the walls back in place for me, then they left."

"Bless that woman. I don't know what we'd do without her. Have you eaten yet?"

"Not really." He'd been so nauseous earlier he couldn't force more than a few bites down. His stomach rumbled petulantly now, so odds were better this go around.

"I'll get you something." She popped up with her empty plate, gesturing for him to sit, then weaved her way around sitting people toward the cook fires.

Trev'nor shucked his jacket and settled down, content to wait. He could tell Danyal was a little sad she'd moved so easily, so he tried to distract the man. "Commander, there's something that's puzzled me for a while. Maybe you can clarify."

"Of course, Raja," Danyal encouraged, setting his own empty plate aside.

"I've noticed that whenever there's a conflict between the men, if Becca steps in to mediate, everyone immediately listens to her. I don't always get the same results when I try. Is this a cultural thing?"

Several of the men sitting nearby shifted uneasily, as if feeling he'd aimed this at them in rebuke. Trev'nor waved it down with a smile, showing he wasn't mad about it, and they gave him ducks of the head and shy smiles in return.

"It is," Danyal answered, shifting to face him more squarely. "The men are the head of the family, the ruling force. Our laws and might come from them. But our women hold the heart of the land. They are the peace-keepers, the ones to mediate conflicts between fathers and sons, and so we listen to them."

"That explains a lot." And here Trev'nor had assumed all this time that Becca had connected better with the army just because she knew how to think and speak military terms and had been the first to don the uniform. That still might have played into it, but apparently it was Khobunter culture more than anything. It certainly explained the positions of Rikkana and Rikkan. "I'll have to remember to send her in when mediation is needed. She'll get better results."

Danyal shrugged agreement, splaying a hand out.

Several of the others listening to this actually huffed a soft laugh, agreeing but not daring to say so aloud.

"While we're on culture terms that don't make sense," Shad inputted, crossing his legs more comfortably, "let me ask this. Am I correct in that you have four different terms for rivers?"

That had also confused Trev'nor, and he wasn't sure he'd gotten them straight yet, so he was glad for Shad's question.

"Hmm, how to explain?" Danyal tilted his head toward the sky for a moment, thinking, then used Solish to break it down for them. "You are familiar with the weather patterns for Khobunter? How we have long dry spells but also rainy seasons?"

"At least until Becca came on scene and messed that up?" Trev'nor responded, getting a chuckle from everyone listening. Grinning, he acceded, "Yes, I know. She had many choice words to say about that on the way up here. You only get three weeks of a rainy season early spring, is that right?"

"Normally, yes."

Becca came back to them, sitting on her haunches to hand Trev'nor a plate of food and a canteen of water. With a challenging glint in her eye, she drawled, "What did I say about Khobunter's weather?"

"There were many words," Trev'nor sniped back, not about to back down. "None of them were clean."

Snorting, she rolled her eyes and retreated back to her spot next to Danyal, which made the commander light up. Seriously, how could she not see what was going on?

Clearing his throat, Danyal forced his eyes away from her and continued the explanation. "Especially near the mountain areas, the water can collect and form rivers, which rush down to the valley floor. But only during that season and for perhaps a month afterwards, the rest of the time those river beds do not contain water, only sand. So we have three terms for rivers: *nahmin alma*, or a river of water; *nahmin alramal*, a river of sand or dry riverbed; *nahmin almutasare* which is a river of rushing water."

That last one had confused Trev'nor. "So what's the difference between rushing water and a river of water?"

"Rushing water is very fast, filthy water," Danyal explained, struggling a little in Solish to get his point across. "It is…gah."

"Like a flash flood?" Becca offered, trying to untangle him.

Relieved, he gave her an energetic nod. "Yes, yes, that. Happens rarely, but dangerous when you come across it. The only way is to go around them."

"And what about *wahah*?" Trev'nor asked, as this was the term that confused him the most. "I've heard that used constantly, usually with some relief or excitement. Is it a pure source of water?"

"Not quite, Raja. It is an oasis."

That made so much more sense. Still, it made Trev'nor a little sad that these people were so water deprived that they needed so many distinct words and ways to describe it. "I feel better for the language lesson. Thank you, Commander, that cleared up my confusion nicely."

Giving him a smile, Danyal ducked into a half-bow. "My pleasure, Raja."

The food looked good, actually, some sort of rice stir-fry with chunks of meat and root vegetables. Most army food was disgusting, or so Trev'nor was told, but Becca had made sure the men ate better from the get-go. He gave it a try, found it perfectly seasoned and not at all spicy, then took a bigger bite.

"While you're eating, let me catch you up," Becca offered.

With an encouraging wave of the hand, he motioned for her to do so, listening intently as he shoveled food into his mouth. Halfway through her explanation he had to stop eating or risk choking on his food. Riyu had left standing orders to torch his own people's homes in order to ward off attackers? Was the man evil to the core? When she finished, he blew out a breath. "Shad. Good job."

"I'm getting a lot of that," Shad responded dryly. "No one's upset that Riyu's dead so far, which really speaks volumes of the man."

"I don't think there's a curse word dark enough to describe that man." Trev'nor rubbed at his mouth, debating if he was too upset to eat or not, but his stomach petulantly reminded him of two skipped meals today and threatened lawsuits if not fed. Determined, he picked his fork back up even as he asked, "So what are we going to do about them? Can we evacuate them somehow?"

"Would you go with an enemy army if they asked you nicely?" Becca asked him pointedly. "Even if their own city tried to torch them, I'm not sure if they'd move. This country has a habit of enslaving anyone taken prisoner. They might think they're faced with choosing between two evils."

Danyal nodded sad agreement. "Our Raya is unfortunately correct. That is likely what they're thinking. I do not advise trying to evacuate them under the cover of darkness. They won't move quietly enough to make it feasible anyway, they'd give the game away and then we'd be dealing with panicked people while fire rains down on us."

Alright, so Trev'nor hadn't thought that suggestion all the way through.

"Instead of trying that, maybe we can block the pots themselves?" Shad suggested. "They're metal, aren't they? Shouldn't Azin be able to do something about them?"

Trev'nor didn't see a problem with that. "Sure. I think we'll need to try this early in the morning, though, give her magic a chance to recuperate. She has to be just as tired as the rest of us."

Becca shrugged agreement but frowned at the same time, as if this caused her problems. "I really wanted to call for surrender today, though, if at all possible. It's hard for us to sit out here overnight, and keep the other army imprisoned out there for too long. If we leave them baking under the suns tomorrow without any provisions, we risk losing people."

All true. Trev'nor fished out his mirror broach, swearing to himself he would attach a case to it or something so he could just keep it pinned to his front jacket. "Alright, instead of assuming, let's ask her. Azin? Azin~"

"*I'm here. Now what's wrong?*"

It was a sad state of affairs that Trev'nor couldn't refute that. "We're having trouble approaching the city. Aside from the magical attacks, and the arrows, they're torching the people living at the base of the city if we get too close."

"*Ehsan told me about that. It makes us both boiling mad. You think I can do something about that?*"

"I'm really hoping you can. The oil is stored in big metal cauldrons along the top of the walls. If you could do something with them, and the ballistas up there, then we can manage the rest of the attacks long enough to get in there and deliver a demand for surrender. What's your energy level right now?"

"*Give me a chance to eat something and I think I can do it. I'm running a little low on power at the moment, but I'm not as bad as you three.*"

Three meaning Ehsan was in the same state as well? Glory. They'd really pushed themselves to the brink on this one, hadn't they? "Alright. We have some pretty good food over here already prepared, if you want to make the trip."

"*Sounds glorious. Orion and I are on our way.*"

Azin, thankfully, had spoken literal truth. After a meal she had the energy required to climb back on Orion and do a quick swoop around the city. Azin kept a hand outstretched as they flew, literally jerking anything with metal away from the battlements and throwing them out into the desert sand below her. Even from the back of the line, Becca could hear the outraged screams from Riyu's soldiers.

She chuckled evilly.

Orion landed at the back, the only clear space to do so, with a few suspicious sounds escaping from his mouth. Azin smacked him lightly on the shoulder as she dismounted. "Stop laughing, you troublemaker. It's not that funny."

"Hilarious," her dragon disagreed, laughing even harder. "Soldiers mad."

Rolling her eyes, Azin let that one pass.

Becca strolled up to him, giving him a good rub along the tip of his nose. "I'm with Orion on this one. It's hilarious."

Orion rubbed against her hand, tail thumping in smug pleasure. "Is."

Azin gave them a glare, but her lips kept twitching suspiciously. "You're both incorrigible. Alright, Warlord, I have made it safer to approach. When do you want to do so?"

"I'd love to go now," Becca admitted hopefully, "but neither Trev nor I have the power to keep a magical shield up. You know they'll rely on the magicians to attack."

"They don't have anything else at the moment to try with," Azin agreed, staring at the city thoughtfully. "At least, at the moment. I'm sure they're frantically hauling more ballistas and weapons out of the armory, but it's going to take time to get it all on top of the walls again. If we hurry, we might make it."

"You have enough power to hold a shield, then?"

"I do," Azin confirmed. "Let's go."

Becca's eyes said the same thing, but it wasn't fair to another magician to just assume things and make demands. Relieved Azin was willing to do one more thing today, after everything else she had done, Becca led her back to the front where the 'command center' sat.

All of the men looked around at their approach, expressions questioning, and Becca answered their silent queries. "Azin is up to holding a shield for us, and she suggests we go now before they get more weapons up there to replace the ones she took."

"I think that is an excellent suggestion," Shad agreed, already reaching for the sword he'd leaned against his chair. "Let's move."

Turning, Becca found Hessen standing aside and asked, "Can you carry Riyu's body one more time for me?"

"Of course, my Warlord," the lieutenant agreed promptly.

"Thank you. Trev, don't you dare try to come with us, you're still recovering."

Trev'nor held up a hand, staying the rest of her words. "Trust me, not tempted. I still get a little lightheaded when I stand for long periods. Go get 'em, tiger."

Glad he was being sensible about this, Becca moved

with her group, not at all surprised when Danyal followed immediately at her heels. The soldiers on the front line watched silently as they moved past, only shifting enough to let their leaders through before closing ranks again behind them. As soon as they cleared the soldiers, Azin stepped toward the front, erecting a mage barrier, then cautioned over her shoulder, "I know that you can't see it, but I just erected a barrier. It's a flat plane directly in front of me. Please don't step in front of me."

"Understood, Magess," Danyal assured her. "Thank you for the warning."

Becca felt it a little ridiculous to have to do this twice in one day, but at least this time she knew that innocent people wouldn't be torched just because she got a little too close. She could feel their eyes as well as she walked toward the city's front gate, peeping out from behind their doors. In fact, she felt like she had eyes on her from all directions—hardly a comfortable sensation.

When she reached the same spot from before, her nerves stretched like an overwrought wire, but nothing happened immediately. Even the magical attacks that she expected didn't come, although she could see multiple magicians lined up along the top of the wall. Had their previous actions shown that rashly attacking never led to good results? Were they now going to wait and see?

Once again, gauging the distance was tricky. Where should she stop so they could hear her? She wanted everyone on the battlements to have a clear view but didn't want to get too close. Besides, they might be tempted to open a side gate and try to capture her, which would defeat the point. But she needed to be close enough that they could see their fallen leader.

In the end, the enemy told her when she got close

enough, as they shot a warning shot into the sand near Azin's feet. Obviously, someone's eyes up there were sharp enough to see Hessen's burden. Lifting a closed fist, she signaled to stop. Praying she had the lungpower for this, she tilted her head back a little and shouted, "I AM WARLORD RIICBECCAAN. WARLORD RIYU IS DEAD."

Hessen took this as his cue to take a step around her and dump the body on the ground in full view before retreating to her back again.

A wail went up among the soldiers, most of them leaning almost perilously over the edge for a closer look, some shouting profanities. Becca more or less expected that reaction and didn't try to shout over them. It went on for several minutes, rising and falling in a crescendo of panic, although interestingly enough not of grief. Riyu was hated even among his own people, eh? Color her not surprised.

Eventually it died down to an unhappy murmur and an officer stepped forward, shouting back at her, "What are your demands, Warlord?"

"Surrender," she responded succinctly. "Surrender before sunset and I will not enslave this people or destroy the city."

Really, in Khobunter, those were amazing terms of surrender. The fact that she asked for surrender was novel in and of itself. Becca knew very well that the officer asking didn't have the authority to agree so she repeated, "Sunset is your deadline. Send someone out of the gate by that point or I level the place."

Another wave of unhappy noises, speaking of fear, passed through the ranks of soldiers on the battlements. Becca prayed they'd have the sense to accept her terms of surrender. Everyone's lives would be so much better if they did. It wasn't, unfortunately, in her power to make that decision for them.

Doing an about face, she led her own men back to the ranks with Azin taking up the rear, still maintaining the shield. As they moved, she asked, "Danyal, I know that the men have been eating in shifts. Has everyone been fed today?"

"The third and last shift is eating now, my Raya." He gave her an approving smile as he answered, pleased that she was thoughtful of her troop's condition.

She didn't have the heart to tell him that she mostly thought about food because she herself was starving. Again. Magical depletion could turn even a hummingbird into a pig. "Good. Let me know as soon as those front gates are open."

"Yes, my Raya."

Hessen cleared his throat and dared to ask, "Raya, if they won't surrender, will you really destroy the city?"

Glancing back at him, she grimaced. "Let's hope that I don't have to."

Nolan called while Trev'nor and Becca ate yet another plate of food. Actually, this was Trev'nor's fourth plate, but no one begrudged him the extra protein. They were once again ensconced in the 'eating grounds' like it was some sort of picnic, although the mood weighed too somber for that. Everyone kept watching the sky, the suns heading steadily toward the horizon, taking the light with them.

Balancing a plate on her knee, Becca caught Nolan up on what had happened, finishing with, "And right now, we're waiting. Danyal is convinced that they'll surrender before sunset, but that only leaves us about half an hour and I haven't gotten any further communication from them, which isn't a good sign."

"They might be fighting over who has the authority to surrender the city to you," Danyal pointed out prosaically.

Frowning, she twisted to stare at the city again. "That is an excellent point. I hadn't thought of that. But of course, if they don't have a designated successor, then that leaves them short of any ruler whatsoever."

Previous warlord really hadn't done his province any favors. Shaking his head, Trev'nor scraped the last of his plate clean and set it in the only clear space available, which happened to be on Danyal's empty plate. They had plenty of space available to spread out, what with a desert being at their back, so why were they all sitting on top of each other? For comfort?

Nolan asked, "How long do you plan to keep the other army out in those temporary holding cells?"

"At least overnight." Becca's shoulders lifted in an uncertain gesture. "Hopefully this resolves so we don't have to keep them in there any longer."

Because really, what else were they going to do with them? It was a logistic headache Trev'nor didn't want to visit just yet.

"Trev'nor tells me that we still haven't spied anyone from Rurick, is that right?" Becca asked.

"Unfortunately. If they're not in Riyu or Sha, then I doubt they're in this province. Which leaves only one real option: Rowe."

"They might still be in Riyu," Trev'nor cautioned. "Let's keep an eye out for them."

"Only thing we can do right now. Is anyone hurt over there?"

"We have a few injuries, nothing too serious. They fell back behind the shields pretty quickly when they realized what they were up against. Why, are you thinking of heading this direction?"

"I've done basically all I can here. And I want to be on hand just in case this does come down to a siege."

Trev'nor couldn't lean that direction without aggravating the wound in his side, so he pitched his voice to carry instead. "I think that's smart. Come over. It doesn't look promising at the moment—"

"FRONT GATES ARE OPEN!"

Well alright, then. Looked like he was wrong.

"Nolan, the front gates just opened, I need to go," Becca said quickly, putting her plate down so fast some of the food slipped off and onto the sand.

"Go, go, I'm flying that direction now."

Trev'nor lost no time in getting up, then had to pause as his head spun. Shadows and light flicked across his vision and it felt like his head detached from his shoulders. He didn't like getting stabbed, who would, but what really drove him crazy was the recovery time afterwards.

Without a word, Becca grabbed his hand and placed it on her shoulder. "Lean on me, less obvious that you're injured if a woman is next to you," she directed.

Truth. And they didn't want to present any kind of weakness to their enemy, especially when said enemy was surrendering. Hopefully surrendering.

People cleared a path for them as they marched back to the city gates. Trev'nor gave no orders but Danyal apparently issued quite a few behind their backs, as they gained a squad of bodyguards as they moved. Azin automatically went ahead of them, raising the barrier once more to protect them from magical attacks. Their respective dragons hovered in the air above them, just out of range, ready to dive in at any moment. Trev'nor didn't blame them for the caution, as neither he nor Becca could fight well at the moment. This battle had cost them both dearly.

Trev'nor had never been this close to the city before and he admitted privately to himself that the walls were a little intimidating. Perhaps the thickness and height of the walls, easily three times that of Trexler's, could be taken as a sign of how nervous Riyu had been governing this place. Even the gates reared tall and wide enough to allow a dragon to saunter through it, a show of power if there ever was one. Soldiers stood near the doors, along the top of the battlements, watchful and grave. Being the focus of that many eyes, most of them filled with anger and fear, sent a shiver up Trev'nor's spine. It took nerves of steel to go right up to the gates instead of stopping far enough away to have a half-shouted conversation. He forced himself to walk close enough for a normal exchange.

The gates stood open with precisely four people framed in the middle of it. Three men and one woman, all older with greying hair, all of them trying to keep a stern face on and failing to show how miserable they felt. The Tonkowacon part of Trev'nor wanted to go and hug them, reassure them that it would be alright, that their lives would be so much better from this day forward. But they wouldn't believe him, not yet. He'd have to prove all of that to them one day at a time.

Because Becca had a cat balancing on one shoulder and Trev'nor on the other, she could only do an abbreviated bow, but she showed respect to the four. "I am Warlord Riicbeccaan. This is my co-ruler, Warlord Rhebentrev'noren."

They didn't quite know what to do with this civil greeting. They exchanged uneasy glances, as if by formally giving their names, Becca had broken some social norm as conqueror. Becca kept a pleasant expression on her face and waited them out without showing the least sign of impatience.

The sole woman in the group cleared her throat and offered, "I am Iesha, Rikkana of Riyu. This is Feisal, Rikkan; Galel, Rikkshan; and General Heydar."

So, the culturally acceptable leaders of the city plus the top military officer. Really, they were the best options for a ruling body. "I greet you, Rikkana, Rikkan, Rikkshan, General."

All four looked thrown at this very polite greeting and it made Trev'nor smile, if a little sadly. For all that these people beat ceremony and courtesy into you, they didn't seem to observe the rules very well. Smile fading, he asked seriously, "Will you surrender the city to us?"

General Heydar took in a breath, expression puckered as if he had just swallowed a rotten lime. "Warlord Riicbeccaan, you said to us earlier that if we surrender to you, you would not enslave this people or ransack the city."

There seemed to be a question there, and Becca answered it. "I did say that. You have my word as a Riic that this people will not be mistreated. We adhere to the First Laws of Khobunter."

Some of them seemed confused on this, as well they should be, as the original laws of Khobunter were not taught anymore, so almost as one they turned to the one person that would know what Becca meant, the Rikkshan. He stared at her for a long moment, not blinking, not even breathing. He looked old enough to have learned the laws for himself as a child, his stooped posture and thin white hair making him look older than even Raile. In a voice gone high and soft with age, he demanded, "The First Laws? All of them?"

"All except the laws on slaves," Trev'nor corrected. "Under our rule, slavery is not allowed. Ever."

"We tweaked a few others to be more humane," Becca

tacked on with a warm smile for the man. "But most of the laws we follow."

Rikkshan Galel turned sharply to his companions, whispering something in a dialect that went straight over Trev'nor's head. He didn't need to understand the words anyway, tone and body language was enough: *Accept the deal now!*

After a very hurried, whispered conversation, General Heydar straightened and faced them once more. "Warlord, most of us can accept your terms, but there are pockets of resistance in the city."

"There always is," Becca sighed in aggravation. "What I want to know is, do you speak for the majority of the city?"

"We do. We surrender."

"Excellent. We'll handle the resistance, then. Don't worry, I won't hold their conduct against you." Becca exchanged a look with Trev'nor, silently asking how he wanted to divide the workload.

Trev'nor really wasn't physically capable of gallivanting all over creation and he knew precisely who should be doing what. Pointing to his own nose, he offered, "City?"

"Army," she agreed promptly. "Rikkana, Rikkan, Rikkshan, please work with Warlord Trev'nor in settling the city. Understand that we want all slaves promptly released to us first, and then we will spend time over the next few weeks repairing the damage and resolving troubles."

Not sure what to think of this, they nevertheless gave a bow of acquiescence to Trev'nor.

"General," Becca continued with a winning smile at the man that instinctively put him a little at ease, "I will have Commander Danyal take over the armed forces inside the city. He will deal with all resistance. Please introduce him as the new commander here and give him capable staff to work with."

"I will, Warlord," the General agreed with a bow, uneasy at handing over the reins of command to someone else, but relieved she was taking the situation so well.

"Also," Becca continued, "We have a lot of soldiers who are currently being held out in the desert. I'd prefer they not stay the night out there. Help me sort them out so that they can go home."

Heydar stared at her as if she'd just sprouted another head. "Go home?"

"General." Becca released a sigh, smile becoming sad. "If the state of this province is anything like Trexler's before we conquered it, then your men have been on short pay for years and have not been allowed to go home at all. This hurts my heart. No army should be enslaved to the state. I want these men to go home, see their families, for the province to pay them proper wages once more. They are *my* soldiers now and they will be given the honor they are due."

Trev'nor watched the almost magical effect these words had on the general and every soldier listening. She really understood how to speak directly to the military heart, didn't she? Trev'nor had a sense that Becca should always be over military matters. It would just make life easier all around. "Perhaps some of those soldiers can go rescue the fled citizens of Jashni?" he murmured to her in Chahirese. "'Cause I'm pretty sure they ran for the coast."

Grimacing, Becca responded in the same language, "I'll take care of it. You get things settled here."

Sounded like a fair division of labor to him. Switching back to Khobuntish, he said cheerfully, "Someone lead me to an office that I can work out of. Let's try and get things settled at least for the night before the suns leave us entirely."

"Well, young Warlord," Raile greeted jovially as he took the seat in front of Trev'nor's desk, "you certainly captured the city easily."

Trev'nor had been hip deep in reports, sending messengers out until midnight, and rising at dawn to do it all over again in order to figure out where this city stood. That didn't even count the scolding he got from Becca, Nolan, and Shad about pushing himself too hard during a state of recovery. Even Danyal had given him the stink eye while delivering breakfast to them. His eyes felt gritty, his joints ached, and it took constant snacking from the tray at his elbow to keep him awake.

If not for Dunixan lingering in Jashni, helping to straighten the city before going home himself, Trev'nor might very well have asked Nolan to create a clone of himself so he could be in three places at once.

"Trust me, Raile, there was nothing easy about it," he groused, pouring himself another cup of tea from the tea set on the desk and offering it to his guest. "So many things went wrong during the battle it's hard to count them all. And there's still pockets of resistance in the city that Danyal is dealing with, and by dealing, I mean with much swearing and threats to cut off people's tongues."

Raile took the cup and gave it an experimental sip. "Battles normally go awry, it's the result that counts. What is this? It's quite fragrant."

"Jasmine tea. Local specialty, so I'm told." Trev'nor found it wonderful and soothing to his low-grade headache. "We count that we have nearly eight hundred magicians for you to take. Three hundred some odd are non-magical but please take them anyway so they can reunite with their families."

"I'll do so," Raile promised, relaxing a little more into the chair. "You'll be pleased to know that after Sallah and I bring this lot back, she'll be headed to the Isle of Strae to collect everyone else. I've been in contact with Garth and he's relieved I'll be doing so soon. He also passed along the message that he's proud of all of you, wishes that he could help, and that if you want to send correspondence home, he'll play messenger for you."

For a moment, Trev'nor's eyes burned with unshed tears as those words meant the world to him. Out here in this desert land, he sometimes felt so far removed from home, uncertain that this path he chose was the right one. Sometimes he felt so homesick the emotion churned his gut, other times so lonely that his heart twisted under the force of it. It took a minute to get his unruly emotions in check before he could trust his voice to not betray him. "Thank you, Raile. I'll take him up on that offer. I've been writing very long letters for my parents and my mentors, explaining what's going on and what our plans are for the future. If you'll give me a few minutes to finish them up, I can send them along with Sallah."

"That'll be fine," Raile assured him. "We've discovered it's best to talk with everyone first, let them know what to expect and who's waiting for them at the new academy. They're less inclined to panic that way. Llona has to get everyone's names first, of course. I expect it to take a good portion of the morning. Just how good is a dragon's memory, anyway?"

"Exceptional," Trev'nor answered bluntly. "You would not believe it. Nolan finally explained to me why they have such short sentences. It's not because they can't learn extensive amount of vocabulary—they have no problem doing that—it's because of how their speech patterns work. They literally don't speak in long sentences. It's completely nonsensical to them. Whatever they want to say, they feel can be said in six words or less, and they simply indulge us when we insist on using more."

"Interesting." Raile took another long sip of his tea, mulling that over. "I do feel that we should bully Nolan into writing a more comprehensive guide on dragons. Our young Fire Mage's efforts in that regard were less than helpful."

"Anemic, is what it was," Trev'nor grumbled. He fully realized just how much Krys hadn't bothered to note down after his own experience pairing up with Garth. "I'm all for it, sir."

Raile took a good look around Trev'nor's—formerly Warlord Riyu's—office. In terms of opulence, it gave Trexler's former office a run for its money, as it had all of the gold edging and gilt plus ridiculous amounts of carved wood trim and paneling. Raile had a particular curl of distaste on his mouth as he looked, and his eyes spoke volumes.

"I know." Trev'nor held up a hand, forestalling what he knew was to come. "Believe me, I know. Trexler's office was just as bad before we took it over. We'll strip this thing down of all the gold and use it to help finance things a little, mostly in paying the soldiers properly until we can get the taxes and economy straightened out."

"Becca mentioned to me that the hard part was always the finances after taking in a new territory." Raile leaned in to pour himself another cup of tea. "She said that Nolan has been invaluable, teaching you two what to do in that regard, and she now fully understood why the Gardeners insisted that it had to be a Prince of Chahir and a Life Mage to come with you into Khobunter."

"We'd be seriously lost without Nolan," Trev'nor admitted frankly, every word heartfelt. "I know that he has his own country to rule, and we can't keep him forever, which honestly makes us both a little sad. Still, we need him desperately now and you can bet I'll keep him here for as long as possible."

"I certainly would in your shoes." Raile regarded him steadily over the rim of the teacup. "Have you considered, young Warlord, where you are going to base your capital city once Khobunter is won?"

Perhaps Raile thought this a trick question, but the three of them had been talking about this for weeks, and Trev'nor knew the answer already. "Rheben."

"Ah. I thought as much. Otherwise why build the academy there?" Raile's eyes crinkled up in the corners in a pleased smile. "You chose it for its history?"

"And location. It's almost dead in the center of the country." Trev'nor shrugged as it all seemed quite obvious to him. "We talked about other locations as well, but really it would look like favoritism if we chose any of the other major cities, and we really don't want to do that. Rheben is our best option."

Raile gave a satisfied nod. "If that is your intent, then we will accommodate you."

Perhaps those words were supposed to make sense, but it went straight over Trev'nor's head. "I'm not following, sir."

"Trev'nor," Raile sighed, almost exasperated, "think. Why did we in Coven Ordan reach out to Chahir to begin with?"

"In my defense, sir, I was five when you came over."

"Ah. I'd forgotten." Raile lifted a shoulder, blasé about this, but then at his age he probably forgot things often. "We were of course invested in Chahir's magical future, but we also had run out of room. Coven Ordan even now is crammed to the gills and there is no room for the next generation. Some of them of course have left and made new lives in Chahir, or Hain, but there are still many of them that wish to leave and make their own paths. I've received inquiries from several of them, wanting to know if they are allowed to come over even if they don't accept a teaching position."

It all sounded quite sensible, so much so that Trev'nor couldn't help but put a hand to his head and lightly smack it, sure that his hearing was failing him. "They want to come over? Here? Why?"

"For the adventure. For the sake of building up the future in this country. Some of them are sick and tired of living under their parents' thumbs and want to carve a future for themselves in a foreign land." Raile flicked a few fingers up, a very Chahiran gesture of 'what can you do?'

Trev'nor was all set to say that they were crazy, who would want to come into a foreign country that was culturally against magicians, in a desert and hostile environment? Then he remembered that he himself had done just that very thing and wasn't sure whether to laugh or groan. "I don't have a leg to stand on. I can't protest that they're crazy."

"In all fairness, Trev'nor," Raile pointed out pragmatically, "you've already blazed the trail. You did the hard part. They want to join us first in Rheben, prove their worth to this country, then branch out from there. They will only occupy the safe areas that you designate to them."

"That...is probably for the best." Trev'nor leaned his

elbows against the desk, resting his face in cupped hands, and thought about it. It all sounded wonderful, of course, but he shouldn't be making decisions without his co-ruler even if he had a good idea of what she'd say to this offer. "Raile. How many people are we talking about?"

"Twenty have contacted me, and I understand that some of them were speaking on behalf of themselves and their spouses."

So over twenty. "I'm inclined to say yes, and offer them full citizenship, but you understand I have to run this by Becca first?"

"Of course. I mention it to you as I'm not sure where she is."

Even Trev'nor wasn't quite sure about that. "She's running about like a crazy woman today. She's settling the army, dispersing most of the troops to go home, overseeing the repair of Jashni, trying to get the resisting forces to surrender, and so on. I'm getting updates sent to me every few hours, so I'm reasonably sure that I'll see her late tonight. I can ask her then."

"That's fine. In the meantime, we'll settle our students and use the city as a large teaching module, fix up what we can." Raile set his teacup on the desk, preparing to rise. "One more thing. What of the magicians still enslaved in the other city of this province? You don't have them yet, do you?"

"I don't," Trev'nor admitted heavily. They still hadn't found their lost friends from Rurick yet, either, which weighed at his soul. "We've sent word to Sha Watchtower about the death of the warlord here and the city's surrender. We hope they'll surrender as well and not make us fight them for it. I'll have an answer for that hopefully soon. The records we have here indicate that another six hundred magicians will be coming your way once we claim them."

"Six hundred?" Raile asked in justifiable surprise.

"I know, much more than usual. Riyu apparently realized we'd come for him next," Trev'nor explained, repeating what he'd learned that morning. "He shifted the bulk of the slaves over to here, hoping to use their magical combat skills or, if necessary, more hostages. Becca foiled the plan by breaking into his war room and forcing him to leave the city before he could give the right orders. In that respect, at least, our plans went right."

"Thank the Guardians for that."

"Truly." Trev'nor didn't even want to think what this battle might have been like otherwise. "Only six hundred magicians remain in Sha Watchtower because of that, so we have the bulk of the magicians in Riyu now. Sir, is there anything that you need?"

"We're managing just fine," Raile assured him kindly. "What few things we've found we needed, Sallah's gone and fetched for us. Our students are quite lovely people, all of them, and are very happy to be free and learning magic properly. I've had more than a few families reunited and have performed no less then sixteen marriages since starting the academy."

Trev'nor blinked. Then blinked again. "Marriages? Seriously?"

"Quite a few spouses requested it of me, having never been formally bound together under the law, and I was happy to oblige. I'm actually an official in Bromany, you know, but they didn't care if I used the Bromanian vows." Raile beamed, pleased with himself in the matter.

Trev'nor felt like a complete idiot. Of course the slaves had never been given the chance to formally marry. Why would they have? "Raile. Before you leave, let me register you as an officiant here in Khobunter as well, so that we make sure it really is legal."

"I think that's a splendid idea, Trev'nor." Leaning in a little, he asked, "And perhaps a small token to congratulate the couples with? To encourage the others to properly marry as well?"

Trev'nor really, really didn't want to think about how many people were not legally married. He so did not want that tradition to continue. "That's a great idea. Hold on." He grabbed the large bell next to him and gave it a good ring.

Sergeant Amir promptly came into the office and came to attention in front of the desk. "Yes, Raja?"

"Sergeant, it's just come to my attention that I'm an idiot," Trev'nor informed him, making the man's lips twitch in a suppressed smile. "It's alright, you can laugh. Wizard Blackover tells me that several of our new magicians are intent on legalizing their marriage. He's performed sixteen ceremonies in his time with us."

Amir smacked his heart with an open palm, expression pained. "Raja, this hurts my heart. Why did we not think of this before?"

"Because we're all focused too much on war," Trev'nor growled, still irritated with himself. He'd lived in a slave pen for ten days, had that not taught him what their lives were like? "Amir, I need help with two things. Wizard Blackover has been using his authority as a Bromanian officiant to marry them, but I'm not sure if that's entirely legal in Khobunter."

"It likely isn't, Raja," Amir admitted before hastily adding to Raile, "No offense meant, sir."

"None taken, young man," Raile assured him. "Every country has different rules on this matter."

"I need you to find the right paperwork to register him as an officiant in Khobunter," Trev'nor continued firmly. "If there isn't one, make one. Respectfully request help from

Rikkshan Galel to make sure that we honor the spirit of the law in this."

"Yes, sir."

"Also consult with Rikkana Iesha and Rikkan Feisal about the appropriate gift to give a newly married couple. Something that won't bankrupt us, please, as we need sixteen gifts, but choose something nice. We want to bless these couples as they've been through enough already."

"I'll make sure to choose something tasteful, Raja," Amir swore. "Perhaps a few more than sixteen so that Wizard Blackover will have gifts on hand for future couples?"

Trev'nor really should have thought of that too. This blood loss thing had slowed his mind down. "This is why you're my favorite, Amir. You anticipate things. Yes, do that. Send thirty. I'm sure there's other couples that haven't dared to ask yet, but that will hopefully change." Looking around, he spotted two of the more ornate sculptures occupying a side table and pointed at them. "Take those two gold cats with you to pay for things."

"It will be my pleasure, Raja." Amir promptly went to pick them both up, securely tucking one under each arm.

"Raile," Trev'nor waited for the wizard to focus on him before continuing seriously, "is there anything else? Anything at all?"

"There is one more thing." Raile hesitated, carefully choosing the words before speaking them. "I know that Sallah wanted to speak to you about this personally, but her hands are full at the moment. I'll ask on her behalf. The little Earth Mage you rescued, Parisa. Sallah wishes to know if you'll adopt her? If not, Sallah wishes to do so."

"About that." Trev'nor also chose his words very carefully. "I'm told that Parisa's parents were sold and sent north."

Raile's thin eyebrows shot up. "They're still alive? She's

not an orphan?"

"I believe that to be the case. I can't prove it at the moment as we still haven't found them. But I want to wait until we know for sure before making any decisions."

"Of course, of course. I'll inform Sallah."

"Thank you. Tell her…" Trev'nor rubbed at his forehead, not sure what the right answer would be. "Tell her I want to adopt her, but if she feels it's better for her to have parents, I won't argue. I'll give them my blessings."

"I'll tell her." Raile gave him an odd look. "You really wish to adopt her?"

"I'm not sure if it's my Rheben blood or my Tonkowacon heritage," Trev'nor admitted honestly, "but I have this urge to adopt everyone. It's a thing."

Amir cleared his throat and offered, "Raja, with respect, you already have. Most of a country."

Until put that way, Trev'nor hadn't realized it. Snorting a laugh, he waved to the sergeant. "There you go. It's an illness, I tell you."

"May it never be cured." Raile grinned at him and rose to his feet. "Is there anything that you require of me, Warlord?"

"No, no. But are you sure you don't want to borrow someone up here to help you with all the marriages?"

"I'll do one big ceremony," Raile said cheerfully. "Then one big party afterwards. Easier that way."

Trev'nor certainly thought it would be. Almost belatedly, he remembered a certain conversation with Sergeant Mose under Jashni, and tacked on, "You might encounter resistance because people here are used to giving bride prices and dowries. But Becca and I are dissolving that practice, so put them at ease."

"Wait, what?" Amir demanded sharply. Then, remembering he was speaking to a superior, immediately amended his tone. "Raja, you're changing the requirements for marriage?"

"We are. Well, unofficially we want to, but we haven't put out an official stance on this yet." Judging from Amir's hopeful expression, this just became something vital. Gently he asked, "Amir, is there someone you want to marry?"

Amir's voice was a little choked. "Yes, Raja. I've been engaged five years, trying to earn the money. I'm not the only one, there are quite a few of us that have been engaged for years."

Trev'nor resisted the urge to bang his head on the desk. "Shrieking hinges, this is ridiculous! Amir, after you've gotten Wizard Blackover on his way, bring the Rikkana, Rikkan and Rikkshan to me. We're dissolving this practice as soon as possible. I'll contact Becca immediately and get her seal of approval on this."

Amir gave him the sharpest salute to date. "Yes, Warlord."

He got a 'warlord' for that, eh? Trev'nor returned the salute, sending both men out with thanks. When the door shut behind them, he picked up the mirror broach lying on the desk and grazed it with a hint of power. "Becca."

There was some fumbling, perhaps a panicked yelp, then Becca's voice in crystal clarity. "—*almost dropped the stupid thing. Hello?*"

"Becca, it's Trev. Look, we need to talk about something."

"*Just tell me that it doesn't involve fighting, as I really want a good nap first.*"

"Don't bring up naps," Trev'nor groaned, his body informing him that was a delightful idea and why wasn't he doing just that? "I can't take one, people keep springing surprises on me."

"*Good surprises? Tell me good ones because I don't think I can handle bad ones right now.*"

Distracted from his main point, Trev'nor frowned. "What's happening that's bad?"

"The residents of Jashni returned, but they're terrified of dragons. As in they almost abandoned the city again when I arrived on Cat. I don't blame them. Llona, Orion, and Garth basically trashed the place, which didn't give them a good first impression. Cat's had to play 'nice dragon' all morning and feed them and everything just to keep them from running out blindly into the desert again."

He really, really should have stopped Garth earlier. Although to be fair, Orion had done the most damage. Rubbing at his forehead, Trev'nor asked, "Anything I can do to help?"

"No, it'll pass. It already is, a little, although people here are still really confused. They're happy to have their sons back, though, and that's helping to smooth feathers while we fix the city. Hang on." Her voice became a little distant as she gave several orders, then a thump. *"Alright, I'm sitting down for a minute. Whatcha need?"*

"Becca. We're idiots."

"Tell me something I don't know."

"We forgot that our former slaves couldn't properly marry each other before now."

She swore long and viciously. *"You're right, we're idiots."*

"Fortunately Raile is helping to cover us. He's already married sixteen couples. I'm having it set up now so that he's an officiant and can legally marry everyone else. I'm sending some gifts along with him, too, on his suggestion. But seriously, I think we need to talk about marriage practices and get this settled. Do you realize that Sergeant Amir has been engaged for five years because he hasn't been able to earn the money to marry his fiancée?"

"It's not just him. Trev, I've been meaning to talk to you

about this. How do you feel about turning some more cultural norms on their heads?"

Trev'nor grinned out over his desk, looking at the cityscape beyond the window. "I'm all for it."

Becca came back from Jashni to a party in full swing.

She landed just outside of Riyu's gates, sliding slowly off, taking in the many lanterns strung up along the streets, the multiple bands playing music, the singing, the free wine that seemed to be passed out everywhere, and couldn't make sense of any of it. Why the celebration? Surely they weren't happy about being conquered? Becca and Trev'nor hadn't been in the city for more than twenty hours and hadn't had a chance to make much of an impression yet as rulers. For that matter, there was still fighting going on in parts of the city, or at least there had been.

Usually they got this sort of response after putting in multiple gardens, but no one possessed the magical strength to start on that project yet. So what had brought this about? More than a little puzzled, she approached the gate guard, a guard from Riyu. She glanced at his right shoulder, reading the ribbons there and addressing him by rank. "Fifth Guard, what's this festive air?"

The guard saluted her sharply, a middle aged man with grey in his beard and a happy smile on his face. "Warlord. Warlord Trev'nor released the news at noon that dowries and bride prices are no longer required. He also removed the Marriage Tax."

She held up a hand to stop him. "I'm sorry, the what?"

"The Marriage Tax," he repeated patiently. "The previous warlord required a tax of ten lieng to gain a marriage certificate."

Becca had to do a few quick calculations in her head, as Riyu used a different money system than the other provinces, but when she finally did convert it, she choked. You could put a down payment on a house for ten lieng! Trev'nor had only asked for approval to change the marriage laws when he spoke to her that morning; she hadn't heard about anything else. Taking in the city with this new perspective, she realized what must have happened, but had to ask it anyway. "Has everyone turned the city into one big wedding festival?"

"More or less," the guard agreed with a wide smile. "When I get off shift, my own daughter wants to marry."

Becca felt more than flabbergasted. These poor people had literally been waiting years, scrimping and saving just to have a basic right. What had Riyu been doing? Was he trying to drive his own people into the ground? "My congratulations to you and your house, Fifth Guard."

"Thank you, Warlord." The man ducked his head into a bow. "You are benevolent rulers to think of our happiness."

And they hadn't even started yet. She smiled at him, clapped him on the shoulder, and continued on with Cat carefully following. As she walked, Danyal appeared from a side street and gave her a salute. "Raya. You made good time."

"I did. Cat was glad to stretch her wings, I think." Turning to her dragon, she encouraged her, "Go eat something, take a nap. Danyal will guard my back."

The dragon looked down at the commander, and they exchanged serious nods, an almost formal changing of the guard. With a flap of the wings, Cat maneuvered about and exited the city once more before launching herself into the sky.

"I'm very surprised to see all of this," she noted to Danyal, who matched her pace so they moved side by side. Truly, her earlier experience in the city didn't prepare her for this. It no longer looked drab and monotone, not with the multi-color lanterns strung along the clothing lines, the bright swatches of cloth draped over every door and window frame, and the multiple banners announcing different couples' weddings hanging along the walls. "When did the party start?"

"Shortly after my last formal report to you. I thought to wait, not spoil the surprise, when you said you were flying over."

"It's a surprise, alright," she agreed fervently. In fact, she still couldn't quite take it in. She stopped and stared at one house, the thick walls around its garden blocking her view, but the iron gates wide open to permit her to see a party going full swing in the front courtyard. She smiled at the sight then moved on, switching back to business. "But what about the two pockets of resistance we still had on our hands?"

"One of them surrendered right after you left. Captain Mosa is taking care of it. The other has locked down tightly in a warehouse on the far side of the city. They have no food or water, so I'm sure we can starve them out in another few days. In any case, most of the city is ignoring them, just avoiding the area." Danyal stepped in a little closer, their shoulders brushing, and confided in a low tone, "Your announcement about the wedding fees was brilliantly timed. People were worried about the in-city fighting up until Raja Trev'nor released the news. Then people were so overjoyed, they seemed to forget the trouble altogether. Our men have actually been welcomed and given free drinks in a few places."

Well now, that was a surprise. "I think it only counts as an ingenious idea if we actually planned for this effect."

"Take the credit," he advised, eyes sparkling with muted amusement. "In any case, it's made our transition into the city much easier."

"Then I have no complaints."

Music blared down the street, coming from a very enthusiastic band who heralded a new couple as they entered one of the houses. Everyone wore white-on-white clothing with brilliant red headdresses and sashes, traditional in this part of the world for marriage outfits. She stood aside to let the wedding party pass, and no one paid attention to her at first, then gave her deep bows when they realized belatedly who she must be. When people recognized her, they became uncertain in their joy, until Becca offered congratulations and blessings upon them. Then their smiles rekindled, happy again.

"Danyal," she said to him in a low tone, keeping her smile up for anyone watching, "I want to know where all that money went. I also want to send a small cake to every couple that gets married today and a card to congratulate them."

"I'm sure that we can do that, my Raya." Danyal leaned a little and said in a low tone, "You're smiling but your eyes are shooting lightning."

"This makes me really happy but boiling mad at the same time. If Riyu wasn't dead, I'd kill him myself for this." She passed a hand over her eyes, trying to fix her expression, as she didn't want to give anyone the impression that she was mad at them. In fact she felt very happy for all of them. The last of the party passed her and she resumed her walk, something that Trev'nor mentioned earlier coming to mind.

"At a guess, how many men in our army are engaged?"

"I'd say about two hundred. Perhaps a little more."

"You give me a list of names and I'll grant them three weeks leave to get married. If we can permanently switch them out with someone else in that area, make it happen so they're stationed in their hometown."

Danyal warned her, "You realize that Sergeant Amir is one that I can permanently switch out?"

Staring at him in dismay, Becca groaned, "Busted buckets."

"Are you sure about that order, my Raya?"

No, she really wasn't. She adored Amir, he was extremely helpful and one of the best linguistics specialists that they had. "Tell him that he has three weeks at the very least and I would take it as a personal favor if he didn't choose a permanent relocation. At least not yet, I can send him home after we have Khobunter under control."

"I'll discuss it with him," Danyal promised. "My Raya, I believe that those two women want to speak with you."

She looked to where he indicated and found a young woman grasping an older woman's arm tightly, both of them glancing in her direction with every other word, as if urging the other to approach. They clearly had something important to say but were scared of doing so.

The hardest thing to do once conquering a place was to get it through the people's heads that any of them could speak with their new rulers without reproach. Becca saw a beautiful opportunity to get the ball rolling on that and marched directly for the women with a welcoming smile on her face. "Ladies. I'm Riicbeccaan. Harmony find you."

They promptly ducked into bows, hands folded at their waists. "Harmony find you, Warlord," the oldest of the two promptly said, the youngest echoing her.

"I think something troubles you. What is it?" Becca urged, using her most compassionate voice to help draw them out.

The older woman started to demur, but the younger straightened, even though she couldn't quite meet Becca in the eye. "Warlord, we are grateful for the changes in the marriage laws. Blessings on you and Warlord Trev'nor for this."

That was not a question, but Becca felt the young woman worked up to something, so she responded, "We are very glad to change them. Many good people that wish to be married have been thwarted by those rules."

"This is true, Warlord." Wetting her lips, she pushed back a strand of curly black hair to rest behind her ear before asking very carefully, "I wish to inquire if there are other marriage laws that you'll change?"

Becca stared at her blankly. What other marriage laws were there to be changed?

The older woman—mother? aunt?—smacked her on the arm and whispered, "It's fine, we'll manage. You're being rude to the Warlord."

Catching on first, Danyal took a half step forward. "I'm Commander Danyal, aide to the warlords. Is there another marriage fee still in place?"

Seeing honest curiosity and nothing more, the young woman pressed forward once more. "Yes. The filing fees are still in place."

Becca's eyes closed for a moment in fatalistic understanding. So they'd missed some. "Tell me—I'm sorry, what is your name?"

"Jamila, Warlord," she responded with another bow.

"Jamila." Aptly named. Her name meant gorgeous woman and Becca had rarely seen a more striking woman.

"Thank you for the gift of your name. Please tell me how much are these filing fees?"

"Several liengs, Warlord." Jamila looked up under her lashes, gauging this response.

Becca promptly turned and used Danyal's shoulder to bang her head against, letting out a muffled scream. "Was Riyu trying to forbid marriage altogether?!"

"Calm, my Raya, calm," Danyal counseled with a soothing pat on her shoulder. To the now nervous women, he smiled and assured them, "Our Warlord has been very upset about the marriage laws for some time now. Some of those dearest to her have been prevented from marrying because of them. It brings pain to her heart."

A little relieved at this explanation, they still watched Becca warily, like a cobra in the sand.

She took in a huge breath, blew it out, and forced herself to at least appear calm on the surface. "Jamila. Can you take me to the nearest city register's office? I need to ask questions."

"Of course, Warlord." She promptly turned and led them a short distance to a plain white building with a tiled roof. Several couples stood in line, straight out the door and wrapping around the sidewalk, impatient and jittery. Hopeful couples ready to register a marriage or get a license? Looked that way.

Becca had to scoot sideways to get past one couple, at least until they recognized the uniform, then they promptly flattened themselves to give her room to pass. Once inside, she paused to get her bearings, but it wasn't that big of an office. A single desk sat in front of the door, manned by three harried individuals trying to keep up with the sudden demand, and a long counter to the left with built in bookshelves that stretched to the ceiling. The counter was armed by a single man, an elderly sort with glasses perched on the end of his nose and a bookish look to him. Becca marched straight for him, ignoring the sudden silence of everyone behind her. "I'm Riicbeccaan."

The clerk's eyes went wide behind his glasses and he immediately ducked into a bow. "How may I serve you, Warlord?"

"Tell me the steps in order for people to get married, please."

Confused, he straightened a little. In a voice gone high in contained panic, he started listing things out, counting them on his fingers as he went. "First they must register the intent to marry with the date. Then they must obtain a marriage certificate. When it is signed by a priest, they return it here, and we file it. The woman then registers a change of name to match her husband's. She also registers for a change of address."

Becca had a sinking feeling about it and had to rein in her temper, as she just knew she wasn't going to like the answer to this question. "And how much does all of that cost?"

"Eighteen lieng, Warlord."

Yup, that urge to scream or kill something was back again. She pinched the bridge of her nose, hard, and breathed deeply.

Danyal put a hand to her back, stroking her spine in a soothing gesture. "Calm, my Raya, calm."

"Riyu was nothing more than base-born scullion, and if his corpse was clean enough, I'd spit upon it," she gritted out between clenched teeth. "Was he trying to beggar his people?"

"The wood has already been turned into a house, my Raya. Focus on what you can do now," he advised, not unsympathetically.

Practical advice. She'd be wise to heed it. "Thank you, sir, for answering my question. Don't look alarmed, I'm not mad at you, just that thrice-cursed whoreson of a goat that used to be your warlord. Hang on." Turning to the other clerks, all of which were alarmed, she pointed a finger at them. "No one do anything until I give you the go-ahead. I need to confer with my co-ruler on this matter."

"O-of course, Warlord," one of the braver men stammered out.

Taking her mirror from a breast pocket, she lifted it to her mouth and said distinctly, "Trev."

It took a minute, as usual, for him to respond and it sounded like he was speaking around a mouthful of something. "*What?*"

"You didn't ask enough questions earlier about the marriage laws."

"*Uh-oh. What did I miss?*"

"There are in fact five different steps to the process. You only nullified one. The total before you changed the marriage certificate was eighteen lieng."

Trev'nor swore loudly and with more creativity than Becca had given him credit for. "*Why didn't anyone tell me?! I specifically asked!*"

"I don't doubt you, but this tells me there's an underlying problem in the city. These poor people have been taxed every way from sundown and they don't know up from down at this point. Trev, I vote that we cancel all taxes for the next few days until we can put a new economy structure in place. Let's just wipe the slate free, start fresh."

"*Like we did in Trexler? I think it's the only sane approach. If we don't, we'll spend months buried in tax code, and I'd rather not.*"

Just the idea depressed her. "Me neither. I'll start

spreading the word down here, I'm at a clerk's office now, and you put an official notice out. Deal?"

"*I'm fine with that, but what about the people that have already paid?*"

"Refund. If they'll show us their marriage documents, we'll refund them in full."

"*Fair enough. Go. I'll start things rolling from here.*"

Ending the connection, she put the mirror back into her pocket. It took another breath and a promise that she would eat cake later to soothe her ire before she could face everyone with the proper expression again. "As you've just heard, we are lifting all taxes for the time being. No fees are to be collected for marriages, births, deaths, or anything else. Honorable Clerk, if anyone comes to you with their paperwork and asks for a refund, give it to them."

He promptly bowed although he looked a little confused. "Yes, Warlord."

"Good, thank you." Becca addressed the waiting couples with a wink. "Now's the time to buy a house if you haven't already. No taxes on that either."

There were several that clapped in delight before realizing what they'd done and folded their hands again, trying to be demure and failing miserably at it.

Becca caught Jamila's hand, ducking her head to force the girl's gaze to meet hers. "Jamila, thank you very much for speaking to me about this. If you hadn't, we might not have known. I want to know, do you want to be married soon?"

"Yes, Warlord," she responded hopefully. "We hadn't the money to pay for all of the paperwork, that's why I wanted to ask."

"Well, you can certainly do so now, can't you?" Becca wanted to make sure on this point just in case they'd missed something else.

"I can," she agreed brightly. "Everything else is prepared except the food. That we can manage in a day, I think. The taxes, when will you give us new ones?"

"Likely not this week. Too much is going on." Becca wanted to reward this bold behavior, to encourage it, and could only think of one thing. "How much will the food cost?"

Jamila shared a glance with her mother (probably her mother), who was the one that answered politely, "Half a lieng, Warlord. We both have large families, so it takes quite a bit to feed all of us."

"Is that normal?" Becca asked, signaling Danyal covertly to give her money.

Danyal, bless him, promptly pulled a wallet out of his pocket and counted out a lieng into her hand. She was going to have to promote him.

"Yes, Warlord, or I should say it is not unusual. Between families, and friends, and such it normally costs that much."

"I see." Turning Jamila's hand over, she put the money into it before firmly closing the girl's fingers around it. "That should cover it, hopefully."

Jamila started to see that much money in her hands and protested, "Warlord, you've already done so much, I don't dare—"

"Hush," Becca ordered although she smiled as she said it. "You've prevented a huge problem by having the courage to talk to me. I know your previous warlord was a bad one, he didn't instill trust in his people, but I want you to understand that your new warlords aren't like that. We're new to ruling, there's many things we don't understand, but we want to do right by our people. If anyone has a problem, we want you to approach us. This is your reward for your courage. Now, go get married, kiss that man, and be happy. Your Warlord orders you."

Jamila gave her a blinding smile, bright enough to be a third sun. "I will. Thank you, Warlord, I will."

"Good." Becca left the office in a slightly better mood than before, especially since she left a lot of jubilant people behind her. As soon as she gained the street, she heard more than a few excited screams. One brave soul, still in the doorway, profusely heaped blessings on her head as she passed him.

Danyal half-turned and observed, "They're certainly happy."

"I would be too in their shoes. I just saved them a lot of money." Becca turned her face up to the sky, taking in a deep breath and feeling better for it.

Danyal put a hand at her waist and turned her a little, gesturing to the street in a wide sweep of the arm. "Becca. This place is full of joy right now. Will you put duty aside, just for a few hours, and share it with me?"

Elation shot through her. Finally, finally, he had asked! It took all she had to not kiss him right there on the spot. Reining the impulse in, she beamed up at him. After a hard battle, an equally hard day of dealing with the aftermath, and all of the stress that came with it, Becca thought partying with Danyal sounded sublime. Teasing him a little, she asked, "That depends, Rahim. Will you teach me the dances here?"

"I will," he promised her, grinning in return, delighted she had used his first name.

"Then let's find dinner and good music. I'm ready to party."

Trev'nor decided to call it quits at sunset. He wasn't really made for paperwork, and yet had done nothing else for sixteen solid hours. His head hurt, his eyes burned, and he wanted to be horizontal somewhere for a while. He'd seen Raile off at noon with his letters, the wedding gifts, and all of the necessary paperwork to be filled out. He'd fixed wedding laws, argued over culture, and tackled one fire after the next. Time to call it quits for the day!

Someone thoughtfully arranged a bedroom for him on the upper level of the fortress, with a very inviting bed that he fell into and didn't emerge from until mid-morning. When he finally did pull himself out of the sheets, he felt whole and well again. With more energy than he had in the past three days, Trev'nor got dressed in the one clean outfit he had left—he had to do something about that—and wandered down to the main dining hall.

Technically, it was meant to be a formal dining area, designed to seat at least two hundred guests. Trev'nor had dismissed that nonsense and informed all of his officers that this was now their mess hall and to eat meals here. The cooks, used to this kind of workload, didn't bat an eye, although they looked a little uneasy to be serving their conquerors. The room still displayed all of the paneling and elaborate trim that marked it as an official residence, but the effect was spoiled with all of the uniformed men in the room.

At this odd hour of the day, the room actually only had about twenty occupants, Becca being one of them. She lingered over a report, a cup of hot tea near her elbow, along with some sort of flaky bread thing that looked interesting. Trev'nor went to her and leaned over the table, getting a good whiff of it. "That looks fun."

"Oh, are you finally up?" she teased. "I've been waiting on you. And yes, it's quite fun. They call it goezeme. It's a sort of flat pancake with spinach, lamb, cheese and spices as a filling. I love it."

"Where can I get three of them?" he asked seriously.

Becca turned and pointed to the side bar behind her. "Get the honey lemon tea, too, it's delightful."

Trev'nor followed her advice and picked them up, plus a glass of pressed grape juice because he felt more than a little dehydrated. Balancing it all took some doing, but he managed to return to the table and put it all down without dropping anything. As he sat, he noticed that while she looked a little tired, she glowed under it all. "Something good happen?"

"Rahim took me dancing last night," she reported with a very satisfied feminine smile.

Trev'nor paused with the food halfway to his mouth. Rahim? Since when did she call Danyal by his first name? And that smile said something. "So you *have* realized that he's trying to court you."

"I realized that he wanted to do so and was working up the courage to approach me," she corrected, that expression on her face positively enigmatic and feline. "I gave him a little time to work up the courage is all. Last night he finally called me by my name and asked me for a date."

"And the date went swimmingly, I can tell from that smug smirk you're wearing." Trev'nor felt more than a little relieved at that. Relieved enough to tease, "Bec, be honest—this whole thing with dropping the dowries and bride prices was just to encourage Danyal to make a move? Or was it for everyone else?"

She gave a dainty sip of her tea, batting blue eyes in wide innocence. "It can't be both?"

Snorting a laugh, he gave up with a shake of the head. "Sure, why not?"

For the first time, a trace of uncertainty flashed over her face. "You're alright with this? I mean, he is a little older than I am."

"Age differences don't bother me," he said around a mouthful. Yum! Becca was right, these were delightful. Was this a regular breakfast food? Trev'nor hoped so. "What I always worried about was that you'd fall for someone that can't act as a guardian for you. Just because you're a full-fledged mage now, you can't just go it alone. You still need people to watch your back."

"And we're now entering the world of politics and such so I really need someone to watch my back?" she finished for him knowingly. "And Rahim can do that."

"Danyal excels at it. And the man adores you. So yeah, if I had to pick someone for you, Danyal would be at the top of the list." It frankly relieved Trev'nor that she was open to the possibility, as he hadn't wanted to see Danyal heartbroken. Besides, even Shad approved of the man, and that spoke volumes. "You realize we should have really promoted Danyal before this?"

Becca's head dropped as she groaned. "I know, I know, I thought about it last night. I kept meaning to, it's just we've been jumping from one frying pan to another and…"

"And it never got done. Well, since you two are now dating, I'd better do it. Doesn't smack of nepotism that way."

She beamed at him. "You're the bestest best friend ever."

"Apparently so. I was slaving away at a desk while you were on a date." The words had no rancor to them, as Trev'nor was frankly relieved she'd been on that date. Less complications in the future for him, as with Danyal at her side, they'd stop trying to pair him up with Becca.

Nolan appeared from behind and dropped into the seat next to Trev'nor. "What date? What did I miss?"

"Danyal and Becca went on a date last night," Trev'nor informed him, unable to keep from smiling as he said it.

"Finally," Becca inserted, blowing on her nails and buffing them on the front of her shirt.

Nolan's eyebrows arched a little. "So you did know he's interested."

"Nolan," Becca responded with exasperation, "a blind man couldn't miss the signals he put out."

Very true. Trev'nor doubted anyone in the army hadn't picked up on it.

"I'm relieved," Nolan informed her frankly. "I like Danyal and I think you're a good match with him. Even when you're chucking lightning bolts at people, he finds it sexy. Not many men would."

Trev'nor had his mouth full, so couldn't add in anything, but he gave several nods of agreement.

"That's because I am," she informed them with a toss of the head. "And if you two dare laugh, I will chuck lightning at you."

Poor Danyal. He had no idea what he was getting himself into. Trev'nor wisely focused on his food.

Nolan cleared his throat and went to a different topic. "Have either of you left the fortress yet? No? Well the party is still in full swing. Everyone is getting married. I do mean everyone. I also understand that the real estate offices are booming with business, and prices for houses have hit the roof overnight. Everyone wants to buy while there's no tax on it."

"Busted buckets," Trev'nor groaned, putting his breakfast down for a moment. A little sadly, as the food was really excellent. "I did not foresee that. Have they gone insanely high?"

"Fortunately not yet, but you might want to step in and put a cap on it before it does. Even then, it hasn't deterred people, as apparently even with the higher price, they're still coming out ahead. I looked into it, and taxes on buying property were insane." Nolan made a sour face. "Riyu was taxing these people to death over the past five years especially. I heard you wiped all taxes off the books for now?"

"We'll replace it with the system we did in Trexler," Becca answered, frowning now into her tea. "We should probably stick with one system anyway, make it uniform everywhere. Less of a headache."

Trev'nor couldn't agree more. "Bec, I know we gave ourselves two weeks here to straighten things out before moving on, but I'm not sure if we can stick to that timeline. I mean, we still haven't heard from the other city in this province."

"I know, and that worries me. We're going to have to put pressure on them." Chewing on her bottom lip, she added apologetically, "It should be at least three weeks regardless. I may have made a decision without you and told every man in our army that if they were engaged, they had three weeks leave to go home, get married, and have a honeymoon."

Not bothered by this, Trev'nor waved it away. "I decided long ago that military matters are completely up to you. It's easier all around that way. That's fine. Although I'm curious, how many men are engaged?"

"A little over two hundred, or so Rahim tells me."

Two hundred wouldn't make or break them. Trev'nor shrugged. "Let's give them a wedding present and send them off today, then."

"Excellent, I hoped you'd say that. Nolan, how fares all of my injured?"

"We're down to the very minor injuries now, and I'm going to just let those heal," he informed her. "Our soldiers are fine, only a few on light duty. The people that were burned out from the shacks had minor injuries, for the most part—smoke inhalation being the most common problem. They'll all recover in the next week without issue. I actually hoped we'd done enough administrative work that Trev'nor could come out and help me set up gardens. But it doesn't sound like that's the case."

Becca gave Trev'nor an once-over, eyes narrowed a little in concentration. "It looks like you're back up to full health to me. How are you feeling?"

"Perfectly fine," Trev'nor assured her hopefully.

"Well, since I partied last night, why don't you take a half day today?" Becca offered. "I'll get some rain clouds formed, bring them this direction, you two go play in the dirt for a while. I'll start in on the paperwork and call you when I need to."

That sounded perfectly blissful to Trev'nor. "Deal. One thing, though, Raile talked to me about something and I feel like we should give him an answer today. He informed me that there's about twenty or so people that want to come from Coven Ordan and become citizens of Khobunter."

He received some of the blankest looks that ever graced a human face. Grinning, he splayed his hands to either side.

"I know. Trust me, I know, I felt the same way when he said it. But apparently by acting as trail blazers, we've inspired people. The more adventuresome want to spread their wings a little and come tackle Khobunter with us."

"If they're crazy enough to ask, I say we let them." Becca grew more excited with each word out of her mouth, hands waving about in the air, and quickly added, words nearly tripping over themselves, "Trev. Do you think they'll fix Rheben for us?"

"That's my plan. Have them fix the city first, then we'll give them the option of where to live in country after that. That way, when we're finally done with all of the battles, we have a home ready to go back to." Happy that she was gung-ho on the idea, he added hopefully, "Can we officially designate Rheben as our capital city now?"

"No," she denied regretfully. "We really shouldn't until it's done."

Probably a good point. Trev'nor just hated waiting.

"While all of this sounds promising," Nolan tacked on with that wise look he sometimes wore, "make sure to specify to your renovation group that about two-thirds of your population will be non-magical. They can't go crazy and duplicate Coven Ordan on foreign soil."

"That is an excellent point and we really should do that." Trev'nor looked hopefully at Becca. "Will you contact Raile, then, and give him the go-ahead?"

"I will. I'll also consult with him about the budget for the project and start setting aside funds for it." Becca rubbed at the rim of her teacup, frowning in thought. "I feel like I'm forgetting to ask an obvious question."

"While you're thinking of it, answer me this," Trev'nor requested. "How much time should we give Sha Watchtower before we consider them to be hostile?"

"No more than two days," Nolan advised. "It sits on the border of the province, they can easily be negotiating with another warlord for protection, hence the delay in responding to you."

Unfortunately, Trev'nor shared the same opinion on the situation. "I have a bad feeling that's the case. Bec, maybe send a message to the watchtower that they have two days to surrender or we march on them. No warlord can get forces to them within just a few days; it'll pressure them into surrendering."

"I'll do that," she promised with a glint of steel in her eyes. With a snap of the fingers, she said, "Of course, that's what I should ask. I assume that you two intend to start a garden in Riyu today?"

"Well, yes?" Trev'nor responded, not sure why she would ask that question. He only had about four hours, it would be a waste of time to go to Jashni.

"If I give you the entire day, will you start in on Jashni instead?" she asked hopefully. "And maybe while you're there, you can make some formal announcements about the taxes, and the marriage laws, do just a little administrative work? We've got a lot of ill will in Jashni still and I think all of that news, plus some gardens, will go a long way to bringing people around."

Nolan inclined his head to her. "She's got a good point, Trev."

Didn't he know it. "Then we'll do that. Bec, just do me one favor, have someone do laundry for me? This is literally my last clean outfit."

"You need a batman," she informed him with a roll of the eyes. "I'll find someone and assign them to you."

Trev'nor had never heard this term. "A what, now?"

"Batman. He's like a valet in the army. He's in charge of

your tent, clothes, meals, the works. He's your support so that you don't have to worry about the daily chores and can just focus on the work."

Oh. That actually sounded great, why hadn't he gotten one before this point? "Do it. In fact, I think we all need one."

"Can't disagree there," Becca acknowledged ruefully. "Although who I'll be able to pick is the question, as I think that it's completely against cultural rules for a man to be in charge of my tent. I'll have to ask the Rikkana. Anyway, that's my problem. You alright with going to Jashni?"

"Perfectly," Trev'nor assured her. "Besides, it was my dragon that made this mess, it's up to us to clean it up."

"I couldn't agree more. Go play in the dirt, then."

Becca worked through several reports on the desk she shared with Trev'nor, approving financial changes that he'd started yesterday and generally reviewing the changes in personnel. Unlike Trexler, most of the officials here didn't seem to be corrupt. Or at least, only in a limited capacity, as Riyu had been intolerant of such and quick to behead anyone he even suspected. A few people were reported to them but not many, and Becca authorized investigations into them.

Dunixan sent her word that he had done what he could in Jashni and was heading home to settle his own army in place. She scribbled out a note thanking him for the help and asking him to return to Riyu in two weeks so they could start planning out their strategy for Von. Then she rolled it up, sealed it, and put it in the courier pouch waiting on the corner of the desk.

She took another hour to do a quick check-in with her other cities, handling whatever questions they had, but fortunately no one had anything serious to report. They'd do another, more formal, meeting later, but Becca didn't want surprises in that quarter. She'd had enough of those for this week, thanks.

With the immediate paperwork out of the way, she tackled the hard part. Threatening a city. She pulled paper and a quill to her, drafting out several letters, but none of them seemed to have the right tone. It lacked force, and short of writing it in blood, she didn't know how to fix it.

A quick rap sounded on her door and she lifted her head with the intent to call for entrance, only to find her brother skip through the doorway without waiting. He had a tea cup in one hand and a smile on his face. "This lemon tea up here is amazing."

"Isn't it?" she agreed. "I've consumed so many cups I'm making sloshing noises when I walk."

"I haven't reached sloshing levels yet, but it's coming." Putting a hip on the corner of the desk, he leaned in to examine her face closely, white hair shifting over his forehead as he moved. "So. You're up late this morning. And you're smirking."

Knowing very well that he'd probably already heard something, she leaned back in her chair and admitted smugly, "Rahim took me dancing last night. And called me by name."

Shad let out a low whistle. "I'm new to Khobunter's culture, but that's huge, isn't it?"

"Extremely so. Even Chahir doesn't adhere to formality as strictly as they do here." Becca gauged her brother's reaction to the news but he seemed pleased, and not in the new-victim-to-beat sense. "You're fine with it."

"The good commander and I have already chatted about this." Shad beamed at her and went back to sipping his tea.

They'd already talked and Danyal had still asked her? Well. Now that spoke volumes. "I see. And what are the odds that I can convince you to recite that conversation?"

"I cannot possibly breach the Bro Code and divulge such information." Shad leaned in a little further, head cocking sideways as he tried to read her latest attempt at a letter.

"Whatcha writing?"

Of course he wouldn't go along that easily. Maybe she could wiggle it out of Danyal later. Giving up for the moment, she let him change the subject. "A letter to the last standing city of Riyu." The obvious hit her and she poked his chest. "Shad. You've threatened people before."

"Loads of times," he admitted cheerfully. "My favorite hobby, second only to beating them up."

"I need to threaten them into surrendering. How would you phrase it?"

Pretending to think about this for a moment, he offered in a dramatic tone with a grand sweep of the arm, "Surrender or burn!"

Immediately regretting her decision to ask, Becca rolled her eyes. "Three words will not suffice."

"Nonsense, the shorter the better," he disagreed, waving his teacup and then softly swearing when he splashed some on his knee.

A knock at the door again, but since it was open, Danyal also just walked through. "Good morning, Riicshaden, Becca."

She couldn't help herself. She beamed at him for using her name, which made him blush in return. Becca had half-feared he'd address her by title, at least while they were working, and if he did she'd really have to kick him. "Good morning, Rahim."

That made him really blush, a ruddy red staining his cheeks. He glanced away, cleared his throat, visibly pulling himself together. "I've come to update you on a few matters. The men who are engaged have been released to go home for the time being. Most of them are being ferried there via dragon, as the dragons for some reason were quite happy about this news and wanted to help in some way."

"Dragons are huge into finding lifelong mates," Becca explained. "It's one of the things they celebrate as a whole clan. I'm glad to hear no one's trudging through the desert. Did you give them all a wedding present?"

"I did," Danyal confirmed, handing her a list of the personnel who had requested leave and then another report detailing expenses. "It was easiest to give them a red packet, especially since they were traveling, so I took the liberty of doing so."

For Shad's sake, as he looked a little confused by this, Becca explained, "A red packet is a traditional gift in Khobunter of a red envelope containing money. Every guest to a wedding is supposed to bring at least a little money to help the young couple pay for the wedding."

"Why can't Chahir have this custom?" Shad demanded. "I could have used that."

"You got married on board a ship; all you had to pay for was two dresses and a marriage license," Becca snarked back in amusement.

Pointing a finger at her, he disagreed vehemently, "You were expensive. I want my red packet."

Ignoring him, Becca asked Danyal, "We were generous, I trust?"

"We were," Danyal assured her, taking the open seat in front of her desk. "After all, we still owe some of the men back pay, although I hope that with the spoils of this city, we'll be able to catch up."

"Riyu certainly hoarded gold like a dragon, it's very possible we can." Becca made a note to herself to follow up on that in her to-do sheet. She'd only been working an hour and the to-do sheet was half full. That was not a good ratio. "Anything else?"

"Sergeant Amir hasn't left yet, he wishes to speak with

you first. I informed him of your wish to keep him with you, and he's very flattered, but he wants to directly ask you a few questions." Leaning forward with his elbows on knees, Danyal confided, "Amir is a military man through and through. He's not interested in leaving it once the war is over. I think he hopes to have a more permanent position among your staff once you settle in the new capital."

"Considering how much politics I'll have to wrangle at that point, I'd certainly put his linguistic skills to use." A thought occurred and she leaned back, crossing her ankles and thinking about it. "Rahim. The boys and I agreed this morning that we've reached the point we really need our own individual batmans."

Danyal nodded instantly. "I agree."

"I thought you might. But I can't have a male batman, can I?"

"No, the people will pitch a fit," Danyal confirmed easily. His tone and expression clearly said who would be the one to protest the most.

Biting back a smile, Becca told herself firmly not to laugh. Danyal would not take it well. "Let's try this, then. I want to ask Amir if he's willing to bring his new wife up, have her travel with the army and serve as my batman."

Humming a tone, he considered this for a moment. "What is that Chahiran phrase you use sometimes? Two birds, one stone?"

"Keeps Amir with us, he doesn't miss his wife, I get the batman I need." Becca ticked the points off on her fingers and shrugged in conclusion. "If she's willing."

"I think we'll need to give Sergeant Amir some time to talk this over with her, but it might work. I'll fetch him and you can ask him directly." Danyal's eye caught the letter on her desk and he frowned at it. "I checked with the semaphore tower not a half hour ago and there's still no word from Sha Watchtower. You think to write them another letter?"

"I'm struggling with it," Becca sighed. "The problem I'm facing is that words just don't have the same impact as a physical show of force does."

"Respectfully, my Warlord," Danyal stated neutrally, "I think you've given them enough time."

Becca's instincts said the same. She appreciated Danyal's effort in speaking to a superior instead of his potential-something and gave him a sharp nod. "You're probably right. Show of hands, who wants to fly out with me and about twenty dragons and scare them into surrender? Both of you, huh. Right, let's do it, then." Glancing at the clock on the wall, she estimated time and such, considered all she had to do today, and made a plan. "I think we should leave in the morning. Trev'nor and Nolan are in Jashni today planting a garden and getting the place repaired. I don't want to interrupt that and there are still a few things I should do here today. Rahim, talk to the dragons and get me a squadron ready to go after dawn. Let's put them in line."

"Understood, my Warlord. Shall I fetch Sergeant Amir now?"

"Yes, please. I don't want to unnecessarily delay him." As Danyal left the room, she asked of Shad, "Can you round me up one of the Legends to go with us tomorrow?"

Shad went still for a moment, expression almost neutral. "You don't like to work with any of the reformed priests."

"No, I don't," she admitted frankly, tone blunt. Taking in a breath, she forced herself to stay reasonable and calm. "But if I had taken a Legend along when we snuck into the city, as people urged me to do, we wouldn't have lost Riyu. We would have been able to track him before he left the city and that whole fiasco with two armies wouldn't have happened.

I like to think that I learn from my mistakes."

A slow, pleased smile took over his face. "My little girl, all grown up. Almost makes me want to cry."

She lifted up enough in her chair to slug him in the arm, not hard, as he half-dodged. "Shut it. As a ruler, I can't afford personal prejudice to interfere with my judgement. And if nothing else, I need to trust the Gardeners. They've never led us astray and if they bring me Legends, I must use them."

"Glad to see you speak sense. Sure, I'll go find Carjettaan and ask her." With a salute of the tea cup, he left the room whistling a merry tune.

Becca huffed out a breath, still a little uneasy with her own decision, but not from a lack of trust. She just didn't know how to deal with the Legends on an emotional level and it would take grit on her part to bear them for any length of time.

Danyal returned with Amir in tow, distracting her, and she stood long enough to exchange a salute with Amir before gesturing him to a chair. "You want to speak with me?"

"Yes, my Warlord." Amir sat at the edge of his chair, hands clasped, looking a little uncomfortable but determined all the same. "My Warlord, I wish to know, what is your plan for after the campaign? Will you keep any of the military officers as personal staff?"

"I certainly will," Becca answered readily, knowing very well what he needed to hear from her. No need to torture the man by making him ask all of the questions. "And I'll be frank, Sergeant, you're one of the men I hope to keep. I realize that's a lot to ask of you, however, as it would mean moving to Rheben, and that's some distance from your family."

Amir raised both hands, shaking his head, trying very hard not to openly smile. "No, my Warlord, I assure you that's not an issue. But truly, the new capital will be in Rheben?"

"It will, although we can't announce that officially yet, not until the city's been restored. I am organizing a work crew to do just that." Danyal was correct, Amir really wanted to move with her. Becca adored people with ambition. Still, there was a problem with this plan because of the man's rank. Although she knew the answer, she still asked the question to verify it. "Sergeant, I believe you are a noncommissioned officer?"

"Yes, my Warlord," Amir admitted, mouth flattening into an unhappy line. "I wasn't able to afford officer's school."

Not a surprise, most men of his humble background wouldn't be able to. His training in languages amazed her, all things considered. "Then let's do this. I want you to head my linguistics division and start organizing a full staff, as I'll need them shortly. I'll sign off on you becoming a commissioned officer, rank of Second Lieutenant, with the appropriate pay raise."

Overjoyed, Amir promptly stood and saluted her. "Yes, my Warlord, thank you!"

Returning the salute, she waved him down. "Good. Commander, make it so."

Danyal gave her a nod and smile, already noting it down on his ever present notebook.

"It'll likely need to wait until you've returned before I can make it official," Becca apologized. "But unofficially, welcome. All of that said, Amir, I take it you plan to bring your wife back with you?"

"I would dearly love to," Amir responded hopefully. "Our support personnel are never in danger, and I know she's deathly tired of waiting around at home for my return, so I thought to bring her back with me with your permission, my Warlord."

"That's fine, but I wonder if I can ask a favor of you and

your fiancée." Becca had thought of how to word this, as she didn't want to pressure the man and make him feel like his new rank would be dependent on his answer to her request. Far from it, she was trying to solve a problem. "And the answer can be 'I don't know' or 'no,' that's fine. I am in need of a batman, you see, and considering my gender it has to be a woman. I wonder if your fiancée would be willing to serve as one."

Amir dearly looked like he wanted to answer the question on the spot, his mouth nearly quivering from the effort of holding back. "I cannot answer for her, my Warlord, she'd skin me if I did such a thing, but I think she would look very favorably on the offer. My Nahla doesn't like to be idle. If you will permit, I'll ask her when I return home and then send her answer back to you via the dragons."

Now that was smart, it would save Becca time. "Please do. I don't wish to hold you up any further. Please go home, have a wonderful wedding, an excellent honeymoon, and if you see anything wrong in Trexler report it to me. It wouldn't hurt to have someone else's eyes on the city."

Standing, he gave her another salute. "I will, my Warlord. Thank you very much."

"You're very welcome." She answered the salute and shooed him out the door, watching him go and feeling very right about the whole thing. "It's so much fun promoting people. I want to promote everyone."

Danyal snorted. "You can't. Not all of them deserve it and we certainly can't afford it."

"Spoilsport." Pointing a finger at him, she ordered, "Go get a squadron together and do all of the necessary paperwork for Amir. I'll plough through as much of this madness as I can so we can leave in the morning without the sky falling on our heads."

"What about the dragons?"

"Garth will organize who goes with us tomorrow, don't worry about that." Leaving the desk, she went to the window and opened it before calling, "Cat?"

"Hear you," her dragon informed her from somewhere overhead. The dragon simply loved the water canals along the outside of the fortress—it apparently made for good perches. As long as the dragon didn't start collecting pillows and hoarding gold up there, Becca was content to let her perch wherever her scaly heart desired.

"I need you to relay a message to Garth. We're going to terrify Sha Watchtower into line tomorrow."

A thump sounded overhead, likely Cat's tail making happy rhythms. It only shook the building a little bit, enough to make the furniture jump and skitter. "Smash city?"

Becca could feel a headache coming on. How was it that the only two Garths she knew destroyed cities? Was it something about the name? And now this Garth had corrupted the others into joining in. "No, Cat."

"Awww," her dragon whined in a high pitched tone.

Sha Watchtower took four hours to reach by flight. Sitting on the border between Von and Riyu, it saw more action than any other city of Riyu's, since Von was the epitome of a hostile neighbor. The Watchtower reflected this as it had thicker walls, more soldiers, and the most alert security out of any city that Trev'nor had seen so far. It looked exactly like Alred, only larger, as if they had copied the plans but doubled it in size. Even the single tower in the center had more girth to it, although not as much height. The city huddled around the base of the tower as if a child clinging to its mother's skirts, with the same monotone sandstone used for walls and buildings, the watchtower the only thing in site made of a different stone. They must have dug deep to find enough granite to build a watchtower that large.

Carjettaan rode with Trev'nor, for various reasons. While Becca requesting the help of a Legend showed excellent progress, Trev'nor knew better than to push her by putting the two women in constant proximity. Becca could admit to her mistakes, but asking her to change overnight was a bit much. Carjettaan seemed to realize where she stood on the matter, as the older woman had politely agreed to help and not demanded anything more of Becca.

Now she tapped Trev'nor on the shoulder to get his

attention and half-yelled near his ear to be heard over the rushing wind: "Confirmed six hundred thirty-two magicians!"

So the reports in Riyu were up to date. Good. Well, partially good, if she felt only magicians, then that meant Rurick's citizens *weren't* here either. Busted buckets, they really were in Rowe, weren't they?

Alarms sounded, gongs going full blast, and even from here Trev'nor could hear them. Soldiers scrambled into a defensive position only to freeze once there, weapons clutched in a half-raised position. Twenty-six dragons, all of them carrying soldiers, likely would put the fear of the Guardians into anyone. In their shoes, Trev'nor certainly wouldn't want to face that many dragons and he absolutely would not antagonize them by attacking first.

Becca signaled for a landing, which they all did, a mere hundred paces from the front gates. The dragons kept their wings half-furled, spaced out so that they surrounded the watchtower on all sides, ready to lift in the air and fight if needed. Not that anyone sane would choose to fight in this situation, but the commanders in Khobunter didn't always fall in the ranks of sanity.

Sand flew in little eddies of air and settled as the dragons landed, the gongs stopped sounding, and nothing but silence remained. Even the wind stilled a little, a rare occurrence in this country, and Trev'nor silently suspected Becca had something to do with that.

The gates of the city remained firmly shut. None of the soldiers on top dared to breathe, much less move. Trev'nor watched them all carefully, muttering from the side of his mouth, "Carjettaan, are they moving about inside?"

"Not an inch. The whole city seems to be in lockdown. They're not even disturbing the slave pens."

Good to know. So they weren't stalling for time to ready hostages? Then what were they waiting on?

A muffled sound came from his pocket, and Trev'nor fished out the mirror broach, eyes still on the walls as he answered, "Yeah, I'm here."

"*Trev*," Becca's voice came through clearly, perhaps a trifle smugly, "*Your turn.*"

Frowning, he turned to look at her, as she sat only two dragons away and a little ahead of him. "My turn to do what?"

"*Demand surrender. I did it with Riyu, so it's your turn.*"

"We're taking turns on that?" News to Trev'nor. But Becca often made decisions on her own and then acted as if this was common knowledge and why weren't you already doing it?

"*Of course. I can only be scary sometimes. The rest of the time I reserve to be cute.*"

Trev'nor heard a masculine chuckle, muted through the mirror, and rolled his eyes. Of course Danyal found that funny. "You know, I could make the argument that now you've demanded surrender of Riyu, you've got more experience than me, so you should be the one to go."

"*I can also make the argument that because I have more experience, you should get some practice in, which still makes this your turn.*"

"I'm not going to win this, am I?"

"*Nope.*"

Resigned, he unbuckled and threw a leg over, sliding down Garth's side. As soon as he was far enough out, he threw up a weapon's shield and strode for the city's gates, trying to phrase in his head what he should say. 'Surrender, please' likely wouldn't cut it.

Well, when all else fails, start with an introduction.

He stopped just shy of the gates, turning his face up and projecting his voice as much as possible. "I AM RHEBENTREV'NOREN, WARLORD OF TREXLER AND RIYU. I HAVE COME FOR YOUR SURRENDER."

Silence.

Oh, for the love of— Trev'nor refused to stand here developing a crick in his neck. He called upon the earth under his feet to create a small platform, then rose steadily into the air until he was level with the battlements. Soldiers screamed and cursed, scrambling backwards until their backs hit the opposite side of the wall, swords and spears at the ready, although no one attacked. From the expressions he saw under the helmets, no one wanted to, either.

"I'm going to repeat myself," Trev'nor informed them as a whole, trying to pick out the commander. Surely he was up here somewhere. "I'm Rhebentrev'noren, Warlord of Trexler and Riyu. I've come for your surrender. Now, who's in charge?"

Silence again, which dragged out for nearly twenty seconds before someone cleared their throat and bravely took a half-step forward. "Warlord? The thing is, our commander fled the city about five days ago."

Five days ago. When Becca sent Riyu's corpse here with a letter asking for surrender? Or shortly thereafter, anyway. Trev'nor felt a headache coming on. "Did he, now. Is there no second in command?"

"Second in command went with him, Warlord," the soldier respectfully answered, a slight tremor in his voice he couldn't quite mask. "As to that, our captain has been leading us, but he's not technically allowed to rule the city or make any decisions for it."

Trev'nor had a feeling he wouldn't like the answer, but asked it anyway, "And why's that?"

"Mother was a slave, Warlord."

Yup, the headache had arrived full force. "I find that a perfectly ridiculous reason to deny someone a position, but alright. I think I understand. So you literally haven't surrendered or chosen to fight because you have no one in this city willing to take responsibility for it?"

The soldier gave him a deep bow. "Yes, Warlord."

Could this situation be more ridiculous? "Rise, please. And stop shaking, I'm not in the habit of eating people. Neither, for that matter, are the dragons. We came here in full force because your silence indicated that there was a problem." Granted, there was, just not the one they anticipated. "We have no plans to demolish the city or pillage it."

Everyone within earshot released a breath, a sigh of relief bordering on a prayer.

Shaking his head, Trev'nor fished out the mirror broach and lifted it to his mouth. "Becca, Nolan, slight problem."

"We're listening."

"So turns out the commander and his second in command absconded about five days ago. That left only one senior officer, a captain, but because of his birth he's not allowed to take responsibility for the city. So they literally have no one here with the authority to surrender to us."

"Well that puts a new spin on the whole situation." Becca sounded very exasperated by the whole point.

"So what do we do?" Nolan asked. *"I mean, if there's no one to argue the point, do we just take the city?"*

"I don't see why we can't. Technically it's ours anyway, since we took the province."

"If they'll lay down their weapons and come out, we'll not attack," Becca offered.

Trev'nor felt that was perfectly reasonable. He didn't

want people to get the idea that his back was a target. "Hear that? Lay down your weapons and come out through the front gate. Do that, we won't kill you, or raze the city."

People immediately dropped their weapons, heading for the stairs with due alacrity. Satisfied, Trev'nor turned and called down to the waiting Garth, "Can you repeat what I just said so the whole city can hear it?"

Garth obligingly lifted up onto his haunches and bellowed out in his best Solish what Trev'nor had said, word for word. Trev'nor had to put his hands over his ears to keep them from being blasted by the sound, but he didn't reproach his dragon for setting his head to ringing. At that volume, no doubt the whole city had heard him.

Retreating to the ground, Trev'nor kept his weapon shield up and watched attentively as the front gates opened wide. Several soldiers poured out, most of them of lower rank, and immediately lined up against the outside wall. Trev'nor hadn't thought to ask them to do so, but it kept the gate from being crowded, so he encouraged them to keep it up.

Somewhat to his surprise, only two garrisons' worth of men came out, some two hundred men. With a city of this size, he'd expected more. Or had Riyu robbed this place of soldiers to defend his own territory in anticipation of their attack? Trev'nor would not put it past the man.

The last soldier to exit was the captain, stripped of all weapons but with his rank still clear on his sleeve. Trev'nor blinked, startled, at his first clear view of the man. He looked amazingly Chahiran. Clearly hereditary traits were at play here, as the man had light brown hair, blue eyes, and a lighter skin tone than anyone Trev'nor had met in Khobunter. With looks like those, it was a wonder he'd risen to a high rank at all. He must be very formidable indeed, not just in fighting strength, but in political maneuvering.

Dropping the shield, Trev'nor went to him, inclining his head in greeting. "I'm Rhebentrev'noren."

"Captain Talib," the captain answered with a sharp salute.

Coming up from behind, Becca returned the salute sharply, as did Nolan. "Captain. I'm Riicbeccan, Warlord. This is Vonnolanen. Is there really no one of authority in this city aside from you?"

"I'm afraid not, Warlord. The Rikkan and Rikkana refused to accept responsibility of the city." Shifting a little uncomfortably, he explained, "We did receive your letter with the corpse, but none of us were quite sure what to do about it after our commander left. There have been heated arguments about what to do ever since. Apparently we took too long in deciding."

"Committees always take too long deciding," Nolan drawled knowingly. "It's alright, Captain, we're just relieved nothing's seriously wrong. Now, is this all of your men?"

"It is, Raja."

Carjettaan, standing behind Becca, leaned in to murmur something that sounded like an affirmation. Becca gave Trev'nor a slight nod to indicate that was correct. Good enough for him.

Taking a half step forward, Becca drew his attention. "Captain, we require two things of you. First, we want all of the slaves released to us. Second, release the men to return to either their homes or the barracks. We'll sort things out ourselves from there."

"Of course, Warlord." Turning, Talib bellowed out orders to the men.

Trev'nor listened in dismay as the Khobuntish he used was so thickly accented half of it went straight over Trev'nor's head. And that was with knowing what the man would say!

He turned, ready to call for Amir, and belatedly remembered their favorite translator was off in Trexler getting married. Busted buckets.

Stepping in a little closer, Nolan murmured in Chahirese, "I suddenly miss Amir. What kind of mouthful of rocks did they chew to come up with an accent this thick?"

"I have no idea, but seriously, I barely understood any of that." Trev'nor felt like finding a wall and beating his head against it. "What are the odds that people up here speak fluent Solish?"

"It's still the major trade language up here, so odds are good. Captain Talib's Solish was impeccable, after all."

True. Anyone of rank would know the language, then. It was everyone else Trev'nor had to worry about. Glory.

Well, his ears would adapt to it eventually. Resigned, Trev'nor marched in with everyone else, standing right beside Becca as they waded in to straighten out yet another city.

Sha seemed a little better off than Alred had been. More box gardens lined the outside of the buildings, for one thing, the streets didn't have much in the way of refuse, and the city stood in rather good repair. Heartened to see this, Trev'nor greeted most of them with a smile, inwardly celebrating that he didn't have to fix yet another city. People didn't know what to make of this friendly attitude and ducked their heads to him, but didn't smile back.

Ah, well. Give it time.

Danyal and Nolan went off to start the very fun process of pulling slaves out of pens and chains. Trev'nor didn't really envy them the job, as while he enjoyed helping people, the slave pens always brought back dark memories for him. The dragons situated themselves around the city, trying not to scare people, and drawing a few of the braver ones into conversations.

Dragons, when they put their minds to it, could be lethally charming.

Captain Talib quickly organized the Rikkan and Rikkana meeting with them in a shaded patio area near the command headquarters. As Trev'nor had been in the suns all morning, he looked very favorably on sitting somewhere cool and promptly took one of the wooden folding chairs. When the two elders entered, he popped back up again to give them each a bow. "Rikkana, Rikkan, thank you for coming so quickly. I am Rhebentrev'noren, Warlord. This is my co-ruler, Riicbeccaan, and our Military Advisor, Riicshaden."

Overwhelmed by this friendly greeting, they stared hard at Trev'nor, as if waiting for the other shoe to fall. When that didn't happen, the Rikkana cleared her throat and offered in a rusty voice, "I am Zahra, Warlord. This is Yasin. How may we serve you?"

Becca gestured them into chairs, answering as she did so, "First, please relax. We have every intention of treating this people well, as they are now ours. We wish to discuss with you what the rules were here, and how they'll be changed, so that you can help the citizens get used to them. Captain Talib?"

"Yes, Warlord?"

"Stay," Becca ordered firmly. "Whatever the previous warlord's opinions about people, we don't share them. No one is a slave under our ruling, nor do we treat anyone like a subclass being. You have been the acting commander since the last one deserted you, have you not?"

"He has, Raya," Rikkana Zahra answered when the captain faltered. "Even though he cannot bring himself to admit it."

"I thought as much." Satisfied, Becca informed him,

"Then sit. I have questions and you three likely know the answers."

"Trev'nor." Garth's head came down a little, forcing people to either move or get squashed. "Llona has found more family."

Twisting sharply about, he demanded, "Who? Is it...?"

"Parisa's parents," Garth confirmed.

A thrill of excitement shot up Trev'nor spine. Finally! Finally he'd managed to locate them. Turning back to Becca, he begged with his eyes to go, only to find her already urging him that direction.

"Go, go, I can handle this."

Beaming, he informed her, "You're the best ever."

"I know that," Becca responded, chuckling. "Go!"

He wasted no time in doing so, climbing immediately on Garth's back and just hanging on without even trying to strap in as the dragon made one giant leap to the nearest building's roof, then several hops in succession to reach the right area. Only then did he stop and extend a leg so Trev'nor could slide down, landing lightly back on the street level.

Llona lay half-curled around the corner, her bulk squeezed into the narrow street, happy as a clam because of all the magicians surrounding her. She lifted her head and greeted happily, "Trev'nor. Come, your family. Meet them."

Magicians all around them, some of them still in the chains, turned and watched him with wide eyes, almost disbelieving. Trev'nor knew their reactions came from seeing a mage in full power walking around unshackled, not to mention arriving on dragon back, and he ignored their reactions. Instead he made his way through them, careful to not jostle them, as a puff of wind could knock most of them over. He did keep an eye out for Rurick's people, just in case, but he didn't recognize a single face in the crowd.

A man and woman stood directly in front of Llona, clutching each other's hands tightly, for all the world looking a decade older than they likely were. Both of them had dark hair, braided and matted, sores from the manacles on their wrists, but their eyes—their eyes were alive with hope. Trev'nor felt like hugging them both, he was so happy to see them alive, if not well. He stopped just short, holding back the urge to smile like a demented gnome. "You're Parisa's parents?"

"Parisa Rheben," the woman said, voice husky, eyes nearly pleading with him. "She's well? You know where she is?"

"I know exactly where she is. She's with our cousin, Sallah, learning earth magic." Trev'nor started hunting for the mirror broach that had fallen somewhere deep in a pocket. Now seemed like a wonderful time to call his cousin, maybe get Parisa to speak with her parents and relieve a few fears.

"Wait, 'our?'" the man questioned hesitantly.

Right, proper introductions should be in order. "I'm Rhebentrev'noren," Trev'nor introduced with a half-bow. "Your many times removed cousin. Your ancestors originally came from Chahir, you see. Sallah Bender was Rhebensallahan before she married. She's an Earth Mage as well, like you and Parisa. Not all of the Rhebens are, you understand, but the bloodline for it runs strong in our family. What are your names?"

"Qadir," the husband introduced himself, growing more animated with every word out of Trev'nor's mouth. "This is my wife, Sahar. You glow so strongly to my eyes, Trev'nor. You say our daughter is learning magic? Like you did?"

"Yup. Not under the same instructor, I had a different mentor, but Sallah is an amazing Earth Mage and teacher."

Finally finding the mirror broach, he pulled it free and winked at them. "Hang on, and you can talk to them yourself. Sallah. Sallah~"

"*I'm here. Sha Watchtower, did you get them to surrender?*"

"You certainly cut to the chase."

"*Shut it, you, we've been on pins and needles all day over here. Did you get in or not?*"

"We did, but speak in Solish, please. I have a lot of listening magicians that have just been freed and are very curious on whom I'm talking to." Trev'nor felt people leaning his direction, fascinated with what he was doing. But then, not many of them seemed to know how to use the mirror broaches, as those hadn't survived very well in Khobunter for whatever reason. "But Sallah, we finally found Parisa's parents!"

An actual squeal of delight rang out on the other end. "*Put them on, let me talk to them! No, wait, they'll want Parisa first. She's in the other room, give me a second. Parisa~! Parisa! We found your parents!*"

Trev'nor had to pull the mirror away when another, even higher pitched squeal of delight assaulted his eardrums. What was with the screaming today? It made his head ring. Lowering it a little, he gestured Qadir and Sahar in a little closer. "Speak directly into the mirror, she'll hear you."

"Parisa," Sahar said, projecting into the mirror, biting her bottom lip uncertainly. "Parisa, honey, you hear me?"

"*Madi!*"

Tears started streaming out of Sahar's eyes and she wiped them with the palms of her hands. "Yes. Yes. My Pari, are you well? Are you hurt, or hungry?"

"*No, Madi, I'm fine. There's lots to eat here, and treats you've never seen before, and the softest beds to sleep in. Madi, is Paha there too?*"

"I'm here," Qadir choked out. "I'm here."

"*Trev'nor got you both out of the chains?*" Parisa asked, her excitement ramping up in her tone, her words coming out faster and faster. "*He got me out and I lived in a castle for a while, with our cousin Garth, and then Sallah came to get me 'cause she said it'll be easier to live here and Trev'nor was still searching for you, which took him a long time—*"

"Hey now, it's only been a month!" Trev'nor protested, not sure whether to find this amusing or be insulted. "And I have to conquer each place before I can rescue people, you know. I can't just waltz in and kidnap people."

"*Why not? It took you forever, Trev'nor.*"

"Eight year olds have no sense of time, I swear," Trev'nor lamented. This was not where he'd intended the conversation to go when he pulled out the mirror, but strangely enough this back and forth seemed to relieve her parents' anxieties. "But yes, they're both out of the chains, kiddo." Looking both parents in the eye, he promised, "I'll make sure they get to you as soon as possible. Happy?"

"*Yes!*"

Qadir and Sahar nodded, smiles and tears intermixing.

"You better be. Spoiled princess that you are." Trev'nor couldn't help himself and reached out, drawing Sahar into a quick hug. He knew only a taste of the terror she'd lived through, thinking never to see her child again. When all of this properly hit, they wouldn't let Parisa out of their sight. "Alright, give me Sallah back. We need to arrange a pickup."

"*I'm here, Trev.*"

"Sallah, our report to you of six hundred and thirty-two was dead on. We managed to get the city to surrender so there's no casualties, thank all the Guardians. These people look rough, though, so make sure there's plenty of food, hot water, and new clothes to go around. I'll raid the stores here and see if I can send supplies with you as much as I can."

"That'll help. We're using an insane amount of magic down here to keep up with the supply and demand."

Trev'nor suspected that was the case. "I'll send the order out immediately. When can you come get people?"

"Give me three hours. Yes, Parisa, yes, you can come with me this trip to get them. Of course, that's if it's safe enough. Trev?"

"Perfectly safe," Trev'nor assured her. "Bring her up."

"Then see you in three hours."

The connection ended and Trev'nor returned the mirror to a pocket, although this time a different one so he didn't have to go on a hunting expedition for it. He really had to stop using that pocket. Seeing the mounting unease on the faces around him, he sought to reassure everyone, "We're just moving you to a safer location. You know the Ruins of Rheben? Yes? Good. That was your ancestor's home a hundred years ago. We're restoring it, and there's a new magical academy there. All of you are going to be living and training there for the next few years. It's very possible that you have friends and family already waiting there for you. Llona—" he gestured toward the dragon patiently waiting nearby "—is our record keeper. If you give her your name, and the names of those you want to find, she'll be able to tell you if they're in Rheben already."

Llona cleared her throat a little, drawing attention to herself. "Trev'nor. Garth told people to search for food and clothes."

"Bless him. Thanks, Garth!"

The dragon gave a huff, a very smug sound indeed.

Now, what else would these people need to know? Right. "You'll be traveling to Rheben via Earth Path. It's a magic used by Earth Mages and it's very, very fast. You'll be going underground during the trip, but it means you'll arrive in Rheben by tonight. Don't be alarmed, it's not dangerous, and you'll be going to a very good place. The dean of the academy is Raile Blackover, a wizard from Chahir. He's one of your ancestors, in a way, so he's family to you."

"Family?" someone objected near his elbow.

Trev'nor turned to face him, an older man that may be in his fifties, a wizard by the look of it. After going through this more than once, Trev'nor knew exactly what to say to put all of their fears to rest. No doubt they wondered at his motivations, at his identity, but he now understood this culture enough to give them a reason to trust him. "Right, family. Look, all of you are descendants of Chahiran magicians. Every single one of you, no exception. Your magic alone bears proof of that. And the Chahiran magicians? They're all related to each other, in one way or another. So you're all family. The reason why I'm here? Me and my two friends? We saw our family in trouble and refused to leave you here."

"Family," Qadir breathed, only now sounding as if he believed it. "You're really our family?"

"I am. Not quite sure how," Trev'nor admitted. "We're still piecing together the family history to trace it back, but I think we're eighth cousins? It might be ninth. Not sure. Sallah is also an eighth or ninth cousin. We can figure it out later. For now, understand that you're full citizens of Khobunter. Slavery is now outlawed in this country."

The same slightly belligerent man from before demanded, "Since when?"

"Since I started conquering the country." Trev'nor shot him a smile that might have had a feral edge to it. "I am Warlord here."

A wave of sound swept through the listening crowd, a mix of emotions that spoke of wonder, disbelief, and perhaps even a touch of unease. Trev'nor overrode it, speaking over them until they gradually quieted. "Slavery, all slavery, is outlawed. You're full citizens, with all the rights you should have had from birth. After your training is complete, you are free to go and do whatever you wish as long as you obey the laws of my land. Oh, and all of those that haven't had a chance to do a proper wedding ceremony? Please inform Sallah and Raile of that. Raile has the power to marry people and has a wedding gift for you."

"I think, cousin," Sahar said shakily, a hand pressed to her heart, "that our freedom is gift enough."

Trev'nor pish-poshed that. "Nonsense. I haven't begun to spoil you. Now, who knows the way to some of the storage buildings? Excellent, several of you. Give your names to Llona quickly, ask what questions you need to, then lead me to the right buildings. Let's get people outfitted as much as possible before we send you to Rheben. Llona, when you're done with someone, have them escorted to the southern gate. We'll gather everyone together to wait for Sallah."

"I will," Llona agreed faithfully.

"Good, thank you." Why couldn't he have chosen a sweetheart like Llona instead of being adopted by a rascal? "Where's Danyal and Nolan, anyway?"

"Other pen," Llona answered, using her nose to point the way. "I told Nolan. He happy."

"I bet he is." Not to mention relieved. They'd all been worried they'd never find Parisa's parents, or worse, find them dead. Slavery was not conducive to a long lifespan. If only the Rurick citizens had been in Riyu too…well. He'd rescue them soon. Hopefully soon.

Shaking off the thought, he grabbed Qadir and Sahar, drew them a little aside and asked, "Now. What other family members do I need to hunt for?"

Becca had her hands full of two reports, a pen in her mouth, all while leaning over yet another report to compare the other two with. If she could juggle this right, she'd be able to reassign all of her new soldiers so they were back in their hometowns, or at least nearby. Most of them hadn't been home in five years or more, which was entirely inexcusable. Helping her with the task was Danyal on the other side of the desk, his mouth silently moving as he read the names.

She found the habit endearingly cute.

It had gotten very late in the day and although she'd had dinner not an hour before, her mouth craved something sweet. After the meeting with the Rikkan and Rikkana—which went very well—the city had settled a little. The citizens still felt uneasy but nothing bad had happened to them, and the only strange thing was the change of rules and the slaves being released, which seemed fine. Becca knew that it would remain this way for a while, although if they followed the usual trend, their attitudes toward their new rulers would radically change once the gardens got put in.

Knowing how to soften their hearts a little, Becca had called in a storm on the ride in, and it rained now in a steady drizzle. She tilted back in her chair, giving her neck and back a break, and checked the storm through the nearest window.

Maybe give it another hour, then send it on. Too much rain in this area would lead to standing water and minor flood conditions, after all. Trev'nor hadn't had a chance to change the soil conditions yet up here.

A knock tentatively sounded on the door, and she put the chair's legs back on the floor as she answered, "Come in!"

Captain Talib strode through, saluting them both. "Warlord. Commander."

"Ah, Captain, come in," she invited. Talib had proven to be very useful during the day, an excellent commander. If he were actually from Sha, she'd leave him here, but he was in fact from Jashni. "I actually had a question for you. You're from Jashni, that's correct? I see. I'm trying to reassign everyone so they can go home, live there and work, but it's proving to be a bit of a challenge. Some people I need to remain in Sha. I know it's a lot to ask, you haven't been in Jashni in nearly six years, but can I leave you here another six months?"

"As to that, Warlord, I would actually prefer not to live in Jashni ever again," Captain Talib stated neutrally. He stood in parade's rest, not meeting anyone's eyes.

Oh boy. Becca had the uneasy feeling she'd just wandered into an area of tripwires. "Ah. I won't pry, you needn't tell me why. You're a very capable person, Captain, the work you've done here reflects that. I want to leave you here as commander. Is that alright?"

Those blue eyes snapped down to her, wide and stunned. "Commander?"

"Yes, of course. Your men trust you, the Rikkana and Rikkan trust you—in fact they asked me hopefully to leave you here, that's how much they like you. I found no major issues in this city. Your previous commander was a cowardly dog that ran off at the first hint of trouble. I can't imagine he's responsible for the city being in such good shape." Becca paused, watching his expression, and snorted when there was no rebuttal. "I thought so. So, Commander, can I leave you in charge of Sha's defenses?"

"I would be honored, Warlord," Talib answered huskily, giving her a sharp salute.

"Excellent. Be aware that two dragons will claim this as home, they'll be happy to help in whatever way they can, and I will appoint a mayor here to govern. You'll work in conjunction with both of them. Any problem with that? No? Very good. Then, sit." Pointing to a chair, she shifted half the paperwork toward him. "You can help Rahim and I sort this out."

Talib sat, a little uncertainly, but he pulled a sheet gamely closer. "How many men do you wish to leave stationed in the city?"

"You didn't have enough men before, so I think double that. With two dragons now in residence that should be enough. If I'm wrong, I'm happy to rearrange things a little so you have more on hand."

"With respect, Warlord, we prefer to keep at least nine squadrons on hand," Talib answered carefully. "Since we're in between Von and Libendorf, after all."

"Ah." Staring at the map with new eyes, Becca felt like kicking herself. She was so used to thinking only about Khobunter that she'd failed to realize Libendorf's borders were *right there* and of course that should be taken into account. Not that Libendorf had the habit of barging in on its neighbors, but still. "Thank you, Commander, that is an excellent point. Nine garrisons it is. Rahim?"

"Riyu has too many soldiers stationed in it, we'll shift them over to here," he responded promptly. "But Becca, not all of them will be from Sha. There are simply not enough soldiers from this city to pull that off."

Growling curses under her breath, she pondered the problem. "Then shift people who are from Riyu first. They've been home for years, they can afford to be stationed elsewhere for a while."

"Sensible," Danyal approved, picking up a different roster.

From outside the window, there heard an exaggerated clearing of the throat, or at least as close as a dragon's throat could get to the sound. A golden eye came into view. "Commander Talib."

Talib startled a little at being directly addressed by a dragon. Gamely, he squared his shoulders and answered steadily, "Yes, Raya Cat?"

"Ask," Cat commanded, tone gentle.

Ask what? Becca shifted in her chair so she could glance between the two of them, not at all sure what was going on here.

His gaze went to the floor, then came up again, radiating uncertainty.

"Will be mad," Cat threatened, sounding more and more like an older sibling scolding a younger one.

Becca's eyebrows shot up. Seriously, what was going on? What did her dragon know that she didn't? And when had Cat gotten attached enough to Talib that she would look out for his interests like this?

Cornered, Talib forced himself back up to ramrod straightness. "Warlord. Did anyone report to you that I am, in fact, the child of a slave?"

"They did." Becca bit back the questions as clearly he geared up for something.

"My mother was sold when I was five. I've been searching

for her ever since. Raya Llona informed me that she has been rescued and is now in the Ruins of Rheben."

Becca stared at him, incredulous, and then shot out of her chair. "Good Guardians, man, tell me things like this sooner! Cat, find me Trev'nor."

"On it," her dragon promised, sounding very smug.

"You," Becca informed her new startled commander, stabbing a finger in his direction, "are going to see your mother tonight, if I have anything to say about it. Trev'nor needs to head that direction anyway to deliver supplies and money. You can just hitch a ride with him."

Stunned, he stared at her for the longest moment before croaking, "You're giving me leave to go? Just like that?"

"I do not separate people from their families, Commander." Becca felt a mix of sympathy and anger that he would even feel the need to hesitate, that it took Cat's urging before he found the courage to ask. "One of the worst things a person can do to another is rob them of family. I'm not that monstrous. Now, the question is, how long can you stay down there with her?"

Danyal cleared his throat. "Perhaps you should ask if she needs to stay in Rheben at all?"

Becca smacked her palm against her forehead. "Of course."

Talib's eyes darted between the two of them. "I'm sorry, I'm not following. Warlord Trev'nor said that everyone needs to stay there until they are trained magicians."

"The thing is," Becca explained patiently, "not all of the slaves are magicians."

Jaw dropping, Talib spluttered, "Wait, what?"

"I know, everyone in this country assumed that if you were a slave, you had magic, but that's not at all the case. About a third of the people we've rescued don't have a trace of magical talent in them. We took them to the academy anyway, as they'll need some education just to have careers and lives after this, but they don't need magical training at all." Becca picked up her mirror as she spoke, activating it with a graze of power. "Hold on, let me double check this with Raile. Raile? Hello, Raile~"

It took a minute for him to answer, sounding a little out of breath as he did so. "*Becca, is that you?*"

"It is."

"*Don't tell me you found more people. We barely got this lot settled two minutes ago, I can't handle more tonight.*"

"You're sounding entirely too gleeful for that to be a complaint," she teased. "I think I need to find another thousand to send to you."

Raile chuckled, not at all bothered by this playful threat. "*Send 'em on! We'll just keep expanding the campus. In all seriousness, though, they're doing fine. Many families reunited today and I performed three quick weddings for the ones too impatient to wait. Young Parisa turned into a tour guide on us, leading everyone around and showing the place off.*"

"I'm glad to hear it. Trev'nor has some supplies and money that he's bringing down to you shortly. It'll be enough to help out for a few days, at least."

"*We'll gladly accept them. Our poor Life Mage is going crazy down here trying to keep the gardens in full production. If Nolan could hop down with Trev'nor, help us establish another garden, we'd take it as a kindness.*"

"I'll ask him."

"*I know you haven't been in there for long, but have you found any genealogy records? I'm very curious why it's named Sha.*"

"You're not the only one. It can't be a coincidence." As both men looked at her in confusion, she explained in a quick undertone, "Sha is one of the more famous bloodlines for Chahiran magicians. We have to assume that this place was founded by a Chahiran ancestor."

Danyal's eyebrows shot into his hairline. "Truly?"

Becca nodded, then shrugged her ignorance, as even she didn't have a theory on how it had happened. At least, not right now.

"*So nothing yet, eh? Well, it's early days, surely you'll discover something soon.*"

"That's the hope. Actually, Raile, I called with a question of my own. I have a son up here that's missing his mother, and Llona says we've rescued her. Commander, what's her name?"

"Kamira," Talib answered, nearly on the edge of his seat as he watched the mirror in her hands.

"*Kamira. Sounds familiar, but give me a moment.*"

Knowing very well that he must be checking the student roster, Becca waited patiently, listening to the sounds of shuffling feet and paper rustling.

"*Aha. There she is. Oh? She's not in the magical section, but the general section.*"

Becca grinned like the cat that not only knew where the cream was, but how to get into it. "Is she now. Raile, I'm about to take a student away from you."

"*Now that's not nice, Becca. I don't steal your toys.*"

"Kamira's son is the newly appointed commander of Sha Watchtower. I can't give him extended leave from this position, I need him here, so she's going to have to come up."

"*Ah. That does make more sense to do it that way. My records indicate she has no other family here, either. Shall I send her up?*"

Becca eyed Talib and while he didn't openly fidget, the man looked fit to burst out of his skin. He did not have the patience to wait until the morning. All things considered, Becca didn't blame him one iota. "No. Commander Talib will come down to fetch her with Trev'nor. But do cue her up that he's coming."

"I certainly will. Is the commander listening in?"

"He is."

"Then, Commander, is there any message you want me to tell her while she's waiting?"

"Tell her," he choked out, "that I'm finally making good on my promise."

Becca didn't need to be a soothsayer to imagine what a five year old would tell his mother before she was taken from him. Just imagining the scene set her blood to boiling.

"I'll do that. Becca, anything else?"

She blinked, banishing the mental image, focusing once more on the conversation. "Give Trev'nor an expense report, if you have one, so we can set up an annual budget for you. Right now I have no idea what your expenses are."

"I won't be able to pull that together tonight, but I'll start in on it. For now, let me go track down Kamira."

"Thanks, Raile." Putting the mirror down, she asked Talib tartly, "What are you still sitting here for? Go! And I don't want to see you for at least three days."

Standing, he gave her the deepest bow she'd ever received. "Thank you. So very much." Standing again, he saluted her, tears standing in his eyes. "Warlord, request permission for leave for three days."

"Permission granted." Becca saluted back then shooed him out with a hand. After he left—and it sounded like he sprinted once he reached the hall—Becca slammed a fist against the desk. "There's too much heartbreak in this country, Rahim. It makes me mad."

Standing, he caught her arm and guided her out of the

chair, drawing her in for a tight hug. Needing it, she hugged him back, letting the solid thump-thump of his heart soothe her ire.

"It's alright, Becca," he whispered against the top of her head. "There's indeed heartbreak here, but you're fixing it. I have faith that when you're done, this people will be able to grasp happiness once more."

The universal way to make friends was service. Trev'nor had learned this at five years old and the lesson had only become more firmly cemented in his mind as the years rolled by. Sha Watchtower's citizens proved no exception as they watched their new rulers improve their city. Trev'nor and Nolan worked steadily in every clear patch of ground inside the walls, putting in gardens and orchards, water canals and irrigation systems, then went outside the city and continued the project. Because of Libendorf's border nearby, Trev'nor built another wall around the new garden to protect it from possible attack, something he hadn't bothered to do in previous cities. He also constructed several landing pads for the dragon pair that now claimed this place as home.

Citizens came out and watched, eyes round as saucers to see sprouting green things jutting out of what used to be infertile soil. Their smiles came more readily as Becca called in daily showers, not only watering the gardens but topping off the water reservoirs. The first time that someone came to Nolan, asking questions about the plants growing, Trev'nor knew they'd won half the battle.

It took six days to get everything done to their satisfaction. Becca made her new mayor, commander, and dragons faithfully swear they'd call the minute something went wrong, although truthfully Trev'nor didn't anticipate trouble. Not from this lot. They seemed more than competent and had things well in hand, although of course they were still adjusting to the new rules.

With relative faith that Sha Watchtower was more or less situated, they left on the afternoon of the seventh day to return to Riyu. Trev'nor still had gardens to plant in that city, irrigation canals to build, and to be honest he had left Jashni half-done. More quality time in the dirt was required for both cities before they could move on to Von.

Which suited him right down to the ground, no pun intended.

They flew back to Riyu at a casual pace, enjoying the coolness of the night air and the general quiet of the rushing wind. Trev'nor loved people, he truly did, but even he sometimes needed a break from them.

Knowing very well the dragon could hear him in this gentle current, Trev'nor pitched his voice forward. "What do you think, Garth? Are the people happy with their new rulers yet?"

"Confused," the dragon corrected. "Happily confused."

That was probably the most perfect summary to date. Confused at the generosity, happy to receive it, not certain if it would continue. That's what this people as a whole felt. Trev'nor cautioned himself, again, to give it time. They'd come around at their own pace when they realized that their new rulers were genuine and this sudden peace and posterity would last.

"Fledgling."

Trev'nor leaned forward in the saddle, the pommel digging into his abdomen. "What?"

"Might be trouble," the dragon cautioned, voice rumbling low, head tilting a little downward toward the ground. "No lights in city."

That didn't sound good at all. "Absolutely none?"

"Some lights in buildings. Tall buildings. Nowhere else."

When Trev'nor had left Riyu, they'd still been in a celebratory mood with lanterns lining the streets. When did that change? Was there trouble in his new city? Surely not an invasion, he would have heard about it before now. "Enemies attacking?"

"No," Garth denied, voice going deeper before he let out a sonorous call, the tone echoing and questioning.

An answer came back in slightly shorter bursts before ending in a long, haunting note. Trev'nor didn't speak Dragonese, but he recognized the tones of unease well enough. "There's trouble?"

"People attacking people. Clan stopping it but people scared. Hide in houses."

People attacking people? "You mean thieves? Bad men?"

"Yes."

Oh glory. Was Riyu heavily infiltrated with criminals? Why hadn't anyone reported this before? Trev'nor could only think of one reason and he dearly hoped he was wrong.

They landed on top of the battlements, one of the clearer spots in the city, and Trev'nor hopped down. He barely had his feet on stone before he could hear Becca striding for the nearest sentry, hiding in the watchtower. "Soldier!"

Tentatively peeking out, the soldier found the dragons either peacefully standing by or taking off again, and gathered the courage to come out with a lantern in hand. Coming to attention in front of her, he snapped out a salute. "Yes, Warlord?"

Becca returned the salute automatically even as she demanded, "Where are the street lights? Why is the city dark?"

The soldier gave her the blankest look of the century. "Street lights?"

Trev'nor came up to stand at her side. "Street lights, man, to keep the streets lit to discourage thieves. Doesn't Riyu have those? And why are the dragons reporting multiple muggings and attacks throughout the city?"

Becca's head snapped around, eyes wide. "They're what?"

"That's what Garth told me." Trev'nor shrugged, indicating that was the extent of his knowledge. "Fifth Guard—I'm sorry, what's your name?"

"Jahid, Warlord." Giving him another salute, the man dutifully answered, although he looked bemused doing it, "Riyu has no street lights, Warlords. The previous warlord deemed them a waste of time and money and had them torn out. Crime's always been a part of the night life here. We stop it when we see it, but for the most part, people stay home after sunset with their doors stoutly locked. It's safer that way. The only exception is during festivals."

And there it was, Trev'nor suspicions confirmed. He hated it when he was right sometimes. "Are you serious? The underworld literally has control of this city at night? It's that bad?"

Jahid spread his free hand in a helpless gesture. "It's too big for us to patrol, Warlord. We do our best, but…."

Becca growled, looking ready to call lightning down as soon as she figured out the target. "I just knew taking this city went too smoothly."

Snorting, Nolan reminded her, "You had to fight an army with three mages, three dragons, and a drowned cat in order to take this city."

"Semantics," she dismissed with a wave of the hand. "Well, this is ridiculous, I'm not going to let criminals run amok in my city. Shad?"

Their mentor popped around and into view, a smile of anticipation on his face. "Do I get to go around beating up all the bad men? Please? Pretty please with a cherry on top?"

Becca pointed to the city in general and intoned grandly, "Go forth."

Beaming, he bounced forward to give her a hug. "You're my favorite sister ever."

"Shad. I'm your only sister."

"Semantics." With a grin, he disappeared down the stairs in a flash, calling cheerfully as he went, "Don't wait up!"

Trev'nor idly thought of suggesting that someone should go with him. Then thought better of it. "Becca, I'm not sure if this is your short-term solution or if you released Shad on them because he was driving you crazy."

"He pestered me the entire flight here about not getting any action for seven whole days," she complained, "and how he was bored, and why couldn't I just send him to Von, he'd fight for us, etcetera."

Right. So she really had turned him loose on the unsuspecting underworld just to get him out of her hair. Trev'nor could almost feel sorry for the criminals, especially with Shad in that hyper mood. Then again, a tired Shad was a well-behaved Shad. A few criminals were worth the sacrifice. "I'm not arguing, he'll be much happier for the next few days. But permanent solution, that's not going to cut it."

"I know," she sighed, drooping a little in exhaustion.

Nolan put an arm around both of their shoulders, leading them back around to their dragons. "Sleep tonight. Shad has this well in hand. We can come up with a plan tomorrow. Thank you, Fifth Jahid. You can resume your post."

"Of course, Raja."

Trev'nor didn't like the idea of criminals running about unchecked, but saw sense in Nolan's advice. Truly, he couldn't come up with a quick fix right this minute anyway. It would take time to fix this problem. Sleep would be best.

Trev'nor slept soundly, enough to give the dead a run for their money, and rose a little later than normal. Sometime while he was gone, a batman had been appointed to him—although he didn't know who—as all of his clothes were laundered and hanging smartly up in the armoire. Someone had even fitted another uniform for him, and he chose to wear that, as he needed to get into the habit of wearing one anyway. Re-braiding his hair took a few minutes, then he was out the door and ready for breakfast.

As usual, he missed the early breakfast rush in the dining hall, and only a few officers still lingered. He found Danyal at the end of a table with a steaming mug in his hand and a report in the other. Trev'nor took a moment to really look at the man and found himself pleased at the changes he saw. When they'd first met Danyal, he'd been a man hardened by sun and harsh conditions, worn thin from life. Now he'd gained some weight, looking healthy instead of gaunt, radiating contentment even while sitting there reading what was probably a very boring report. Becca likely had something to do with that.

Smiling at the thought, he fetched himself some breakfast and went to join the man, sliding onto the bench with graceful ease. "Morning, Danyal."

"Morning, Raja." Setting the report down, he greeted his warlord with a smile. "You slept well?"

"I did, thank you. You're up earlier than I expected."

"I do not sleep much," Danyal explained. "I did pass Riicshaden on the way in. He looked a little tired, but pleased, and there were no injuries. He said that he located one of the major gangs last night and dealt with them."

Of course he had. "Then he had fun. Good. A bored Shad is a terrible thing. I take it he's sleeping now?"

"Yes, or at least that's what he indicated to me."

The man had been up all night fighting, after all. "I think we were supposed to have a war council today and discuss what to do about Von, but I guess we need to concentrate on this problem first, catch up on anything that happened while we were out, and think about conquest tomorrow."

"Likely a better plan, Raja," Danyal agreed placidly, "as I doubt anyone is up to the discussion today. You all worked very hard and with very little rest in Sha. Take today easy."

Trev'nor could feel the exhaustion pulling at him, even though he'd slept fine last night, and had to concede to good counsel. "I think I will. I noticed I acquired a batman at some point. Who is it?"

"Sergeant Mose." Mouth quirked, Danyal chided him gently, "Don't look so surprised. The man thinks highly of you and when I sent word out that you needed a batman, I had more than one volunteer. I understand a wrestling match went into deciding the matter. Mose won."

Trev'nor hadn't thought he had enough fans in the ranks to garner that kind of competition. "I'm flattered, truly, but also confused. I mean, Mose is a man of rank after all."

"A batman actually has a higher rank and better pay than a noncommission soldier," Danyal explained patiently. "He's far better off in this position and it gives him security. He can now invest in a family and put them in a fixed place by serving you."

Oh. Ohhhh. That was certainly interesting. "Well, I'm certainly happy to have him. Mose is one of my favorite people."

"I had a feeling that was the case. I'm glad it worked out this way, then."

"So am I. While we're speaking of personal things… Danyal." Facing the man squarely, he met those dark eyes with his own and tried to make it clear how sincerely he meant every word. "I'm not sure if you realize that all of us are pleased you're courting Becca."

The man's polished professional exterior slipped and his lips parted in bemusement. "You are? I would think…."

"What? That a soldier wouldn't be a proper fit for her?" Trev'nor snorted. "Danyal, I think you're laboring under some misconceptions, here. Nolan aside, none of us are from prestigious families. Becca's family are poor fishermen. I'm from a long line of blacksmiths. Shad's family were all soldiers. Trust me, we don't look at you and find you lacking. Our backgrounds are the same."

Danyal's mouth moved, searching for words, and only producing a croaking noise. He didn't seem to know what to do with this information and he sat there pondering it for a long moment. "Is that why she so easily accepted me?"

"Part of it, I'm sure. And why she went through considerable trouble to make sure that Khobunter's customs changed so you knew you *could* approach her. But Danyal, I want you to understand that being the partner to a mage like her is going to be true work in some ways."

"I don't understand," Danyal admitted. "You think that the mage part of her requires more of my attention than her warlord status?"

"Yes." Trev'nor abruptly became glad he started this conversation. Apparently Danyal needed to be clued in on a few facts. "Let me explain. You've seen Becca work her magic several times now. You know how distracted she gets while her head is literally up in the clouds. Well, all mages are that way. We all have familiars for that reason, to help protect us while we're focused on something else. Becca's familiar is Tail, but he's ancient as the hills and I honestly don't give him another five years. Maybe not even two. When she loses him, she'll lose a major helper and support."

Danyal's expression lit up in understanding. "I'll have to be that for her."

"Exactly. I'm sure Cat will help, but Becca needs more help than most mages, due to the nature of her magic." Trev'nor hesitated to say anything else, some of this was personal, but the man did need to know. "Did she tell you that she is the last of her bloodline?"

Shaking his head, Danyal protested, "But she has family."

"None of them carry the talent for magic. She is literally the last. The Gardeners told her at eight years old that if she failed to have children, if she died before doing so, the talent for Weather Mages died with her." Trev'nor leaned his elbows against the table's surface, voice going rough with intensity. "Danyal, listen to me. We absolutely cannot lose her. The reason why she, and she alone, has an appointed Guardian is for this reason. You must also understand that if you choose to marry her, you absolutely must have children. It's not an option. This world cannot afford to lose the Weather Mages. Khobunter looks like this—" Trev'nor gave a general wave of the hand to indicate the country surrounding them "—because we had none for two hundred plus years."

Staring back at him, Danyal sat still as a statue, barely breathing. The weight of what Trev'nor told him settled on him visibly, not smothering, but deeply impactful all the same. Then he took in a shuddering breath, and another, accepting it. "I understand. Thank you for telling me, Trev'nor."

Delighted the man had finally used his name, Trev'nor

grinned back at him. "You're welcome. Don't worry, I'll guard her too. She's one of my best friends, after all. I just thought you should know. I have a feeling she hasn't told you everything yet because she's a little afraid of scaring you off. Becca's somewhat complicated."

Danyal actually rolled his eyes a little at this. "Life is complicated. I do not find her to be so."

Yes, those two would be just fine. Trev'nor felt infinitely better for their conversation and finally focused on breakfast, a flaky pastry of some sort that melted in his mouth and made him regret only grabbing two.

Trying to sound casual, and failing miserably, Danyal inquired, "Perhaps you can tell me a little of Chahiran wedding customs?"

So the man really liked her well enough to propose? Trev'nor swallowed the bite in his mouth, trying to keep a serious face on. He really wanted to cackle madly, as getting Becca married off would free him of people's expectations, but that might scare Danyal off. Better to cackle internally. "I'd be pleased to. Where do you want me to start?"

Becca had no idea what had gotten into Danyal, but she liked it. He'd followed her after lunch to the rooftop and then, without any care for who might see them, pulled her into his lap, loosely hugging her around the waist. This from a man who could barely bring himself to hold her hand in public, too aware of his position as her subordinate to do anything more than that.

Leaning more firmly against his chest, she told him seriously, "This cuddling on the job is very nice. I approve."

Chuckling, he pressed a quick kiss against her forehead, startling a blink out of her. He'd never done that before in public either. Seriously, what had gotten into him? "Focus, my Mage," he chided teasingly.

"You start cuddling me and then expect me to focus on clouds?" The man had lost his mind.

"Yes, I do."

Becca had not been around Nolan this long without learning some negotiation skills. "Fine, I'll work, but only if you tell me what's gotten into you today. I want to make sure it happens again."

His teasing mood sobered a little, voice more serious against her temple. "Trev'nor spoke to me after breakfast this morning."

Not sure where this was going, but mentally planning to kill her best friend if he'd said something unnecessary, she prompted, "Oh?"

"He told me several things I needed to know. I thought you were from a prestigious family until he told me otherwise."

Turning in his hold, she gave him a dumbfounded look. "When did I ever give you *that* impression?"

"You walk through this world with the confidence of a queen and the fighting prowess of a lion," he answered with a proud expression on his face. "What else was I to think?"

"Well, when you put it that way…" she demurred, getting another chuckle from him. "But truly, you didn't know? I thought I'd mentioned it at some point."

"You only told me that Riicshaden had to rescue you from southern Chahir. I didn't know your family are fishermen."

Ah. Whoops. "My bad. What else did he say?"

"He explained how important it is to protect a mage while they are working," Danyal continued seriously. "I didn't realize you were the last Weather Mage, or the importance of having an appointed Guardian. He also reassured me that everyone is quite delighted that I'm courting you, which is flattering."

Now his courage in being touchy-feely in public made more sense. It looked like Becca wouldn't have to murder her best friend after all, which was a relief, as she didn't want to run this country by herself. "Then are you up here to steal hugs or learn how to protect me while I'm working?"

Danyal blinked at her, the epitome of innocence. "Both, naturally."

"I approve of your multi-tasking," she informed him with a smirk. "Alright, then, first lesson. When I turn my face up to the sky, you'll know for sure that I'm working.

I have basically no situational awareness when I'm using magic. I need someone to watch my back."

"Understood. What else?"

"Let me walk you through the types of clouds, so you can recognize when I'm working and what kind of storm is heading your direction. I might not always have the time to give you a full explanation before diving in." Turning back around, she situated herself more comfortably in his lap before pointing toward the sky. "For instance, the clouds up there are cumulus clouds and they're a natural byproduct of clear days when the sun heats the ground directly below. I rarely create these and usually it's just for shade. Then you have stratus clouds."

The lesson continued, Danyal sometimes asking questions, sometimes repeating what she had said to make sure he had it right. Becca found it strange, this lesson, as she had never attempted to explain anything about weather before to another person or teach how her magic worked. Then she realized that this might very well be good practice for the future, when she had children of her own.

"So these cumulonimbus clouds, they're the ones you use for heavy rainstorms?"

Becca nodded, her hands gliding up as she steadily pulled on a weather current heading their direction. "Right. You can see the edge of them now, approaching from the west. I don't normally have to form every single storm, sometimes I find one over the ocean and gently herd it our direction. It's less work and magic on my end—" Frowning, she glanced towards the stairs. "Is someone calling me?"

Danyal cocked his head, listening. "I think so." He gently lifted her up, freeing himself, then headed to the top of the staircase. "Ah, Serg—forgive me, Batman Mose, what is it?"

"Sir, is Raya Becca up there with you?" Mose sounded

completely out of breath, as he should be, if he just sprinted up five stories of stairs.

"She is," Danyal confirmed, voice sharpening. "What's the situation?"

Mose chose to come up the rest of the stairs, seeking and finding Becca, before reporting, "Raya, Commander, we just got an emergency message from Ascalon, addressed directly to the Raya and Rajas, and Raja Trev'nor urged me to find you with all speed and meet him in the war room."

She did not like the sound of this at all. Pushing up to her feet, she rushed past both men, taking the stairs as quickly as she dared. Becca didn't run anywhere if she could help it—mostly because she was a slow runner—but she made an exception in this instance. By the time she arrived three stories down, she felt more than a little winded, and paused just inside the room to catch her breath.

Trev'nor, Nolan, Shad, and even Dunixan were already there. Becca knew the other warlord was due to arrive next week, to help them plan for Von, but she hadn't expected him quite this quickly. He'd had a lot to settle in his own territory after the last battle. Had someone called him in or had he just decided to fly in early? With a nod of acknowledgement to him, she turned an expectant look on both boys.

"It's from Xiaolang," Nolan answered, as if she'd asked him aloud. "A private message to us, and bless him for it. He's received a report that Rowe has gone to Ascalon to ask for reinforcements, to prepare for our invasion. They've apparently offered a non-aggression treaty, trade concessions, and the like."

"That does not sound good." Becca found the nearest chair and fell into it, absolutely certain she would need to be sitting down for the rest of this conversation. Danyal came to stand just behind and to the side of her chair, his hand resting on her shoulder. "Does he say what Ascalon's reaction to this is?"

"Mostly confusion," Trev'nor responded, waving said letter in the air. "Rowe has not been the best neighbors, although not actively hostile, and have never made any friendly overtures before this. Ascalon doesn't know what to make of this sudden offer and they're not highly inclined to take it, all things considered."

Nolan shrugged, spreading his hands palm up. "Who can blame them? Ascalon's policy before has been to leave Khobunter's issues up to Khobunter, stay out of their politics altogether, and that practice has served them well. But they might be tempted by this offer if it means finally getting some peace from their northern neighbor."

"I don't like that theory," Becca informed him, her mind already whirling.

Shaking his head, Nolan took the seat next to her and admitted, "I don't either. Unfortunately it's a possibility. Xiaolang makes two points in his letter we need to address. First, we've not made any official stance to the other countries about what we want or who we are. It makes Ascalon especially nervous, but we have to consider Warwick as well, possibly Osmar and Q'atal. They're all neighbors and I think we need to meet them, reassure them, before Rowe turns us into an enemy."

And the day had started out so well, too. Becca put her mental lamentation aside and tried to think three steps ahead. "Shad, when you saw Xiaolang before, did he mention any of this to you?"

"He did," Shad admitted, still looking a little tired from his all night battle. "He didn't think it would come to a head this quickly, though."

Hence why Shad hadn't mentioned it before now? Likely

the case.

Trev'nor pointed to the map on the table. "I know we wanted to tackle Von, but they're not making any moves right now, and Rowe is. I think we better handle Rowe next."

"Agreed." Becca rubbed at her temples, mind whirling at high speed. "We need time, I think. I say we send a message back to Xiaolang, ask him to delay the talks if he can, and give us the time to get down there. Maybe send a message to Warwick, Osmar, and Q'atal stating our intention to meet in Ascalon for diplomatic talks."

"Get them to meet us all at once rather than take the time to visit multiple countries?" Trev'nor leaned back in his chair, staring at the ceiling. "It's certainly more expedient that way."

"Worded right, letters of invitation to meet in Ascalon will work," Dunixan put in. "But I advise that both of you go. Especially since you are co-rulers, they'll want to meet both of you and they will likely ask you questions that you can't answer without the other being present."

Shad shook his head, disagreeing. "All three of them need to go. Nolan can make it clear that Chahir is aware of what's happening in Khobunter and supports the new leaders. They'll need that additional support behind them. Besides, he's more versed in politics, he'll know how to play ambassador."

"Truth," Nolan concurred without an ounce of false modesty. "But that leaves us with a sticky problem. I don't feel that we can leave Riyu just yet in the current leadership's hands. There's still a few major problems to solve and letting them stew for another week while we straighten all of this out will just leave the wounds to fester."

Dunixan raised a hand. "I'll stay."

Becca looked at him, then felt like kicking herself for

overlooking the obvious. Of course, Dunixan was a perfect choice as a deputy governor. He knew their new laws, the lay of the land, and had the experience to govern. "I'm perfectly fine with that. Trev'nor?"

"No complaints here." Turning to Dunixan, he asked apologetically, "Do you mind fixing things while we're gone? I have solutions for them, just haven't had the time to give orders to the responsible parties yet."

"Brief me on what you want done and I'll take care of it," Dunixan promised with a quick smile. "Don't worry about Riyu, you have enough on your plate."

"Bless you, Dunixan." Becca let out a soft breath of relief. The Gardeners had certainly known what they were doing when they chose this man to help them. An experienced warlord was a blessing straight from the gods in this situation. "Now, how did this message get to us from Xiaolang and can we send a reply back the same way?"

"It came via courier, and it would be too slow to go that route," Nolan answered promptly. "I vote we load the courier on a dragon and fly him back."

"I'd take him down," Trev'nor said apologetically, "but I don't think Ascalon would take that well. And it would rather defeat the purpose."

All true. Becca pondered this for a moment before agreeing slowly, "I think that's our best option. Time is of the essence. Let's do that and pray the man isn't afraid of heights."

Nolan's head turned and he let out a sonorous tone with three sharp clicks in it. Lighting up in a proud smile, he announced to everyone, "Llona volunteered to take him down."

Their best dragon speaker when it came to Solish. Excellent. That would help in many ways. "Ascalon's semi-used to dragons because of Krys and Kaya, right? She won't be in danger?"

"Not a lick, especially not bearing a military courier. She'll be fine," Nolan assured her. "How we'll get messages to the other countries' leaders, that's my question."

"Q'atal you can invite in person," Shad reminded him. "We can contact Krys in Osmar, have him pass along the message. I'm sure Xiaolang knows how to send a message to Warwick through official channels. Send the letter along with the courier with the request it be passed along."

"Send a copy of that message to Ascalon as well," Nolan advised, "so they know what you're saying to another country. They'll be too paranoid to pass it along otherwise, afraid it will indicate them in something they want no part in. We should also politely ask them to play host for this party, since they're neutral ground."

Becca doubted that last part. "Will they? Be willing to, I mean."

"I think so. I hope so, anyway, I don't know how else we'll pull this off." Shad pondered for a moment, rubbing the pads of his fingertips together. "If they won't, Q'atal certainly will. But let's ask Ascalon first. Xiaolang might be able to put a good word in for us, which will go a long way."

There were too many ifs in all of that for Becca's piece of mind. Still, they had to try, and trying cost nothing. Her mind skipped back to the situation in Riyu itself, and Von. Although she hated what she was about to say, she couldn't think of any way around it. Standing, she turned to face Danyal.

He met her eyes levelly, expression saying he already knew.

Taking in a breath, Becca said it anyway. "I need you to stay here, take charge of the army while I'm gone. There's still a good chance Von will take the initiative and come to us."

"I understand, my Warlord. I will do so." His lips twisted a little into a sad frown, and in that she read his own disappointment that he couldn't go with her.

Trev'nor cleared his throat a little to draw their attention. "I think it's high time we properly promote the man so he actually has the authority to run the army. Co-ruler, I put forth the motion to promote Commander Danyal to the rank of First General. Any objections?"

Danyal's mouth opened on an instinctive protest.

Becca rode right over them. "None. Motion carried. General, update your uniform, we'll get the paperwork sorted out before we leave."

Spluttering, he stared at her, then jerked around to stare at Trev'nor. "You can't just skip ranks like that!"

"Just did," Trev'nor observed, amused.

"It was long overdue anyway," Shad agreed flippantly. "Stop fighting it, man, they like you too much. You're going to be a general no matter what your argument. I raised that one, I know how stubborn she can be, so I advise you give up the point. Now, we have a lot of messages to write, a courier to toss onto a dragon, and some general housekeeping to do before we can leave. I think the summit should be within the next few days, which doesn't give us a lot of time, but we can't put Ascalon into a difficult position. Delaying even a few days will be hard on them. The sooner we get there, the better."

"Nolan, you write," Becca directed, getting a nod from him in return. "You'll know best how to phrase it anyway. Trev, update Dunixan. I'll handle the military, as usual. Leave in two days, is that our plan?"

Trev'nor winced. "Two days. Busted buckets, I'm not

going to sleep any if you want to leave in two days."

"Sleep when you're dead," Shad advised, not unsympathetically. "Move."

It took roughly twelve hours to fly from Riyu to Ascalon. Since no one thought arriving at night on dragons was a good idea, they broke up the flight a little by going to Rurick and staying overnight there. Trev'nor was more than relieved to find that the soldiers who had returned home at the beginning of their campaign had followed directions to the letter and kept all of the gardens alive. Not just alive, but thriving. They met their leaders with happy smiles and fruits harvested that morning. Nolan found something that dissatisfied him and he went off to plant things in the dying afternoon suns.

Trev'nor was pretty sure it was just an excuse to go play in the dirt after a long flight.

They rose early the next morning, putting on dress uniforms and braiding their hair as tightly as they could to stick under their riding helmets. He'd likely have helmet hair on arrival, but hopefully not too bad.

The morning air heated slowly, the wind whistling around them, taking the edge off so Trev'nor didn't sweat in his very hot formal uniform. The tan color was understandable in this desert, but why on earth did it require him to wear three layers? And the outer coat had considerable bulk to it, making him look far heavier than he actually was.

Interestingly enough, it did not have that effect on Becca's figure. Trev'nor suspected cheating on her end.

When they came within sight of the city, Trev'nor lifted a mirror broach out of his pocket and contacted Asla. Garth obligingly slowed to a mere glide so he could be heard. "Aunt Asla. Aunt Asla?"

"*I'm here, Trev'nor. Have you arrived already?*"

"City just barely came in sight. Can you ask them very nicely not to shoot us down?"

His aunt just laughed. "*Don't worry. Your Uncle Xiaolang already took care of that. He explained to the warlord here that you three are his students and he'd prefer you without any holes.*"

He had? That hadn't been the plan at all. "How did they take the news?"

"*Mixed, I'd say. But you're safe to land and have permission to enter the city.*"

Trev'nor huffed out a breath. "I'll take it. Thanks. We'll land in about fifteen minutes."

"*I'll tell them. See you soon!*"

Connection ended, he put the mirror back in his pocket and waved to the others with thumb in the air, indicating success. At least they'd passed the first hurdle.

Llona shot into the sky seemingly out of nowhere, twirling around Nolan's dragon form in mid-air, as graceful as a dancer. The two of them said something to each other, a happy greeting apparently, as Garth and Cat joined in. She must have been bored to tears waiting on them to arrive.

They didn't land inside the city, of course, there was no room for that, but outside of the gates lay a good clear section of open field. Garth landed gently, wings unfurled for a moment, and he paused there, displaying. Trev'nor rolled his eyes but nothing would keep his dragon from trying to put a healthy dose of fear into people. Ignoring that, Trev'nor creaked a little as he unbuckled himself and slid out of the saddle. Two days of straight flying made him age a decade. Lifting his hands over his head, he stretched upwards, then sideways, then finally with his head to the ground, working out the worst of the kinks.

"Fledgling. Gates open."

Already here, eh? Straightening, he doffed helmet and goggles, stuffing them back into the saddle bags before he went to stand in front of Garth, joining Becca, Nolan, and Shad. Tail looked visibly unfazed by the flight, curled up around Becca's shoulders as usual. If Becca's hair was any indication, they did indeed have helmet hair. He decided that since he couldn't see his own head, he wouldn't worry about it. Besides, these people were all soldiers as well. Surely they wouldn't judge a person's travel-worn appearance too much.

Four people in dress uniform came marching out, with four more guards on both sides in patrol formation. Trev'nor searched and found Xiaolang's figure, giving him a quick smile, then focused on the other three men. Having rarely been in Ascalon before, and certainly never in an official capacity, he didn't know these men by sight. Shad had briefed him, though, even making up a silly limerick so it would stick. How had it gone? Something like:

Long in the face is Svante, his smile has nowhere to go;

He's always fighting with Rada, with the amazing red nose;

Xiaolang of course is with them, wise and mysterious is he;

Which only leaves Vanya, who's lost his hair because of the three.

Becca had begged him to not make any more limericks up because that one didn't even rhyme, but Shad of course only sang it louder, which meant it had been stuck in Trev'nor's head permanently by the first night. He now picked the men out without any trouble, as indeed Councilor Svante had a very thin and depressed look to him, Councilor Rada had one of the ruddiest faces he'd ever seen, and Warlord Vanya was so bald the sunlight glinted off his head.

The men stopped five feet away, close enough to talk, far enough away to snatch a sword free if need be. Trev'nor knew that distance very well. He didn't try to cross it, just smiled and gave them a bow. "Greetings. I'm Warlord Rhebentrev'noren of Trexler and Riyu. This is my co-ruler, Riicbeccaan, our ambassador from Chahir, Prince Vonnolanen, and our military advisor, Riicshaden. But I believe you gentlemen know him already."

"Indeed we do," Vanya acknowledged with a very dark look at Shad. "And I'm still not pleased with his decision to leave, nor have I approved your resignation, Riicshaden."

Shad chuckled but didn't respond, just rocking back and forth on his feet.

Really? Ten years, and Vanya still hoped to win him back?

"I am Warlord Vanya of Ascalon," Vanya responded with cool cordiality. "These are my councilors, Svante, Rada, and De Xiaolang. I believe you know Xiaolang already, however."

Smiling at this repetition of his words, Trev'nor agreed, "We do indeed."

"Tell me," Vanya challenged, a trace of heat entering his words, "which one of your mentors taught you to conquer countries you don't like the politics of?"

The good one. Trev'nor had to bite his tongue to keep from saying that.

"The good one," Shad informed him cheekily.

Fortunately, they had Shad for the improper remarks.

All three of his former students coughed, badly disguising their laughter. Xiaolang didn't bother, his chuckles coming out openly. Head creaking about in degrees, Vanya glared at his military advisor. "I do not find this amusing, Councilor Xiaolang."

Recovering himself, Xiaolang cleared his throat. "I'm aware, Warlord. But unlike you, I know very well how badly these three were provoked into conquering that country. I think you will find that, after you've heard their story, you will be whole-heartedly agreeing with them."

Vanya didn't seem at all sold on this possibility but kept his peace. "Warlords, I bid you enter so that we may discuss matters. I've instructed my men to give your dragons all due hospitality and your companion, Llona, has made sure our accommodations are adequate."

Llona's head came around to bump against Vanya, tail twitching happily. "Vanya nice man. Give cows."

Of course she'd charmed him into feeding her whole cows. Trev'nor rolled his eyes, not even surprised.

Vanya gave her a quick scratch under the chin before pushing himself back upright, restoring his dignity with a jerk of the jacket. "Please follow me."

They marched inside the city, Trev'nor dearly wishing he could snag Xiaolang for five minutes for a debrief and realizing that he likely couldn't. Everyone they passed on the streets stopped and stared, whispering behind their hands, which made his skin crawl a little. Still, he felt no hostility here and Xiaolang would never have let them enter if there was any danger. Of course people would be curious, and talk to each other, there was nothing wrong about that. Trev'nor ignored it as best he could.

Becca skipped two steps to walk right next to him and whispered, "Is my hair as bad as yours is?"

"Probably." And that answered that question.

"I'd dearly love to be a witch right now," she grumbled under her breath.

So would he. He'd barely completed the thought in his head when his hair and clothing abruptly moved, tingling and rapid, settling within seconds. Reaching up, he patted it, but couldn't really feel much of a difference. Giving up, he looked to Becca, then Nolan, finding that everyone looked pristine. Knowing very well who must be behind it, but unable to not look, he turned his head, searching until he found her in the crowd. Then he gave his Aunt Asla a grin, mouthing, 'Thanks!'

She winked back at them, waved, and disappeared back into the crowd.

"It pays to have an aunt that's a witch," Becca approved. "We'll have to thank her later."

"But I liked your scary-hairy looks," Shad bemoaned. "Ow! Bec, not the shins!"

"Will you two stop?" Nolan hissed at them. "You can't have a sibling brawl in the middle of the street, in a foreign country, on your way to a summit meeting!"

"She started it," Shad grumbled petulantly.

Someone nearby snickered at this byplay. Trev'nor shook his head, sighing in resignation, reminding himself that Shad could actually be an adult when he wanted to and everyone in Ascalon was fortunately used to the man. They wouldn't take offense at him here.

In short order they arrived at what apparently would be their meeting hall. It did not look like a government building, rather more an assembly hall, with a U-shaped table in the center of the building and an amphitheater of seats in a half-circle around it. It had no decorations, just gray stone and Ascalon's banners lining the walls every few feet. The place had a cold, echoing feel to it.

He blinked to help adjust his eyes to the relative dimness of the interior. He could hear other people already inside, gathered around the table, but couldn't see around the men in front of them for a clear view.

"Warlords, Remcar-ol, our new neighbors from the north have arrived." Vanya stepped to the side and gestured toward them, making the introductions in a booming voice. "This is Warlord Rhebentrev'noren, Warlord Riicbeccaan, Ambassador Vonnolanen, and Advisor Riicshaden of Khobunter. It is they that have called for this meeting."

And with that said, Vanya sat down.

All his councilors immediately sat as well, Shad following suit on the opposite side, the only area not already claimed. Trev'nor abruptly had no one standing with him except Becca and Nolan, leaving the three of them facing the other rulers with no formalities or guidelines to go off of.

Which, fortunately, Nolan took as his cue. Stepping forward with a smile on his face, he turned first to his right, where Vanya and his group sat. "Thank you, Warlord Vanya, for hosting this. We know it was terribly short notice and we thank you for the kindness. To the Remcar-ol, we greet you. Thank you for coming."

An Meiling and Li Shen both gave a half-bow back to him, wide smiles on their faces. "We are pleased to come," An Meiling assured him.

"Thank you." Turning to the next group, Nolan inclined his head. "Warlord Casimir, you have journeyed a long way from Osmar. I am very glad to see you, as we did not know if our message would reach you in time."

"Your friend Haikrysen flew directly to me to make sure

I received your invitation," Casimir responded, his black beard so thick one couldn't see his mouth. "I was impressed with his urgency and had him fly me here. Exhilarating experience, that. I trust, young Ambassador, that this will be worth my time."

"On that, sir, you shall not be disappointed," Nolan assured him wryly. "Warlord Gaidar, you honor us as well. We were especially anxious to speak with Warwick and meet with you, considering you share a border with Khobunter."

Gaidar, lean as an alley cat, spoke with the depth and volume of a mountain. "I, too, am very anxious to speak with you. I was glad to receive the invitation to this meeting."

"Hopefully by doing so, we can put many fears to rest. You all are familiar with mages, and the oaths we take, so you no doubt wonder what drove us to conquer Khobunter. If you would care to listen, I will relate the tale." No one spoke, all eyes riveted on Nolan. Seeing this, he took a deep breath, and began.

Trev'nor watched faces more than he listened, trying to decipher how people took their story. The Remcar-ol were by far the easiest to read, dismay written over every line and gesture, despite them knowing most of the tale already. Gaidar kept his hand over his mouth, hiding half of his face, and his eyes stayed narrowed the entire time. Vanya's expression gave nothing away, still as a statue, although his clenched fist on the tabletop gave some clue how he felt on the matter. The skin was white, he held on so hard. Casimir looked perturbed, either by the lawlessness of Khobunter, or their own actions, Trev'nor couldn't tell.

Nolan must have been rehearsing this in his head on the way in, as he didn't give the winding tale they'd told their mentors, but a much more truncated version that focused on what had been done to them, their own motivations, and then a succinct summary of each battle afterwards, ending at Riyu.

When he ended, Trev'nor took a half-step forward, giving his friend's voice a break. "I know that was a lot to take in. Are there any questions?"

Casimir lifted a pinky finger, summoning his attention. "I have one, young Warlord. When all of this first occurred, and you won free, why did you not call for help?"

"We did," Trev'nor protested mildly. "Of the one politically neutral power available to us. And the dragons came."

"By saying this," Vanya finally showed some emotion, expression shrewd, "are you saying that you have no intention of dragging other nations into Khobunter's power struggles?"

"I will certainly do my best to avoid doing so," Trev'nor responded honestly. "Truthfully, sir, Khobunter has enough politics going on within its borders. The last thing we need is another political player in the mix."

"You say that," Casimir argued, "but you have the Prince of Chahir as your ambassador."

"Chahir's interests lie solely in rescuing our descendants that have been enslaved," Nolan responded smoothly. "We have no other interest in Khobunter aside from that. I am here to safeguard that intention and to help as a mage."

"So Chahir will not be offering any support other than your services?" Vanya asked doubtfully.

"And a few teachers for those rescued magicians that need training," Nolan tacked on, not bothered by these semi-accusations, a permanent half-smile on his face. "That is the extent of Chahir's support in this endeavor. When they are done, I will leave and return to my home country."

Vanya finally spoke. "That is an interesting stance for

Chahir to take. Ambassador Vonnolanen informs us that you did not conquer Dunixan, but instead took Warlord Dunixan as an ally. Why him and not the other Warlords?"

"There are certain conditions that a warlord must agree to in order to become our ally," Becca explained, her voice pitched a little louder than usual to be heard. "First, they must free all of the slaves and hand them over to us. Second, they must change their laws to the ones we issue and adhere to them. Third, they must accept us as their rulers. If they do all of this, we allow them to keep their positions as warlord of that province. Warlords Riyu and Trexler found this to be intolerable conditions and fought instead."

The other warlords stirred, speaking to their own advisors, words indistinguishable but tone indicating that even they found this list of demands to be a bit much. And listed out like that, it was, but no one could argue that Khobunter didn't need an overhaul in leadership.

Gaidar lifted his voice to be heard above everyone else. "Dunixan agreed to this? Why?"

"For two reasons," Becca answered again. "First, he had seen with his own eyes what happened to a province after we took control of it. We install irrigation systems, gardens, water reservoirs, and change the economy of a city so the people are no longer living on the brink of poverty. Dunixan saw that we are trying to build in Khobunter, not destroy it, and he wanted that same future for his own province. His second reason, or so he confided to me, was that he was very tired of being in constant fear of attack from his neighbors. He wants peace in his lifetime and he felt that by allying himself with us, he'd finally see it."

An Meiling stood, drawing attention to herself, smiling at the three at the head of the table. "May I make a comment? Thank you. Since the new warlords have taken control of

Trexler, we have observed a noticeable difference in the people. The threat coming from that side of the border has disappeared altogether and we've actually established a very satisfactory trade agreement with the nearest city. We of Q'atal do not approve of wars or fighting, but I certainly can approve of how they are running the country once they have control of it. I'm perfectly delighted with my new neighbors."

Trev'nor wanted to go hug the woman. He sent her a mental hug and knew she'd felt it when she gave him a quick wink as she resumed her seat.

Casimir regarded her for a moment before speaking, a slight frown on his face. "Forgive me, but aren't you directly connected with two of their mentors?"

"I am," she agreed equably, not bothered by this statement. "I also had no idea what they were up to until Warlord Trev'nor showed up on my doorstep with almost five hundred rescued slaves in tow, asking for help."

"Help you gave," Casimir stated neutrally, his words not even a question.

"Of course. He had people with him in dire need of help. He did not ask for our aid in fighting, we did not offer it, and the only assistance we've supplied is serving as a midway point for traveling purposes." An Meiling faced him down with all of the aloofness of an ice queen. "You realize that he could have asked for more than that and we would have done our best to support him."

Casimir spread an open palm, accepting her statement although he didn't verbally agree to it. "Warlord Rhebentrev'noren, Warlord Riicbeccan, I would dearly like to hear what your ultimate goal is."

"To restore Khobunter to the country it once was," Trev'nor responded promptly. "I realize no one fully understands what I mean by that, and I'll try to explain, but be patient with me. It's a little complicated. When we first freed ourselves in Rurick, we did some research into the culture and history of the country. We did a more extensive job of it in Trexler and discovered that the original laws of Khobunter were quite fair. The original government worked well and every record we could find indicates that the people thrived under that system. The laws were corrupted some hundred years ago to justify conquering Rheben and turning its occupants into slaves, then twisted further after that into the obscene mess it is now. What we are doing is restoring Khobunter back to its original laws and government."

Gaidar's eyebrows lifted in mild surprise. "Why not copy a governmental system and set of laws you already know? Chahir, or Hain's, for instance."

"We respect the culture of Khobunter," Becca explained patiently, leaning slightly on the table with her fingertips in order to see him better. Both Trev'nor and Nolan blocked her view with the way they stood. "On a fundamental level, they're a good people, they've just had some very bad leaders the past several decades. We don't want to turn them into a copy of some other country, but to be true to their heritage. It's far easier to reset them into laws they once had, something that's half-familiar, rather than force them into something brand new. It would be a very uncomfortable fit, like ill-sized shoes."

"Our second goal," Trev'nor tacked on, "is to restore the land of Khobunter to what it should be. The desert it is now is not natural. We're working steadily to fix that, recondition the soil to accept water, plants, and of course Becca brings in a steady stream of rainstorms to help water it all."

Vanya's jaw dropped and for the first time the man lost his cool aplomb. "You want to turn an entire *country* into some sort of magical garden?"

Trev'nor grinned at him. "Yup. It's going to take us a while, probably a lifetime, but we've got a good start on the project."

No one knew how to take this statement. Even the Remcar-ol were taken aback in surprise.

With a shake of the head, Casimir moved past this point. "Your goals are admirable, certainly. And after you are done conquering Khobunter, will you turn your full attention to this large-scale project of yours?"

Trev'nor took that to mean, 'after you've gotten a taste of conquering, you sure you're not going to turn your eye onto your neighbors?' "We will. Well, that and governing Khobunter itself, of course. I'll be heartily glad when all the fighting is done, personally. I'm more of a builder by nature. This fighting ill-suits me."

Vanya accepted this with a provisional nod. "And what of your co-ruler? Warlord Riicbeccan, do you feel the same?"

"I do. Gentlemen." She planted a hand on one hip, expression one of exaggerated patience. "You do all remember that I'm a Balancer? That it's my job to literally fix the weather patterns of this *world*? I'm running a country in my spare time, here, and I need sleep at some point. One country is enough for me to manage, thank you very much, I don't want any more than that."

Trust Becca to bluntly state what everyone else was dancing around.

"Well." Gaidar regarded her with open amusement. "That was refreshingly honest and frank. Thank you, Warlord. I think you've addressed most of our fears, and while I find the concept of three teenagers conquering and ruling a country to be unorthodox, you're apparently doing a decent job at it. At the very least, you're doing better than your predecessors, and that's an improvement I'm happy to accept. I only have one more question that I need answered by you. What will you do about the remaining two provinces?"

Becca glanced at him, and Trev'nor signaled to her silently that he'd take this one. "We always send a message to the warlord ahead of time, listing out our intentions and demands, and give them a chance to negotiate with us. Honestly, Warlord Gaidar, we'd prefer to not fight if we don't have to. Khobunter's sand has soaked up enough blood, I think."

"I happen to agree." Gaidar relaxed back into his chair, body language more comfortable than before. "Thank you for the frank answers, Warlords. I am content with them."

Vanya cleared his throat. "I agree with my brother Warlord, but I do have an additional question. I wonder at the timing and urgency of this meeting. Why now?"

Nolan took this one, voice smooth and unhurried. "We received a report that Warlord Rowe had reached out to you, offering a peace treaty in return for troops. We did not want to drag another country into Khobunter's affairs or encourage the possibility of another battle."

"So by coming here, speaking to us, you hope to convince us to leave Rowe up to you," Casimir summarized, very careful to keep any inflection out of his voice and face. Nothing about his reaction indicated how he felt on the matter.

Trev'nor really wished people would just state what they felt in negotiations, but apparently that was some major no-no in politics. He found it frustrating trying to read the man. "I came here hoping to prove to you that I'll be a good neighbor. I'm not interested in more conflict. Rowe is extending a hand out to you, trying to convince you that they won't attack in the future, that they'll be a better neighbor than I will. It's not true. I hope to prevent all of you from being dragged into our war by believing in that lie."

"The Warlords of Khobunter are willing to hammer out peace and trade agreements at this summit meeting," Nolan announced to the table in general. "They have no desire for further conflict, certainly not with any of you. My question to all of you is this: Will you accept Rowe's offer? Or will you choose the one we bring before you?"

If there was one thing Garth hated about his job, it was the politics. The Trasdee Evondit Orra lived to make his life difficult, and while he got better at dealing with them as he grew older, he'd never learned to enjoy the cat and mouse game he played with them.

Which was why, as he stared at the report in his hands, the selfish part of him really wanted to ignore it. He'd expected this for some time, was in fact surprised it took this long for them to act, but finally the notification came through that the Trasdee Evondit Orra was dispatching two of its members to detain Trev'nor, Nolan, and Becca with the intent to try them for ethical violations.

For a moment, he didn't feel like he was in his chair, in his office, in an academy he'd built from the ground up. Just for a moment, he was back to being sixteen and faced with a council of strangers he knew precious little of, with no control over his magic, in a foreign land he didn't understand. Garth remembered that feeling all too well, and it left a bitter aftertaste on his tongue.

The office door opened and his wife stepped through, their daughter on one hip, gnawing on her favorite stuffed owl. Chatta had her mouth open to say or ask something, but when she saw his expression, it visibly changed. "What's wrong?"

Lifting the report up in illustration, he said succinctly. "Trasdee Evondit Orra."

"Oh no, are they finally going after the kids?" Chatta hurried around to his side, bending her neck to read the report sideways. "I wonder why now?"

"I'm wondering that myself. It could be good timing for them, seeing as how all three of them are currently not in Khobunter."

She looked confused for a second, then snapped her fingers. "Right. The summit meeting in Ascalon started this morning. They're very quick to react, aren't they?"

"They've had three days warning that the meeting would be in Ascalon, after all. Enough time to prepare and head this direction." Barely. Garth didn't doubt that was the reason, though. The Trasdee Evondit Orra did not have the guts to go into Khobunter after those three, not with the power they currently wielded in the country.

He hated the whole situation but wasn't quite sure what track to take. His students had proven to the world they could take care of themselves. The Gardeners had validated their right to be in Khobunter, doing exactly what they were doing. Garth was no longer a Balancer, not really their teacher anymore, with no real right to interfere in any of this. They'd asked him for support, nothing more, which he'd happily given. Shouldn't he respect their independence?

Chatta regarded him with a knowing look. "You're going to head them off."

Groaning, he let his head thump against the desk. "In my head, I understand that this isn't my battle. But...."

"But your heart has rebelled and you're going anyway," Chatta finished neatly, not even surprised.

Lifting his head, he looked at his beautiful wife, who

always seemed to know what he was going to do before he could actually get around to doing it. "I just feel like they have so much on their plates already. One more thing might choke them."

"You'll get no argument from me. Besides, Garth, have you thought about what will happen next? When they're done with our three favorite problem children, for better or worse, you know the next thing they'll demand is all the magicians out of Khobunter."

Swearing, Garth let his head drop again with a solid thump against the desk. No, he had not thought that far ahead yet. "You're right. You're completely right. Shrieking hinges. It's going to be one battle after the next, and they really can't afford to spend that much time in Ascalon. They've got a war brewing on two different fronts right now."

Chatta gave him a sympathetic smile. "I know you hate to deal with them, but...."

"No, I need to go. It's about time that the council understands that not all of the magicians in the world belong to them anyway." Garth flicked the report aside and double checked his desk calendar. He had one more class today, in about thirty minutes. "I'll teach this last class and then leave. I don't know when I'll get back, though."

"I'll pack while you're teaching," Chatta reassured him. "And call Asla so you can stay with them. Don't worry about the rest of the week's classes, I'll arrange substitutes."

Standing, he gave her a quick kiss. "You're the best wife ever."

"I know," she agreed sassily, grinning up at him.

The baby in her arms squawked protest around the toy in her mouth, holding both hands toward her father. For a moment, he laid aside his worries, chuckling at Annie's reaction. "I'm sorry, did you need a kiss too?"

Annie looked entirely indignant to be left out of the proceedings until Garth leaned down and put a smacking kiss on the crown of her head. Appeased, the baby went back to snuggling with her mother.

Shaking his head, he wondered rhetorically, "How is she so adorable?"

"Because she takes after me," Chatta informed him drolly. "Now, scoot. We have a lot to do if you're to leave this afternoon. You need to take the boys' meurittas with you as well, because if those two are left here without supervision another day, I just might strangle someone."

Too true. The meurittas did not handle being away from their mages well. He would happily cart them to Ascalon and drop them off. Garth gathered up teaching materials with a few efficient moves, warning her as he did so, "I can't promise to be home anytime soon."

"I expect you to be home when the job is done. Don't rush back here, we'll manage. And give the kids a hug goodbye before you go, otherwise I won't hear an end to it."

He was planning to do that anyway. Ellis especially was a daddy's boy and did not take long separations well. If this were a different situation, Garth would take him along, as he loved playing with Xiaolang and Asla's crew. But this wasn't a situation that he could take a ten year old along.

As he turned for the door, Chatta called to his back, "And honey? Remember, you can lead them to water, but you can't drown them."

Drown them. What a tempting notion. Glancing back over his shoulder, Garth pointed out hopefully, "Shad would be perfectly willing to help me with the bodies. Eagle and Hazard would too, come to think of it."

"No, dear," Chatta responded placidly, as if he joked.

Garth wasn't entirely sure he was joking.

Honor Raconteur grew up all over the United States and to this day is confused about where she's actually from. She wrote her first book at five years old and hasn't looked back since. Her interests vary from rescuing dogs, to studying languages, to arguing with her characters. On good days, she wins the argument.

Since her debut in September 2011, Honor has released almost 30 books, mostly of the fantasy genre. She writes full time from the comfort of her home office, in her pajamas, while munching on chocolate. She has no intention of stopping anytime soon and will probably continue until something comes along to stop her.

Her website can be found here: http://www. honorraconteur.com, or if you wish to speak directly with the author, visit her on Facebook.

Made in the USA
Monee, IL
13 August 2023

40942301R00194